GULLIVER
HOUSE

By John Leggett

Novels

WILDER STONE

THE GLOUCESTER BRANCH

WHO TOOK THE GOLD AWAY

GULLIVER HOUSE

Biography

ROSS AND TOM

GULLIVER HOUSE

JOHN LEGGETT

৶৳ ৳৶

Houghton Mifflin Company Boston

1979

Library of Congress Cataloging in Publication Data
Leggett, John, date
Gulliver House. I. Title.
PZ4.L512Gu [PS3562.E38] 813'.5'4 79–827
ISBN 0–395–27759–0

Printed in the United States of America

P 10 9 8 7 6 5 4 3 2 1

For René and Veronica

GULLIVER
HOUSE

1

My father was a dreaming man. Curiosity and wonder were his gifts and with them he painted the commonplaces of his turnstile life.

That is what I was thinking one Saturday morning while I sat on the bed of his small room at the Landon, sorting through his belongings — a pair of gold cuff links, a dozen narrow ties, a sewing kit, a few recent biographies, a bank book with a balance of $407, a framed picture of me in midshipman's uniform.

In the afternoon I wandered the city, remembering other Saturdays when I used to come in from Rye to meet him and how, for a few hours, he would make New York into a carnival for us. In Grand Central I found the shoe shine stand deserted, but we had sat there once, side by side, on those tall, marble thrones, looking down on the hats of preoccupied travelers on their way to the lavatories downstairs, while old Italians went snap, snap, snap with their strips of felt, squeaking my scruffy shoes until they gleamed.

Going downtown on the subway, I took the head car and stood in its forward end as we used to, peering into the city's dusky intestines. Red signals turned yellow at our approach, then green to let us pass, and we glided toward the bright dock where new passengers were waiting for us with hopeful faces.

He had led us on to the Flea Circus, the knickknack auctions, and the Automat, all the gritty entertainments of the street. Now, Hudson Terminal was a tomb, its hosiery and fruit shops shuttered. A derelict slept under the newsstand counter in a stain of his urine. I looked for the trick store, where a monkey of a man with a mischievous voice had drawn a circle of us around him to watch the vanishing of coins and handkerchiefs, but the store was gone.

We had bought a metal tube from the monkey man. You could hide it in your hand and the elastic, which was attached to the tube and which you pinned inside your coat, would whisk away the little square of silk as you tucked it into your fist. Dad did the trick, explaining how the magic lay in the patter, in making me watch his left hand, while his right one fooled me.

At Christopher Street Pier, I spread my newspaper on a timber, as we had done, and sat looking onto the river where a tug worked a barge upstream. The waterfront always used to start him thinking of getting away. He'd told me here about the Mediterranean cruise he'd taken as a young man, and acted out the Lebanese snake charmer, the camelback ride at Giza, the beggar in Port Said who had cried "Gully-gully-gully," as he drew live chickens from his mouth.

From Africa, he had brought me red slippers with curly toes and a crop of rhinoceros hide. Once, when I had exasperated Mother by my stubbornness, she had used it to whip me. I had imagined I could still see the welts when I showed them to Dad that Saturday — but he said he could not see any.

Joe Leblang's was gone. It had been a burrow under the Broadway pavement where, half an hour before show time, Joe would call out, "A pair for the Lyceum at a dollar and a half." Dad would nod for them and we were off, climbing to a balcony as the curtain rose on a cut-rate play. Afterward, we would decide if it had made us believe and if it had touched us in some way.

At the Forty-third Street corner, there used to be a Childs where a huge black man in the window put on a performance. He was crowned by a tower of white and from his pitcher came rounds of yellow batter to bubble for a moment on his griddle; then, with a grin and a flash of his spatula, he sent pancakes flying to alight again like dappled, golden birds. In the next minute he had them stacked and sleight-of-handed off to a waitress with a pencil in her hair. Oh ambrosia, those cakes, and so was the cocoa that spouted from the tongue of a silvery lion's head at the Automat a couple of blocks to the north.

There is a changeless, Times Square fugue — a lowing of taxis, an ambulance wail, a xylophone arpeggio, trumpet laughter — and an equally characteristic blend of Times Square smells — the funkiness of subway tunnels, the toxicity of exhaust fumes, the cheap sweet of Karmelkorn, the smoke of a chestnut cart, and that fragrance of ersatz orange and sizzling hotdogs that is unmistakably Nedick's.

These brought to mind a horse's head swinging toward me. The nose was gray and, to my apprehensive touch, unbelievably soft. Far above, a policeman in puttees peered down at me like Jove, from the summit of his huge beast. Electric signs soared like fireworks into the night — vast blankets of incandescence, winking with flags and ballerinas, telling us the time, spelling out the news.

I suppose the ugliness, the filth in doorways, the hopelessness of taxi dance halls, the abused faces, which is what I see in Times Square now, were all there — but then my eye was untrained for signs of despair. I may not have known what despair was, or, if I did, believed that it was a private agony of my own and that if only I could be like the others here — like those boys and girls in the theater party — I need never know it again.

The Saturday outings, always begun in hope, often ended in betrayal, for while we watched the skaters in Rockefeller Center or browsed the counters in Brentano's, Dee would appear. Then I would have to share my father for the half hour that remained before I was packed off again for everyday Rye.

I always felt it was Dee who made Dad elusive, but maybe that was Mother's fault. When he disappointed me, when he promised to come to the lake on summer weekends and didn't, she let me know where he was. So, even as he made the trough for the skyrocket, even as he set the first one soaring out across the water to burst in a shower of green against the dark sky, even as we packed for our camping trip, I was afraid Dee was near, ready to steal my father away again.

He was my god — tall, wise, infinitely resourceful. And though I know it was a child's eye that saw him so, I go on believing he was a magician, capable of whatever astonishments he chose, or cared, to pull off.

A week earlier, at Bellevue Hospital, it had been hard to believe this was my father — this skull against the pillow, with its fringe of wild hair and the madman's eyes fastening on me, yet seeing nothing, the mouth working, but making no sound.

"Dad, it's Lloyd. I'm home."

"He doesn't hear you. His mind's gone," Dee said. She was squablike, her rosebud mouth receding between cheeks, gone gray in the face as well as the hair.

I was counting drops of clear liquid as they fell from a bottle toward the needle in his forearm.

Dee said, "You can come home with me. There's a room for you. It's only an hour."

"Prognosis poor, you said in the cable. What does that mean?"

"The doctor's phrase. He said it would help you get leave. But now I don't know if we should have brought you all this way. He's dying, Lloyd. It's his heart."

Then Dad spoke. It was not his natural voice, but the ballooning one with which he had played officious roles for my childish amusement. "This way," he ordered. "I can see where we're going. Over there, where it's getting bright. Way awa-ay, awa-ay."

"What is it, Dad?"

His eyes closed. Except for the steep rise and fall of his chest, he was still.

Dee said, "I wanted to write you three months ago, when I found how sick he was, but he wouldn't let me. He said there was nothing you could do out there in the Pacific."

"No," Dr. Winter told me on the phone, "I don't mind if you call in a Navy doctor. If it reassures you, go ahead. But your father's heart is big as a melon. It fills his chest. I think he'll die in forty-eight hours, and it's doubtful he'll regain consciousness. The nurse tells me he had a lucid moment the other night. He asked where he was, and then her name."

"He'd want to know her name. He's always uncomfortable about being waited on. He'd want her to know he appreciated it."

"We don't get many of those," Dr. Winter said. "Well, leave me your number and get some sleep."

From the bedside I could look down into Avenue A, sleek with rain, where a boy on metal crutches waited for the bus. I was thinking of the last time, eight months previously, when I had seen my father.

He had come through the door of the Harvard Club with the air of a man entering a strange church. He was tentatively giving his name to the porter as I approached. As we clasped hands, his eyes took in my Navy blue and gold, and they were moist with pride.

At lunch we were waited on by a big, Teutonic man with grudging gestures, and when I asked for the brown sugar Dad liked on strawberries the waiter replied, "No, we don't have that now. We used to, for one of the old members, but he's gone now."

It was such a gratuitous *memento mori,* here in the headlong clatter and enterprise of the dining room, that I laughed, but Dad looked shaken, as though it were a warning.

When I asked about his health, he said, "It's blood pressure. I haven't taken enough exercise you know, living in the city, sitting at a desk all day. I suspect I won't have to worry about that much longer."

"What do you mean?"

"When George French retired, I lost my last account. All I do is odd jobs for the younger men. Frank Cochrane keeps me on because I'm a familiar sight. He'd have to explain my absence." Dad always spoke without self-pity, smiling, exaggerating so that I never knew where truth stopped and hyperbole began. His hands moved in graceful arcs, as though he were conducting an ironic accompaniment to twenty-five years of staff meetings, client lunches, and accounts pursued, gained, and lost for C & C.

"Why don't you look for another job?"

"I think about that. I had an offer from Dancer's, but I passed it up, thinking there'd be others. Besides, I owed Frank loyalty, and there was still a chance of being a partner."

"Could you go to Dancer's now?"

"I'm nearly sixty, Lloyd. I don't really care anymore."

"You would, in a new situation."

"Maybe — some entirely different line of work." He made a pruning, then a digging gesture.

"I've always imagined I'd come looking to you for a job."

He shrugged indifference to his profession.

"If the war were over in the morning, what would you suggest I do?"

"Whatever you want to do."

"You don't care?"

"Of course I care. I hope you won't decide to be a ballet dancer." He paused for me to laugh. "But if you do, I'll try to hide my disappointment."

Loving him for such faith, I said, "Whatever it is, first we'll take that trip."

"You'll have a girl. You'll want to be with her."

"No, first we're going to do our bicycle tour."

He warmed to the familiar sound of it. "You know, I found the boat we can take. It sails from Liverpool and calls at the Isle of Man before it heads up the Solway Firth. We can land at Penrith and cycle the towpath along the Eden to Windermere." He was pedaling the country lane we had seen in an issue of *National Geographic* fifteen years earlier.

"They say the war will be over in a year. If you really are out of shape, you ought to start getting some exercise."

"The doctor's got me on toe-touching and a thing I do lying in bed, raising my legs."

"There's a gym here, with weights, even a bicycle."

"Too late, Lloyd." He smiled. "Too late for Herpicide." It was the slogan under a bald head from an old hair-tonic campaign that always tickled him.

"Maybe leaving C & C is a blessing. You won't have to stay in the city. You can move out of that room at the Landon, maybe get a place in Connecticut."

"It's convenient there. I'm used to it. They know my idiosyncrasies."

"Do you spend a lot of time at Dee's?"

"Not so much now. She's going to marry — someone she's known for years."

"That's incredible."

"I can't blame her. I've certainly had my chance."

"I feel badly," I said. I was remembering the time he had asked my advice about marrying her and I had said I didn't like her.

"You needn't feel responsible. It's all my own perverse doing. I'm not very good for women, as your mother would have been the first to concede."

"She was difficult," I said.

He shook his head in pain and doubt. "Disappointed. I'm sorry you only knew her in those last years. She wasn't always that way, but she'd expected something different of life."

"A bigger house? Servants?"

"Richer, in some way."

"I didn't blame you for leaving."

"Well, it isn't so simple. I often feel that I was the one, that I made her that way, with my own lack of understanding."

"But you did understand."

"Never mind, Lloyd. It's too late to mend. Tell me what you do on the Downing."

I was communications officer on a destroyer, and as I told my father about the routine of our patrols, I went on thinking of his own humble, culpable view of himself, which I was unable to accept. In my opinion he was the victim of the women in his life. I had always loved him more than my mother, who'd indulged, even spoiled, me.

She'd had an arbitrary nature. Trivial things — the purple curtains she had to have, the kids who stole some tulips — obsessed her, put her in week-long, silent rages that made the house an agony. He deserved better, this fine, gentle, imaginative man across from me.

After lunch, we stood awkwardly at the club door, sensing it was an important parting. "You must have things to do, girls to see," he said. "I'll be getting along." He touched the brim of his hat and I watched him go down the steps, watched his back until it disappeared down Forty-fourth Street.

Oh, what my father might have been. If only others could have seen him as I did — his understanding, humor, and intelligence.

At eleven the night nurse looked in, adjusted the intravenous feeding tube, smoothed the sheets and, with a rustle of starched skirt and a click of the latch, left us alone again. Whereupon Dad's mouth opened, as though he expected to be fed, and from it, at each intake of breath, there issued a series of groans, not of pain but of accompaniment to a dream.

I rose to stand beside the bed and look into the face with its halo of gray and its stubbled chin. I put my hand around his wrist; it felt no larger than a pencil.

"It's Lloyd," I said. "I've come back to see you."

"The sea's higher," he announced suddenly. "That's a big one breaking over there. Come on now, boys, we've got to bail." His eyes were unfocused. He was in a dream, one that I imagined was prompted by the sound of my voice, but as I wrapped my fingers around his, there was no response. His eyes closed and he slept.

I wakened at the sound of his clearing throat. In the dawn light, I saw that his eyes were open, and then he spoke, evenly, distinctly, as though we had been talking together.

"It's always seemed long. You think it's going to last forever, and then it's over."

"Dad, it's Lloyd. Do you know I'm here?" I took his hand and imagined I felt the slightest pressure, but his head did not turn toward me.

After a moment he spoke again. "We get off course and founder." He was silent, and then he whispered, "Or do *some* find the way to port?"

"Dad, do you see me here?"

His head turned at last and his gray eyes were as I remembered them — clear, gentle, and perceiving. "You shouldn't have come. You must be busy."

"The war's over. I'd be here anyway."

His thin lips quivered. "Thank you." Now his hand clutched mine. "I've been thinking of you," he said, turning to the ceiling again as his eyelids fluttered closed.

The funeral was in Rye, and notices in the *Times* and *Westchester News* brought a handful of mourners into Christ Church. Dee, in a dark-lady outfit, was weeping as she entered, playing a widow's role. What a drab little woman she was. How could Dad, so fastidious in every way, have found her appealing? To my dismay, she came to sit beside me.

I saw Frank Cochrane, looking like a Tammany judge, come in, glancing at his watch. Dad would have been happy that

Frank, the man at C & C who twenty-six years ago had hired him and six months ago had fired him, took the time to come out from town to say good-bye.

Ethan Poole, a man Dad had admired, was there too.

After the perfunctory service, the undertaker's men brought the coffin out the side door and I watched them roll its collapsible carriage along the pavement, across an incline to the street, and up to the rear of the hearse, which took it in a swallow.

Frank Cochrane came down the steps and moved toward me for a handshake.

"Thanks for coming."

Nodding, he asked, "You looking forward to being a civilian again?"

"I like the Navy."

"If you think better of that, come and see me."

"I might, thanks."

At the cemetery, watching the dirt scatter over the lid of the coffin, I had a sense of my own suffocation, as though the grit and humus taste of it were sifting through my lips, filling my nostrils, darkening the sky. Yet, as I turned from the hole that would soon close over him, I felt an exuberance too, as though I had shed a harness.

While he lived I had been indentured, not only to Dan Erskine's morals and attitudes, but to his attainments as well. Not that he didn't want me to exceed him. He was a truly humble man. But for me to have outrun him was to have dishonored him, to have demolished the Dan Erskine of my heart. Now I was released, all injunction dissolved.

Ethan Poole had lingered. He was leaning against the fender of a car, lighting his pipe.

"I'm glad you came," I said to him. "I know how much you meant to Dad."

"I hadn't seen Dan lately," Ethan replied, his voice tart, like cider going hard, "but I'll miss him. We used to ride the eight-twelve and the five-forty together — every morning and evening for a dozen years."

"He looked forward to the train, to sitting with you. I remember."

Ethan moved off. "Good luck, Lloyd. Look me up sometime, will you?"

"I will."

"You know my office?"

"I'll find it."

I did find it, that Saturday afternoon following the funeral, expecting it would be closed. But the door, lettered Ethan Poole & Co., Publishers, swung open to my touch. Although the cluttered foyer was dark, I could look into the corner office and there, in light filtering through dirty windows, was Ethan. He looked up from his desk and waved as though he'd been awaiting me.

"Sit down, Lloyd," he said as I entered his office. "What brings you to town?"

"I've been going over old ground, thinking about Dad, revisiting good times with him. I've been putting his stuff in order this week. I was surprised by the books on his shelf. He wasn't much of a reader but he'd bought half a dozen books in the past year, two of them yours."

Ethan nodded. "He used to ask my advice about them. He'd buy a book but rarely discover his own enthusiasm for it — which was odd for someone so perceptive."

"You thought him perceptive?"

"He was intelligent and articulate. He had a sensitive spirit, a feeling for human behavior."

I was suddenly moved by his words. "That's an epitaph I'll settle for."

I found myself scanning Ethan's bookshelves, picking out titles, wondering what had attracted Dad to the books I had found among his things.

"What are your plans, Lloyd?" Ethan asked.

"On Monday I'm supposed to start back to the Pacific, but I don't want to go now. I wish I were a civilian."

"What would you do with yourself?"

"I'd look around. I'd take some time about it — but not too much. One of the last things Dad said to me was about the shortness of time, that there isn't much for any of us. 'Whatever it is you want to do, better not put it off.' "

~§ 2 §~

On the threshold of 3436 Q Street in Georgetown, I gave three taps with the tail of the silver dolphin and, presently, Charles Cushing, in uniform, and an even grayer eminence than I recalled, opened the door.

"Come in," he said. "Come in, Lloyd," and with a perceptible brusqueness he led me off to his library. There was the fragrance of a meticulously kept house, a medley of wood wax, metal polish, and camphor, traces of perfume and fresh tobacco, and beneath these astringents, almost but not entirely camouflaged by them, a juicy promise from the oven.

Charles Cushing's bookshelves held leatherbound sets of Hardy and Galsworthy and a collection of sextants. There were photographs of yachts, student groups, and ship's companies. On his desk I spotted a paperweight bearing the rampant cat of the Fly, my Harvard club.

I said, "I'm sorry to have put you to all the trouble."

"It's no trouble, Lloyd, but I hope you'll give it another think. The peacetime Navy's a good life, and there's a big interest now in converts, particularly from Harvard. If order and composure appeal to you, as they do to me, you could do worse than stay in. Even the form of it is good. I like wearing it all on my sleeve, the getting and giving of respect." He held up his own three stripes. They were in mint condition, a rebuke to my lovingly verdigrised one and a half. "What's your dilemma, a taste of sweet civilian life?"

"No, sir." I wavered, wanting his approval. Four years ago, when I had first seen Charles Cushing, I was struck by his easy authority. In the spring of 1941 he had come back to the Fly for a club dinner and told us about his return to the Navy. His obvious pleasure in it had made me choose it as my own wartime service, and as a midshipman, I had gone to him for help with a duty assignment. "The Navy's been good to me."

"But?"

"When I wrote you," I explained, "I had no clear idea of what I'd do as a civilian."

"The regular Navy's no stopgap."

"I know that. It turns out that, as a legacy, my father left me a hint about what to do."

"What's that?"

"I used to imagine myself in advertising, like my father. There seemed no harm in persuading people to buy this gasoline over that. I think that was what first interested him, but in the end he lost whatever respect he'd had for his work, and for himself as well. He told me that it does matter what you do. So I want to go back to New York and find some kind of work I can believe in."

He nodded and, after a moment, asked, "Must it be New York?"

"I think so."

Charles Cushing rose and walked to the garden window, jingling coins in his pocket. We watched a girl emerge from the house through French doors. She knelt to examine a potted azalea, plucked a dead leaf. Then, in a continuous, graceful motion, she rose, lifting the plant, cradling it, and reentered, closing the doors behind her.

I'd had only a glimpse of her face, seen no more than a corner, but it suggested the rest was fair. Looking at Cushing, I guessed that the women around him would be so.

"Why go back to New York?" he asked.

"Why not?"

"There's no need for all that noise and bad manners. Oh, if you want to work on Wall Street I suppose you must put up with the push and squeeze of the subway. Is that what you have in mind?"

Before I could answer, there was a knock at the door and the girl we had seen in the garden appeared. So often a partial glimpse of a girl offers a promise that, once she is seen in the round, goes unfulfilled, as though the observer projects an aspiration of his own and binds actuality to disappointment. So it was a surprise to find the girl was even more handsome. Eyes, guileless as a summer day, were set in a broad, serene face. Her mouth was wide and determined, yet at the same time there was a fullness, a susceptibility to pleasure.

"I'm sorry. I didn't mean to interrupt," she said.

"This is Lieutenant Erskine. My daughter, Andrea."

She seemed a woods creature, grave one instant, coltish the next. I guessed she was eighteen, and the way she looked at her father suggested a powerful admiration for him.

"It was Andy who postponed our meeting this afternoon," Charles Cushing explained. "She arrived unexpectedly from college and I had to go to the airport to meet her." It was a reprimand of some kind, not lost on her. Then he dismissed her, saying, "I'll be free in just a minute, my dear."

As she smiled and left us, I had a sense of déjà vu, prompted perhaps by our uniforms, the order of authority, the milieu. I saw very clearly the headmaster's house at Montague School with its steeply pitched slate roof, the low, coffered ceiling of its living room, the grass-papered walls hung with Samurai prints.

We went in groups of twenty for Sunday night cocoa. Across from me sat Susan, the youngest of Colonel Emmett's daughters. She was fifteen, with straight, black hair that shone like satin in the firelight, and her hands went this way and that, birds flying in the hangman's game we played. Her eyes were large with wonder at the palpable yearning she had started in the score of us encircling her.

I said to Charles Cushing, "I don't want to interfere in your evening."

But he was not quite finished with me. He said, "Tell me, Lloyd. If you were that girl's father, would you let her go off to Harlem to work and *live* in a settlement house?"

"She wants to?"

"For her nonresident term. A couple of months up there — living right among them."

I hesitated. "I suppose I'd see all kinds of dangers for her."

"They're very real, those dangers."

"Yes, sir. I'm sure they are."

"What would you do then, if you were in my boots?"

"I'd let her go. Because I'd suspect there was more danger in thwarting her than in any back alley."

"I disagree there. She cannot possibly meet these people on their own level simply by sleeping in some rat-infested tenement. It's a masquerade. No one will be deceived but her."

"Still, if she doesn't discover the truth for herself, she'll find another way — and another danger."

I felt that I had antagonized him by taking his daughter's side and that he now wanted to be rid of me. Rising, I said, "Well, I'm grateful for your time."

"You're withdrawing your request to integrate? Is that right?"

"Yes. With thanks."

"Anything I can do, then?"

"I'm going to make the rounds of the publishers."

He was nodding, guiding me out. On the way, he paused to introduce me to his wife. She was in the foyer with her daughter, arranging flowers in a bowl. "This is Lloyd Erskine, Alison. We've been talking about a man's work."

"And a woman's too," I said.

Andrea Cushing's mother was a good-looking woman, smartly dressed, her gray hair cut modishly. She gave me a bland smile and stepped back to appraise her bouquet of anemones. "Do you like it?"

I said, "It's lovely."

"Simplicity. I think that's the secret, don't you, Mr. Erskine?"

"I'm all for simplicity," I said, "and the bowl is handsome too." It was a delicate, creamy porcelain, inscribed with blocks of Chinese calligraphy in pale red. "Do you have any idea what it says?"

She deferred to her husband as though she felt he might reply, but it was Andrea who said, "It's a Ming bowl. Grandpa brought it from China, and that's poetry, isn't it Mother?"

"Yes," she said quietly, "but I can't translate it. I don't know Chinese."

"Anyway, it's pleasing to look at," I said. "I'd like to be able to draw those characters. I'd fill a wall with them."

She smiled, nodded, and then Andrea saw me to the door. With a hand on the knob she asked, "Do you need directions?"

"I'm just going to Union Station. I know the way."

"New York?"

"Yes. To look for a job."

"Good luck. I hope you land one."

"What about you? Your father said you want to go to Harlem."

"I do. I've been trying to persuade him all afternoon."

"For whatever it's worth, I put in a good word."

"Did you? Thanks."

"I don't think I changed his mind."

"No. It isn't an easy one to change, but I have the rest of the vacation. I'll work on him." There was resoluteness in her smile. "What kind of job will you look for?"

"Yesterday I talked to a man about publishing books. He's got me interested."

Just before the door closed, she said, "So long," in a way that left me thinking of her all the way to New York.

"What do you want, Lloyd?" Ethan Poole asked. It was eight-thirty. The others had not yet arrived and we were alone in his corner office. "Do you want to make money?"

"That's not the main thing, surely. My dream of rolling

stock and real estate washed overboard somewhere in the Pacific."

"What's the main thing?"

"I don't want to waste my life."

"How'll you manage that?"

"I'll try not to get swallowed by another man's ambitions."

Ethan laughed. "Well, you *are* serious. Been looking around?"

"I had an interview at Doubleday's yesterday. There's hustle and possibility in the halls. That's appealing, and they pay pretty well — but they're big, like the Navy. I wonder if one can understand the whole of a place one only knows by the parts."

"In time."

"What I like about Poole's is that you see it all. There's no deception."

"Why have you settled on publishing?"

"You strike me as a man who knows what he's doing."

"It's a pain, Lloyd. Affects every part of the body."

"You get pleasure out of it too."

"All right," he conceded. "I do."

"Do you know why?"

"I like books." He waved at the wall of them. "They're ideas in negotiable form, ideas about us and our times, what's good and bad about 'em. If I must be busy with something, and I must, I'd prefer to be trading in them, than in . . ." He was peering at a window across Thirtieth Street lettered LIB-ERTY BELL FOUNDATION GARMENTS, and through it a large woman could be seen removing the dust cover from her typewriter. ". . . than in corsets, essential as they are."

"Ethan," I said. "Could you put me to work?"

He looked surprised. "I don't think you'd want to come here, Lloyd. Not much to attract a young man."

"I've looked around the shops," I said, "comparing Poole books with the others. Yours seem to be books that wouldn't get on other publishers' lists easily, as though you don't want to be popular. Is that right?"

"Mebbee. Though it doesn't follow that all popular books are bad ones."

"Anyway, I liked your books. I could see why they appealed to you, and it occurred to me that your policy is to choose books that interest you."

"You're mistaken, Lloyd, if you think I don't want my books to sell. I take on a book because I believe that if *I* like it, I can find another seven thousand readers who'll like it too. But that's where the trouble starts, finding those seven thousand people."

"I think I could find them."

Ethan was distracted by the appearance of a woman in the doorway, getting out of her coat. Her hair was gray, her face alert and agreeably pedagogical.

"Oh, Mia," Ethan called. "This is Lloyd Erskine, who thinks he wants to get into publishing."

"I'm Mia Penrose," she said in a fresh-mint voice as we shook hands.

"Take him away and straighten him out, Mia," Ethan said.

"Sure, I'll do that." Her quick, black eyes were already frisking me. "Come along."

Mia Penrose shared an office with a typist and an accountant, already at their places, but she had put her mark on a corner of it with a kneehole desk, three daisies in a flask, and a sketch of Rebecca West.

"I'm production manager," she explained, nodding to a work table piled with paper and printing samples, "but Ethan is always sending me home with a manuscript to read, and I enjoy that. I've been doing it all my life, one way or another. What's your professional experience?"

"None at all."

"Then what do you hope to do?"

"To start anywhere, wherever you need me. I think I have some taste."

"What *is* your taste?"

"You mean *now?*"

"Or then."

"Well ... John Steinbeck, of course. And Thomas Wolfe. I liked *Of Time and the River*."

"*Did* you?"

"I grew up on Hemingway and Fitzgerald," I managed, "along with everyone else. I guess I have rather plain literary taste — but I know when something's good."

"Most of us feel that way until we've made a few mistakes." In the center of her desk was a page full of figures that she'd begun to decorate with doodles. "What other writers do you like?"

"I've tried Joyce. I can appreciate him, as I do Faulkner, but I don't get caught up, if you know what I mean. I don't enjoy Joyce."

"Joyce isn't easy."

I hurried on, mentioning Dreiser, desperate to find some bridge between us. Clearly Dreiser was not a favorite of Mia Penrose's.

"Have you read Gide?" she asked. "*The Counterfeiters?*" I shook my head. "Virginia Woolf? Have you read *Mrs. Dalloway*? No? Or Huxley?"

I surrendered. I was certain I had read Aldous Huxley — was it *Antic Hay?* — but my mind was an abandoned room without a curtain at a window nor a bulb in a socket. This was so apparent that she set out to rescue me, asking what English courses I had taken at Harvard. But it was too late. I was speechless, my own ignorance laid bare before me.

"Do you know Ethan well?" she asked. "He's the most extraordinary man. I know. I've worked at other publishers and Ethan's unique, a bona fide saint." With that, she led me out and toward the elevator.

Here, as I was pressing the button, Ethan caught me and asked me to wait in his office while he had a word with Mia. He returned looking pleased with himself.

"Let me help to purge you of this folly, Lloyd." Settling into his chair, he said, "Publishing isn't a business in the usual sense. If I were you, setting off in life with expectations of a family and a decent existence, I'd give serious thought to the manufacture or distribution of some necessity — whiskey, for example."

"But you don't believe that."

"Well, I'm a little crazy. Anyone will tell you that, and I've never known any other profession." His desk was piled with correspondence, some of it dog-eared and sooty, as though it had been awaiting his attention for months. He tapped the stack that looked most immediate.

"Here's a bank loan overdue, along with a letter from an author — a damned good one, incidentally — saying he's leaving us. We've built him a little reputation and he's taking his new book uptown. For the money, of course, but it's also my own inattention. They're like children, authors are. They can't get enough affection." He lit his pipe and puffed with contentment. "So you see, ours is a world ruled by disappointment."

"All the same, you seem to rejoice in it."

"Oh, I do." A smile grew on Ethan's lips, at once benign and mischievous. It seemed to say, "I know something you don't, but keep on and you may get it."

"Because it's yours?" I asked.

"Mebbee."

"I'll think it over," I said, and rose reluctantly, feeling dismissed with this lightheartedness.

But instead of a farewell, Ethan gave me a sly smile and said, "If you're so desperate to learn the business and you're willing to work long hours at coolie wages and do some selling for us — pack your sack with the spring line and see if you can take some orders from a reluctant public — come ahead, Lloyd. I think we can find you a corner here somewhere. But take some time to think it over."

Riding uptown on the subway, I did have misgivings, felt it was foolish to take a five-thousand-dollar-a-year job. I had pretty much made up my mind to call Ethan Poole and say I had decided against the offer when I noticed the man across the aisle. He was about fifty, shaggy and worn in every respect.

Although not handsome, his face, among the vacant ones, was remarkable for its absorption. He was reading a manuscript. Whether or not he was an editor, he fit my conception of one, a man doing what most interested him.

When I got home I called Ethan and told him I wanted that corner at Poole's.

⌇ *3* ⌇

CALLING THE CUSHINGS' number in Georgetown, I hoped that if Andrea did not answer, her mother or a maid would, but it was Charles's voice, "Hello? Yes, Lloyd. How you getting on?"

When I summoned the nerve to ask for her there was surprise and chill in his response — "You want to speak to *Andy?*" — as though I had asked to borrow his car, and then doubt, "I'm not sure she's here. She was going off with her mother."

But in a moment she did come on, saying, "Oh, hello. Did you find that job?"

"It seems so. At Ethan Poole's. Did you ever hear of it?"

"No, but I only know the names of a few."

"It's partly selling. I've always thought selling was a thing I'd never do, but Mr. Poole . . . Ethan persuaded me that selling's how you learn. He's not paying me much either, but it's a small place, a Bob Cratchit office on lower Park Avenue. It's obviously an impulsive act."

"But, as you say, it's a good place to learn."

"Yes. Exactly," I said. "Listen. I was wondering. Are you coming to New York?"

"Next Tuesday. On my way to college."

"No Harlem?"

She hesitated. "It's in doubt."

"Could you stop over for an hour or so?"

"My train gets into Penn Station at twelve-ten."

"I'll meet you. We can have lunch."

"I'd like that."

Waiting at the foot of the escalator, an eye on the several gates from which travelers were spewing into the city, I felt a rising excitement. The hands of the clock, which hung like a moon over the concourse, stood at just 12:10, and I sought her shape, imagined straight, light hair falling to the collar of a camel's-hair coat, a canvas valise swinging at her knees, her gray green eyes skittish until we joined, until I could take the valise and guide her toward the taxi stand.

I was planning on the upstairs dining room at Le Chanteclair, to which Mia had introduced me last week. From our table at the back, Mia had pointed out the worthies. "Do you see the man with the pretty girl there? The one with the pepper and salt mustache? Know who that is, Lloyd?"

"He looks like William Faulkner."

"He *is* William Faulkner. He comes here when he's in town. Random's just around the corner. This is a favorite of the agents too. That's Henry Volkening holding up his martini, and the lady in the large hat is Elena Wallace."

I was dazzled and grateful, nodding tractably as she went on to tell me about Ethan Poole. "He's such a dear man that he allows himself to be put upon by everyone. You'll see that, Lloyd, and how there'd be nothing left, really, if I weren't around to say no for him and look after details. So I'm hoping you'll check with me on what he actually needs to be bothered about."

Her mandate was so smooth and laced with smiles, it was only when I was back at my chores, with wine and charm wearing thin, that I realized how deftly she had slipped a hobble on me.

The station clock had jumped to a quarter past, while underfoot I felt the coming and going of trains and before me young women of every shape but Andrea's passed. For the first time it occurred to me that she might not come to me, that she had told her father and he had forbidden it, or that she herself had thought better of it and had gone directly to the Green Mountains.

The thought of being forsaken, expectations of the Chante-clair lunch suddenly replaced by this void with its shadows of rejection, led me back to uncertainties of my new job. The dinginess of the office, the threadbare salary, a distaste for sales-manship uncoiled at the edge of my consciousness.

It was 12:30 and a woman, all business, at the information counter told me, "The Congressional? Oh, it's come and gone. Yes, twenty minutes ago."

Gray with remorse and chagrin, heading for my sooty corner beside the men's lavatory, I passed Ethan's office and saw there was a girl at his desk. She wore a blue coat and her hair was chestnut brown — definitely pretty — and something about the way she sat, arms folded like his, suggested this was Ethan's daughter. I was past the door when he cried out, "Hey, Lloyd, what's your hurry? Someone here to see you."

Confronting the girl, I found her smiling, embarrassed at my own confusion and failure to recognize her. She seemed about to say, "You don't remember me, do you?" and for a second more I didn't. Then, as in a film dissolve, the image of the girl I had just been seeking, the fair-haired one, became the dark-haired, brown-eyed girl at Ethan's desk.

"Andy," I said. "I was so disappointed at not finding you in the station — and I hardly expected . . ."

Ethan laughed. "I should have let you go by. We were get-ting along fine."

At Schrafft's counter, while waiting for sandwiches, Andy said she had been impressed with Ethan, understood why I enjoyed working for him, and I told her how he was training me for my first road trip.

During the past week he had begun my conversion to a sales-man, assigning me the spring list as reading, along with a list of New York State accounts, the bookshops from Poughkeepsie to Buffalo, with his own notes about the idiosyncrasies of each buyer.

All my qualms about salesmanship erupted in a distaste for one of the books, an English novel I would be selling. Persuading anyone to buy it seemed a hypocrisy. Even though I knew it for a kind of disloyalty, if not grounds for dismissal, I did confess my feeling to Ethan.

His response was typically capricious and jovial. No, of course I wasn't to lie, but like people, there was something good in the worst of books, and if I hadn't found it, that was because I hadn't read carefully enough.

When I replied that the book was such a depressing one, he laughed. "That's it, Lloyd. Tell 'em about the convincing gloom. Some readers dote on despair. They seek it like an alcoholic does his drink."

I had kept Andy entertained by the account and she was delighted with Ethan's lesson in salesmanship, but when I asked about her nonresident term, she turned abruptly sullen and picked some shreds from the paper doily.

"Can I trust you?" she asked.

"Of course."

"The Bennington campus is closed and I'm not going back — but I've told Daddy I am, that I'm going to stay at a faculty house. I can get Mr. Morris to cover for me if the family should call, and he'll forward my mail." Now Andy looked into my eyes. "I've never been deceitful, but I have to. Do you see, Lloyd?"

I nodded uncertainly. "Yes. I guess so."

"I'm going up to Goodwill House and see what it's like. Can I leave my bag with you? Can I give Mr. Morris your number? I could check in with you every day."

"You know your father got me into the Navy, and into sub chasers when I wanted them, and now he's gotten me out. He's a good friend. I don't like the idea of lying to him."

"Oh, you won't have to. And really, if you don't want to be involved, I'll understand."

I weighed the betrayal of a man I admired against the sight of his daughter, all anxiousness and suppliance beside me. There was a clarity about her. It shone like sudden truth. I wondered what she thought of me, if I seemed a sort of uncle, her father's ally with a coat that might be turned — or a possible lover.

"At least I'll take your bag home with me." I wrote the number on a matchbook cover. "I'll be there by six. And if you like, we could have dinner."

Andy called at six-thirty to report that Goodwill House was a former elementary school and there was a makeshift dormitory but as yet no mattresses on the beds. She had called the Barbizon and asked them to save her a room.

We met at the Astor Place subway stairs and I took her to El Faro, a Spanish restaurant on Greenwich Street where the paella was good and the crowd reminded me of a Brueghel feast.

Andy had been disappointed in her first impressions of Goodwill House. It was a dark building in need of repair and a thorough cleaning. There was more staff in evidence than children and the officious woman in charge had been more concerned with her new office machines than the lack of kitchen and playground equipment.

However, Andy had made friends with a girl from Oberlin and they had resolved to do some recruiting and at once do something to make the place more attractive.

As Andy talked I was thinking that against this background of raffish bohemians, her face seemed a child's.

"Why are you smiling?" she asked.

"Because you seem so young to be doing this. I don't know what to make of you."

"I know. I do have an innocent look. At college they protect me — you know — keep things from me."

"What things?"

"My roommate came back from a Dartmouth weekend with the top of a boy's pajamas, blue ones, and when she wore it, the other girls laughed. There was some joke and they wouldn't share it with me."

"You don't know what it was?"

"I do now. My roommate and another girl had crawled

through a dormitory window and spent the night with two boys. The blue pajama top was what she wore — and she kept it, as spoils."

"*Were* you shocked?"

"Not really."

"Envious?"

"Interested, not envious. I was angry, though, that they tried to keep it from me, as though it might taint me."

"And it wouldn't?"

She smiled and cocked her head. "Of course not."

For the first time it entered my head that she was ready for a love affair and that I had had an invitation. Now I recalled her bag, waiting just inside the door of my apartment on Thirtysixth Street. In stopping for it, we'd see.

Viewing my monkish one room through Andy's eyes — the door and sawhorse table with its load of books and galleys, the narrow bed and bleak kitchenette — I said, "I'm not here much. It's just a place to work and sleep." But she had already found things to admire, my scarlet curtains, the jacket drawings I had hung, and she marveled that a man could cook and clean and sew for himself.

"Would you like a drink?"

"No thanks. I have to be up early."

It was as though my hands were bound to my thigh bones, and although she stood before my bookshelf, waiting and vulnerable, tension lay like a wall between us. I heard my voice saying foolishness about the new books and finally it was I who escaped, grasping her valise, leading her out my door and down three flights to the street.

In the taxi, going uptown, some courage returned. "I want very much to kiss you," I said. "Do you mind?" Her murmur, more no than yes, confused me, but I leaned into her darkness, found her mouth and we kissed, inexpertly, as though she hadn't been expecting it and hadn't much experience, but it was a relief, and afterwards she said, "Thank you — I didn't mind that at all."

"Can we do it again tomorrow, then?" I asked as she headed for the hotel door.

"Sure," she said, and disappeared through it.

She arrived late at El Faro, explaining she had lost her way. It had been that kind of day. Mrs. Ginter had vetoed the plan she and Betsy had proposed for recruiting more children. At lunch, Sidney, the only black on the staff, had accused Andy of prejudice, and then Mr. Randolph, the program director, had taken her from the counseling pool and sent her to the Welfare Department on 116th Street to collate five years of truancy reports from the files. It could take the rest of her nonresident term.

"You mustn't let them do that to you, Andy," I said. "Get mad. It isn't as though they're paying you. You're there for the experience. Tell Randolph that."

"Oh, I wish I could, but you know I can't complain because they've all been there longer and I don't have any kind of a degree. They're doing me a favor. The worst of it though is the scorn of Sidney. He looks at me and sees a rich white girl — a caricature of a rich white girl, damn him, just as Daddy said."

"What about your mother? I couldn't tell if she was rooting for you or not. She was busy with flowers. I remember you had to prompt her about that bowl."

"Oh, Mummy knows all about the bowl. After she was married, she studied Chinese art at the National Gallery and she was going to Formosa, but then Daddy got sick so she couldn't. They have a joke about his miraculous recovery. She's devoted to Daddy, but it's a gyp on her, it really is."

"How did she feel about your wanting to spend the term in Harlem?"

"She understood, but she didn't interfere. Once Daddy had decided, that was the end of it."

"Well, don't let the gyp be on you."

"Oh no, I won't. It's just the first day. It's bound to be better — thanks." In what seemed an extraordinary act of affection she put her hand in mine and the remains of the tension wall between us melted away as if it had been a mirage.

Struck once more by her beauty and her unconsciousness of it, I said, "You're beautiful, you know."

She blushed, looked into her lap and murmured a denial.

"What do you mean? Mustn't I say so?"

She frowned, but said, "It's all right."

"What then?"

"I don't know what to say."

"You don't have to say anything, but it makes me feel good to tell you."

"It makes me feel good too, even if it isn't true."

"But it is true."

She looked up, making a helpless gesture, as if to say that if it were, she couldn't honestly take any credit for it.

Riding uptown, she said, "It's easier for men, isn't it. I mean you *know* you're ambitious."

"Am I? I *don't* know."

"Oh yes. It shows in the way you walk, the way you look, your curiosity about everything."

"Is that bad?"

"No."

"Good?"

"Oh yes. I think so."

"I'm puzzled about girls," I said. "What do *they* want? Is it children? Do you think about having children?"

"Not particularly."

"What then? What do you dream about?"

She shook her head but a moment later she said, "Well, there are a lot of girls leaving college to get married. Two of my friends decided over the holidays. That has a demoralizing effect on the rest of us. I don't know why, except it's exciting, going off like that, and a sociology course suffers by comparison. We have to keep telling ourselves that our education is important and real life will wait for us. But then, when you're in love, I guess that's all that counts."

"Love, then? That's a girl's ambition?"

"If she's in love, I guess it blots out everything else. From the moment she falls, she lives for the man, believing in him, looking after him."

"How does that appeal to you?"

"Oh, I suppose it's glorious, when you're ready for it, but right now it seems threatening, as though it'll catch me if I don't watch out, a snare that'll catch my foot just as I'm starting to run, just as I'm feeling how splendid it is to run. My friend Betsy was chased last night by a man coming out of a bar on Lenox Avenue. He was right behind her for blocks and blocks, but she outran him and she says she wasn't frightened at all because she knew she was faster, and she was just exhilarated. You know what she means?"

"Yes," I said. "I do."

Andy took it for granted that we would stop at my apartment, and this time she accepted the drink. When I had got the lights right and put on a Segovia record, I sat beside her, wondering again at her beauty and why it had been left to me to persuade her of it. Now I had a sense of sharing in it. As we kissed, it seemed to me that until we had come together, neither of us had understood our worth.

Exploring, I was sure she wanted to leave inexperience behind her, and indeed there was a little of the teacher-pupil relationship at first, an awe of me, an anxiousness that some awkwardness of her own might put me off, but soon her lips found comfort, then some freshets of passion, on mine. Willingly, Andy skinned out of blouse and bra and it was she who turned down the covers of my bed and was first to get in.

"I am . . . you know," she whispered in my ear. "I am a virgin."

"Does that frighten you?"

"No. But it may not be nice for you."

"I think it will."

I woke to the sound of the shower and rose to put on some coffee. Andy appeared fully dressed, and although she let me kiss her, she laughed and drew away. "It's the whiskers. I feel as if I have a sunburn."

She was preoccupied, letting me see her independence and that, however distasteful the job, she was going to be at those files by nine o'clock. Watching her across my table, as she sipped from my coffee cup, I sensed that last night's initiation had, ironically, left me more attached, more in need of Andy, than she was of me.

Thus some captiousness crept into my thoughts. I began to see her urgency as bravado — the weakening of her own resolve to survive against the indifferent and hostile social workers uptown — and to suspect her true commitment.

"Why not start the day with a confrontation," I said. "Tell old prune face you only have eight weeks and you want to see some action."

"I told you, I'm in no position . . ."

"Sure you are. You don't owe them anything. I have a feeling that I'll go off on this sales trip for a week and come back to find you're buried in that file cabinet. That's crazy, unless you like filing."

"I'm going to like it. I'm going to make it useful to them and to me. I wish you'd stop."

"You know something, Andy? If you really cared about doing something up there, you'd find a way. You'd change the place somehow . . . or go down trying."

She was furious, springing up to carry her half-empty cup to the sink and dump it. "You don't understand what it's like up there. I do, and I can handle it. I can get out of it just what I want." She fixed her scarf in the mirror and started out my door.

From the landing I called down, "Next Thursday, the night I get back, there's a party. Will you go with me?"

There was a delay before her answer floated up, bits of wreckage from a sunken ship. "You'd better call me." The front door slammed.

While I was away on that first selling trip, I thought about Andy all the time. I repented the thoughtlessness that had so offended her and at the same time realized that her insecurity at Goodwill House was not just concern over her effectiveness in the surprisingly hostile environment, but her guilt at deceiving her father.

Each day away from her persuaded me that Andy was essential to me. When I thought about making amends, I told myself how important it was to encourage her in whatever she was now doing at Goodwill House.

When I did return and, after leaving several messages, did reach her, she was reluctant to talk about how her work had been going. However, walking across Fifty-seventh Street to the party of my classmate, Loomis Pitcher, she admitted she was still at the welfare files.

When I agreed that the material itself, the relation between welfare and schooling, should be interesting to a sociologist, she brightened and said she was already starting a paper on it for her Bennington course.

The party turned out to be an all-liquid dinner, tall drinks followed by vegetable juice, two kinds of soup, and a runny dessert, so that there was soon a queue at the bathroom door. Andy was no surer than I of the point of his joke, but she was captivated by Loomy, as he was by her.

Indeed, Loomy took her off into a corner to show her his photographs, lingering over an album of nudes he had taken in woods and on dunes, their heads drawing close enough to start some jealous pricklings in my chest.

When Andy went to take her turn in line, Loomy came over to say, "That's a real girl — and she likes you."

"How do you know?"

"She asked about your girls."

"What did you tell her?"

"The truth — one romantic misfortune after another."

"Really, what did you say?"

"What difference does it make? She's yours."

"Oh, Loomy," I said. "I wish that were so."

Later, in a booth at Kip's, our hamburgers ordered, I told her about my trip. I had been as far as Utica and had the tenderfoot treatment all the way. Buyers would keep me waiting deliberately, while they gossiped with customers and clerks. When they did receive me, they told me how other publishers gave them a better discount than Poole's and had a fairer returns policy. When at last I got around to our new books, they would often yawn and shake their heads. Sometimes the day's orders failed to cover my night's lodging.

However, I did find a consolation in the fraternity of the road, finding I could spot the publishers' travelers by their threadbare look. There was one who took pride in repairing his eyeglasses with friction tape. I found they were like anglers, sharing their knowledge of the stream. Waiting to see the buyers, killing time in the lobby of the Goshen House, standing in the aisles of small-town bookshops, we would tell each other we weren't in it for the money, but for the peculiar satisfactions of the bookman's trade. I began to believe they were real ones, that what we carried in our sample cases was vastly different from that of other kinds of drummers. We carried man's thoughts — dark ones about his fate, soaring ones that open the mind to possibilities, and frivolous ones to gladden his heart.

When Andy asked if I did feel like a true drummer, I told her I'd made a discovery about that. While in Albany, having dinner with the Houghton man, we talked about an Australian novel on his list. We both liked it but differed on how we thought it would sell. He'd decided it was too remote, that American readers weren't curious about everyday life in Melbourne, while I argued it was a good book and they could overcome that resistance. Finally I asked him whether, if it had been up to him, he'd have published it.

He told me that was the editor's decision, and his job was simply to sell books. This surprised me and I asked if he didn't want to be an editor. He said no, making those decisions didn't interest him. He'd as soon leave them to someone else. While I was fully aware that editing was only one of the half dozen functions of publishing, to me it was the crucial one and the others seemed like novitiates for it. I couldn't imagine going through this selling experience without the hope of graduating. In fact, I had begun to see every book less in terms of who wrote it than of the man who decided to publish it. Would I? Why? Was it a courageous or an easy decision? A sound or a shoddy one?

"Did you tell that to Mrs. Penrose yet?" Andy asked.

"No. Not yet."

"Well, if you really cared, you would," she said, "or go down trying."

I laughed and said, "Right. I'm getting ready to tell Ethan."

When I asked about Loomy Pitcher, Andy said, "Oh, I liked him."

"What were you talking about?"

"You."

"What did he say?"

"That he was very fond of you — and that you needed to be looked after."

"I do, right now."

Andy licked a dab of ketchup from the corner of her mouth and smiled. "All right. I think I can do that."

At one moment in the middle of that night together with Andy, I remember opening my eyes to find that hers were open too, round with astonishment and unity with me, and I felt she had been persuaded to the roots of her being.

I woke late to find the sun reaching across our covers and realized we had slept the night in each other's arms. Even as Andy rose, looked at the clock, and calculated the time she would need to get to the welfare office, there was a languor in her movements, and once, as I was squeezing orange juice, she came alongside to kiss me.

Then, just as she was leaving, my telephone rang. To my dismay, a voice said, "This is Charles Cushing speaking. Is my daughter there?"

"Hello, Charles," I said. "It's Lloyd, Lloyd Erskine."

Across the room, Andy was shaking her head.

"Morris, her instructor up there, tells me Andy's gone to New York. He gave me this number. Would you have any idea where she is?"

"Well, I do. Yes."

"Is it her social work? Has she gone up there to Harlem?"

"Charles, I think she is hoping to get in on some opportunities she's found here. I think it's research at the Welfare Department. I'm sure she's going to be all right. I'll be here to see she's safe. I'll be looking after her."

"That's all very well, but I want to talk to her. When will you be in touch with her? Sometime today?"

"Yes, I think I will."

"Tell her to call me, will you? It's not like her to disobey me."

Hanging up, I told Andy, "I think it'll be all right."

"You didn't have to say that — about seeing I'm safe. You're not looking after me. I'm looking after myself."

"You can tell your father when you call him."

She started into the hallway and I asked, "Will you? Will you call him before noon?"

"When I'm ready," she said, and ran down the stairs.

Before noon, Andy reached me at the office. In a chastened voice she said she was in Grand Central, on her way back to Bennington. "And I'm sorry about this morning. It was unfair. I know you were trying to help."

"That's O.K. Will you be coming back?"

"I'm going to stay in Bennington."

"What if I want to see you?"

She seemed uncertain. "Well, you could come up, I guess."

Each time I saw her, Andy took further room in my heart. As I look back on that time now, I think she was still more my own design than truly Andy Cushing, but each meeting left me new shards of the real Andy.

I gathered them thirstily, trying to preserve and store them in memory. Apart, I was forever at my tessellations, correcting old faults or recollection, tiling-in lacunae, sculpting and resculpting the shape I would carry in my mind until next we met. My need to compare the likeness I carried with the real thing brought an urgency to our plans and I yearned for the time when Andy and the image of Andy would be one.

I suppose that the matrix of my love was essentially the void left by my mother, and the image may even have resembled her in obscure ways, but it was also a reverse cast of her. Where Mother had manifested disappointment, I sought joy — joy for the mind and spirit and, of course, for the body; joy for eye, for ear, for hand, and for the heart.

It was the first of March and Vermont winter was relenting. A pale sun made pools in the snow and a cataract in the rainspout of Dewey House. There were already signs — cars studding the horseshoe drive of the red barn administration building, a janitor opening the commons doors — of students' return.

We walked along the path under bare branches, crossing the field between the dormitories toward a bench that was sheltered from the fresh wind. Andy looked solemnly across the low stone wall that bordered the campus, to the lavender hills beyond.

I reached for the notebook she carried and found its pages filled with notes on poverty and unemployment, written in her careful hand.

I told her about Ethan's most recent schooling. He had been giving me manuscripts, asking me to work up a page that would focus on the book's appeal. I had brought him drafts of these and he had studied them, picking away at weaknesses, looking for ideas I had missed. I had revised them and we had conferred again, until we got it right.

When the draft was right it became the description. It was also the catalog copy and then the flap copy for the jacket and, in turn, the key to everything good that might happen to the book — the forecasters, the reviewers, the buyers, and finally the readers.

I had even made a dent in his reluctance to include me in editorial decisions. After putting me off for several weeks, he gave me a manuscript, a biography of Herbert Asquith, and asked my opinion. Clipped to the title page was Mia Penrose's carefully reasoned report. She didn't like it.

I did, and yet I was intimidated and finally persuaded by Mia's authority. I took care to do my reasoning separately but in the end agreed we should decline the book.

As always, Andy seemed absorbed by my apprenticeship, and I guessed she felt I was enjoying exactly the experience she had sought in the past two months. It was her vicarious enthusiasm that opened the way for my proposal.

"I don't know what you really want to do with your life, Andy," I said. "I don't know if you're committed to social work, or even if you believe you are, but if you do want to find out, you should try it for a year. You could do that with me."

She had seen my serious question coming for days, but still she was frightened, an animal cornered and looking now for escape. But she put her hand on mine to say, "Oh, Lloyd, I'm not sure of anything, except that I'm nineteen years old and I'm very green. I think I do love you. Do you know that?"

"No."

"There are times when I'm very sure of it, times when I'm listening to music or seeing something beautiful like those hills, and there are other times when I feel that I do, only not enough yet, not enough to be all that you want me to be, and then I'm not so sure — and this is a good place to be when you're not so sure."

"But all I want you to be is you. I want you to be all the things and do all the things you want to do. I know you think that marrying is the end of freedom, that you'll be gobbled up in obligations to me and a household and children, because that's what you've seen, but it won't be that way with me. I want you to be you. I want you to go on with college if that's what you want, or with welfare if that's what you want. You only have to choose. You can share my career if you like. There's plenty of excitement in publishing, plenty for two of us."

"But what will I do for you, Lloyd?"

"While I was off on the sales trip, I was terribly lonely. I never knew there was such loneliness. It was like an illness. There was a chill in my fingers and toes forever creeping toward my heart and I knew it was because I was missing you, that you were the light and warmth that could make me well. I would see that kind of light through windows, walking along a street at night, looking in at people having a good time together. I want to live in the midst of the light we make together. That's what you'll do for me."

Andy had been staring out at the hills, as though she had escaped me there, but now she turned to me and looked at me gravely for a second and then she said, "Well, you do understand, dear Lloyd, and against that, I don't think I can hold out any longer."

A week later, Andy called from Washington to say, "Lloyd, I think you're going to have to ask Daddy. Really. I want you to be friends, and no I don't know what he'll say. I'm not guaranteeing anything, but I do think you'd better come down. I'm not going to *elope* with you."

"But have you told him?"

"Yes."

"What did he say?"

"He asks why I'm so impetuous."

"Two months? That's an eternity. So much can happen in only one month — to you, to me."

"Tell him that. Don't worry about telling Daddy what you think."

But I was worried as we confronted each other the following Sunday. He welcomed me at the door of the house on Q Street with his customary cordiality, but as he led me off to the library and sat down behind his desk, there was a stiffening, a girding for an ancient conflict.

"Well," he said, "things between you and Andy have certainly progressed."

"Yes. They have. I love her."

Charles Cushing nodded. "She's a lovable girl. We all know

that, but I wonder if you're ready to take on a wife who's still very young and full of all kinds of unrealized ambitions."

"I want her to realize them, and I think she will." I watched him look darkly into his folded hands. "Charles, I'm sure I'm not at all what you had in mind for a son-in-law. I have no wealth, no position, not even a family."

"That's not the point at all, Lloyd. As you must know, I'm fond of you, but I've been talking to Andy about finishing her education. I thought she set considerable store by that. You'll remember she was quite angry when she felt *I* was interfering with it. Now just a few months later she's thinking of pitching it all over. I want her to think about that."

"She can go on with her education in New York."

"Well, it'll be a very different sort of thing from Bennington, night school and so on. You'd want her with you, not running around the city to classes. I know about such things. So I've suggested she wait awhile, a year perhaps, to see how things go. Then, if you're still fond of each other . . . I'm going to suggest the same to you, Lloyd. What have you to lose?"

"Andy."

"If you're truly fond of each other, you won't lose her. You'll be a year more sure."

"Is Andy not sure?"

"I think she has some doubts."

After a moment I said, "I dread a year's wait — but if Andy is doubtful I must. Is she really? Could we ask her, or is this just between us?"

Deliberately, he rose and went into the hall. At some distance I heard him call her, and then they came into the library together, Andy looking pale but with a sympathetic smile for me. She sat on the window seat and looked from one to the other of us, tension adding years and extra beauty to her face.

Charles spoke gently. "We were talking, Lloyd and I, about whether you had any doubts about his plan of marrying in a couple of months."

Andy frowned at the toes of her shoes and then said, "Sure I do. But Father, I'll always have those. I do want to be married in June."

There was a silence then between us, until Charles said, "All right, then." He rose and went to Andy to kiss her. When he turned to me I saw that his eyes were filled with tears. Taking my hand he said, "Well, from what I hear, you're off and running in this publishing career of yours." He smiled. "Tell me, Lloyd, you going to let her go up to Harlem?"

~§ 4 §~

WE WERE MARRIED on the seventh of that June in 1947, at Trinity Church, across from the White House, with Loomy Pitcher as best man and Ethan Poole standing in for my family. I remember Ethan browsing the room where our wedding presents were on display, pausing before the Ming bowl. "It's beautiful," he told Andy in his avuncular way, "but now that you're marrying into the publishing business, you need gifts of a more practical nature." Whereupon he produced his — a jumbo, Malacca-handled umbrella of crimson silk. His card read, "No forecast here of rainy days, but a rosy shelter just in case."

In the first year of our marriage, Andy and I made endless discoveries about each other, yet I don't remember any of those moments of discovery half so vividly as I remember our first quarrel. Perhaps the vividness was due to the setting. It was Austria. We had gone on our first holiday abroad and were to stay at the Gasthaus Chesereng in Zurs, which charged four dollars a night and included a breakfast of pinwheel rolls and coffee. Even for 1948 that was cheap, and Frau Chesereng didn't let you forget it.

As I dipped the nib pen to scratch *Mr. and Mrs. Lloyd Erskine, New York,* into her register, the clamp of her mouth suggested I had taken too much ink. She withheld all curiosity about our journey, every semblance of welcome. If it was her tongue's reluctance to tangle with English, that did not forgive the worn carpet of our room, the grudging towels, the barred bath, the distant cell that was our toilet.

While Andy unpacked I walked through the town, peering in at the bar of the Alpenrose and crossing a snowfield to look in at the Lorünser's dining room, where a dozen people were still at table. Farther on, the lights of the Zurserhoff beckoned from arched, mullioned windows, as though from a royal *Schloss*. There was dancing at the Zurserhoff.

Back at the Chesereng, I crawled in beside Andy, who had gone to bed. "We've got to move."

"M-mm. I'm asleep."

"The town is full of places, every one better than this."

"I'm tired."

I rolled toward her down the incline of the brass bed's sag. "I just wanted you to know we're moving in the morning."

"They're probably all expensive."

"We didn't come three thousand miles to save a few bucks. We'd have done that better at home."

She was silent and I decided she had gone back to sleep, but then she said, "I thought we came to ski?"

"It's my first trip to Europe. I want to see what it's like. Don't you?"

"I'm seeing more than I can possibly take in. Why don't we give the Chesereng a chance."

"It smells of cabbage and bad plumbing and something else I can't put my finger on. Maybe it's Frau Chesereng. At the Lorünser there are English and Americans. I could hear them. I'd never realized what a lovely language we speak."

"I didn't come three thousand miles to hear American. I could have done that better . . ."

"Oh, you know what I mean. This was a dumb decision."

"I don't think it was a dumb decision. We're not going to spend our time in the room. We'll be skiing."

"It's God-awful." I found the cord to the bedside lamp and

pressed a switch. A hole was scorched into the yellow shade. Looming over the bed's foot was the flimsy clothespress where Andy had hung her jersey dress and overcoat. The curtains were printed with unlikely flowers in wan colors. "It makes me want to weep, this place."

"Then turn off the light."

I did, and edged away, up the slope. We lay silently for a while, but I could tell from her breathing that Andy hadn't gone back to sleep. "You know this is stupid," I said, "arguing about where we're going to stay, but this is a dump. What makes you want to stay here?"

"I don't care that much."

"I do. I've always imagined what coming to Europe would be like, and this isn't it. Wait'll you see the other places."

"But we have reservations for a week."

"In the morning, you get your skis and go to ski school. I'll move us. I'l pay her for the whole week if she likes — a month if necessary."

"Other places may be booked up."

"Leave that to me. We'll meet some place for lunch and I'll show you where we live."

"Lloyd, I don't understand you. It's one-thirty and we're dead tired and you're fretting about this not being a classy enough place. Are you afraid somebody's going to *see* you here?"

"No. I don't think it's that."

"Then, why?"

"Because this place depresses me."

She did not reply, but I felt her creep farther away, and then I did too, getting a hold on the edge of the mattress and pulling myself toward it, then crossing my arms, as I used to at sea, securing myself. "Look," I said. "You stay here if you like. I'll move and we can meet sometimes. I'll invite you over for a drink."

In the morning, after the rolls and coffee, I went out and got us a room at the Lorünser, which was twice as expensive but cheap I insisted, by any reasonable standard.

Our new room had a huge bathtub with brass fittings and towels big enough to wrap a horse. From its tall windows there was a grand view of the Mahdloch.

"Isn't this more like it?" I crowed.

Andy smiled and asked, "What *is* this need to . . ."

I said, "When I was in the fifth grade, there were rich kids who went to Europe for vacations. One family had spent a summer in Nice. That name, the sound of it, has always seemed unbelievably beautiful to me, a symbol of all the sybaritic illusions I'd drawn from books and movies. Isn't it that way with you?"

"No."

"I thought everyone did that."

"Aren't you trying to be someone else?"

"No — I don't think so."

"Appearances matter so much to you."

"Yes, I guess they do. It's what you must go on, mostly. Appearances matter to you too, Andy. You worry about our effect on total strangers in the train."

"I don't want to offend them."

"With me it's more my own vision of myself. I'm trying out a romantic idea I've carried around for years, the vision of being in Europe for the pleasure of it, to see if the dream isn't a truth of some kind."

"But do I have to act out your dreams?"

"I'd assumed you had a set of your own."

"Maybe I do," Andy said, "but they're different."

We stayed in Europe a month and when we came back to New York we rented an apartment in Chelsea. It was in an old house and we peeled the plaster off one wall, wire brushing away the last of it, washing down the bricks with muriatic acid, and finally waxing them with such passion, as if a clear and shiny wall would reflect our happiness.

Andy hung old family photographs; I offered her a picture Dee had taken of Dan, posed against the Carnegie Library lions. Looking at it through Andy's eyes, I was struck by how little there was to go on; half his face shaded by the fedora's brim, eyes behind the gold-rimmed specs, surprising jowls over the stiff, white collar (he'd seemed so skinny to me then), hands in pockets of a boxy, black topcoat, the vest, and the dark foulard — protective colorings all.

But Andy's lips were parted in wonder, as though he were coming alive for her, and she said, "Yes. I see *you*, and I see his intelligence, the kindness, and a reticence." Her fingertip hovered over the corner of his eye.

I said, "To me, looking at him now, he's elusive, just about to go. That's how I remember him too, never having enough of him. Saturdays I'd have him sometimes, and maybe a week in the summer. Once we planned a camping trip. He'd camped as a boy and remembered good times and we did, finally, get all the junk in the car and set off for the wilderness, but it rained for three days and we were eaten up by the bugs that got through the mosquito net and the food got soaked and we came back early, but we went on planning another trip together. It was to be a bicycle trip to Scotland. We'd pore over a map of the British Isles, saying the names of the towns we were going to visit — Portknockie and Lossiemouth." My lips pursed and I whistled the ten notes, down then up the scale, still as plaintive to me as those of a mourning dove. "That was our secret call."

"Oh, I wish I'd known him," Andy said.

"The job at C & C claimed him. He was excited by it in the beginning and then gradually, over a lifetime, he soured on it and never had the spirit to clear out."

"Did he want you to do something different?"

"I asked him that, and he said, 'I don't want you to do anything for me. Do it for you.'"

Andy said, "That doesn't sound like an unhappy man."

"Not self-pitying surely, but bereft. As a kid I always sensed that he was as lonely as I, but we never talked about it. And the women he knew disappointed him. I don't know if it was bad luck or bad taste or a lack of courage."

"What about your mother?"

"There was an old photograph of her wearing a long white dress and a bow in her hair. She's peering out over the lake with an expression of delighted expectation. But whatever she was expecting never came in and I remember a woman whose moods changed like the weather, from adolscent gaiety to fury and despair. Some days she was remote and some days she'd spoil me. Life seemed to fail her, so she resented it and failed it back. She ran a little real estate business and she was always in trouble with some tenant or owner. She'd promise things and then forget."

"Were there men?"

"I don't think so. She'd grown suspicious of them. Hostility ran just under the surface of her gaiety. She'd gone faintly mad, really, and had come to look a little askew, as though she'd lost the sense of how she appeared to others. She died of a typical carelessness."

"How?"

"If she was late for an appointment, she'd take a cup of coffee with her. It spilled while she was driving, and she put the car over a bank."

Andy shook her head. "What do you feel for her?"

"Lately I've felt some pity, but beyond that I don't feel much, one way or the other."

Andy's fascination with publishing and quick grasp of its dynamics made me realize what a good counselor she would be. A few months before our son was born, I gave her the proofs of an English novel about a married woman who, at the time of her father's death, returns to her childhood home. She took a week to read it and afterward said that she'd enjoyed it, thought it well written.

I said, "Did you feel he was right about fathers and daughters?"

"Yes," she said, "that's what I liked about it."

"What about the scene after the funeral, when she makes love to her husband? Did that ring right?"

"Yes, I thought that was probably the way it would be."

"Come on, Andy. Did it send you right out of your socks, or just sort of interest you? If you're going to help me you're going to have to read aggressively, pick a quarrel with the author, and then be articulate about it. You can do that. Your antennae are fine, but you tense up."

"Why do you want my opinion? Aren't you sure what you think of this?"

"I'm never so sure of my judgment that I don't want it bolstered. Besides, the editorial process involves checking your enthusiasms against others', building confidence in your own taste and that of the people around you, knowing whose you trust. That's the ultimate puzzle — *which* book, out of the thousands, you publish. I ask every editor how he does it, and I've had only one satisfactory reply."

- "Which was?"

"My wife tells me."

Andy laughed. "I wonder what the wife feels about that, if she's happy being the silent partner."

"I'm sure she'd be pleased — wouldn't you?"

Andy raised her eyebrows, nodded uncertainly.

"Besides, it's a profession, and you're learning it."

"Do you like me learning yours?"

"I want you to share in it. And you don't have one of your own, do you?"

"I could — one day."

"Remember your commitment to social work? It was such a passion with you. I thought you married me because your father wouldn't let you go to Harlem."

She laughed. "It was."

"I don't believe you've lost all interest in it. It's your kind of thing. If you got into it again . . ."

"I've been thinking about that, and why I cared so much about going to Harlem that spring. I had to prove my own will against father's strong one. I love him, but I didn't want to be like Mummy. She's made herself into what he wanted, into a good sailor's wife, and there's no trace left of what she felt about things."

"What about being a good editor's wife?"

She looked at the proofs.

"Yes, of course, I want to be a good reader for you."

"You've got to tell me what to publish."

"I'm going to. Don't you worry."

At the office, I now grasped every opportunity to offer an opinion on what we should publish. When I discovered the who-was-Shakespeare controversy through a manuscript that came down on the side of the Earl of Oxford, I was convinced by it and said so in my report.

Mia disagreed. "This is shoddy stuff," she explained to Ethan. "The author has not acknowledged his debt to Herbert Crowe and he seems quite oblivious to the Marlowe possibilities. There's an ingenuous charm to the manner but these are unsafe waters for an amateur. A waste of your good time bothering with this."

I felt Mia was unfair both to the book and to me and I began to wonder if Ethan wasn't being taken in by her, but he dismissed my gripes. "You don't know enough yet to hold a respectable opinion," he told me with the affectionate smile that made my apprenticeship more endurable. "You'll have to be cuffed around a bit before you do."

Yet my feud with Mia continued by way of an anthropology book that I admired and recommended. Mia, of course, knew better. "This book is readable enough, but pedestrian, and I suspect it's been all over town before coming to us." A few months later, Macmillan announced the book's forthcoming publication and their tall expectations for it.

I made sure Ethan saw the ad, with a note, "Poor Macmillan's. They aren't going to know what hit them when they try to put this one over on the trade."

From that moment I felt I was going to be a match for Mia Penrose, and the field for it came about through a classmate,

Billy Maxwell. In the spring of 1950, Billy came into the office one day with the manuscript of his comic novel about the Air Force.

I enjoyed *Solo*, laughed aloud at it, and felt it was good enough to publish. I hoped Ethan would share my enthusiasm and made the mistake of taking it directly to him. I knew he was busy, yet I hated to see the manuscript untouched on his desk all week. I wondered if this was more of his hazing.

When Billy called to ask about prospects I went in to Ethan and, for the first time, showed some spirit. "You know how anxious I am about my friend Maxwell's manuscript, Ethan. Can you let me know something soon?"

Ethan nodded soberly and carried *Solo* off to Mia Penrose.

"I'm afraid I don't care for Mr. Maxwell's slapstick at all," Mia wrote in her report. "The humor, which turns on the stupidity of senior officers and the sexual bragging of the cadets, is adolescent and often just plain coarse. While it no doubt pulls some guffaws in the barracks, I think any intelligent reader would find it embarrassing. There is no need to dignify this with hard covers — certainly not ours."

"It's not Mia's kind of book at all," I told Ethan. "That's why I didn't show it to her. But it's very accurate. Any serviceman will recognize that. Can't you look at it yourself?"

"I did."

"And you feel as Mia does?"

"No. I suspect you're right, but you know it's not our style, and because of that I think we might fail with it, where a racier house might succeed."

"Why shouldn't *Solo* be our style? It's a funny book. As for our not doing as well with it as another house, I'll see that we do."

Caught as I was in my duel with Mia Penrose, I was losing the objectivity of sound editorial judgment. Still, if I gave way in the gentlemanly fashion Ethan was expecting, I knew I would be unable to live with myself.

In the end, Ethan relented. "Okay, Lloyd. After — what is it? — four years of putting up with me *and* Mia, I guess you deserve it. Go ahead and contract with Mr. Maxwell for his book." The mischief returned to his eyes. "And . . . let it be a lesson to you."

All the while, Ethan was sharing his knowledge with me — his pleasure in typefaces, rich paper, and the fine linen cloth that bound Poole books. I began to delight in beautiful printing and the feel of good cloth, the craftsmanlike binding that rewarded the eye and hand.

But as I grew to know Ethan, I began to see him as a man with limitations. Even as a bibliophile I suspected he was an amateur, that he knew what he liked but lacked the professional's understanding of why he liked it. When he spoke of the editorial function, of procuring the best available manuscripts for us to publish, he told me it was largely a question of socializing, of seeing the agents and feeding them a drink and a good lunch now and again.

Our own authors, he said, were an equally important source. If you "stayed with good people," you would get good books. By good people he meant literary people — writers, editors, academics, but especially those you trusted. I guessed that just "staying with good people" was a pleasant but haphazard way to go about acquisition. His integrity, rather than his business sense, was at issue. He was loyal to friends and went about putting together his list with more heart than mind.

Nevertheless, Ethan Poole was a good publisher. He published books because he thought they were good ones, and secondarily because he thought they would make money. The Poole list reflected Ethan's taste and he *was* putting his stamp on his times.

He believed less in his brilliance, or even his taste, than in his own sensitivity to honesty, shrewdness, understanding, kindness, and the belief that the qualities he admired would prevail in a mischievous and untidy world where, as a rule, baser motives had the upper hand.

⊸§ 5 §⊸

DURING THE POST-COMMENCEMENT weeks in the spring, scores of fresh graduates wrote, phoned, and came unannounced in search of a job. One day, Ethan asked me to see a young man just out of Harvard and recommended by a friend.

Joel Rossbach strolled into my cell as though paying a diplomatic call. His hair was a tossing sea, his nose a blade, and if not handsome he surely was, in dark, well-cut business suit and tasseled loafers, elegant. He was smiling without a trace of an applicant's humility.

"Do sit down," I said, nodding at the hard chair beside my desk.

He reset it with a flourish and, seating himself, he crossed his knees and clasped them, alert and at ease. His eyes shone with pleasure as he took me in, as though he liked me on sight.

In his furry, resonant voice he spoke of common ground in Cambridge, Eliot House, the *Lampoon,* of which he had been an editor, and the Signet, where we had both been members. His vitality and sense of fun were contagious and in a few minutes he had me laughing at an account of Paul Revere's latest ride through the Yard.

I found myself wanting to please and entertain him, to give him a favorable impression of both me and Poole's, but I warned, "I hope we haven't got your hopes up. As you can see we're just a handcar crew here and there's not likely to be any opening you'd find tempting."

He waved away my concern as though to say he understood and that it was my time he was concerned about wasting.

"We only do about forty books a year," I went on, "and we do them because we think they're good books and believe that if they really are they'll sell enough to pay the rent."

"And they do?"

"Yes."

"I wondered if there were an angel somewhere in orbit."

His remark confounded me. I had no idea whether Ethan subsidized his firm. It had never occurred to me.

"No. Not to my knowledge. But I'd be ashamed to tell you what I make here. It's no way to get rich."

"An occupation for gentlemen?"

"Hardly. On Tuesday I was picking up books at the warehouse in Queens and delivering them, out of the back of my car, in Stamford. This morning, for an hour, I was tending the switchboard."

"Still, it's a very classy operation. I can tell." He grinned without malice. "Not even a token Jew around."

"I don't think that's purposeful. There are only a dozen people here."

He was no longer concerned. His eyes had found the boxes of manuscript on my radiator cover and he asked, "You do some reading?"

"We're all first readers here."

"Then you're lucky. It's a good job. I can see why you're jealous of it. You get to do everything."

"That may be an indulgence for a man of thirty with a wife and a child on the way. But perhaps I'm not ambitious."

"I doubt that." Joel Rossbach laughed. There was an appealing quality, both sensitive and exuberant, to his laughter.

"I have the feeling you're interviewing *me*," I said. "Now tell me about you."

"Well, I'm *not* interested in making a lot of money. My father's interested in that. What interests me is good writing."

"Agreed."

"I've known for some time that I want to be a good editor."

"The Maxwell Perkins legend?"

"The great Max set the pattern for shrewdness all right. He recognized the Ernests and Toms and Scotts when they came along, and he knew how to behave with them. I give him full marks for that but I simply do not believe his famous humility. False modesty gives me a pain in the ass. I think he was probably worried about seeming too big for his breeches and offending Charlie Scribner. The books a house gets, the authors it keeps, are what makes a house great, and that's all up to the editor. To pretend otherwise is a dishonesty."

"The irony is that for all his protesting against thanks and notoriety, he got plenty of both."

"Oh, Perkins is a real legend, and it'll be the ruin of this business, all the illusions of it."

"O.K.," I said. "I certainly agree that deciding what to publish is the big mystery, and anyone who does it well is some kind of magician, but I have an idea that the trap for all of us lies right there, in the editorial hubris, the notion that we have, not just discretionary, but real creative power. Agents and authors keep suggesting to an editor that he does, simply by publishing this person and not that one. If he's not careful he'll come to believe he can *make* an author. Even to *suspect* he can is dangerous, and that's why Perkins's modesty wasn't false. He knew that."

"You gents," he said, and we both laughed.

"Joel, you sound as if you've had a lot of publishing experience."

"In my sophomore year I started a literary magazine, *Gimlet.* It lasted three issues, but it gave me a taste for making my choices, for betting on them. Then I put in a couple of summers as a salesman for Holt. I learned to look over a list like yours" — from his pocket, Joel produced the Poole catalog, ticked along the margin — "and see the plumbing. Now there are some good books here, but I would guess there's no title that's going to sell a thousand copies a year. I'm puzzled. I've always assumed that a quality operation like yours can't run in the black without twenty-five years of backlist."

"We have a backlist, some history and biography that keep active at five hundred a year, or thereabout, and Poole's putts on."

"You must have a good accountant."

"Our accountant seems to get the accounts so snarled we have to hire another to come and straighten them out."

"Charming," Joel said, "and I don't believe that either. From what I've observed, a successful publishing house is always two men, one with the editorial flair, and the other with a mind ruled like a balance sheet."

"That doesn't apply here."

"You hire people just because they need a job?"

"Ethan's a kind man. A year ago he took that accountant to lunch with the intention of firing him, but he put it so delicately the accountant came away believing he was getting a raise — and so he did."

"My God," Joel laughed. "I don't understand, but clearly Mr. Poole is some kind of genius."

"He's stubborn and doesn't give much of a hang what anybody thinks. He avoids fads and does things his way. If he likes a book well enough to buy, he figures he can find enough readers who feel the same way. Often he does."

Joel Rossbach squinted at his watch. "Lloyd, I've taken too much of your time. You've persuaded me there's no job here but made me very curious about Mr. Poole. Could I meet him?"

"I think he'd like to meet you." When Ethan came on the phone I said, "I've discouraged Mr. Rossbach all I can, but he'd like to hear it from the boss as well."

"I've got five minutes," Ethan said. "Send him in to the lion."

"He's in the corner office," I told Joel. "You can go right in."

In my doorway we shook hands, and as he went off I called, "Let me know if I should clean out my desk."

He waved. "Not a chance. I'm not qualified."

Later, when I asked Ethan about Joel Rossbach, he said, "Yes, he's a bright boy. We'll be hearing from him. What did you think?"

"I found myself liking him. He made me curious about how, with so small a backlist, we manage financially. He suspected a subsidy."

"That *is* impertinence. Lucky he didn't ask me."

"Supposing I do?"

He frowned. "Oh well, in the first few years I was always dipping into the sock. Once I took a second mortgage on the house in Rye, and I've been known to tamper with the children's education money. As you know, I still trot off to the bank in lean months, but *no,* I'm not a rich man, and if Mr. Rossbach's interested, each year our backlist is more fruitful."

"Thanks. A good answer to that question."

"There's another?"

"He observed the prevailing, Protestant air and said he felt unqualified to work here. No Jews — was that a matter of policy? I said no, but I'm not altogether sure."

Ethan's eyebrows raised at the challenge. Then he smiled and tossed me an apple from the bowl on his desk. Selecting one for himself, he polished it on the sleeve of his shirt.

"I have no policy about anything, Lloyd, except for a policy of not having a policy. What's yours?"

"At least I know I'm against anti-Semitism. But of course I do have an ambivalence, a fast-eroding sense of social advantage, alongside the suspicion I'm inferior, that in the end some circle of Jews where I most want to be is going to exclude me."

Ethan pondered his apple and took a careful bite. "Well, I tell you, Lloyd. I come to work because I like it here, and I try to keep it that way. Where I can, I surround myself with people I enjoy. Generally speaking I prefer attractive ones to unattractive ones, intelligent people to stupid ones, and friendly, approachable people to sullen ones."

"I should think Joel Rossbach would qualify on all those counts."

"Perhaps this is a shortcoming of my own. God knows I have a number. But I'd be a little afraid of him."

"In what way?"

"There's such a thing as too *much* get-up-and-go. It would be hard on the rest of us."

We did hear more of Joel Rossbach — first a note from him saying he had taken a job at Crowninshield & Company, and then one announcing he had found an apartment on Bank Street. He wanted me and my wife to come to the house-warming.

In the garden apartment of a brownstone, Joel had mustered a roomful of youngish people, recognizable by the stuffed brief-cases in the bedroom, the darting, *qui vive* eyes framed by horn rims, and some gypsy affectations among the women, as fellow publishers.

"Mostly Crowninshield's, you'll find," he explained, "but there's an infiltration from other houses, also some agents and an author or two. I'll take you around if you like."

"No, please," Andy said, wanting to let him off that chore.

"We'll look after ourselves," I assured him.

Andy was good at parties, tending to anchor. Her looks and composure attracted strangers. A good, sympathetic listener, she learned about people, and her passive deployment for the social skirmish generally succeeded.

I tended to roam. My eye went searching for the live, attractive ones, and curiosity drew me toward them. So we had settled on a strategy. If I discovered someone interesting, I would tow my find to Andy's corner, or come back for her, all the while keeping an eye out to see what her net had caught. And we enjoyed the game, knowing that, unlike most guests, we would be leaving together.

I left her as she asked Joel about a row of new Crowninshield titles laid out on a trestle table, and moved toward the bar where a fellow with an insolent cherub's face was addressing a respectful audience.

"We're so smug," he was saying, "pretending to be art patrons or taste makers or whatever, and behaving like businessmen. I've got nothing against businessmen, so long as they know what they are."

"Hello," I said to the dark-haired girl beside me. She had a penetrating but friendly eye. "Enjoying the lecture?"

She smiled and said, "I've heard it before, actually. I'm Kay Sondheim. Who're you?"

I told her and she took charge in an easy way, leading us past the buffet for a plate of shrimp and out toward a bench in the garden. She asked intelligent questions about Poole's and spoke so knowledgeably about publishing that I asked, "You're at Crowninshield's?"

"I'm an *author*."

"Sorry. I should know."

She shook her head. "My first story's in the new *Paris Review* and I'm *thinking* about a novel, which explains Hughie's interest. It's Hughie that asked me here."

"Hughie?"

"The one doing the talking. I thought *every*body knew Hughie Severance. He's the boss's son."

"Is he a good editor?"

"I think so. He's in earnest, and he guesses I'm a comer. Of course, I don't have a novel so it is a kind of farce. I feel like the maid mistaken for the princess, but I'm no fool. I'm counting on a lovely dinner out of it, and maybe an invitation to Greenfields."

"What's that?"

"The family compound in Duchess County. Is that your wife talking to him?"

Through the French doors I saw that Joel had indeed brought Andy over to meet Hugh Severance, Jr. "Yes. How did you know I was married?"

"A smart girl can tell if a guy is really looking around for someone, or just keeping his hand in. It's also a clue if she sees him come in with a pregnant woman. Your wife is beautiful. Could I meet her?"

When we approached, Hugh Jr. was asking Andy, "It's unpleasant, right?"

"Well, it's cumbersome," she replied without visible embarrassment. "That's what's surprising, the hippopotamus feeling. I'm no longer sure of where I stop, and I take the measure of every doorway."

He laughed in a way that seemed presumptuous and coarse, and I liked him no better for it. When Kay Sondheim introduced us, Hugh Jr.'s hand was indifferent and his eye cold. "Your wife's been telling me about Poole's. You like it there?"

"Very much."

"There must be an advantage in being small and independent, but why not do something with it?"

"We *do* do something with it," I said. "And how we do is a matter of opinion. Ethan Poole's is that we do very well."

"I hadn't noticed," he said.

"Do you do a lot of controversial books at Crowninshield's?"

"I try," he replied.

"And you *can't*?"

"Oh, I don't get any special treatment," he said. "I'm just one of the finks. Isn't that so, Joel?"

"Yes, sir," Joel said, and there was laughter.

When Andy and I exchanged the time-to-leave glance, I noticed that although Kay Sondheim still hovered, Hughie Severance had turned his attention and a roving hand to a shining blonde from Viking. Then, as I looked for our coats in the stack on Joel's bed, Kay came in.

"You getting that lovely dinner?"

Kay shook her head and, with a clownish smile, said, "You were right. Any editor who'll turn me down for Miss Atlantic City there is frivolous. He's just lost an important author."

Joel spoke from the doorway. "Kay, have dinner with me,

will you? We'll have to wait for the stragglers, another half hour maybe."

She was tugging at the sleeve of her coat. "No charity, thanks."

"It's a selfish invitation," Joel said.

"You mean that?"

"Dead earnest."

As Andy and I left, Kay was busy emptying ashtrays and I said to Joel, "He's odd, isn't he, young Severance?"

"We make allowances for Hughie," he smiled. "He's not nearly as bad as he seems on first encounter."

"I can believe that," I said.

In the cab, Andy opened the book Joel had given her to the title page, where he had written, "Andy — for your lying-in, and the touch of immortality it will bring you — ever, Joel."

"I like your friend Joel."

"Ethan felt he was too much on the make."

Andy closed her book. "I don't think it's *all* business with Joel. He has a real concern for people. I'm sure of it."

"One can't help liking him — as opposed to young Severance, say. I thought he was a major pain."

"Really? Isn't that funny. I thought he was simply unsure of himself."

"Unsure? Did you see him feeling-up the blond girl in the center of the room?"

"But he's pathetic about that. He doesn't attract women, surely not effortlessly as Joel does, and he knows that. No, Lloyd, Hughie's not at all certain that way, nor as an editor. You really got to him. Working for his father's house must haunt him. I saw a sad young man."

"You *were* taken with him."

"Don't be silly."

"When I came in, it seemed to me you were flirting with each other."

"Oh, Lloyd. Nobody flirts with a pregnant lady."

As I let us into the apartment I said, "You know we might

give a party. Maybe Ethan should have a look at the competition. Would you like that?"

"Drinks and a casserole? Sure, if we can do it in the next couple of weeks. Who'd we ask? Joel's crowd?"

"I'd skip young Severance, but I thought Kay Sondheim was fascinating."

Andy paused in hanging up her jacket, fitting it onto a hanger and weighing it in the crook of a finger. "I noticed. I thought you didn't care for aggressive women."

"I don't find Kay aggressive. She was funny about her book and candid about her feelings."

"Changing her opinions of people in the instant of their usefulness? Would you like me if I behaved according to what, or who, would help me most in my career?"

"You couldn't, Andy. It's against your nature, and the way you were brought up. Anyway, that was different tonight. That was a publishing party."

"But publishing's where you live, Lloyd."

Later, we did discuss a guest list, but we did not agree on it, as though a deeper issue lay between us, and finally our party gave way to parturition.

The eroticism of Andy's full belly and breasts dissolved as she became more careful of herself and withdrew into the clinical world of childbirth. Her mother arrived, bringing an air of urgency and momentousness. I would come home to find them consulting lists and stores, conspiring in pediatric mystique.

When I emerged from the refuge of a manuscript to complain, Andy and her mother reacted with surprise, as though to say, *You still here? But your function's done. Now, do have the grace to stay clear of these big doings.*

So I counted the days until our life would return to normal.

I was unprepared for the miracle itself, the moment of peering into Lenox Hill's nursery for a first glimpse of William Cushing Erskine, and being struck through the heart. *That is me again, only better by Andy. I am the creator of that small man, presently helpless in his basket there, clenching, unclench-*

ing his miniature fingers, making fishy kisses with his minuscule lips, blinking his new, blue eyes in surprise at our air and light, frightened (and well you might be, Will), yet joyous to be here among us (and doubly well you might be, Will), and capable of anything. Yes, Will, you small replica of us, if only you choose — you can change the whole fucking world!

It was as though God's own voltage had just passed through my index finger, exactly as through that of Michelangelo's Adam. I had felt the force and exaltation of it and I *believed*. But such headiness had the life of a butterfly. It was all but forgotten by the time Will took up residence with us on Twenty-second Street. Within a week his outcries were shattering the once-reflective bourbon hour and the hour of profoundest sleep, at three in the morning.

"Why don't *you* go this time," Andy would propose as we listened to the rising of Will's alarm.

"Because he wants you."

"He wants a warm bottle. He wants to be picked up and held for a minute."

"By his mother," I would say, pulling up the covers to muffle the sound. "My time'll come."

Throughout Will's infancy, I kept thinking — this is a phase. In another week or so, we'll be back to normal. Andy'll be less tired, less anxious about him, and Will about us, less worried that we'll go away and leave him, or whatever that terror is which speaks in the top note of his anguish.

But it was never quite the same again. Andy never entirely shed the fatigue of her efforts for him, nor her preoccupation with him. Even as we made love now, I sensed her ear cocked for his need, and there was always a slight difference between us on how to respond to that, on when he was sick enough to want the doctor, on his bedtime, on the appropriate toy.

In the end, of course, I deferred to Andy. She was a good mother, and I was not, but she was never again so mine as she was in the days before Will joined us.

~§ 6 §~

To MY PLEASURE, and Mia's and Ethan's surprise, Billy Maxwell's *Solo* took off. The *Reader's Digest* condensed it. For two weeks it kept a toehold on the best-seller lists and became the most successful book of our season. Ethan was gracious about it, but a little hurt, as though I had taken advantage of his permissiveness and brought home a stray dog he suspected of having fleas. I decided he really did shun easy money. It threatened his most precious values.

Nevertheless, I began to feel like a real publisher and bold enough to take a cottage on Martha's Vineyard for August.

After Labor Day, when I got back to my desk, I found a message there from Hugh Severance, Jr. I had not thought of him since the evening of Joel's party, but I was oddly pleased to find that he sought me. I had been savoring a taste of success, yet suspecting it was entirely in my own mouth. Perhaps it was this eagerness to confirm my sprouting self-confidence as an editor that turned my resentment of Hugh Severance Jr. into curiosity and anticipation.

"Oh, Lloyd." Hugh Jr.'s voice was that of a comrade, as though we'd been through something together and had an understanding. "Do you know the Editors' Lunch? Well, there is such a thing. Old boys, full of themselves. My father refuses to go anymore. It's often a waste of time, but I thought it might interest you. Would you like to come along — next Thursday?"

"I would."

"Pierre's, on Fifty-third. Twelve-thirty. Meet you at the bar."

It was true, then, that it doesn't take much, perhaps no more than a book that clings for a couple of weeks to the bottom of the best-seller list, to change the way the world regards you.

Hugh Jr. was twenty minutes late, but unapologetic. Crowding by waiters, he led me through the restaurant into the kitchen, an inferno where white devils stirred oaths into their caldrons and, with a flash of blades, carved the flesh of pale creatures.

We climbed a narrow stair to a room where wine bottles rose in tiers to a painted arbor overhead. A dozen men and a single woman were gathered around the table, and while some looked up, waved at Hugh Jr., gave me a welcoming glance, there were no introductions. We took empty chairs and ordered drinks.

Looking around the circle I found I was lunching with the bosses. I recognized Bennett Cerf, opposite; and learned it was Ken McCormick beside the woman, Helen Everitt; that the ruddy face was John Farrar's; and the guardsman's mustache belonged to Alfred Knopf. There were younger men, silent, attentive, in the presence of the elders.

The conversation ran swift in the shallows of the morning's washroom wit and the company gossip, relating the affairs and divorces which swept like February colds through publishers' offices.

Pierre, the amiable boniface, interrupted, pad aloft, proposing "the scallops, truly benign creatures who slept last night in the cool, green waters of Sheepshead Bay and even now are simmering gently in fresh Vermont butter, with just a suspicion of shallots. Or perhaps you would prefer a rack of tender spring lamb, flavored by herbs gathered with utmost care from the holy mountain tops of the Himalayas? And of course we also have the specialty of the house, a most exquisite *boeuf bourguignon* — tender, juicy morsels of prime beef and infant, spring vegetables swimming in a poem of *sauce pommard*. I cannot recommend it too highly . . . and besides it is left over from last night and we would like to bid it *au revoir*."

"I'll have the steak," said a voice.

"What a brilliant decision, Mr. McCormick." Beaming, making a flourish on his pad, Pierre turned to Helen Everitt. "Madame?"

As lunch was served, talk moved to the trade's deeper waters and the season's big catches. There were several versions of how the agent Elena Wallace had arranged the release of an author from Scribner's and offered his new book to McGraw-Hill. No one from McGraw-Hill was present, but there was agreement the house had paid seventy-five thousand dollars for it, and a lively dispute over whether it would get its money back.

Now came tales of authors lost and won, of advances sought and paid, of gratifying sales and the effects of serialization and favorable publicity on particular titles. There was talk of books that had taken a firm into, and out of, financial difficulty.

As the anecdotes bubbled forth, the laughter grew more intense, eyes and ears alert for information. The faces around the table reflected joy and envy at daring, successful ventures that brought in the season's big harvests. Just as clear was a there-but-by-the-grace-of-God-go-I sense of relief at stories of disaster. There was palpable uneasiness at the mention of a man who, a year ago, had been a member of this group. Today he was making the rounds for a job, and some had already forgotten him.

But the stories that gave the most pleasure were those that had the flavor of legend about them — John Farrar's recollections of Frank N. Doubleday, "Effendi," as they had called him; Bennett Cerf's of Horace Liveright, under whom both he and Dick Simon had served their apprenticeship; and stories of the old agents, Ober, Matson, and Collins. These figures of the past, already bas-reliefs of publishing, came alive at the table, often as petty and difficult as the day's counterparts.

Indeed, the stories had a common thread that pleased this audience — the triumph of guile. It was as though they most enjoyed acknowledgment of the double standard of ethics, the impeccable one they professed and the real one by which they functioned. They relished tales of greed along publishers' row, ones in which ambition, cleverness, and power triumphed over good intention and good will. Clearly it was accepted here as the way of its world.

Walking down Park Avenue with Hugh Jr., under a promising, September sun, flowing with the postprandial crowds — brokers emerging from the Racquet Club, secretaries and models from Schrafft's and Bloomingdale's — returning to the afternoon's demands, I had the most extraordinary sense of well-being.

I had drunk some good wine with lunch and was tipsy, but my elation went beyond that. I felt a routing of self-doubts, a sense of coming into my own. Across the Avenue, from a torn battlefield of rubble and twisted wire, rose the partial skeleton of a tower. As I watched, a crane set a new bone into the sky. Someone's office. It was being made for a man as yet unchosen for it. Being me, being alive on this September day of 1951 was an exquisite piece of luck.

We turned in at Crowninshield's Louis Sullivan building on Forty-eighth Street and, on its fourth floor, entered a reception room whose moss-green walls were a gallery of the house eminences, Melville and Hawthorne, Twain and Thoreau, Cather and Dreiser. Recessed cabinets displayed current titles in crisp jackets, the pick of the new crop — two big novels, a popular science book, a biography — and I felt like a man leaning on his scythe to watch a reaper cut a swath through his field.

As we walked along the corridor toward Hugh Jr.'s office, I saw faces remembered from Joel's party, and then Joel himself. He was in shirt sleeves, emerging from the submissions pool with an armload of manuscripts.

"So, Lloyd," he said as though my being there was no surprise, "you've come to look us over and see how a real outfit works. About time, too. When Hughie's shown you around, come see me. I'm right in here."

Hugh Jr.'s office had a zebra skin on the floor and some photographs of Egyptian ruins on the walls, still it was not an office to impress visitors. His secretary, a slim, pretty girl, said "Hi," and I knew her for an indifferent typist.

He shuffled some messages on his desk, but they failed to interest him and he said, "Let's see if the old man's in." He dialed, asked, "Is my father there?" Presently he said, "I have Lloyd Erskine in my office. Could I bring him by for a minute?"

I followed, past the receptionist and two secretaries. The younger, a striking, dark-haired girl, smiled our sanction, and we entered the wide, chaste office of the president of Crowninshield's.

Hugh Severance sat at a writing table, head bent over it, so that my first impression was of a steel furze cresting a palisade of brow. Only when he had finished his task, penciling a note in a margin, did he look up. It was a grave face, the spare mouth bracketed in soft dewlaps. Seams became him, as though time's erosion had made off with only dross, leaving him the more durable.

Examining me, deep, close-set, brown eyes were bright as a boy's and for an instant I felt an old inspection chill, some fault overlooked, now detected. Then the mouth forgave. Hugh Severance rose and came around the table, amused and tolerant, to take my hand. The fingers were cool and powdery as they touched mine.

"Well, did I miss anything at Pierre's?"

"The old malarkey," his son replied. "There was a tiff between A.K. and Marshall. I couldn't make it out."

"That Goncourt prize winner. Each has a translation he claims is the authorized one." Mr. Severance smiled at the discomfort of his competitors. Then his eye fell upon a procession of photographs propped against the baseboard, and he said, "Come have a look at these."

Standing, he was taller, straighter than either of us, and he led us around the display, explaining it was the work of Margaret Bourke-White, taken during her recent journey through the Soviet Union — peasants at a café, a sleigh on a lonely road, a *dacha* in ruin, a city balcony.

"What do you think?" He was asking our opinion. "Would you buy a book of these?"

"Pretty schmaltzy," Hugh Jr. replied. "I guess they didn't let her in the salt mines."

"But beautiful, sir," I said. "The moon through the trees there is quite marvelous." Ethan's schooling guided me. "Who buys books of photographs anyway? People who don't read?"

The Severance brown eyes met mine with a merriness. "Some of that all right. Gifts for people who lack literary taste, or keep it secret." He frowned at the band of schoolchildren. "Still, pictures alone won't do it. We'd need some cachet."

"Bourke-White?" Hugh Jr. asked. "She has all the cachet you're likely to get in a photographer."

"You might add to it with some text," I proposed, "by a Russian. A poet perhaps. Pasternak?"

I felt there was some logic to my suggestion, enough to be taken seriously and, possibly, to reveal me as a brighter boy than his own. But Hugh Severance was not responsive. He nodded, as though to say he had heard and understood me, but would not reveal what he thought of the suggestion. Reassurance, even for politeness' sake, was clearly not his line.

The older of the two secretaries appeared like a stern concierge at her window. "There's a call for Mr. Severance, Jr.," she said. "Will you take it here?"

"I'll take it in my office," Hugh Jr. said, and hurried out, while his father nodded me toward a chair. As I took it, he noticed the light struck me in the eyes and he turned to adjust the blinds. Sitting down across from me, he made a chin rest of his hands.

"My son tells me you work for Ethan Poole. I've barely met him, but he seems an interesting man. What do you do there?"

"I've been selling, and writing copy, a little of everything — learning the ropes. Ethan's very good about the ropes."

"What sort of ropes?"

"Why people buy books."

"Why do they?"

"For information, primarily, but sometimes for pleasure."

"Does he tell you how to spot the good ones?"

"No. I haven't found anyone who'll talk about *that*. But Ethan has ideas about human nature, and he shares them. We talk about the sales pitch, really, about how you describe a book, and sometimes where."

"Where?"

"Whether we should try mail order or find some unusual place to spend our money, whether there isn't a more imaginative place to blow it than the *Times*."

"Do you get into such Socratic discussions over *taking* a book?"

"No. Ethan takes on a book because he likes it. Then he asks the sales questions."

He seemed surprised. "Perhaps I should have guessed, from your list."

"Is it such an odd one?"

"It's an interesting but erratic list. It reflects the taste of one man. Wouldn't you agree?"

"I can say this, that walking into Crowninshield's is awesome for me. Major authors, going back over the years. You turn out monuments as a matter of course. Is it fair to ask? How *do* you stay out in front?"

"People." Hugh Severance shrugged at the simplicity of it. "Editors with a taste for quality. Businessmen with" — his hand became a gull in flight, tipping this way, now that, trying the air currents — "a sense of balance. Would Mr. Poole differ?"

"Ethan is a man with a lovely curiosity, a New England canniness, and he uses it in sizing up a book and its author, very much as if he were choosing a friend for a journey. When he decides to take a book it's a matter of loyalty and commitment, very much a matter of the heart."

Hugh Severance was interested. "It's remarkable he can maintain that kind of publishing luxury in this day," he said. "I certainly envy Mr. Poole. But from this editorial floor, it seems like play. It's putting the man and his particular, possibly idiosyncratic, tastes ahead of the business."

"But how else? How is it done here?"

He laced his hands behind his head and looked at the ceiling. "It's hard to separate the two, of course, but we try to publish books that are good for the house. Not for our egos, surely. I would hope to publish a book I disagreed with, even disliked, if it were intelligent and well written. That's the function of a publisher — to put the best of every point of view out and let the readers choose." Hugh Severance lowered his eyes to mine. "What do you think of that?"

"I agree. Though of course, deciding on those . . ."

". . . is easier said." Hugh Severance laughed, making a moment of simple understanding between us. It was an exquisite moment, and I wanted to please *him* now, to excite his admiration as he had mine.

But then, as though overcome by shyness at this intimacy, he withdrew, turtlelike, retracting soft parts. His face changed, one moment accessible, the next, snapped shut, impervious. The skin had taken on the quality of granite.

He spoke now of how in most cases the difficulty in editorial decision was overcome by practical knowledge of the market. His hands made mandarin gestures. Thin, tapering fingers carved delicate designs between us, moving carefully, certain of their deftness.

I sensed he was Ethan's opposite. Where Ethan trusted his heart, even as it failed him, Hugh Severance distrusted that organ above them all. I wondered if this was an answer to my question about Crowninshield's eminence.

Casually, he said, "You've had a gratifying success with *Solo*. Is that the sort of thing you like? What kind of books *do* you want to do?"

"Well, no, not humor necessarily, but all sorts." I struggled for some candor. "I'm not a scholar, but I think I know, within a first chapter, if a book is good. I think I can tell when a book has . . . intelligence. I want to publish those."

He cocked his head in doubt.

"You don't believe that?"

He shrugged. "You make it sound so easy."

A buzzer interrupted. He spoke into his telephone. He would be with someone directly. I was dismissed. Tilting back in his chair he said, "But you mustn't be put off by me. I'm an old and cynical campaigner."

Rising to go, I said, "But I still don't know. How *do* you tell which books to publish?"

"Every available sensibility." Smiling, he laid a finger alongside a nostril. "Particularly this. The longer I live, the more I'm sure it's all in the nose. Good-bye and good luck, Mr. Erskine."

Passing through the outer office, I caught the severe secretary's glance and there was no interest in it. I felt I had been denied Hugh Severance's approval. Suddenly, everything I had said, about the Russian photographs, the books I wanted to publish, seemed fatuous and my presence here a disloyalty to Ethan.

I saw by the reception room clock that it was ten after three, too late now for a call on Joel Rossbach. Standing in the core of Crowninshield's, I could feel the energy of important undertakings in the air, all going forward efficiently, authoritatively, in the way of the elevator doors, which opened for me with a sigh of powerful pistons. I hurried aboard.

The midday elation, that sense of possibility which had overwhelmed me on Park Avenue, turned shadowed and cold as I scurried back to my office. The rise and fall of expectation had left me queasy. That night, at home, I answered Andy's questions about the Editors' Lunch, but I did not report my visit to Crowninshield's.

However, a week later, Joel Rossbach called and asked me to meet him for a drink at the Harvard Club, and at six, mingling with the others at the bar, waving to friends, he was silent with me. He thrust his hands in and out of his pockets as though unsure how to put something to me.

"You know, Lloyd," he said at last. "You're wasting down at Poole's. I know you've learned a lot from Ethan, but you're the kind of guy who makes a burden of his debts."

"I don't think Ethan's exploiting me."

Joel raised his eyebrows. "How many books, that you can take the credit or the blame for, will you do next year?"

"Ethan doesn't work that way. With one horse, there's one driver."

"And you're how old?"

"Thirty-one."

Joel spread his palms, resting his case. "How much do you make? Oh, come on, Lloyd. I'm your friend. I couldn't abuse your confidence."

"Seventy-five hundred."

"And you've been there five years?" He wagged his head in disapproval, then beckoned me to follow. We took a table in the deserted card room and Joel said, "You never know your reach until you try it."

"All right. Suppose I am up a creek. What would I do about that?"

"Crowninshield's will make you an offer if you ask."

"Should I?"

Smiling, Joel held up his glass and squinted at it. "Let me give you a peek into my crystal ball here. Hugh Severance is sixty-three."

"He seems a young, vigorous man."

"Nevertheless, if he keeps to his own rules, he'll retire in five years. He's an old man. So are the others on the executive board. Tyler, Waterhouse, Gore are all in their late sixties. The two younger ones, Finlay and Sid Broyles, are not editorial types. The editorial people will always run Crowninshield's."

"How do you know?"

"Because that's the way a good house gets that way and stays that way — a good editorial head counseled by a good business head. Never the other way around. Hugh knows that and he'll see to the succession."

"Won't that be Hugh Jr.?"

"Need you ask? Don't you trust your own judgment?"

"It was you that told me he's no fool."

"What I said was not to mistake Junior. He's intelligent.

On occasion he's a very likable fellow. He has sound ideas. He's knowledgeable about the business, but your first impression was accurate. Hughie has a big problem, and it's measuring up to Pa. That's constant torture for both of them and the reason he fucks up. We can count on Hughie to do something gauche, irresponsible and dislikable once a day, testing his own authority and his father's patience. Hughie wasn't born a trial but he's making himself into a beaut."

"Young men with expectations have a way of outgrowing their faults."

Joel shook his head. "Hughie is twenty-eight. He has a taste for booze and variety in women. His books top the remainder list. You have to understand that Hugh Severance isn't playing at publishing like an Ethan Poole, nor is it simply a business for him either. He's the emperor of Crowninshield's and he's responsible to it. He took Crowninshield's when it was in receivership back in the twenties, and using his wisdom and guile, his ability to manipulate people, his instincts for books, he built it into the realm it is today. He's simply not going to blow all that, not going to deliver it to a son who will dissipate it. Crowninshield's is Hugh Severance's immortality."

"You're in the line of succession?"

Joel reflected, nibbling at the corner of his mouth. "Times are changing, Lloyd. No single person will succeed Hugh. Nobody is rich enough to own, as well as run, Crowninshield's. It's too big. It'll be a bunch, and I could be a member of that bunch. It' a great house, and it can be greater. That will depend on how wise the bunch. Which is why" — Joel pointed a finger at my chest — "Crowninshield's wants you."

"*Does* Hugh? I felt I'd made a poor impression."

"Hugh's not an effusive man. He liked what you said about his pictures."

"He's going to do that Russia book?"

"No." Joel smiled.

I leaned back in my chair, dizzy with the prospect. "Well, you know how I feel about Ethan, but you're right in many ways about him. I'm complimented, of course, and interested."

"Think it over. No rush. It's not as if there were a vacancy we have to fill. Incidentally, I haven't been authorized to make you a salary offer, but I'm sure it would double what Ethan's paying you."

We reflected for a minute, thinking separate thoughts, and then I asked, "You don't think we'd be competitive? Wind up slugging it out for points?"

"No."

"How come?"

"Because you're a *starker*, Lloyd. It means you make things happen. You've got class. You play from an open hand. I like having you for a friend. If I were in trouble I'd want to talk with you about it. I hope that works both ways. I want to be in business with you sometime. I think we'd make a hell of a team."

"We might."

"We're different in obvious ways. From what you say, your father and mine would not have understood each other. My old man thinks I'm going to starve in publishing and he's going to wind up supporting me again. He doesn't believe publishing is a real business. But somehow you and I are alike. We're interested in the same kind of accomplishment. We understand each other without explaining. I wouldn't worry about competing, not if we're together. We're going to be too useful to each other."

Over the past five years Andy had come to feel as I did about Ethan Poole, that he was a rare man, a source of benevolence and the fulcrum of our lives. I felt sure her advice would be to stay. So, while she put Will to bed and prepared our supper, I delayed telling her about Joel's proposal. I wandered about, half listening to her account of a visit to a nursery school.

Late in the evening, after we had washed up the dishes and Andy had turned to some sewing on the curtains, I opened my case, saying, "You'd think Mia would be letting up a little."

"I wouldn't think that at all," Andy said. "Why?"

"We scrapped again over a book I like and she doesn't."

"Can't you talk it out with Ethan?"

"He's protective of Mia. He seems to enjoy our spats. Or do I just imagine all this?"

"No," Andy said. With a sailmaker's palm she was forcing her needle through boat canvas. "You don't imagine *all* of it. Ethan doesn't mind your making money so much as ending your apprenticeship. Maybe he thinks *Solo* is giving you airs and ambitions that are going to affect him. Is it?"

"I don't know, Andy. Do you?"

"Well, I don't *think* Ethan wants a partner. Perhaps you're growing up too soon." She broke off a thread and heaved me the finished curtain. "Would you hold that up so I can see how it looks?"

I climbed the stepladder while Andy, in jeans and denim shirt, long hair gathered in a crimson ribbon, nodded at the effect. She wanted our Chelsea apartment to have the simple, seaworthy look of a Maine house.

"As for Mia," Andy went on, "you're a thorn to her as well. It makes a nice balance for Ethan, keeps you both interested in your work. I seem to remember that's how it goes in the Navy and, for all I know, everywhere else. If you don't like it you can quit."

"Well, that's the point," I said. "You see I've had a sort of offer today, from Joel. He wants me to come to Crowninshield's."

"I'm surprised you'd consider it."

"Why?"

"Young what's-his-name. The boss's boy. I thought you disliked him so much."

"Severance. He's been agreeable lately. Took me up to the Editors' Lunch last week, then back to meet his father."

"You never told me that." She was both surprised and hurt.

"I know."

"Funny. I thought you told me everything. Don't you really?"

"Maybe I hide a few things from myself. I'm not sure why I've changed my mind about Hughie Severance, whether I find him newly likable or it's just the flattery of his attention."

"Would you really prefer to work with those people than with Ethan?"

"I feel exactly as you do about Ethan. I love the man — and yet that may be just the reason I should get out, and into the world. Maybe this is the big chance and if I don't grab it I'll regret it the rest of my life."

There was a wail — Will's waking from some fright — and Andy went off to comfort him. Returning, she said thoughtfully, "Lloyd, I think you should go. You're an intelligent man. And you're lucky too. You'll do all right. Of course I'm sorry about it . . . but it's time. You *should* try the ocean."

I deliberated for several months before bearding Ethan. Except for a sweeper somewhere emptying baskets, the office was still. Telling him was surprisingly exhilarating. His eyebrows rose in amusement, as though he'd expected this all along. I was hoping he would respond with an offer that could change my mind about leaving, a demonstration of his affection and faith, even the promise of partnership.

"I'm seriously tempted by this chance, Ethan," I said. "What do you think I should do?"

"It's your decision, Bub," he said sharply. "And it's a fairly easy one if you want to be involved with that kind of people."

"You mean Hugh Severance?" I took his silence for assent, suspecting some bitterness beneath that benign façade of his, a feeling of being excluded from the faster, more aggressive race where Crowninshield's ran. "Isn't he an eminence? Is he something less than his reputation?"

Ethan was uncomfortable. "I don't know anything from firsthand experience. I've been in a room with Mr. Severance. I may have shaken hands with him. People who have dealt with him say he can be difficult, but I don't know him, so I ought not to talk about him or his business."

"Is it that they're merchants up there? That they try to make

money out of books? That Hugh Severance is more business-
man than bookman?"

"Could be."

"Is that so bad?"

"If it's what you want, Lloyd, you'd better go."

"Do you know something about Crowninshield's that I
don't?"

"Not really. My feelings may be simple envy. It's a powerful
and successful firm — and I reason that that must be at the
sacrifice of human relations. That's all, but that's enough."

"O.K. I understand. The big, predatory fish. The swimming's dangerous, but it has its appeal for me."

"Lloyd," he said. "The future's bright here too."

"How? I'd like to hear about that."

"Well, first of all there's working with me."

"That's an advantage, I'll admit."

Ethan was filling his pipe, tamping it thoughtfully. "Tell
you what I'll do. I'll give you a nice fat raise if it'll make you
any happier. I think I can afford to pay you ten thousand dollars next year."

"That's generous. I appreciate that, Ethan. Can you tell me
one more thing? Do you foresee a time when you might take
me in? When you might let me share fully in the agonies and
joys around here?"

"Ah-h." He lit his pipe, leaned back now, and tilted away
from me so he could look out the window. "Anything is possible. However, I'd as soon you didn't ask that because the answer depends on how we live together. Maybe Poole's isn't for
you. By considering going to work for Hugh Severance you've
suggested that. If it's true, I wouldn't want us to make promises to each other we'd find it hard to keep. Be a good fellow,
Lloyd, and unask that question."

"All right. I'll unask it, and ask another. If I go up there
for a couple of months and don't like it — can I come back?"

"This here is a bridge you'll burn as you cross it, Bub." It
settled between us, a slab of ice. Presently he said, "Well, next
thing I know I'll miss my train." He gathered a manuscript,

some unanswered correspondence, and a pair of pruning shears, stuffed them into his briefcase, and took hat and coat from the closet. "Unless I hear otherwise, I'll presume you're quitting me."

"I'd like to think about it overnight, but I guess so."

As he went out the door, Ethan said, "I suspect you'll be sorry."

～ 7 ～

HUGH SEVERANCE had built a lively, purposeful world on Forty-eighth Street. Coming into the building from the wandering aimlessness outside, you could feel the hurry and urgency of its corridors, a sense of well-being, like alcohol in the bloodstream.

From my first day at Crowninshield's, in January of 1952, I savored that particular vitality. It was a house that rewarded intelligence and social sensibility, and I felt I would do well here. I liked people and could charm them. I had an instinct for muzzling my own ego and putting myself in their shoes.

I felt I had a certain intelligence particularly suited to choosing books — common sense, common touch, an instinct for that smack of just-rightness in words that gets to a truth about life.

Finally, as Andy had said, I was lucky. I had a sense of being looked after by an extrahuman force that liked me, had the power to grant me special indulgences and put me in the right place at the right time.

My office was a windowless, partitioned area beside Joel's identical one, and when he had settled me there, he gave me the tour, down a flight to meet Ben Dockery, the production manager, a grizzly of a man whom we found thrusting proof into the hands of an assistant and fuming, "I don't know why they can't understand English."

But Dockery greeted me amiably. "You'll like it here, Lloyd." Waving at the tables beyond, where work lights made a brilliance of shirt sleeves, he said, "We do a hell of a lot of books and it's frantic most the time, keeping up with schedules. Always something getting fouled up, but we usually deliver the goods."

As we left, Joel confided, "And sometimes they're pretty sorry goods."

"I've always thought Crowninshield's books were handsome."

"Usually, but Ben keeps his job with a sharp pencil, and the result, when he can get away with it, is shoddy bookmaking." Joel took a book from a stack by the fire door, and, peeling back the jacket, felt the slick binding, and sighted along the boards. They were cambered from a fast pressing. Opening to a page, he squinted at the type. "Look, it must be ten-point. Need a magnifying glass." Dropping the book, as though it had soiled his hands, Joel led on, saying, "Beware. When you see sample pages, watch out for Dockery and his economies. He'll be testing you to see what he can get away with."

We turned into the advertising office and found Alice Margolies at her desk. She was a bony woman, elegant and ageless. As she shook my hand, offered me a cigarette, her arms flew about with such spasmodic energy I was reminded of a fretful bird.

"Welcome to Crowninshield's, Lloyd Erskine. From everything I've heard, we're going to get on like old campaigners." Alice Margolies's voice was fathoms deep. "You'll be hounding me for space before long, and I'll be giving you less than you want." She laughed huskily. "But we'll stay friends all the same, because you'll realize soon enough that advertising does a lot for the author's vanity, and the editor's too, but it rarely sells books."

"As it happens, I have some ideas about that," I said, "and I'm anxious to learn more."

"You've come to the right place," and she answered her ringing phone.

In the corridor, Joel said, "Alice has a vision of herself as

Madame Récamier, you know, terrific taste and knowing everybody. Not quite accurate, I think, but she does have verve and
guts and she'll make much of you, particularly if she thinks
you're going to be important around here, which you are."

"How is she at advertising?"

"When she's good, she's very, very good, and when she isn't,
at least she's amusing about it. You'll see in the meeting."

Joel caught at the sleeve of a rumpled man who was bearing
a paper cup of coffee along the corridor as though much de-
pended on its safe delivery to his desk. "And this here is Dexter
Barnes, our publicity director."

"We've been waiting for you, Lloyd," Barnes said in a cozy
Carolinian accent that contrasted with the frisking of his eyes.
"I'm going to send out a release on you. Put your name in the
paper. Come in and tell me about yourself when you have a
minute."

When we were out of earshot, Joel said, "There's a power
broker for you. If you ever want to find out how your stock is
selling, just pass by Dexter's office. If he gives you that halibut
eye, it's at a new low — Hugh has left you off the party list or
your book is getting creamed in *Newsweek*."

"What should I know about publicity?"

Joel shrugged. "We talk about it all the time, as though it's
a supernatural force and needs a medicine man, but actually
it's a service, getting the word around. If you begin to think
the lack of publicity is what's ruining your book, you've gone
paranoid." Joel paused at the gates of the sales department.
"Now, in here is Sid Broyles's place."

An amiable-looking man was shambling toward us. His
short, blond hair was graying, yet there was a boyish spring to
his step and the crack of a smile as he grasped my hand.

"By God, Erskine, we need you around here, particularly if
you're any kind of a Giants fan. We've got a box at the Polo
Grounds, and lately I can't get rid of the seats." Broyles
scowled at Joel. "This one here is a tremendous disappointment to me."

"I'm glad to hear that the company encourages us to spend

our afternoons in the out-of-doors," I said. "I had no idea."

"Nothing to do with the out-of-doors. It's the Giants that are company policy. They give us transference. We can worry about the team instead of why the books aren't selling. Maybe you can help us out with that too, Erskine . . ." His bray was resonant and a comradely hand came down on my shoulder.

Leading me away, Joel said, "You can detect the faint aroma of cow barn around Sid, but don't be taken in. I mean he's a yahoo all right, but he's shrewd too. He knows what's going to sell and what isn't. He sets the print orders and as a rule he's right on the nose — which is discouraging since he hasn't the least literary taste."

"He takes that on faith — from the editors?"

"No, just sales instinct." Joel shrugged.

"Isn't that hard on the literary books?"

Joel nodded. "Which is why our list isn't as fine as Knopf's, say — not as fine as it could be."

"Maybe we can change that."

"Maybe we can — but not Sid. He knows, and so does Hugh, that it isn't literary books that keep us all in Brooks shirts."

We finished up with a call at the president's office, pausing for a *laissez-passer* at the window guarding it. A girl's face appeared. At the sight of us, playfulness welled in her eyes, as though she sensed some mischief between Joel and me and wished to share in it.

"Hi," she said, tucking back a strand of hair. "Want to see the boss?"

"If we could," Joel said. "Ceremonial visit for the new man here. This is Lloyd Erskine, Flavia."

"I know," she said, putting her hand through the window. "I'm Flavia Moore."

"I remember . . . from my last visit."

She looked within, frowning at the possibilities, and was joined by the senior secretary who, with a shake of her patrician head, said, "Sorry. H.S. is busy. I don't think there'll be a minute before lunch." There was a sound of laughter from within the office. "I'll call you, Joel, if there's a chance, but don't count on it."

Leading me off, Joel said, "Very influential lady, Corinne. She runs the place, especially when he's away. A maiden, of course, a very elegant one — still, they all operate on the same principle. She adores him, anticipates him, and has become his *Doppelgänger*. Incidentally, that's another thing I envy H.S. — a classy, loyal woman to mind the store while he's at play — the mark of a true Florentine."

"He seems remote."

"H.S. is that."

"Kind of a cold bath after Ethan. I passed him in the hall this morning and he didn't even nod. It was as though I'd become transparent. Does he not remember?"

Joel laughed. "He remembers everything. And it isn't rudeness — he's not like that at all. It's simply his concentration. He's so intent on whatever he has on his mind that he dismisses all other sights and sounds."

When Joel released me to look around on my own, I passed the corner office whose windows looked into Forty-eighth Street. At the desk, an elderly, basset-faced man waved and called, "Come in." As I shook hands, he said. "You're Lloyd Erskine. Can you sit down for a minute? I'm Guy Waterhouse. They call me the treasurer here, which means I've been around for years. I hope you will be too. Getting settled in?"

"Joel Rossbach's been showing me around. It's a little bewildering at first."

"I should think so." He peered at the face of a grandfather's clock whose hands stood at a few minutes short of noon. "You have lunch plans? If not, I'll tell you what I can about this place."

Across a table at The Players, Guy Waterhouse told me that he'd worked at many trades in his quarter century with the firm. He had sold college texts as well as trade books, been sales manager and a trade editor, until recently, when he had been "kicked upstairs."

"I still have a few authors, old-timers like myself. Been in to see Hugh?"

"Not yet."

He caught my disappointment and said, "You may as well know right off that Hugh is self-contained and he expects the same of the rest of us. Let me give you a piece of advice, Lloyd. Build yourself a list. Be a house within the house. That's the way you'll get along here. Hugh runs Crowninshield's, no doubt about it, but don't expect an embrace, certainly not until he sees how you're doing." He reflected on that and then said, "Anyway, you'll get your share of house books. But if you make a reputation here, it won't be from house books, no matter how well you do them, but from the books you bring in on your own hook, and that depends on how well the agents like you, whether you impress them as being able to deal with what they give you — how you'll like it and, if you do, how you'll publish it. Can you get the money? Can you build up excitement in the house for it? Make it go? You know the agents?"

"One or two."

"You'll want to be close to three or four of the good ones."

"I've been thinking," I said, "that if I had ten good authors, if there was a sense of trust and enthusiasm between me and ten good authors . . . wouldn't I be O.K.? Would I be that house within a house?"

Guy Waterhouse shrugged. "All right, yes. It's a way to go about it. But there's no system to editorial success. You learn from doing it, from the success and failure of others as well as your own." He smiled. "And I should say it's a good idea to be right, to be very right, some of the time."

"Because Crowninshield's is *not* a benevolent monarchy?"

"Well, such things are relative. Hugh believes in free competition. If you don't, you should never have come to work for us."

"I came *because* of it. But are people here anxious about their jobs?"

"A company like this is a family in many ways. There's jealousy among the children, but it's not bad, Lloyd. It sharpens the wits and it's good for business. We live with it."

Walking back to Crowninshield's, Guy Waterhouse said, "If you like, I'll see if I can stake you to one of my authors. I'll say you're the comer here, and as a matter of fact I think you are. You seem sensible enough. I'll call some of the agents and tell 'em that too."

When I asked Joel about Guy Waterhouse he said, "Yes, he's still on the executive committee, and I wouldn't be surprised if Hugh asks his advice now and again. I think Hugh beat him out years ago. Probably hatchets buried there, but I don't believe Guy cares anymore."

Next morning, Guy Waterhouse delivered me two partial manuscripts along with arrangements to meet their authors and, if agreeable all around, become their editor.

"Don't thank me, Lloyd," Guy protested. "At least wait until you see the books delivered. They may turn out clinkers. And Lloyd, make up your own mind about how Crowninshield's works. Your instincts are sound enough."

The board room was on the top, the fifth floor of the Crowninshield building. Its dark, walnut wainscot, the mantel, the framed letters and manuscripts hung on the linen-covered walls, had been brought from the old building on Chambers Street. So, the Wednesday meetings, held here under the stewardship of the president and chairman of the executive committee, had a dramatic sense of publishing history — past, and in-the-making.

The meeting began at ten, editors taking chairs to the left and right of H.S.'s central one, around the vast, oval table, arranging their notes before them while the sales and promotion people took the places opposite. There was some whispering, an exchange of jokes about the thermostat which, in its sensitiveness, invariably ordered a thermal overdose which required either a fetching of sweaters or a loosening of collars. The tension, marked by bursts of nervous laughter, was thick as a summer night at the approach of a storm.

H.S. was normally the last to arrive, bustling in with an armful of papers and, as he took his chair, looking over the top of his spectacles at each of us, as though calling the roll. He would offer a benediction to begin, some dry assurance that all was well. There had been triumphs in the week just passed.

At the first performance I saw, he announced, "At their meeting on Thursday, the Book-of-the-Month Club judges decided on the Hughes as their October selection, so I think we can anticipate a good run for our money there . . . and perhaps afford some prominent advertising. Can we lead off with that in the fall announcements, Alice?"

To which Alice Margolies beamed and replied, "Oh, indeed, Hugh. I'm dreaming up something exquisite. Something for the cover of *Publishers Weekly* that'll knock 'em cold."

With this flourish, like the note of a pitch pipe, the meeting was under way, Hugh nodding to Sid Broyles, who began calling off the active list — Crowninshield titles that were recently published or so successful they continued to sell in quantity.

For a book just about to appear, Broyles would report the advance sales and his hopes for continuing demand — what cities, what jobbers, and what stores were enthusiastic about it. Dexter Barnes would add favorable advance comment from the trade and the press, along with what he had been able to do in displaying the author, while Alice told of her plans for advertising.

To this strategic trio, and really the whole council, the book's editor now appealed for more of everything to help his ward.

Joel was always quick to plead for a book of his, asking, "I think we must have a small ad in the daily *Times,* Alice. That's such a good quote from Warren, and nobody's going to know but us."

Books that were in production had their dust jackets held up for general comment, a barrage of amateur art judgment enjoyed by all but the art director.

Books that had been published and received with indifference, were stricken from the list. As Broyles drew his pencil through a title, we could hear it tumbling down the shaft of oblivion, carrying with it the editor's hopes. These would be revived only when a new book of his took its place on this master roll of house accomplishment.

The last book on the list was reached and dealt with at eleven o'clock, marking the end of the meeting's first act. The second, and final, one began without intermission. As the sales and promotion people filed out the door, they passed editors in special fields, as well as junior editors and readers, who entered the room silently to fill the empty chairs.

H.S. seemed to relax now, leaning back in his chair. This was the part he most enjoyed and he signaled the start by a nod to the editor at his left, who would tell us his accomplishments since our last meeting — a book successfully published, a contract for a new one signed, but particularly what he was thinking about, some new idea, one for a series of historical interest perhaps, or an article in a magazine which had suggested the possibility of a book.

The editor would report on what his own authors were doing, how much progress they had made on their projects. He would also note what books and authors were being successful on other lists and what might be learned from these experiences. If he had been lunching with agents, he would tell what authors he had discussed with them, whether any prominent ones were unhappy and open to invitation, which ones might be approached for a special project, and what projects might be thought up here at this table which would be attractive enough to bring new authors to Crowninshield's.

As Hugh nodded to each in turn, some editors were terse, telling a few facts about their preoccupations, uncomfortable at this scrutiny of their ingenuity and aggressiveness. But for the most part they seemed to enjoy Hugh's spotlight. Joel in particular took the opportunity to talk about himself, to describe the people he had written and talked to, and leave us the impression of an alert, adroit fellow moving knowledgeably through the intellectual communities of the city.

*

I still suffered with the feeling of remoteness from Hugh Severance. I had imagined immediate acceptance as a trusted apprentice, and he had scarcely acknowledged me. So when, in editorial meetings, he turned to me, a curiosity lighting his eyes, to inquire, "Lloyd, tell us. What have you been up to?" I was always astonished to find that he *did* recall my name, that he was expecting something of interest from me, and I longed to supply it. That intermittent radiance upon me was ample reward for all possible effort.

Those first Crowninshield years of the early fifties were propitious ones and my self-confidence grew. The interview that Dexter Barnes arranged, resulted in a flattering piece about me in *Publishers Weekly*. It said that my Poole's experience had been a training ground and Crowninshield's had recognized in me the makings of an able editor. I was a man to watch.

This, and the luck of my first few books, gave me a cachet. I could sense it in the house, the new deference from secretaries, from associates in the college and religious departments whose names I did not know. When I called agents, they were eager to meet and lunch and tell me about their clients.

The young agent whom we spoke of as the Ace of Hearts offered me a first novel by a twenty-three-year-old Berkeley student. I wasn't wholly enthusiastic about it, and I knew it had been turned down by at least two clever editors at houses the Ace would have preferred, but she piqued me. At our first lunch she said I was an able editor but at the wrong house, one which was too much Hugh Severance's instrument to allow me the scope I would need.

I took the book, in part at least, to prove my independence. While it sold less than two thousand copies in our edition, it was favorably reviewed, won the William Faulkner Prize, and was bought, at a modest price, for reprint. The author was off to a good start, and so was I, for the Ace of Hearts spoke well of me where it counted, and her favor spread like ripples in a pond.

One of Guy Waterhouse's gifts, a biography of Willa Cather, became an alternate selection of the Book-of-the-Month Club and was praised on the front of the *Times Book Review*. There was also fruit from my Poole's years. Billy Maxwell showed me a second book about the Air Force. When I wrote Ethan, saying that Maxwell wanted me to edit and publish it at Crowninshield's, we had a painful correspondence.

"You simply cannot do that, Lloyd," Ethan wrote. "Maxwell was not published by you, but by Poole's. It was our collective enthusiasm, time, and money that went into the building of his reputation. Surely it is understood between us that your leaving Poole's for the greater glories uptown does not mean you are free to walk off with those effects, real and intangible, that are rightfully the property of this house . . . There are lots of fish to be had in the brook, Lloyd," Ethan concluded. "No need to be greedy about those we've landed together. I cannot believe you won't agree, once you've thought it through. As always . . ."

"Certainly there's logic and fair play on your side of the argument, Ethan," I wrote in reply. "I can hardly deny that. I have no intention of poaching on Poole authors, nor anyone else's for that matter, and yet the fact remains that Billy Maxwell and I are friends. We have been friends since long before he came to Poole's (which he did because of that friendship) and we remain friends today. Indeed, Billy and I have become closer, so that he wanted me to read some of the work he's been doing and get my advice about it. I've already done this.

"Now, as you know, I'm perfectly happy to do this for him as your author, but realistically, Billy is going to *want* to be published by Crowninshield's because I'm here, because, whether it's true or not, he feels that I'm his chief advocate, and that it's only fitting to be published where I work.

"I think you'll also admit that Billy's book was not a great enthusiasm of your's and that *Solo* would not have turned up on Poole's list were it not for my obstinacy over it. In any case, I think what's going to be decisive is, not what you or I feel is right, but rather what Billy feels is right. It was you who taught me that no publisher wants to keep, nor will he, an unhappy author. Ever . . ."

"This is all very graceless and distasteful between such good friends as you and I, Lloyd," Ethan replied, "and I'm certainly not going to jeopardize my own self-respect, or yours, by further brawling about it. Take him. But before you do, have one last think about it. Do you really believe any single book — a new William Maxwell comedy, however risable — is worth the slippery rationalizing that enables you to encourage Bill to leave us? Ruefully . . ."

My enthusiasm for the new Maxwell, which we called *Grounded*, was vindicated. For seven weeks it flew the bestseller list and, at its zenith, was bought for a movie. In the auction for reprint rights it went to Bantam for sixty thousand dollars.

Several times in the course of *Grounded*'s flight I tried to compose a letter to Ethan, explaining that I had not anticipated the financial success and was more pained than pleased by it. This was true in a way, but I could not make it sound so. In the end I did not write him.

Six months later, when I caught sight of him at a P.E.N. party, I joined the cluster where he stood. He acknowledged me, introduced me to the others, but he did not ask after Andy, nor how I was getting on. The chill was palpable.

Saying good-bye I touched Ethan on the sleeve, hoping for a sign, his squint and flicker of a smile, that I was forgiven. But he did not even offer his hand, and as he turned away, I had a wholly unanticipated feeling of forlornness.

But at Crowninshield's there was little soil in which remorse could root. I came to the office early, half an hour before the official opening of the editorial day at ten. Spread upon my desk lay the morning mail — letterheads of William Morris, Curtis Brown, Russell & Volkening — bringing hints, offers of books to be. Here was a Bennington girl's novel about the vagabond expatriates, an Englishman's about the ascent of Everest, that of a well-known author whose publisher would not meet his terms. It was a feast, and I felt my appetite was growing sharper, and more discriminating.

When Elena Wallace asked us for dinner, Andy told her we had a previous engagement and turned her down.

"You what?" I asked. "Andy, she's one of the most influential agents in town. An invitation from her is a summons. You don't turn it down."

"And you don't pull out on your friends just because a better invitation comes along."

"You do if it's important. That's what friends are for. Cathy and Fred Ryan live in the real world. They'll know who Elena Wallace is, even if you don't."

"I know perfectly well who she is." Andy was spooning applesauce into Will's plate. "But I believe in sticking by my promises. Cathy's having people she wants us to meet."

"I understand all that. We can have them all here sometime. But that'll keep and Elena Wallace won't."

"She said she'd try us again."

"I doubt she will."

At the end of an hour's silence, I heard Andy on the phone, explaining to Cathy Ryan, "I'm mortified about this, but something important to Lloyd's business has come up. Can you possibly forgive . . ."

Next evening, when I came home, Andy said she had reached Elena Wallace and, swallowing gobbets of humiliation, explained she had been mistaken. We were free, and if we were still wanted, could we accept for Friday? We could.

After such a fuss, I suspected Elena Wallace's party would be disappointing, but I need not have worried. She greeted us effusively, as though she had known us as children, complimenting Andy on her dress and giving my forearm a squeeze. She steered us into the room where her guests were assembled, making the introductions and adding a compliment for Crowninshield's.

"He's so grand, your Hugh Severance," she told us. "I adore him. He's one of the last of the real, gentleman publishers. My first husband and I used to go over to Greenfields for the Sunday luncheons. They had simply everyone — Charlie Chaplin, Osbert Sitwell, Martin Luther King . . ."

I decided she must be at least sixty, but a mainmast of a woman, six feet of her straight into the air and a fierce eye that warned she generally got her way and sent managers of first-class restaurants scurrying to find her a good table.

Guiding us to a couple who seemed our destination, she whispered, "Surely you know Lansing Fosse. He's had such a lovely success with his latest book."

Fosse was wiry, springing on the balls of his feet like a boxer. He assumed our knowledge of his work and an interest in it. He spoke of himself, the writer, with a remove, as though that part of him were a bustling small business which he could admire without loss of modesty.

His redheaded wife was even less inhibited, explaining that *You Bet Your Life* had brought them a threat of legal action from three of the big Hartford insurance companies, "but in the end they backed down because Lans was right about all that and they *knew* they'd look all the worse in court."

It was Beverly Fosse, too, who gave us a first insight of "the *new* book." It would be an inquiry into the tobacco business and promised to raise more controversy than the last.

"The Tobacco Institute already has the wind up," Fosse told us. "I was shot at last Sunday, in front of my own garage."

We sat with the Fosses at dinner. He told stories well and both he and his wife played up to me. I was flattered, but Andy was less impressed. She ignored Beverly Fosse's suggestion we drive up to see them in the country over the weekend — which is what we discussed going home in the cab.

"I think we ought to go," I said. "Couldn't we get someone to stay with Will?"

"I don't think he'd put up with a whole day of Mrs. Hammond, and as for the high school girls . . ."

"Is it Beverly you don't like — or do you think the book is a lousy idea?"

"Did you believe that stuff? The sniper from the Tobacco Institute?"

"I don't know. He dramatizes. It was probably some neighbor's kid with a BB gun."

"Or some neighbor."

"I'm going on Elena's enthusiasm. She thinks he's good. Did you hear her say she felt instinctively that Lans should be with Crowninshield's?"

"Yes. Did that influence you?"

"Well, she *knows* him. She's brought him up as a writer. She wouldn't be investing her energy and reputation in him if she didn't have faith."

"What about yours?"

"O.K.," I said. "Still, you know it isn't liking or not liking these people, as though they were simply acquaintances."

When I had let Mrs. Hammond out the door of our apartment, I looked in the bookshelf and found an old copy of *Atlantic* in which there was an excerpt from *You Bet Your Life.* Sitting down, I read it at once, deciding it was able writing, sometimes perceptive, and consistently entertaining. Laying it on Andy's bedside table, I said, "I wish you'd take a look at that. It's a piece of Fosse's last book."

She yawned and snapped out the light. "Too tired tonight. I'll try in the morning."

"Why don't you like Fosse?"

"Awfully taken with himself," she said drowzily.

"But Andy, that's an occupational requirement. And it isn't as if we were driving to Bridgewater to make *friends.*"

"I know. But is Fosse's book the kind you went to Crowninshield's to do?"

"They liked you enormously, Lloyd," Elena Wallace told me on the phone, "*and* your enchanting wife. I think they're going to ask you out next weekend, but of course you and I ought to have an understanding before you go. Now, as it happens, I've just given Morrow's a little hint about what could occur, and they're not happy about it, but of course, in the end, they'll let Lans go. I'll see to that. Still, I don't want to go to the bother if you're not sure. You *are* sure, aren't you? I mean *I* thought you were getting on just beautifully . . . but I've been mistaken. How *do* you feel?"

"I've been doing my homework. I've read the book and all the Fosse articles I could find. He's good, no question. An intelligent man."

"And a young one," Elena put in. "A publisher could look to a long, as well as fruitful, relationship." Whereupon she read off Fosse's sales figures and told of negotiations for subsidiary rights.

"Well, yes," I said tentatively, "I do like the idea for the new one. It's very scary, our smoking ourselves to death because it's good for the tobacco business."

"Well, then, you ought to ask how much I want for it. Don't be shy with me, Lloyd."

"How much?"

"Fifty."

"Thousand?"

"Yes, my dear. It's cheap. And if you have cold feet, don't do it. But tell me quickly. There are a dozen publishers who would give their eyeteeth for this chance, Lloyd. Oh — if I were you, I'd talk to Hugh about it."

Although I came away from Corinne Perry's office with a feeling my collar was dirty, she assured me of an audience with H.S. I waited until the afternoon's end for it. At a few minutes before five, I was summoned.

"I'd like your advice, Hugh," I explained. "I have a book about the tobacco business by Lansing Fosse."

Hugh kept busy with small papers, but he nodded. "I know the name. The life insurance book."

"Fosse is just beginning it, and Elena wants fifty thousand dollars to take him away from Morrow's for us."

"Sounds high." He looked up. "Do you think he's worth it? How's his sales record?"

"Surprising. *Bet Your Life* did twenty-seven thousand in the trade and had a good reprint sale."

"You don't think this will do as well?"

"Every bit. Fosse sees in the tobacco business an even greater conspiracy to . . . you know, exploit human weakness. Plots within plots. He'll have a book."

Hugh's phone rang and, as he spoke into it, his eyes met mine without seeing me. Hanging up, he asked, "Have you talked to Broyles about his expectations? Have you worked out a manufacturing estimate? You ought to be able to project some kind of financial picture."

"Yes, a sketch." I shrugged. "But all based on ifs. Of course, as Elena points out, we're pretty sure of a paperback sale."

"Then what are you worried about?"

"Well, I think it's because Lansing Fosse is a *competent* writer with a good eye for the contemporary subject. He has a kind of knack for the sensational. He won't do a bad book, and he may do one that'll make us some money, but it won't be a good book either. That's my reservation. It's not the book I had in mind for my first, big, fifty-thousand-dollar effort."

I had hoped for a sharing of that dilemma, some Ethanlike reflection that would lead us to a philosophical base for it. I could imagine Ethan's fondling his pouch and pipe as he lit up to muse about tobacco, perhaps to note that we all pay a high price for it but that smokers agree to it and no amount of persuasion will prevent them from paying, since it offers comforts they won't be denied.

But H.S. was returning my hopeful smile with indifference. Over the tops of his glasses the Severance eyes were without interest. He looked at his watch. "Lloyd, I'm afraid that's a problem you must settle for yourself. Sorry, but I'm pressed for time."

Now I walked through the familiar arroyos of the Forties, puzzled by Hugh's refusal to respond. Was it the pressure of his own affairs? Or had he been impatient with the idea of a compromise with quality, which I had admitted? I peered into the faces of commuters hurrying toward Grand Central and read the headlines from the stacked, final Wall Street editions of the *News* and the *Post,* recalling all the old truths in which I believed — to beware of a book in which I lacked faith, to beware the enthusiasm of others, and above all, to beware ignoring my own inner voice, however softly it spoke.

And yet I felt that this was the way opportunity always looked, beguiling, chancy, and blurred around the edges with misgivings. It was a phenomenon that asked for courage, and how humiliating to fail it out of caution.

At home, I found Andy on hands and knees, pinning the pattern of a skirt over a square of Indian madras. When I had made myself a drink, I prowled around her until she asked, "What's the matter? Something go wrong today?"

"Not really." But after a while I said, "I still can't decide about the Fosse book."

"That's not surprising." She was intent on her shears, cutting a scimitar of blue green tartan from the top. "You haven't read it. I should think you'd ask for a look at it first. That's only fair."

"You don't understand. Nothing's *fair* about this. Elena wants enthusiasm on past performance and her own faith in her client. It's a test of my loyalty and courage — don't you see?"

Andy began to unpin the pattern and, when she had, folded it carefully. "Well, you don't have to play that game if you don't like it." When I didn't reply, she asked, "Do you like it? Elena Wallace isn't the only agent, is she?"

I lay down on the window seat and watched her tie up the scraps and put them away in a drawer. "I want to be a good editor, Andy. I have to recognize good books — not just the ones that are to my taste."

At the kitchen counter, she put two ice cubes from a tray into a glass and added a low tide of bourbon. "What do you really think of Fosse?"

"As a writer, he's clever, skillful. He knows the extent of his gifts and how to use them — exactly the man we met at Elena's. He can do this kind of book — but no, he's not profound."

"Well, there you are," she said, and took a sip of her drink.

*

Joel understood before I had finished explaining, and interrupted to say, "Well, that's expensive all right. And she'll get it too. If not from you, from somebody else. When she springs Fosse from Morrow's she'll be out to get every nickel she can."

"So you'd forget it?"

"Not at all. It can't turn out to be a real dog. There's more to win than to lose. What's bothering you?"

"I wish Fosse were trying to write a good book instead of a sensational one, because I really believe that sales come *because* of quality."

"Quality's in short supply. It's a real world, Lloyd."

"Nevertheless, we water down our reputations — yours, mine, and that of the house — with every mediocre book we do."

Joel took off his glasses and polished them on the tail of his necktie. "Not really. Everyone's attracted to success, all kinds of it. That's the light that brings authors through our doors."

I put in the call to Elena Wallace and she came on at once, cool and suspicious. I felt a great joy in saying, "Oh, Elena. Yes, we'd like to take the Fosse book. Shall we draw the contract?"

When I had hung up, I sat for a minute, listening to the babble float over the partition, and felt a strong urge to tell Hugh the outcome.

As I entered his office, he asked immediately, "Well, what did you say to Elena about your tobacco book?"

"That we'd take it, sir. I didn't argue about the price, but I think it'll pay its way." Saying this gave me a feeling of relief.

Hugh rose from his chair, though this time it was not to dismiss me but to straighten the long, surprisingly youthful body which had been desk-bent throughout the afternoon. He stretched, kneaded the muscles at the back of his neck. "I guess you'll have to wait and see about that."

But as I took my leave of him, H.S. was regarding me with fresh interest, and he said, "We must get you and your wife around to dinner some evening."

~§ 8 §~

THEY BROKE INTO our apartment. During an afternoon while Andy was out for a stroll with Will. They jimmied the lock and made off with a hi-fi, a fur coat, two of my suits, and the steam iron. They went through our drawers, contemptuously spilling our stuff onto the floor. Nameless, faceless people.

At first, Andy seemed resigned, agreeing when I pointed out that everyone gets burgled sooner or later and we were lucky to get off so easily, but a few nights later I came home to find her resentful.

"Daddy was right about this city. Everything seems hostile now, iron grills to keep people out, or in, square miles of cement to smother leaves and grass, and filth in every corner. I'm seeing mean faces everywhere I turn, like sharks idling, waiting for prey. Why must we live here, Lloyd? Why Will and me? *We're* not on call for publishing alarms."

When I'd thought about it for a while I said, "Maybe it is time. I'm counting on a good raise next month. If I get it, we can afford to think suburban."

Our first car was an MG two-seater with enough room behind for Will. That spring we went community shopping. We went along the Hudson where the Victorian mansions were neglected, or cared for by funeral companies, then over to Rye to show Andy the house where I grew up.

I scarcely recognized it under the fresh paint our successors had added, nor the elementary school with its new wing. "Not here," I said. "Not Rye."

Andy had a preference for Darien. "The school's good," she pointed out. "It hasn't that awful stylishness of Greenwich, and yet it's a decent commute."

"But it's nondescript," I argued. "It doesn't know its own nature, the way Westport knows it's arty and the way New Canaan has class. In New Canaan, even the A&P looks like a country club, and it's a literary town."

"In what way, literary?"

"Maxwell Perkins lived here, though I didn't know that until last week. I remember coming to a party here once, in a really beautiful house. A girl whose father was an architect." I stopped the car in front of the red saltbox I recalled as his office. There was another name, Charles Ogleby, on the sign.

When I knocked and inquired about New Canaan real estate, Ogleby himself offered a tour of the town's winding lanes. One handsome field was Ogleby's, the last section of an estate which he had bought and subdivided.

I liked Ogleby before Andy did, for his intelligence and modesty. He had skinny, sandy good looks and was a year or so younger than I, but he spoke with such sensible authority on Fairfield County real estate, on taxes and 5 percent mortgages, that in half an hour he had convinced me we should forego buying a house and undertake the adventure of building one. With Charles Ogleby's help, of course, we would express ourselves in wood and stone. We would build our house overlooking the brook, and the pond we would make of the bog, right here at the end of Oenoke Ridge Road.

At first Andy was cautious about such an investment, but that night, when she came around, she did so with all her exuberance. She began a notebook, pasting it up with illustrations from magazines and her own sketches of likable features that might adapt to our plan.

When we called on Clip Ogleby, as we did now each Saturday afternoon, it was Andy who did the talking. Clip would listen to her ideas, often of buildings recollected out of child-hood travel. We realized that Andy had architectural sense. She recognized not just the effects she liked — the rustic, durable ones, the steep slopes of Norman roofs, and the weathered, clean-swept openness of Cape Codders — but how they were achieved.

She could communicate it all to Clip in a word and a quick sketch on the back of an envelope. While I was still puzzled, he would smile and nod and in a stroke of his own pencil, put it on the shelf of our possibilities.

In Vermont I had seen a house with a tower. A resourceful ski instructor had converted a silo to a snow room with an overhead loft, and I was so intrigued with this, with the way it might look at the end of our house with its witch's hat roof, how its ground floor would make a cozy study and library, that I proposed it as one of the ideas we'd like worked into our plans.

Andy was interested and Clip found the prospectus of a silo manufacturer in Iowa. With typical open-mindedness he said, "All things are possible, and that includes towers." He went to work on a rough drawing and sent off for specifications and a shipping estimate.

But on her return from a trip to New Canaan, Andy said, "Here's some bad news for you, Lloyd. Your tower's got to go. Clip says it's going to add at least seven thousand dollars, and maybe more. But he can give us the little study right next to the front door."

When I dug in, saying it was probably the only house I would ever build and that I wouldn't give up so easily on something I really wanted, she said, "But it's so impractical. Doors, windows, everything will have to be made to order, and it's wasteful in every way — heat, light, space. I don't understand. What's so important about a tower?"

"I don't know exactly. It *could* be something Freudian, but I don't think so. I just like the idea. You don't see many towers. It's a statement of self. I thought that was why we're building."

"Exactly," she replied. "Why *we*'re building. For the first time there's a chance for me to have a hand in the way we live."

"I'm for that. What about my hand? What have you got against towers?"

"A house we expect to live in for the rest of our lives oughtn't to be a joke. It ought to reflect our good taste."

"I don't think a tower made out of a silo is bad taste. There's fun in it. A tower would make them wonder, and laugh."

"I don't think making people wonder and laugh is the point of a house."

"Clip Ogleby tells me that a house should state, as much as building material can, something about the people who built it." I sensed we had entered some uncharted and possibly hazardous waters of our marriage, but I smiled, anxious to keep this lighthearted. "If that's so, do you really want to deprive me of my First Amendment rights?"

"You know something, Lloyd?" Andy said rigidly, "you don't have the least notion of what you're like."

"What am I like?"

"You think you're so fair-minded."

"And in fact I'm just the reverse — a tower of ambition and ego?"

"You do want to have your way in everything. If I didn't shout and wave my red flag every now and then, I'd be two-dimensional."

"O.K." I sighed. "It was an idea, no more. I really don't want to make a big issue of it. It's impractical. Let's let it go at that."

"But you're disappointed."

"Yes. Of course."

"I'm sorry."

"Forget it," I said as grandly as I could. "I'll settle for an ordinary house in a spectacular setting. I'll cut down the trees in the bog and scoop out our lake. Lake Erskine will be one of the wonders of Connecticut and people will come from miles around to marvel at why so spectacular a lake lies beside so commonplace a house."

In victory, Andy was gracious. "Let's wait and see then. Maybe there'll be a way for your tower." She laughed as she added, "But you are so obsessed with appearances. It's as though you were always outside yourself, looking back at yourself. You're never at home with you. Sometimes I wonder if *I'm* for appearances."

"You are. You shine forth as my beacon in a naughty world."

My tower fell before the keen, inexorable edge of the contractor's estimate, and my disappointment was deepened by Andy's insouciance. Clip Ogleby seemed to share her view, speaking of the tower as a whim, no more reasonable than if I had proposed a row of gargoyles.

But I was busy with two books that particularly interested me, and glad enough to leave the building of our house to Andy. Her taste was sure, and we had come to an identity of preference in color and style. It came about through our interdependence in the first years of our marriage. We went to galleries and shops together, pointing out what we liked and didn't. We shared our sensual pleasures, the tastes of food, the sounds of music, the look of clothing, and talked about them, knowing that agreement was part of the joy of marriage.

I liked shopping for clothes with Andy, helping her choose a dress or a pair of shoes. But, if at first I had imposed my own love of quality and simplicity, of boldness and surprise, on Andy, I soon realized she had a strong, independent taste of her own, and I began turning to her for aesthetic judgment of every sort.

Andy was on our building site several days a week and reported the progress on excavation and pouring of the foundation. She would glow over each new development and, as the skeleton rose and the floor pattern took shape, the solving of each new difficulty.

One Saturday as I perched on the threshold, looking out over the churned earth and rubble that would be my lawn, I watched Andy and Clip on the tailgate of his pickup truck. They were reading a blueprint, her finger tracing a line, and she said something I couldn't hear, but he laughed and touched her. His fingers brushed hers for just a second, and their heads inclined together in such an intimacy I was embarrassed to have intruded upon it.

As we drove home, Andy said, "You're awfully silent. Anything wrong?"

"Yes. Watching you and Clip today made me realize how much I love you."

"What do you mean?"

"I'm in agony," I said, "at the thought of losing you."

She put a hand on my elbow. "You're not going to lose me."

"I don't have to be told. It sticks out on you like a tusk. I can feel it. I haven't cried since I was twelve, but I'm close to it now." I was not exaggerating. I was shaken by that glimpse of my wife's affection for another man, made aware of what an emptiness there would be in my life without her.

We rode along for several miles, threading through parkway traffic, passing through a tollgate, Andy's silence all the confirmation I dreaded.

"I've been trying to sort it out," she said finally, "and I guess you're right. You're a little right, anyway. I am attracted to Clip."

"Well, you have a right, everyone does, to whatever happiness he or she can snatch from life. I know that, and I'm not asking you to stop whatever . . . It's only that it's painful for me, and I'm going to ask you not to do it so I can see. Will you do that for me?"

"There's nothing," Andy said, ". . . nothing like that. Oh no. Maybe there's some sneaky little idea in Clip's mind. I suppose there is, but he has a perfectly nice wife, as I do a husband. I wouldn't hurt you, Lloyd, not for anything. The house is very exciting to me, and I've been a little giddy, but don't worry. From now on, I'm going to have it very much under control."

After a while I asked, "You haven't slept with Clip?"

"No, Lloyd. Of course I haven't. You must know that."

"Did you kiss him?"

"Yes. Once. It won't happen again."

I was almost certain that it wouldn't.

Lansing Fosse proved his professionalism. There had been a new chapter of *Winston-Salem* on my desk each Monday, and the book had glided toward publication as though on rails. There was only one adverse review and, as Joel had promised, Dexter Barnes delivered me an advance copy of it, smiling.

The *Time* man had decided that at least one of Fosse's charges was unsubstantiated and dismissed *Winston-Salem* as the kind of journalism that used to snatch some circulation in the newspaper wars. Even though *Winston-Salem* reaped a substantial commercial success, and there were assurances from Joel, Sid Broyles, and Elena Wallace that this was a worthwhile venture, the *Time* review was like a blister on my heel and I promised myself that henceforth I would avoid the merely commercial ventures and put a stamp of excellence on every book I did.

The invitation, our first to dinner at the Severances on Beekman Place, came along in midwinter. It fell on a Christmasy evening, with a light snow covering the city's everlasting soot, and I can remember the Dickensian look of the house as we alighted from the cab and stood in the little courtyard waiting for the wreathed, oak door to swing open for us.

A maid in a lace headband admitted us to a house that gave an impression of a more civilized community, Boston or Georgetown. Through multipaned windows I had a glimpse of bare branches, a slope, and bridge lights beyond.

Enid Severance, unmistakable in the imperative rake of her chin and cheekbones, the sure sweep of her long legs, came to meet us. Clear, gray eyes appraised us, making me feel uncertain. Her voice was cellolike, deftly cutting into Hugh's conversation to introduce us to Edmond Pigott. Hugh was in an agreeable mood, warming to Andy at once, and explaining Pigott to us.

"He's a partner in the firm that bears his name, and a fine host to me when I'm in London."

Smiling, Pigott blinked behind his spectacles. He seemed shy of our attention, but likable.

"He's in town," Hugh went on, "to sniff out some good books for his British market, and he's brought some from his own list which he may just offer to a New York editor who treats him well."

Then, of me, Hugh explained, "Lloyd's one of our young editors who'll know the choice books coming up for us. He may find you something interesting, Edmond."

Pigott beamed at me. "Yes. We shall have to chat."

I nodded, but was distracted by Enid Severance, who was telling Andy that Hugh Jr. was yet to come, bringing someone unknown to her.

"I'm glad to hear that," I said, turning to give her my attention and letting Andy fill my place between Hugh and Edmond Pigott. "I haven't had a chance to talk to Hughie since he's come back. I'm anxious to hear about California."

"Are you?"

"I'm sure he's had some adventures."

"I dare say." She left a gulf of silence between us, inviting me to fill it.

"Your son's been very gracious to me." I was all eagerness to please. "He took me up to the Editors' Lunch while I was still at Poole's. A real initiation."

"Hugh Jr. isn't my son. He's Hugh's by his first marriage. But never mind that. What interests me is that you find him gracious."

Stunned by Enid Severance's spininess, I stammered. "Well, yes . . . lately, though I must say . . . Hughie takes some knowing."

She considered, making a judgment of me, and simply turned away.

"Incidentally," Pigott was asking Hugh, "you'll be over this spring?"

"Yes," Hugh replied, "not so much for the books. We haven't done so well with our English titles lately. Buying in order to justify the trip is such an easy mistake. Often it's wiser to come home empty-handed. But I do have to call on you, Edmond. We must do our ceremonial lunch at the Garrick and, of course, there's my tailor. Otherwise I wouldn't be sure it was April."

As Hugh took Andy off to admire the view of the river, Edmond Pigott asked, "What are you at work on, Erskine? What would be of interest to our readers?"

He listened to my description of *Winston-Salem*, nodding politely before pointing out it was unlikely for his audience, but he brightened at my mention of a mountaineering book. As I was promising to show him galleys, my eye strayed to Enid Severance and I caught the surprise and irritation on her face as Hugh Jr. came into the room. With him, fresh and childlike here among her elders, was his father's younger secretary, Flavia Moore.

Hugh Jr. shambled over to join us, grinning, and apparently oblivious to his effect on his stepmother.

"How was California, Hughie?" I asked.

"Unreal. We do business by the pool," he said. "Nobody reads books, but they buy and sell them, and that's why they call them a property. The price is set by how many people are expected to turn out for the movie. It's all ass-backwards and they can't understand why we don't want to make a book out of a screenplay. It's crazy, and I love it."

Pigott seemed embarrassed, and saying, "I think I'll just . . ." he moved off to join Hugh.

"People are always talking about starting a publishing house in California," I said, "but nobody ever does."

"I'm afraid if I lived out there it wouldn't seem funny anymore. That's too big a risk."

Enid Severance joined us and, ignoring me, said, "What an indelicate thing to do, bringing your father's secretary. I'm sure it's great fun for you, but it doesn't amuse me in the least."

His laugh was brave but uncertain. "Last minute change of plans. Couldn't be helped."

"You might have warned me," she said, and abruptly left us.

"Well," I said, "it's hard to please more than one woman at a time."

Hughie shrugged. "She's always like that."

Enid Severance seated us, Edmond Pigott on her right, me on her left, and started conversations, like so many lamps, around her table.

Reaching for his glass, Hughie tumbled it, spilling a red stain across the linen. "Oops," he said, righting the glass, smiling, making me think he had done it deliberately. I wondered if it was to be ignored or joked about, until Enid whispered to the maid as she bent with a serving dish.

While the fresh napkin was spread across the stain, Hughie said, "I'm sorry, Emily. I've made a mess here." His eyes rose to Enid's and fell. Then he brought the refilled glass to his lips and drank off half its wine.

Enid Severance turned to me now, and in an uneasy effort to prime a conversation, she asked, "What about you, Mr. Erskine — what brings you to publishing?"

"Reading books and getting paid for it. It's the last of the gentlemanly professions."

She smiled wanly. "Rubbish. I'm serious. I'd like to know what sort of influences have brought you to Forty-eighth Street."

The others were attentive, even Hugh at the far end of the table. "Publishing good books *is* important to me. That always sounds pompous when I try to explain it, even to myself, and it must be very parochial and boring to anyone outside."

"Nothing about Crowninshield's is boring to me, Mr. Erskine," she said. "You'd make a great mistake in believing that. Why is it important to you?"

I was becoming frightened. "I suppose it goes back to childhood reading," I said. "I've always liked to read, as escape, as vicarious experience. I can't imagine more interesting, more important work. We ought to pay to do it."

"That's a very romantic view." She was unappeased. "And not really an answer. I was asking about you as a person, about your background, because I think that forms your predilections as an editor. Are there publishing influences in your family?"

"No." My tongue struck. I felt cornered and terrified by Enid Severance. She seemed like an elegant, predatory bird whose sharp beak sought my vulnerable parts. I could neither divert nor propitiate her.

In desperation, a need for some compassion, I let pride go. "My mother was a pragmatic woman," I said. "She wanted an orderly, irreproachable life — and my father was a failure, by her standards."

"By yours?"

The price of a drop of kindness from her was to be total exposure, but I did not shrink. "Yes," I said, "because he believed he was. He was in the advertising business. He worked at the same agency all his life, but when it was too late for him to change, he tired of it and wished he had done something else. He had a friend in publishing, and the more he learned about that, the more he envied him. Then, toward the end of his life, he was fired from the agency. I saw him lose the last of his self-respect in one short note from his boss."

I did not look up at her, but I asked Enid, "Is that what you wanted to know?"

"Yes," she said. She relented now, but in her expression I sensed a distaste, as though I too had made a mess at her table. There was embarrassment all around, and I was the source of it.

Hugh came to my rescue, asking, "Why don't you tell us what you think of our current list, Lloyd? Tell us what's good and bad about it. That will interest Edmond."

"It's the envy of the business," I said, pulling myself back into the party. "Our strong suit is politics, books with a Washington point of view, books by historians and academics, books by established writers on important themes. But we could make it more exciting by doing half a dozen first novels each year."

"Include me in," said Hughie.

"Well, of course," Hugh said, "it would be a lovely world where we could just publish the books we like, but in the end, we're a business."

"We've missed out on the angry young men," I said. "Doubleday's doing a very good business with *Lucky Jim*."

"As our London scout, I'll have to plead guilty there," Hugh said. "But the trip is just luck. Odds are all against your turning up in the office of a British publisher on the day a really promising new author is available. And if you are lucky enough to bear off your Birmingham rebel to the hotel room, chances are, reading him with a bleary eye, you'll miss him."

"Even so," Hughie said, "we'd like a try at it."

"I'm sure you would," Enid Severance said. "So would Joel Rossbach, who'd be awfully good at it, by the way."

Edmond Pigott said, "I'm afraid we've missed out too. It is difficult. We had a chance at John Wain, and passed him up."

"Perhaps it's easier for us," I suggested, "as Americans."

"To spot them?" Enid Severance asked. "What makes you think so? It takes an angry young man to know one."

"I'm angry enough for that."

"I don't think you're angry at all." She smiled. "Anyway, I can put your mind at rest about the London trip. Hugh won't be giving it up for a few years yet, and I don't think Crowninshield's will suffer as a result." Rising from the table, she said, "Shall we have coffee in the next room?"

Pouring brandy, Hugh urged Edmond Pigott to describe the changes he had noticed here since his visit of a year ago and Pigott answered amiably that the moral climate was clearly in a nose dive.

He was stopping at the Elysée, "aways a favorite with us, you know, because it's small and they know us and cater to our peculiar British tastes. They'll serve us tea in the bar without making a fuss — but I've become most uncomfortable . . . Surely you've been reading in the paper that it's now the haunt of expensive call girls."

Hugh laughed, and Pigott protested, "But it's quite true, you know. One of the wretched girls tried to strike up a conversation with me this morning. Can you imagine? At nine o'clock? Good heavens!"

Eyes brimming, Hugh set down his cup and saucer to prevent an accident. "Edmond, I've been waiting all day for this moment. Ian Ferguson's in town. He came by this morning."

"Oh yes. He's stopping there too. I saw him in the lobby this morning, and he's equally concerned."

"Just after he left you, Edmond, he went into the dining room to join his wife who'd gone ahead to order breakfast. As he sat down, she asked him, 'Wasn't that Edmond Pigott with you?' Ian said yes, it was, and Heather replied, 'Well, that's what I *thought,* but when I said good morning to him in the elevator, he turned away as if I were some kind of toad . . .' "

"Oh *Lord,*" Pigott cried. "I *couldn't* have." He covered his face with his hands. "I know Heather Ferguson very well. I don't see how I could have failed . . ." Enid and the others were laughing, too, and presently, lowering his hands from fiery cheeks, Pigott joined in. "It was unexpected, seeing her *here* you know. Oh, how ghastly."

Hugh comforted Pigott now with an account of his own trials with London hotels and then came to sit down with me and Andy, to say that he had been thinking, since I had mentioned it at dinner, about what brought us to publishing.

"In my case," he said, "it was by accident. I'd been working at Morgan's, hoping to be sent to Paris. That was what my first wife and I most wanted, a nice, cushy job and life in Paris. But I found the work boring. So, during my lunch hour, I went looking for something different."

"I stumbled into the old Crowninshield building on Fulton Street, and a man I later discovered was Henry Crowninshield looked at my blue suit and starched collar and asked if I was too swell to sell books. I was, you know, but I've always been one to take a chance. And a year later I was in the midst of things when the defalcations were discovered. The partners had been helping themselves to money when they needed it, and we were bankrupt. We had to salvage what we could and start over. Those were hard days, nothing like the Paris ones we'd planned . . ." Hugh looked across the room to where Enid was talking with Edmond Pigott and Flavia Moore. "And they lost me a wife, but in the end they settled my career for me. I'm grateful for that, most of the time."

"*Your* father had no interest in publishing?" I asked.

"No, no. He was a delightful man, devoted to my mother, who was a really lovely woman, a great beauty of her day." He smiled, recollecting. "I can see him perfectly, but I don't recall his reading anything but the sporting news, races of all kinds, boats and horses. He had both. He was a playboy, really, a handsome and delightful man whom my mother was forever trying to discipline."

"I'm always doubtful of accidents where careers are concerned," Andy said. "Is there anything in your school or college days that pointed you to publishing?"

"No." But Andy's question had pleased him, sent him rummaging. "Really the most conventional upbringing for a fortunate boy of my time. We went to Newport in the summer, and occasionally to Europe, to economize. I recall Switzerland vividly, the Park Hotel in Gstaad, where we always stayed. I went to Groton and had the starch taken out of me, and the fear of God put in, by Endicott Peabody. And Harvard, of course, where I learned as much, and no more, than a gentleman should."

Now Hugh raised his eyebrows. "I think perhaps my real education began with that old convention, the Grand Tour. Being at college, I'd just missed the first war and as a sort of compensation I was permitted a year to roam before I got down to work. At first, the trip bored me, really. All those European capitals. But then in Shepheard's Hotel in Cairo, some old African yearnings took hold.

"As a boy I'd read my Edgar Rice Burroughs assiduously and at the zoo acquired a liking for the crocs and hippos. Also, as a very young child, I'd once substituted for my father, escorting my mother to an illustrated lecture on Africa at the Museum of Natural History. She was quite taken with the African explorers, Speke, Livingstone, Stanley, and Baker in particular. Baker took his wife along.

"In any case, I met a fellow in the hotel bar who persuaded me to take a steamer trip up the Nile, just overnight. I ended by going all the way."

"How far is that?" I asked.

"Four thousand miles." Hugh sucked appreciatively at his cigar and blew the smoke above our heads. "My friend left me at Khartoum, where the river divides into the Blue Nile coming down from Abyssinia, and the White, the longer, which crosses Sudan and rises all the way to Lake Victoria and the heart of Africa. It's the most extraordinary journey in the world. You go from desert to swamp and jungle, to forests and hills, and then the falls, the Murchison and Ripon, and finally to ice and snow, the Mountains of the Moon."

"Is the river navigable all the way?" Andy asked.

"Only parts of it. There are small steamers and boats for charter. At a place called Kodok I hired a boat with a crew of three Shilluks, dour-looking tribesmen, to take me through the swampy part, the old sudd. It was hard going, poling really, through waters choked with vegetation. The boatmen would climb out and chop away at the stuff with their billhooks, or pull us with ropes when there was any sort of bank.

"Finally they gave up. The river was lower than expected and they said we must go back, but I climbed a little rise and saw what I thought was clear water ahead. I remembered from that childhood lecture that Baker had gotten his whole flotilla through the sudd by building a dam behind it.

"I tried to show the boys how we might do this, cutting bundles of reeds, making fasces, and stacking them to catch what flow there was and float us forward. While I was demonstrating, wading into the ooze to plant a bundle, my footing gave beneath me, as though I'd stepped into a suck, and I called for help. The Shilluks made no move toward me. As I thrashed, trying to save myself, they crouched on the bank, staring and waiting.

"The old one, the captain, until now a very grave man,

laughed, and I realized that not only was there to be no rope, no pole for me, but that they had hoped for this, even planned it. They were after my money and pack in the boat.

"My bundle of reeds saved me. I had dropped it, naturally, because it was heavy, but now when I grasped for it, put a little weight on it, there was just enough buoyancy to it so that I was able to pull myself toward firmer ground."

"How did you get on with the boatmen then?" Andy asked.

"I think they felt they'd witnessed a miracle of some sort. They were newly respectful, and when I told them to unload the boat, that we'd go on by foot, they did so. We walked for several more days, through the mounds of earth made by the white ants, swarming with swamp flies. It was fierce and yet beautiful. I have never seen such beauty as Africa's." He smiled at Andy. "Yes, there's a point too. My journey was different from what was expected of me. Until I met the Nile I was a pretty conventional fellow, but here I'd tried something, just for the hell of it, and it was the richest experience of my life. I might have died, but I didn't, and so I was the better for the danger of it. Ever since, I've been tempted by new things, adventures of one sort or another. The Nile was a useful preparation for publishing."

When it was time to leave, I determined to avoid Enid Severance on the way, but at the door it was impossible. Hands in pockets, I said to her, "I offended you, but I don't know how."

"What makes you think so?"

"The inquest."

"I was trying to find out about you." Enid nodded. "And yes indeed I did. I'll tell you sometime. Good night, Lloyd." She sent me off with an agreeable wave, as though it had all been a game. "And to you, Andy. So glad you could come."

On the way home, I said, "I'll say this about a party at the Severances, you don't know what misery is until you've been to one. What did Enid have in mind? Why was she wielding her gelding snips?"

"I don't think she was."

"Andy, there was nothing I could say. She quarreled with me for not knowing Hughie was her stepson and for saying he'd been kind to me. Then she drew me into that agonizing explanation about my father."

"She *is* sharp."

"Oh, you noticed that?"

"She's an original. She says what she means and expects it of others."

"I was being polite."

"Maybe she felt you were overdoing it."

From New Rochelle to Stamford, we rode in silence toward our new home in New Canaan, and then Andy added, consolingly, "Listen, just be glad you're not Hughie, having to measure up to that terrific old man of his while Enid razzes him. A wonder he isn't a blacker sheep. There *is* a man to feel sorry for."

That night I dreamed of Montague School. Its antiseptic smells and dark halls, the lining up in snow and rain for the march to meals and classes, make a stage for my subconscious wanderings. I am there again, walking a path near the old infirmary, believing the man ahead is Dan Erskine, come to see the parade.

But it is too late for me to catch him now, for I hear first call blown and I must run for the assembly, knowing my shoes are scuffed, my rifle misplaced. Then I am in company-front and we are passing the reviewing stand. At eyes-right I search for him and don't find him, but Edith Emmett is there, beside the colonel. From under a wide-brimmed, leghorn straw, a lock of her gray hair stirs, then the hem of her silk print dress, like the parade ground grass, riffles in a sundown breeze.

I look to Mrs. Emmett's cameo face, hoping she is picking mine from our long file, and find she is Enid Severance, her mouth made up in a smile. But it is the parade which pleases her. She doesn't see me.

≈§ 9 §≈

I HAVE NEVER FELT so close to, so open to, so illuminated by, and affectionate toward another man as I was toward Joel Rossbach during those years of the late fifties and early sixties when we rode the New Haven together. Each morning we would set out from our leafy bivouacs to join up at the little New Canaan station. Here we would board the branch train to Stamford, transfer point for the 8:32 into Grand Central.

This journey, through blighted Westchester and Yonkers, finally tunneling down under Harlem to emerge within the city walls and the very center of its strife, was a daily siege. It was just that kind of warrior's comradeship we felt, Joel and I.

During the two hours of each day that we spent together on the train, I found most pleasure in the honing of our editorial judgment. We traded manuscripts and came to trust the advice, the caution or daring, we offered each other.

I learned from Joel that an editor practices around the clock, each perception continually on the alert for good ideas and good writing. Even while it sleeps, the editorial mind is sorting experience, selecting what's worthwhile from the slag of daily impressions. Above all, an editor does not wait for writers and ideas to swim to him, but rather he fishes the periodical streams where the new ones are spawning.

Joel rode with a lapful of periodicals — *Scientific American,* the *Nation,* the airmail editions of the *T.L.S.* and the *Observer* — and I envied the easy way he glided through them, plucking ideas — on farming the sea, the trouble with the schools, the new Africa.

I soon had my own lapful — *Harper's, Newsweek,* and *National Geographic, Esquire,* the *New Yorker* and *Paris Review* — and although I could match Joel idea for idea, I lost no admiration for the ambition of his mind. It was so quick at recognition, so deft at getting to the core of things.

Without any need to voice it, we understood that the originator of any idea was its proprietor. While he might call upon the other for further advice and encouragement, if the idea was viable, he alone would pursue it.

We shared the frustrations of train delays and rising fares with the cheerful resignation of old campaigners, along with the joys of unfolding our copies of the *Times* each morning and exchanging our perceptions of the world.

We groaned together over each new banality that Eisenhower uttered, mourned over Adlai Stevenson's defeat, and watched the market in publishing stocks.

"Look at that, Lloyd," he said, his finger on the Crowninshield quotation. "Up another quarter. You made twenty-five bucks yesterday without even knowing it. How's about the capitalist system?"

At the office, we had fallen into an easy, parallel stride, each of us finding five or six books for every list, meeting similar successes and failures with them. There was so little competitiveness between Joel and me that the other editors took us for a team.

Then, at the close of one Wednesday editorial meeting, Hugh altered that. He had been speaking of how agents were anticipating the growing market for paperbacks by asking more money for their books.

"We'd better get used to paying bigger advances for the books we want," he warned us, "and needing to earn more money from the books we do publish. It's taking more money

just to operate. Let me dispel any doubt in your minds —
publishing's gone big-time."

While we drank this in, he made a second announcement.
From the papers before him, he selected a letter and studied it
a moment before speaking.

"This is news I'm sad to bring you. It's a letter from Guy
Waterhouse in which he tells me he wants to retire at the beginning of next year. Guy, as you all know, has a house in
Mexico of which he is particularly fond, and he wants to spend
more time there. I'm reluctant to accept this, but I'm afraid I
haven't much choice."

Over the top of his glasses, Hugh looked around the table.
"Guy's leaving will have a further significance to some of you,
of course. It will open a position on the executive committee.
I think it's safe to say we'll be making an appointment from
among the people at this table."

Hugh smiled. The gray eyes brightened as they swept around
the oval, hesitating slightly on Hughie, then Joel. I thought
they paused on me as well. So the meeting ended. There was
a shuffling of papers, a shoving-back of chairs and I saw that
Joel was watching me.

Waiting for the elevator, I said, "Well, Joel, there's a challenge for you."

"Yes," he said. "That had the sound of a starting gun."

The next day, as I was signing some letters, I looked up to
find Loomis Pitcher smiling at me. I had not seen him since
the wedding, and fifteen years had changed him. Delicate features had thickened and there was a clearing in the once-dense
forest of his hair, but the flamboyance with which he used to
make wonder among us was undiminished. He was elegant, in
a biscuit-colored suit and a polka dot bow, and pleased at having eluded the receptionist in order to take me by surprise.

"Loomy." I pumped his hand. "How *are* you?"

Seated by my desk, he told about London, about a girl, an
Irish poet he had loved, about an adventure in French wine
which had been profitable, and another in an international art
magazine which had not.

In his mixture of earnestness and self-mockery, he went on to say that although his life *seemed* diffuse, short of the work-of-art he had so fervently promised me, he was making progress.

"Never fear, I'm going to leave life more beautiful than I found it," he assured me. "That's the responsibility of having enough so I needn't hustle."

Then, in contrast with this creed, he said that he had returned to New York a year ago and had taken an office downtown, a single room on the Bache & Company floor at 36 Wall Street. Interest in the stock and commodity markets, the solving of financial puzzles, had been a pastime. Now he had turned professional, putting out a weekly market letter for brokers, interspersing his advice with bits of philosophy, comments on new books, plays, and art shows, even some of his own poetry. He liked to think the letter was literate and informative, and it was certainly profitable. Although he had just raised the subscription price to a thousand dollars, this only increased demand — and here Loomy laughed, pleased as ever at human folly.

Now he looked at his watch and said, "I know you're busy, Lloyd, and I mustn't take more of your time, but in fact there *is* a reason for this call. I'm doing some publishing stocks and I'm curious about Crowninshield's. Is there going to be a merger?"

"I don't believe so," I replied, although the prospect had begun to worry me. "I suspect that the big money men are a threat to a place like this."

Loomy crossed his feet on my radiator and looked at the jacket sketches on my wall. "Still, Lloyd, you ought to see yourself in perspective. Crowninshield's is impressive. It's very tempting as a partner to a rich company. That's why I suspected there was truth in the rumor about a Crowninshield's merger."

"I think I'd be told if that were true."

"Who knows?"

"Hugh Severance."

"Can I ask him?"

I hesitated, but then liked the idea. I felt Hugh would be intrigued with my precocious friend. "I have a Mr. Pitcher in my office," I explained to Corinne Perry. "He's putting out something about us in his market letter and wants to ask Hugh a question."

"I'll see, Lloyd."

Hugh's voice came on. "Lloyd, there's someone with me, and I have another appointment in half an hour. Can you make my apologies to Mr. Pitcher?"

"Of course."

"What's he want to know?"

"Our plans — mergers and rumors of same."

Hugh laughed. "Tell him to believe nothing he hears, and that I'll be glad to talk to him another time."

Five minutes after Loomy had left, Hugh called back to say that if Mr. Pitcher was still here, he could see him.

"He's gone, Hugh, but you know, *I'm* curious now."

"Come on in."

H.S. was in an easy mood and I said, "Everyone seems to think we're going to make a corporate alliance. I'd like your assurance that if there are such plans, they won't change the nature of my job."

Hugh nodded. "Whatever you want to know, Lloyd. Ask away."

"For instance, my friend Pitcher — he feels there's truth in it. Wondering about the rumors makes me uneasy."

Hugh laced his fingers. "They're real concerns. I can worry you further by saying I believe in change. To stand still is always tempting, but petrifying. You're buried before you know it. If you don't believe that, look around at some of the firms that were leaders in the thirties. But I can assure you of this, Lloyd, the key to change here has always been the trade editor. The editorial mind is most important to us, and so long as I'm in charge here, editors will run Crowninshield's — cautioned, naturally, by a good business head. An editor who proves himself in that way will be rewarded here."

"You mean money?"

"Money, of course, along with more responsibility and the freedom to do what he wants to do. He shares in the company destiny, so he has more rewards — of every kind."

"Affection too?" It was a joke and I expected another in response. However, Hugh frowned.

"Emotions tend to compromise the situation," he said. "I've always thought a good house is the triumph of mind over emotion. What else, Lloyd? Anything else you'd like to know?"

"Yes, I'd like to know what it's like, being the head of a house like this."

"I'm very attached to it." He smiled at his understatement. "You know Crowninshield's has sustained me nearly forty years. It's a community, united in purpose, and I feel toward it as, I suppose, a mayor feels toward the town where he's grown up and spent his life. He must behave in ways that make the town proud of him, and lead it as well as he can — listen to his constituency but in the end make decisions according to his own best instincts and intelligence."

"I like that, Hugh, and it puts my mind to rest about rumors of merger. There isn't a need for it, is there?"

"Well, I think your friend Pitcher is right, Lloyd. Often it's worthwhile to have a look in the Wall Street mirror. We must guess what publishing is going to be like in a couple of years and think about meeting demands the future will put to us. Of course we'll have to expand in some areas simply to give us the capital to keep up with changes."

"I'd certainly be for expanding, if it keeps us clear of mergers. Is that an acceptable point of view?"

"Acceptable?"

"For a candidate. Guy's successor."

Hugh smiled. "Oh, yes. I suspect the new man on the executive committee will be one of you younger people who's proved his interest in the course we take, because naturally he will have an influence on which of the rumors about us develop some substance. So it interests me very much what you and Joel, and young Hugh of course, are thinking about . . . as well as what you're doing."

"How our books are doing?"

"Exactly."

"Understood," I said.

As I rose to go, Hugh touched two fingers to an eyebrow, and away, in mini-salute. "Good luck."

I grew increasingly anxious for signs of Hugh's favor. I looked for these everywhere, and indeed found some. He had begun to ask my advice about his own books and I realized that the clamshell of his confidence had opened by a crack.

Dozens of manuscripts came to Hugh — work of the firm's oldest and most distinguished authors, work of their friends, the best of what the agents had to offer us, and work of his enormous professional and social acquaintance — all asking his attention.

Bearing one of these, H.S. would come into my office to say, "Lloyd, if you're not too busy, I'd like your opinion of this. I've had a glance at it myself, enough to know it's interesting and maybe up your alley."

These often proved marginal manuscripts, competently written and sound enough to require a thorough reading. In the course of this I would discover Hugh's stake, often that the author was an acquaintance, that he had encouraged him, offered an option or contract perhaps, so that if I responded unfavorably it was to disagree with Hugh's own inclination. I was wary of that, of course, but however anxious to please, I could tell him no less than the truth as I saw it.

I had misgivings over a book on aging which, I realized, had been written at Hugh's suggestion, by Hugh's doctor.

"I don't know what you want of me on this book," I said in returning it to him, "and of course I'll take it on if you say so, but I think I owe you a candid opinion of it."

"Shoot."

"I'm sure he's a very good doctor, but he can't write. It's not just that the language is a bramble patch — that would be relatively easy to fix — but the organization's hopeless. He gets lost in his own arguments. Have you put out money on it?"

"Not enough to worry about." He had begun a rueful nodding. "Go on, Lloyd."

"I could go to work and see what can be salvaged, but I don't believe the ideas are original, or strong enough to make it worthwhile. I'm afraid my advice is to junk it."

He sighed. "I guess you're right, though I was hoping you'd tell me otherwise. I must have got carried away with my own enthusiasm for a ripe old age and the Doc's palaver. He's a smooth talker."

This new dependency, an intimacy really, which permitted me to say no, for and to him, seemed grounds for confidence, and I was rejoicing in it when H.S. asked my opinion of a book called *Pleasures of Collecting* by a William Stickney. Although it was an interesting manuscript, telling of the author's absorption in collecting books about the presidency, how this had brought him divers pleasure, his most valued friends, and a good return on his investment, in the end I found it disappointing. Andy confirmed my judgment.

When I told Joel I would be delivering Hugh some advice he wouldn't like on the book, he said, "H.S. *is* a great editor, but along with the rest of us he has his weaknesses. Unlike the rest of us, though, he knows it. He really does want you to tell him what to do about Stickney. He's probably someone Hugh sees at dinner parties and he wants to pass on the responsibility of turning the man down. Christ, Lloyd, don't worry about Hugh's sensibilities. They're steel — and you're doing the dirty work."

Still, bringing Hugh another no was disagreeable. I began by saying, "The first part is O.K., but the last chapters, on training 'the collector's eye' and applying it to life as a whole, puts him on very thin ice. Good taste *isn't* that important. It doesn't replace feeling. He's proposing to get a decorator in to deal with all our problems. Unless the author's willing to cut that, or revise it drastically, I wouldn't recommend our doing it."

Hugh shook his head. "I don't believe Stickney will take to

substantial revision. The last chapters are important to him."

"Who is he?"

Hugh's eyebrows went up in surprise at me. "He's head of a broadcasting company."

"Oh, *that* Stickney. Well, I suppose his position alters the prospects, but not my opinion. We might remind him of Job's lament, 'O that mine adversary had written a book.' "

Hugh laughed. "You may be right, Lloyd. Still, Stickney's often incisive." He picked up a report, pondering it for a moment. "And Alice Margolies feels rather differently." Handing me her summary, he went on, "You'll see she thinks it will appeal to a great many readers."

My eye was caught by a line in Alice's report which noted that Mr. Stickney was an influential man who would not let his book fail.

"It offers some insights to the author, surely," I conceded. "Still, I doubt it will add much to our reputation."

I found H.S. smiling at the possibility of my being wrong.

In the months that followed, Hugh did see I was acquainted with every small victory Alice had with the Stickney, the ease with which Dexter Barnes coaxed feature stories from the press about the author, and the respectable advance sale. While the *New Yorker* shared my view of *Pleasures of Collecting,* there was a prominent and favorable account of it in the *Times.*

It seemed a comradely ribbing that ran between H.S. and me over the Stickney book. I took it good-humoredly. I told myself I had not been proved wrong, and that even if I had, I couldn't be right *all* the time. Still, I suffered.

Editorial decisions became agonizing in the knowledge that they weighed so heavily in the competition between Joel and me for appointment to the executive committee. The books and authors we brought in made our constituency and the measure of our worth.

In the midst of these semifinals between us, I happened to go down to the basement cafeteria during the noon hour for a sandwich and a carton of milk. As I settled at a table there, Flavia Moore sat beside me, laying out salad and fork and flattening the pages of *New American Review*.

"Hey," she said in a conspiratorial whisper, "is it true your secretary's leaving?"

"She's just getting engaged."

"If Pat goes — and between you and me I think she will — would you want me for a secretary? Think before you say no." Flavia laughed and tossed a lock of hair off her forehead. "When you ask Corinne she'll tell you I'm a lousy secretary. She's right too, because I don't like doing her donkey work. But for you I'd be good, and I'm a *hell* of a first reader. I really am." She held up the *N.A.R.* "I read the literary reviews, the fly-by-night quarterlies, for pleasure. I really love looking for the new ones, and I can tell 'em."

"I used to think I could. The more I do it the less sure I am."

She smiled, nodded. "I *can*. Try me. I'm going crackers working for Corinne. I'm about to quit anyway, so there won't be any problem about stealing me from the boss. Please?"

The heat of Flavia's appeal had made her look especially lovely and she had drawn the attention of the other girls, who were watching us and smiling among themselves. I noticed that she wore a wedding ring.

"Bring me something," I said. "Bring me something you like."

"O.K." She rummaged in a leather sack at her feet and brought forth a copy of *Partisan Review*. "Know someone called Bryce?" She flipped the pages, turned down a corner. "Read this. He's a friend of Hughie's, but don't let that put you off."

That same evening, going home on the train, I opened the *P.R.* to the turned-down corner and found it was the start of a novel, a complex story about some Americans in Cuba in the early fifties, the end of the Batista regime. It was obscure, but I was intrigued by it, by the language, the intricate characters, the slowly growing tension, and it clung in my thoughts as I turned to other manuscripts later in the evening.

"Yes," Andy agreed, giving back the Bryce piece at bedtime. "Whoever he is, he's good. I'll bet other people have got to him."

Next morning, Flavia Moore said, "Hughie's read it but he hasn't done anything about it. Anyway, I don't think a friend makes a good editor, anymore than he makes a good lover. Why don't you see what you can find out? And incidentally, how do I look as a job applicant?"

"Better," I said. "I'll let you know."

A call to the *Partisan Review* revealed that Morgan Bryce's agent, and this seemed a favorable sign, was Elena Wallace.

"Oh, you're onto Morgan Bryce too," Elena crowed over the phone. "Well, that's clever of you, Lloyd. Yes he *is* very fine, and I'd adore to see the novel at Crowninshield's, but there are complications. Others have asked before you. I've made no promises and I may very well put it up for competitive offers, but you know he's an old friend of Hugh Jr.'s, don't you? Morgan's part English, rather grand English, actually. He's the natural son of an earl and his mother was the journalist Polly Atherton, very Bloomsbury and advanced for their times, but it makes England difficult for Morgan even now. He was at school here with young Hugh and spent some holidays at Greenfields. Anyway, it will be hard to send it to Crowninshield's and avoid all that. Still, I may be able to find a way to get it to you. Let me think about it, Lloyd."

Flavia brought me first word that the incomplete Bryce manuscript, *Fulgencio's Game,* five chapters of a projected twenty, had arrived in the house. Two copies had appeared on H.S.'s desk with Elena's explanation that because of widespread interest, she was making multiple submissions of this new author and would contract with the publisher who showed most enthusiasm. The two manuscripts were because she knew of his son's, as well as my own, interest in Bryce's work.

"He's an interesting boy," Hugh said when he handed the manuscript to me, "with literary blood in his veins."

At the editorial meeting in which we were to discuss making an offer on *Fulgencio's Game,* I expected my voice would join in a chorus of enthusiasm. Hughie surprised me. Instead of claiming Bryce, he spoke of reservations. "There are so many characters, I can't keep them straight. Too much history of these obscure political parties. And it didn't seem real to me, you know. He's invented this Havana and it shows. Morgan's talented — that's clear enough — but I wouldn't want to invest heavily in this book. Not with a friend. That would be awkward."

The others were ambivalent, balancing Bryce's feats of imagination against the style which they found self-conscious and occasionally impenetrable.

Joel, who had barely glanced at my copy of the manuscript said, "Well, it's the kind of book we ought to be doing, but not at too great an expense."

H.S. summed up, saying, "I admire Bryce's fine sense of violence, that unmotivated cruelty and terror which we all suspect is waiting for us, just outside the door. Still, this is hard reading and I can't imagine a popular sale. I'd surely want to see more before making an offer."

I was dismayed, and questioned my own judgment. Here at our table, Morgan Bryce was drowning in indifference. I thought of Andy's certainty about Bryce, of Flavia Moore's excitement over the eight chapters she had just read, and of my own sense of discovery in Bryce's perceptions. On a swell of indignation I went to his rescue.

"I've never set eyes on Bryce," I told the meeting, "but he's the most talented writer I've come across since I've been at Crowninshield's. He's trying a huge novel here, one that's challenging all his ability, and I see plenty, along with the weaknesses. I suspect the language difficulties can be edited out to nearly everyone's satisfaction, but we mustn't miss out on Bryce."

I could feel the skepticism all around me, and the decision was postponed until I could meet with the author. This was not easily brought about. Even with Elena Wallace as mediator, Bryce broke several engagements before actually turning up one midafternoon in the Oak Room bar.

He had arrived first and had chosen the darkest corner, so I could barely make out his pale, handsome features under a thicket of dark red hair, as tangled as his most labyrinthine paragraphs. He was shy and withdrawn as he sipped his drink, and I sensed an arrogance in his greeting, a curiosity as to why this stranger, not a Severance, had come to talk to him about his book.

"I want you to know right off," I said, "how much we all like *Fulgencio's Game*. We hope we're going to be the publisher."

He waved away my politeness to ask, "What did Thumper think? Did he like it?"

"Thumper?"

"Hugh père. That's what he's called at Greenfields."

"I've never been there."

"I used to come down, from school."

"Well, of course . . . Hugh liked it. He went on at great length about your way with motiveless evil and destruction. He was very impressed."

"Ahh." Bryce warmed perceptibly.

"If you *were* to come to us, would you want Hugh — either Hugh — for your editor?"

Bryce thought about it, puffing on his cigarette and watching someone behind me. "Young Hugh and I were schoolmates — and we've done some drinking together. I doubt we're suited as editor and author. But I have an extensive respect for Thumper's shrewdness as a publisher. In many ways he's the wisest man I know."

"I understand."

"So I'd want him there, you know. But I know he's occupied with many things."

"Would you accept me as stand-in?"

Bryce blew two puffs of smoke before saying, "Perhaps."

"Could you take some advice on cuts and revisions?"

"We'd have to see about that."

He was not an easy man, but we were making progress.

When I asked Bryce about Greenfields, he said, "I'd been separated from my semblance of a family in England for a year, and enduring the monkish life at St. Paul's for some months, so it seemed like heaven, that first Christmas I spent there. I was made a provisional member, and quite suddenly exceptional among exceptional people. It seemed both affectionate and great fun, with games and lovely drink and meals and fascinating new people. There were writers mainly, which interested me, but there was a senator, too, and a British actor and people who knew my parents, turning up for lunch. Oh, it was very difficult indeed, packing off to Concord again."

"You got on with Enid Severance?"

Bryce, who had been enjoying his reminiscence, was surprised. "Of course."

Next morning, reporting to H.S., I was still excited by the interview and the feeling of a triumph within reach.

"To begin," I said, "Bryce is aware he has the pick of publishers, but he's interested in Crowninshield's, mainly because of you. He cared very much what you thought of his book."

With a quizzical look over the top of his glasses, he asked, "And how did I come off?"

"Oh, very well. I said you were a great fan."

"Am I?"

"Oh yes."

"Good."

"So, although Elena will make us bid for him, I think we have a fair chance to get Morgan Bryce."

"How much would you be willing to go?"

I looked at the partial manuscript in my lap. "I think we must have this." It was Maxwell Perkins's phrase of utmost enthusiasm, one that had stuck in my mind. "I'd want to go high enough to take it."

Hugh's lower lip reached upward in doubt and caution. "Surely you'd put yourself some kind of limit. Whatever virtues I saw in the manuscript, I'm also recalling the excesses, those dense, perplexing, endless sentences. I suspect reviews will make much of them. We've only seen a quarter of the book. Morgan may very well disappoint you. Even if he doesn't, how many copies do you think we'd sell?"

Surprisingly, my own enthusiasm was having a reverse effect on Hugh, reinforcing his doubts of Bryce. It was as though he was pushing me toward a lonelier and more dangerous commitment. It brought a sharp memory of previous discomforts in this chair, of his urging me toward his inclinations.

Rebellion bubbled in my throat. "That's not the point," I said. "Don't you see? Bryce is a darkly and enormously talented writer. That's the difference. Whatever it sells, whatever the reviews say, we should do this book."

Hugh leaned forward, folding his hands on the tabletop. "You may be right about this book, that the rest of us with our more guarded enthusiasm will look foolish in the light of its performance, but you might want to look at it the other way 'round and speculate if you haven't gone overboard on Bryce. There's always a danger there, I think, for an ambitious editor to take the part of the author and forget his role as publisher. This is Crowninshield's, remember, and I doubt the passing up of any single book, however fine, is going to prove disastrous to us."

"Yes, of course it's occurred to me that wanting to pick a winner has clouded my judgment. But Hugh, I can only bet on that judgment and take my chances. I'd think a great deal less of myself for being cautious about a book I believe in — and less of Crowninshield's, too, if it failed to publish a good book because it wasn't going to sell."

"All right, Lloyd." It was as though he had counseled my stubbornness as long as he could and now I must find the truth for myself. "Feeling that way, you'd better go ahead and buy it. Good luck."

He was already busy with the correspondence Corinne had brought for his signature.

❧ 10 ❧

I KNEW that the race for the executive committee was running along two tracks, that in addition to editorial accomplishment we were being tried for corporate expectancy — which of us could best guide Crowninshield's in policy — but it had not occurred to me to enter into management concerns until I was invited.

Then, one noontime, I saw Joel lunching at a table across from mine at the Italian Pavilion. The man who came to join him was a gray-complexioned string bean of a fellow whom I recognized as Philip Lerner, one of the pocket book pioneers. His voice was adenoidal, penetrating the hum of restaurant conversation, bringing me snatches of talk about newsstand sales and reorders.

Joel seemed embarrassed by my discovering him in this company, and later, when I asked, he was reticent. "Oh, Phil was telling me what's wrong with our paperback line."

"Learn anything?"

He shrugged. "That it's another world." Although I waited expectantly, he divulged no more, and it struck me there was something up between him and Lerner that he didn't want me to know about. We had often spoken of our weakness in paperbacks and how it might be turned to strength. If he was doing something about this, it would surely be a score for Joel.

Editorially too, Joel's inclinations, once close to mine, were diverging. He was more alert to political possibilities than I. Saul Diamond's *Times* dispatches from the Middle East didn't interest me, but he saw a book in them from the first, and he made it a fine one, *Fire in the Desert*.

On his annual New York trips, Edmond Pigott had become a regular visitor. When he dropped by my office to go over our forthcoming list, I failed to mention *Fire in the Desert*, and that night, on the way home, Joel asked why.

"Diamond's an American journalist," I said. "He's not known in England."

"Oh, really? Well, Pigott *was* interested. He wanted to see galleys. Lucky I ran into him."

"I'm sorry, but Edmond asked me to be selective, pick out the books that had a particular British appeal. It didn't seem to me . . ."

"I'm sure you didn't neglect any of yours."

"No," I replied. "I'm sure I didn't."

A few days later, riding into town, Joel pointed out an article in the *Reporter* on Bernard Berenson, the art critic, noting that he was an interesting subject for a biography, and I took the article to skim some paragraphs and then to ask if he was going to pursue it.

"I think there *is* a perfectly adequate book on him," Joel said. "I forget who did it, but I'd guess it fills the bill."

The article was by a Polly Dupee and I read more of it, absorbing her admiration for the old man and seeing a wit in her writing that saved it from sentimentality. When I finished the piece, I said to Joel, "Maybe we should have another biography. This girl writes well."

"Did you think so? I thought it very schoolgirlish."

"She's up at the Metropolitan. She must know *something*."

Joel shrugged and turned back to his *Times*.

It was several days before I got around to looking up the Berenson book and discovered it was published by a university press. Encouraged by Flavia, who also liked the piece, and intrigued with the notion of proving Joel wrong about Polly Dupee, I called the museum and reached her at once.

"Oh, yes," she told me cheerfully, "I've had several inquiries, but I haven't made any commitments yet and I'm pleased you're interested. Even before the *Reporter* piece appeared, I was thinking of a book."

Polly Dupee went on to say she had plenty of material and would have time, in the course of the summer, to put in the work.

During the week in which I met Polly Dupee and liked both her and her eagerness to do the book for Crowninshield's, Joel was out of the office with a cold, but on his return I told him that I had taken her to lunch and we had gotten on well.

Not amused, Joel said, "You're a fast worker."

"So's she. There's an outline done and a summer vacation ahead of her. All ready to go on a book."

"What makes you think it'll be any good?"

"Faith."

At the next editorial meeting, I proposed we contract for the Berenson. I spoke favorably of the subject and author, and the other editors offered opinions. Noticing that the usually voluble Joel had not spoken, Hugh asked, "And what do you think, Joel?"

"I like the idea very much," he said. "It was mine."

For a moment no one spoke and then I said, "That's true, only you didn't want to do it. You didn't like her writing."

"Last week," he replied, "was an unfortunate one to have a cold."

Hugh smiled and asked if there were other proposals ready for the executive committee.

After the meeting, I looked for Joel in his office, hoping to set this straight between us, but he had already gone to lunch. When I told Flavia what had happened, she shut the door and drew her chair to the edge of my desk.

"You have more solid books on the list than Joel does, and more coming," she said. "You are ahead of him, and you'll win in a fair race. But he's going to stick you right between the shoulders. He has to. I don't know if you care about your future around here, but I do. I want to see you on the board. So fight for it. Play a little dirty yourself."

"Joel's my friend."

"I wonder if he remembers that while he's running you down." Never taking her narrowing, defiant eyes from mine, Flavia said, "Have you seen his friend Lerner? He wears white-on-white shirts and talks out of the side of his mouth like this. Did you know Joel brought him in to see Hugh yesterday? They're talking about bringing Lerner in as a consultant to re-organize the department. I think it's all an idea to score off you."

"Flavia, I'm just as ambitious as he is."

"Joel's more ambitious than you can even conceive. He lies awake nights thinking of how to discredit you — with Hugh, with Guy, with the office boys, with people at other houses, with the agents. Did you know he's having lunch with Elena Wallace today?"

"He's free to. I don't have the franchise on Elena."

"You're such a bunny. He hasn't any of her authors. Can't you imagine what he's up to? He's trying to screw you out of Morgan Bryce. Bet you a drink I'm right."

Later, I called Elena and we met in the Drake bar for a pre-train drink. Settling herself into a divan she told me that at lunch Joel had spoken enthusiastically about the Bryce book.

I said, "I don't believe he's read much of it."

"He's mentioned it to someone at Harper's too. They inquired today."

"That's not helpful, starting the other hounds."

Elena said, "Well, don't worry about Morgan Bryce. I've written him that you're interested and want to talk about publishing him. He's gone home to Sussex, you know, living in a little house on what used to be his father's estate."

"You're not showing the manuscript?"

"No-o. But if you're nervous about it, perhaps you'll want

to contract for it now. I'm asking an advance of ten thousand dollars. How does that sound?"

"With Joel talking it up around town, it's sure to be more next week. Let's agree on that."

Now, when I passed Joel in the corridor, we averted our eyes. In the evening I often took the earlier train, or he the later, but on Friday evening we both took the 6:12, and I saw him seated beside a stranger. As I passed, he looked up from his manuscript, but we did not speak.

At the New Canaan station, Kay Rossbach stood by our car, talking to Andy, and when she noticed us approaching from opposite directions she asked, "You guys still on the outs?"

Joel headed for their little Italian car mumbling, "Lucky to get a seat at all. Pushy new people. Better the subway any day."

Driving home, Andy said, "You and Joel are behaving so foolishly. Incidentally, it's hard on Kay and me. Can't you have a talk?"

"No."

That very night we both turned up at a neighborhood dinner party, to spend an hour eyeing, and avoiding, each other, then to be drawn, like duelists with an appointment, onto a deserted porch.

We faced each other across a table made from a four-foot slice of elm. Joel's eyelids drooped with menace and I wondered if we would grapple here, like schoolboys in the cloakroom.

"You wanted me to lose the Bryce, didn't you — or pay too much? Admit that, Joel. I'll admire you for it."

"If you get the Bryce," he said, "I'm happy for you."

"Bullshit. I know all the things you're doing behind my back."

"What things?"

"You were a sphinx about Morgan Bryce at the meeting. What did you really think? Did you want him for yourself?"

Joel's hand shot out for my lapel and yanked me close.

"Whatever I do, I don't wait until you're sick to poach your ideas. I don't steal your authors, because I don't have to."

"Get your fucking hands off me." I pushed him against the table and heard my lapel rip. "If you mean Polly Dupee, you didn't want her. You said she was a schoolgirl writer and you weren't going to follow her up. Well, you're memory's short and you were *wrong* about her."

"I found her. I liked her. I showed you the piece — or do you deny that? How's *your* memory? Why didn't you say you were going after her? That would have been the decent thing to do. Who's the sneak, Lloyd?"

"And you're learning about paperbacks, right? Finding they're another world? Well, I know all about Lerner, that you're getting Hugh to take him on and reorganize the place."

"I didn't know there was a law against improving the company."

"When you do it deceitfully — when you lie to me about it."

"Don't call me a liar, God damn it." He lunged at me with such force that I fell backward, grabbing at his neck, bringing him along as I tumbled over a child's cart, cracking my head against the table edge as I fell. The sharp pain made me strike out, catching him full on the mouth with my fist.

Before he could hit back, Andy was between us, kneeling, her hands on mine, saying, "Oh, stop this, you stupid idiots."

Kay, coming up behind her, pulled Joel to his feet and led him toward the light to see the damage of his mouth.

An oozing lump on my forehead and Joel's swollen lip kept us from returning to the party, and we hovered in the shadows of the porch. While Andy kept between Joel and me, Kay went inside for drinks.

When she returned with them, we perched in a line on the top of the steps leading down to a rock garden, sipping, thinking, listening to the pulsing of crickets in the field beyond.

Andy said, "I wish you two would remember that you're good friends."

"We were," I said. "We're becoming ugly enemies. You

promised we wouldn't, Joel. You said there would be plenty of room for both of us at Crowninshield's."

"There is," he said. "Of course there is."

"Think what really lies between you," Kay said.

"It's Hugh of course," Joel said. "He's running us against each other and undercutting Hughie in the bargain."

"I'd like to think that — " I said, "that it's only Hugh trying us."

"It is," Joel said, "and we hadn't better let him do that any-more."

Together we trailed up through a vegetable garden. The turnaround in front of the barn was bright with moonlight. There, before getting into our cars to go home, Joel and I shook hands, and hugged each other's wives. It was not quite a heal-ing of the wound, but it would do.

Soon after that night Joel told me that he was tired of com-muting.

"That's a difference between us. I know how you love that house of yours, but ours is just a place to keep out of the weather and to send the mail. I'm dreaming of an 8B some-where in the Seventies. I think we'll move back to town in the fall."

"Kay feel the same way?"

"Kay's two people, you know. She's a bundle of female in-stincts, and a novelist manqué. The rejection slips eat away at her, make her resent it when I enthuse over a writer and con-tract for a book."

At Crowninshield's the pressure of the competition went un-relieved and I was anxious as ever at news of Joel's triumphs — his contract for a big Washington book, and the knowledge, learned by Andy through Kay, that the Rossbachs had been to the Severances for dinner.

Both of us looked for signs of how much longer our race would run and which of us had the lead at the moment. I tried to read them in Hugh's expression and behavior. When he proved inscrutable, as he invariably did, I tried to read them in the tone of Corinne Perry's voice when I asked for a moment with Hugh.

I suspected that Guy, or even Sid Broyles, as members of the executive committee, might have some knowledge, and I searched their faces when we passed, attaching importance to a dour or cheerful greeting, as though my destiny were as much in their minds as my own.

Then Flavia brought news of a threat I had not even considered. "You know about Hughie?" she asked. "He's got something going. He's brought in some lawyers from the California News Union. They've been in with H.S. all morning."

"The News Union?" Joel said. "They've been talking to Viking. They're looking for a house to buy."

When Joel and I confronted him, Hughie confirmed it, explaining that he had met some people in California, the Axelrod family, who controlled the coastal newspaper chain and a group of Western magazines. "They've made a good thing of the journalistic side, and now they want to get into book publishing."

"But what's in it for us?" I asked. "What will they bring that can possibly do us any good?"

"Money," Hughie said. "The old cash flow."

Going home, Joel and I talked of Hughie's prospects.

"To me," I said, "it isn't even plausible that Hugh would fall for it. Why a newspaper chain? He won't give 'em the time of day, will he?"

"He won't reject it out of hand," Joel said, "because he's Hugh. He'll listen to them, hoping to learn something, and also because it's Hughie's idea. Whatever he thinks of Junior's judgment, he has to hear him out, right? But I agree with you. In the end, he's not going to give Crowninshield's away."

After a minute's pondering I said, "Unless . . ."

"What?"

"It's a juicy deal. Suppose they come up with a plan that gives him access to their corporate funds, so there will be no limit to what he can do here, and promise to keep hands off the place, editorially."

"I wouldn't believe them, would you?"

"No."

"Neither will Hugh."

"Suppose they add a temptation — a stock transfer that would make him, and Hughie too, twice as rich."

Joel considered. "I don't know how rich Hugh is, but... O.K. I'm worried."

Next day the Californians departed, to be followed within the week by Hughie's glow of expectation. But the suspense was to continue infinitely, no doubt the essence of Hugh's design for us, and as I adjusted to permanent anxiety, I cared a little less, even accepted that Joel would be chosen over me, not so much on accomplishment as on style, the hubris which so appealed to Enid Severance.

Then, on a Friday morning in late March, while I was going up in the elevator, the usually taciturn Corinne Perry surprised me with a smile. "Isn't it a lovely day, Lloyd?" she said.

When I mentioned this to Flavia, she nodded thoughtfully, chewing at the corner of her mouth. "They met last night. Good news, I betcha."

"Come on, Flavia, you don't *know* anything — do you?"

She winked. "Just what my female intuition tells me."

A moment later, Guy Waterhouse came in. "Hi there."

"Hello, Guy, what's up?"

"Wanted to be sure you were in. There's a meeting I think will interest you."

At ten, Hugh put his head in the door to say, "Oh, Lloyd, do you have a moment to spare?"

His face was masked with preoccupation and his shoulders hunched purposefully as he led the way to his office. Guy Waterhouse awaited us and he gave me a grave nod.

I took the chair beside Guy as Hugh went behind his desk, settling himself, collecting his thoughts. "Lloyd," he said, "the agony has gone on long enough, perhaps too long. You fellows are going to have to work together, to depend on each other in a very intimate way for years to come — long after Guy and I are put to pasture. I don't want to feel that in trying to arrive at a fair decision, we've made that more difficult for you."

"I don't know, Hugh, if this is good or bad news you're giving me."

He smiled. "What we have for you is not, at least on the face of it, bad news. Last night, the executive committee appointed you its fifth member."

Said this way, without emotion, I could not believe it, and the silence grew around us. It was only when Guy said, "Congratulations, Lloyd," and reached out, touching my shoulder and taking my hand in his for a shaking, that I managed to say, "I'm really stunned, and very, very pleased."

Hugh rose and came around to take my hand, saying, "The job may prove to be more a burden than a joy for you. You'll be sharing in some uncertain problems and the making of often painful decisions about the course Crowninshield's will take."

"I hope I won't disappoint you."

"I wouldn't worry about that. You've done well here. But I'm particularly concerned right now that Joel, and to a certain extent young Hugh as well, not take your appointment as cause for unusual resentment. Joel, unless he's dealt with considerately, is not beyond looking around for an offer, and he'll get one. He's spoken of setting up on his own. I would feel remiss if I let that happen. In your new role, as well as your old one of Joel's friend, you can be helpful in seeing that he stays."

"I'll do all I can, Hugh. The last couple of months has put a strain on our esteem for each other, but I know what a good editor he is and how valuable to the house."

"Good," Hugh said. "And you'll understand why we aren't going to make a big fuss over this."

"Of course."

New silence told me that the austere ceremony was at an end. Rising, I said, "I'm grateful as hell and I'm going to do everything I can to justify your decision. I know just how hard it was."

"You're too modest, Lloyd," Guy said. "It wasn't hard at all."

For a day, perhaps two, I was pneumatic with triumph. I shared it with Flavia, who did an Indian dance around the office before giving me a hug. Andy, I thought, took the news stoically, as though she had been certain of my victory all along. Although Will was barely eleven, he was alert to my toplofty feelings. On Saturday morning when I explained that I had had a promotion, he listened attentively, and later, when I went into the bog with the chain saw, he trailed along to perch on the end of a log and to watch me with new curosity as I felled the trees.

There were scores of small joys to be found in my own reflections. Waking, falling asleep, I would have a fleeting thought for how an old friend would be proud, or an old enemy might have a taste of gall, at my news. I lingered over Enid Severance, wondering if she had cared, and been overruled. Then, in my new confidence, I realized that I had imagined her hostility. Flavia and Andy knew me better than I knew myself. Rather than the uncertain fellow I sometimes saw in my mirror, I was enterprising, intelligent, and strong.

৺ৡ 11 ৡ৺

THE RECONCILIATION between Joel and me occurred in the way of a recovery from long illness. I had come to think of our feud as chronic, but in fact there was an imperceptible remission each day until, to my delight, I discovered it gone, or nearly gone. What remained was a scar, and a susceptibility.

The Rossbachs had returned to town to live that spring and Andy had invited them to drive out and spend Sunday with us. Friday night, when she met me at the train, Andy said that Enid Severance had called, asking us to Greenfields for Sunday lunch. Remembering the time she had said no to Elena Wallace, Andy had not refused, but she had promised a reply to-night.

"Wouldn't you know," I said. "Our first bid to a Green-fields lunch, and we have Joel and Kay coming. I wonder who they're having. Did Enid say?"

"Just that there were people she wanted us to meet."

"Oh hell . . . I wonder if Joel and Kay would understand."

"Yes," Andy said. "All too well."

"O.K., you're right. We can't possibly put the Rossbachs off. You'd better tell Enid we can't."

But at the house, the phone was ringing and it was Joel,

cheerfully asking, "Lloyd, how would it be if we put our visit off a week? Will we still be welcome?"

"Yes, of course."

"Enid called to ask us to Greenfields on Sunday. She seemed fairly urgent about it. Someone must have dropped out."

"That's funny. We were asked too. Look, why don't you come out tomorrow. Come spend the night with us. We'll make a weekend of it."

On Saturday morning, Andy returned from the village with a bell glass filled with dragées, like robins' eggs — blue, lavender, and pink ones — explaining it was a gift we'd bear to Greenfields tomorrow.

"Isn't that kind of a nothing present?" I asked. "A candy jar?"

"It's a lovely shape," she said, "and it isn't too much. *I* think it's just right."

That night I dreamed of the bell glass. In my dream it was on a linen-covered table, along with rose-shaded candles, glasses of wine, and plates with exquisite, buttery morsels which were being forked toward fastidious mouths.

Crouching outside on the dark porch I can see the diners' hands, the rings, bracelets, and carmine nails, but I cannot make out the faces. Still, I know they are comely, the older ones healthy and well groomed, the young ones ravishing. The smells — lime, rum, spices, fruit, marigolds, perfume, cigars — are like yearnings.

I can see it is crowded. Waiters hasten with casseroles and bottles. There is a chanting of conversation and the tinkling of silver and crystal as utensils glide from tray to table, from plate to mouth — a syncopation punctuated now and then by glissandos of women's laughter.

The shaded candles reflect a common affection and pleasure here. There are no anxieties; no one is concerned about paying the check, or being welcome. It is an admiring and affectionate company. That is what makes the light so warm.

If I could just make out the particulars of the faces. If I

could see the mouths, the eyes, as plainly as I see the hands reaching to touch others, I know they would be affectionate; they would be joyous at being here with this friend, this brother, this mother, this lover or wife.

"That's it," Kay said. "That's the turn . . . at the GO CHILDREN SLOW sign."

I turned in through sentinels of rhododendrons and stone palisades, skirted a pair of ponds, and broke from woods into an orchard. The road climbed through it to the largest of several houses, a low, stone building whose deep, arched windows were framed by white shutters. Pots of flowers and clusters of outdoor furniture gave the terrace an inviting look, and we saw Enid Severance. In canvas apron, she was pruning back an ilex which threatened to overwhelm the wall, but at the crunch of our arrival she dropped her shears to wave and came striding toward us, hands outreaching.

"I'm so glad you've come early and it's such a grand day. Why don't I show you around, and then you can just do as you like until lunch." She was leading us down a flagged path toward a clay court and a roof, just visible through new leaves. "I'm afraid it's chilly for the pool, but there's tennis, and if you look for Hugh, he's over the hill with a new toy."

We followed her up the steps of a cottage as Enid explained, "This is the playhouse. It's always been the children's favorite and you can make it yours for the day. They're all away now, except for Hughie."

The big room at the front of the cottage was done up with new chintz but it had a nostalgic smell, a Champlain, summery one of wicker and grass rugs, of a cool place on a hot day. While the others left, I stayed, absorbing it. Under the record player were slipcases of Dorsey and Glenn Miller recordings and, in the book case, old Grosset series, yards of Tom Swift and Hardy Boys, even a foot of Percy Keese Fitzhugh.

I held a copy of *Pee Wee Harris and the Bee Line Hike* in my hands, sniffed its muskiness, and read half a page, feeling myself drop a few fathoms down the well of time, the very print evoking dim outlines of a summer house and some terrible adolescent poignance, half expectancy, half loneliness and loss.

Through the window I saw Enid sitting on the grass, legs tucked under her like a girl, Kay beside her, while Joel and Andy perched on the wall. She waved as I came onto the porch and said, "Come along, Lloyd. We're going to the summer house."

We trailed after Enid as she climbed a path toward a hex-agonal, hilltop teahouse. From its scrollwork porch we could see a bend of the Hudson and Enid was saying, "We rarely use it now, too far really to ask the girls to bring tea things, but I always remember Isak Dinesen here." She made a conjuring gesture toward empty rush chairs. ". . . and Edith Sitwell, talk-ing of differences in manners and publishing ways."

As we murmured appreciatively, Enid said, "Now I must get back to my gardening, but Hughie'll be along soon and he can give you more of the tour."

"Is Hughie here?"

"He will be very soon. He's gone into town after a girl." Her bold gray eyes looked into mine. "Perhaps you'll come along with me for a moment, will you Lloyd?"

I trailed her steps on the stones, through an arbor and then an alley of boxwood hedges which, in the warming sun, gave off another evocative smell.

"Do you have any interest in gardens?" she asked. "I am fond of my roses."

"I can see why." She was leading me among the beds, nam-ing the varieties, the bluish reds and delicate yellows, then the pear trees, espaliered against the stone wall of the laundry yard.

Sitting on a bench, Enid turned to me and I admired the freckles June had brought to her forehead and an even more welcome change in her susceptibleness.

"I wanted a little private audience with you," she said, "to ask your advice, really. As you can imagine, it's about Hughie."

"A girl?"

"No, I think it's a rather nice one he's bringing to lunch. I'm quite happy about that, actually. No, it's what's going on at Crowninshield's that troubles me or, rather, troubles him."

"My getting onto the executive committee?"

"Unquestionably that has something to do with Hughie's mood, which is blacker, I'm afraid, and more unruly than ever. He was in a fury last night, making it clear how disappointed he was at the turning down of his newspaper plan."

"I'm sorry."

"No reason you should be, but I would like your advice and, just possibly, your help in this. His father thinks, and I agree, that it's important he have some responsibility in the expansion, which now seems assured. Hugh feels he must be given a share of it or he'll be drawn to destructiveness of one sort or another. He's made it plain he feels rejected. What's your advice, Lloyd?"

"I don't know if Hughie has any interest in pioneering, but he does like California, and we all tend to neglect the West Coast. Maybe we could set him up out there as an editor."

"Do you really think that would keep Hughie happy? If he were sent off to a branch office in San Francisco, wouldn't he feel more the remittance man than ever?" At the sound of footsteps on the gravel, we looked up to see a large, tousle-headed woman approaching. ". . . Oh, Marcella. This is Mr. Erskine — Mrs. Stickney. Ready for the dogs now, Marcella? Lloyd, would you like to have a stroll to the kennels with us, or would you rather find Hugh? He's just over the hilltop, showing off his pigeon shoot. That might be more fun for you."

Joel sat on the playhouse steps, watching Andy and Kay afloat, side by side, in a net hammock.

"I've just met Mrs. Stickney," I said, "who must be wife to the collecting Stickney. What can Hugh have in mind — a joke on me?"

"I wouldn't take it personally," Joel said. "They're old buddies."

"Maybe he has a new book," Andy suggested.

"Then why not Alice," Kay replied, "instead of us."

"You don't suppose . . ." I brooded.

"We don't suppose what?" Joel asked.

"It's a sell out?"

Joel considered, and said, "Could be."

I followed a path through the pine woods and broke out in a hollow. A hundred feet away, at the rim, stood a new, wooden platform. Hugh, in checked cap, leaned against the rail, talking with another man. As I approached I saw they were handling a shotgun and that several more lay on a table along with boxes of shells.

Hugh introduced me to Bill Stickney — tall, gentle mannered, handsome, and with a royal presence, as though he were used to giving orders in a quiet voice.

"I read your book," I said.

"Yes," Stickney replied, "I know."

"You doing us another?"

"Someday perhaps."

"I've been picking Bill's brains about our problems," Hugh explained, "getting the good books, putting them out in the best possible way, and he's kind enough to be interested. I thought you might tell him how you see it, Lloyd, coming onto the executive committee as you are. I think yours is a rather different point of view."

"Yes," Stickney said, "I'd like to hear about that." Selecting a gun from the table, he loaded and closed it, saying, "You want to give me a couple of birds, Hugh?"

Two clay pigeons sailed forth from the arms beneath us and Stickney raised the gun to his shoulder without haste, sighted, squeezed, and with a *blam, blam,* the discs exploded.

"All right, Lloyd," Hugh said, handing me the gun, "let's see what you can do with this." He sent the pigeons flying out for me, so serenely they seemed to stand still in the air, and while I missed the first, I shattered the second.

"That's damned good, Lloyd." Hugh touched my shoulder. "You must have hunted."

"Never." I returned the gun and watched him expel the empty cartridges. "It's beginner's luck."

"You have a fine eye. You led the second one instinctively. We can make a good shot of you."

"You were going to tell me about publishing," Stickney said.

"What would interest you about it?"

"Hugh's been telling me about the changes in your business, the need for more money in order to be effective."

"I explained Hughie's plan, to involve us with California News," Hugh said.

"Oh? I thought we'd disposed of that."

"Still," Hugh said, squinting through the barrels of a gun, "there are lessons to be learned — in retrospect."

"And lucky we are to have learned them."

"Which ones are those?" Stickney asked.

"That we'd lose our independence, and our character."

"I wonder," Stickney said. "Why?"

"Hello," said a sonorous voice, and I turned to find we had been joined by a young man in crisp seersucker. He was a bantam of a fellow, with a shock of black hair and a shiny, eager manner.

"This is Paul Peeling, Lloyd," Hugh said and Peeling grasped my hand as if it were a pleasure he had been anticipating.

"Here you are, Paul." Stickney offered him a gun. "Try your luck."

There was some difficulty with the trap, which unexpectedly flung out two clay pigeons, and Peeling quickly raised his gun, sighted, and fired twice, shattering both.

"Good work, Paul," Hugh said.

"Lloyd?" Peeling asked, ejecting cartridges. "You next?"

"No, no thanks. I've done my shooting."

While Hugh and Bill Stickney resumed their match, Paul Peeling leaned against the stair rail and produced a roll of Life Savers, offering me one. "I understand you're to be congratulated on a new appointment."

"Thank you. Yes. I start next month."

"As the new blood, are you going to bring some fresh ideas to Crowninshield's?"

"I hope so." I looked across the platform at Stickney. "I'm flattered at all the interest. Are you an associate of Mr. Stickney's?"

Peeling nodded. "I'm a futurist at United Broadcasting, and I've been looking into publishing for what might be of use to us. We're after similar goals aren't we — what interests the public? If we could discover the nature of that, we'd have an advantage all right. Crowninshield's has been my study area."

"Learn anything?"

"That a good house still bears the character of a man. Hugh, there, *is* Crowninshield's. That's grand for a man like Hugh, but in marketing I think you're still in the nineteenth century. There's a way to bring publishing up to date."

"I'm curious," I said. "Is it just coincidence, your being here? Or is there something of a business nature afoot?"

Peeling glanced at Hugh and Stickney, who were laughing over a point in their score. "It wouldn't surprise me that between two friends there was some business."

"What do you mean?"

"If I were you, Lloyd, I wouldn't worry about it."

"No? I would."

"Pull!" Hugh said, and we watched Bill Stickney aim and fire, shattering one pigeon while the other escaped to settle gracefully into the bullrushes at the field's edge.

Back at the playhouse I found Andy and Joel playing tennis, and Hughie, just arrived, bringing a rangy, angular blond girl from San Francisco named Nancy Nevius. There was darkness and thunder in Hughie's face and I felt it directed at me, the thief of his future, lolling here on the steps of his past.

"We've been viewing the background of an enviable childhood without the main character, Hughie," I said. "Will you show us around?"

"That would be boring, believe me."

"What about the croquet?" Nancy asked.

"Yes," he said. "There is some scheduled activity now upon us," and he bounded toward the playhouse.

"Can I help?" I asked, following.

Dragging a large, wooden case from the closet, Hughie said, "You can bring those mallets, as many as you can carry."

Beyond the court and the tall privet hedge lay a lower terrace, level and smooth as a putting green, and here Hughie set to work grimly pacing off distances and driving posts and wickets into the turf, while I trailed him.

"I've just met the Stickneys," I said, "and a man named Peeling. I'm trying to make out whether this is a social lunch or if we're all gathered here for some reason."

"Here," Hughie said. "You take these and do the west side. Line them up with mine, a foot in from the edge."

As I did so, I called to him, "Am I right — you just don't want to talk about it?"

"That's right."

"Hughie, I know how you feel about the executive committee. I can only say that I'm going to do what I can to make life agreeable for all of us. It must be clear that there's work cut out for you, that whatever part you want to play . . ."

He was tapping in the last stake and now he stopped to lean on the mallet and say, "Lloyd, you know, you really don't understand. I *am* pissed off, but I'm not pissed off at you, so don't worry about that."

Now the others arrived, led by Enid and Marcella Stickney, already dressed for lunch and talking earnestly about Vietnam. Hughie drew mild protests and laughter as he announced tournament rules and paired us off, Andy with Bill Stickney, Nancy Nevius with his father, Kay with himself and me with Marcella Stickney. Peeling, denied the role of umpire, was left as spectator.

Between turns tapping our way around the course, we clustered to watch each shot.

"Oh, Thimble," Hugh called to his wife as she sailed a ball cleanly through a pair of wickets, "good going!" and Enid laughed and poked out her tongue.

The Severance's playground spirit touched us all, and Marcella Stickney said to me, "Oh, watch Thumper now. That's a hard one."

Amid the cheers for his angle shot, Hugh looked at a stoical Hughie and asked, "See that, Bimmy? See the old back-spin working?" And Hughie nodded reluctantly, not quite willing to be drawn back into the childhood world they were summoning. But there was a special laughter now. With the afternoon sun gilding the lindens which shaded the west side of the court, dappling the Norman roof of the playhouse beyond, the chirp of mallet on ball, and the sound of the voices, the summery feel of things, I thought maybe everything was all right.

"I think that's the real attraction between Bill and Hugh," Marcella Stickney told me, "their past and their trust. They have known each other for years — since London and the war. They were both in the OWI together. Did you know?"

As we watched, Hughie's ball ticked Stickney's and stopped short of its intended wicket. Whereupon Hughie took a position over the tangent balls and, placing a foot on his own, raised his mallet and with an exultant clout sent Stickney's sailing into the marsh below.

"And that," Hughie said to the astonished gallery, "is what I like about this game. It's like life, with its sudden reversals."

I went ahead of the others, looking for Hugh. There was no one on the terrace. A table had been laid with bowls of crackers and a cheese board, but no one had arrived and I waited, listening to the lament of a mourning dove and the hum of distant traffic from the Taconic Parkway. Then I heard Hugh's voice from a remote part of the house and presently he appeared, carrying bottles in a hamper, and followed by a maid with a tray of ice and glasses.

"You thirsty, Lloyd?"

"No rush about that." I watched him arrange his bar and make us a drink. "I'm glad to have this moment, though, before the others come. I wanted to ask about Bill Stickney."

"What about Bill?" He sliced a wedge of Camembert.

"Does he want to buy us? Is that what's going on?"

Hugh placed the cheese carefully on a cracker. "Do you want to try this? It looks like a good one."

"Thanks." I tasted it, watched him cut another slice for himself. "Yes. It's excellent."

"Well," he said, "I find it hard to believe myself, that Crowninshield's is of interest to Bill. For years, you know, we've talked about possibilities of every sort, and very few of them have become reality, but in fact, yes, Bill is interested, and for the last couple of weeks we've been looking more closely into the advantages on both sides."

"Is that who Mr. Peeling is? The advantage man?"

Hugh smiled. "Something like that."

"How about you? Are you persuaded by these advantages?"

"There are some, Lloyd, as I think you'll see."

It suddenly occurred to me that the deed was done. I looked out to the lawn where the others were scattered, talking, and slowly making their way to join us on the terrace. I turned back to Hugh. "Wasn't there some kinder way to tell us?"

"Kinder than what?"

"Inviting us to a party that turns out to be a beheading."

"Oh, it's hardly that, Lloyd. Give me some time to explain. After all, you're here. Nothing's been irrevocably decided yet. But if it is decided, it won't change the nature of Crowninshield's, not in the essentials it won't. At my age, I'm not about to change *my* way of life, but there are likely to be advantages of several kinds in a good merger. Some personal advantages for me and my family, I'll admit, but advantages for all of us too, tax advantages, capital advantages, the money to compete for the big books and their multiple possibilities. Keep in mind that the hardcover book is going to be the dodo bird very soon. The revolutions in printing and distribution and electronics have begun."

"You tell me nothing's going to change . . . and everything's going to change," I said. "I can't believe both."

There were voices and I looked up to see Enid emerging from the front door with Nancy Nevius, who wore her croquet prize, a straw boater with a scarlet Stevenson band. From my perch on the wall I watched Joel present Enid with a long, rose-colored package. Unwrapping it, Enid cried with pleasure over a convincing green sea awash in a clear cylinder. They took turns tipping it, making a tempest and watching it calm.

Nancy Nevius came to sit beside me and said, "I've been meaning to congratulate you on your new job."

"Thanks, but as I've just learned from Hugh, it's not much of a victory."

She gave me a questioning smile. "Oh? Sure you can't do something about it?"

"I don't see how. Does Hughie?"

"He was doing his best on the croquet court."

Hugh carved the corseted cylinder of brown-pink flesh with surgical skill and simultaneously told a story about Bill Stickney's resourcefulness during the blitz, leading their OSS staff to refuge in the wine cellar of the Connaught.

This attention had lowered Stickney's habitual reserve and turned him ebullient. Encouraged by Hugh, he began to tell about his experiences after the war, the joining of several New England stations that had multiplied into United. It was an effortless, urbane account, for which Hugh was the most responsive of his audience, reminding Stickney of incidents that were amusing or showed his friend in a particularly favorable light.

It was so graphic a display of the bonds between them, once comrades at arms and now at business, that it seemed to exclude us, to thrust us further from them, even as it seemed to be a sharing of their friendship.

Nor was that the only irony, for I caught a glimpse of the scene we made here, in the smoky mirror that filled the wall over the sideboard — a reflection of all of us seated about the table with its flowers and silver and glasses, looking for all the world like a group of dear friends, gathered in affection.

In midmeal, Hugh stood and raised his glass in a flourish to Marcella and Bill Stickney, saying, "This is a propitious moment and I'm glad you're all here for it. I think you're all aware that Bill and I have been talking about some preliminaries that could bring about a relationship between our company and his, and at the moment things look encouraging. We think a pooling of resources is going to be rewarding and I think you'll come to agree. I'm very glad you're all here to join in a toast to this very promising new association."

"What are they?" I asked. "What are these advantages? I can't imagine what they would be." My voice sounded as though it came from another room and, in fact, no one seemed to hear it except Peeling, who smiled back.

Stickney rose to respond to Hugh, saying, "As Hugh knows, I'm a great student of the crystal ball. That's how we survive in our business, anticipating what broadcasting will be like next year, and ten years from now. You know there were fellows who saw the first television receivers and decided they were toys, and the American public hadn't the patience for their flickering images."

"Will you give us a glimpse of the future, Bill?" Hugh urged.

Stickney nodded confidently. "Technically, of course, it's going to be very sophisticated with all these remarkable electronic devices, and one result is going to be specialized programming. Tomorrow's viewer will be able to choose what he wants to see when he wants to see it. That's the cable you know, with its sixty-eight channels, and the cassette libraries. We'll be able to invite our friends for dinner and when we're ready, we can command that a story be told or performed. The fine house of Crowninshield is going to be a rich mine of literary material for us — and there's equal advantage to you and your authors." He beamed straight at me. "So you see there's no need to take a glum view of our joining. The prospects are very bright all around."

Listening to Stickney I had been staring at my own reflection in the mirror and was stricken with a sense of disappointment and betrayal. It was only dimly that I heard Hugh's voice addressing me, saying, "Lloyd, you're so awfully silent there.

Would you want to say something about your view of the future. I think it might be appropriate."

I emerged from the tunnel of my thoughts to look from one face to another, to Joel's, Marcella's, Paul's, Enid's, and it was the face of Enid Severance that unstuck my tongue. "I'm sorry," I said, and I could hear terror in my voice, like fear in drowning, "Mr. Stickney, I don't really believe what you've just said. I don't believe you're going to make television dramas out of our books. In the whole of this country there are perhaps a hundred thousand people who care about a good novel and can find the eight dollars to go out and buy it. If we reach a quarter of those people, it's a success for us — and if you reach them all, it's a failure. The only important thing about your audience is the number. Ours is different. They'll never be identical."

"We're going to see about that," Stickney said, his attention waning.

"Do you really think you can raise the public taste by offering it better fare?" I asked even as he turned to Hugh for a change of subject. "Come to think of it, someone who's been responsible for the kind of junk I see on television must have a crisis of conscience now and then and I suppose he does swear that once he gets the kids through college and the swimming pool paid for, he'll atone in some way, but I don't believe he will. I don't believe he can. In the end, what most viewers want is games and soap opera and that's what they'll get. Why not be honest and tell us that there's some tax advantage for you, or that you've always wanted to own a publishing house and you're rich enough to do it? I could believe that."

"Go Lloyd." It was Hughie's muffled voice.

Turning to Hugh I said, "I can't share in this celebration. I don't understand why we're doing this. Why are we trading our independence for wealth we don't need?"

"If you don't understand the problem," Peeling said, and he laughed, "maybe you're part of it."

"I'll tell you what the problem is," I said. "The problem is bigness. And there may not be anything wrong with bigness, but it isn't interested in little problems, like artistic problems, like human problems. Bigness is only interested in what turns up on the quarterly report. It doesn't put anything about failures in the quarterly report. It doesn't understand that for a publisher, failure is the norm, and the right to fail is the most important part of what he is. Recognizing the need of writers to fail in order to mature and develop is what makes a house like Crowninshield's great. Does a stockholder, a United Broadcasting stockholder understand that, or care about that?"

I had Hugh's, Stickney's, Enid's skeptical attention, but it was Peeling's laugh which intruded. "You sound afraid of the dark. Productive people, productive departments, needn't worry about an enlightened management."

Enid asked, "Joel, what's your opinion?"

He looked uneasy but said, "I think it can work out to everyone's advantage. I can see that. I'll admit I've been thinking of it in terms of new cash, that it can give a boost to our paperback growth, give us the money to put out three new lines."

"Who's going to tell us — " Hughie asked, "who's going to tell us what to publish, what not to publish?"

"There'll be no change there," his father replied.

"I don't believe you," Hughie said, and for a moment there was not a sound in the room.

Nancy Nevius broke the silence. "Am I allowed to say anything? Because I don't really understand any of this, but it seems that if Thumper's decided, it's going to be all right, and I'll drink to that, but first I'd like to know what Thimble thinks."

"Oh," Enid smiled at Nancy, rotated the stem of her glass a quarter turn, "I believe in a kind of inevitability. I believe the times shape the course of corporations as much as they do men, and I think these two men are aware of that, and I trust their instincts and intelligence." She raised her glass and then sipped from it.

"Change, Lloyd," Hugh said as he raised a glass to his wife. "Like it or not, we must all give way to change. It's a mistake to fall in love with the past."

Betrayal swept through me like water in the veins. Beyond the dinning in my ears I could hear Joel's voice cheerfully telling something about paperbacks, a story about the Mafia's conquest of a news company. The laughter it brought was a fresh extremity to my torture.

Enid's voice roused me. "Oh, Lloyd." She was holding the bell glass with its cargo of dragées before me, saying, "Do be careful of these. They're hard as glass. You could break a tooth."

We drove back to New Canaan like mourners after a funeral, but Andy found a bright spot. "You don't *know*," she insisted. "You can't be *sure* what the merger will do. Maybe it's a marvelous opportunity for everybody. After all, we wouldn't have been there if Hugh hadn't wanted you to share in it."

"Maybe," Kay agreed warily. "Maybe Papa knows best."

"He's turned us out," I said. "Each of us now."

"Well," Joel said, "I had a premonition."

"Why didn't you tell me?"

"I wasn't sure. I didn't want to be wrong about it."

"The thing I still don't understand," I said, "is why Hugh appointed me to the executive committee."

"I can give you the reason," Joel answered.

"What is it?"

"Guy Waterhouse made it a condition of his retirement."

"How do you know?"

"Enid told me."

WHEN HUGH INTRODUCED HIM to the editorial meeting, Paul Peeling responded with unlikely modesty. "I'm just a tourist here," he told us. "Hugh asked if I would like to look in, and of course I couldn't resist because I know this is where the important decisions are made, and I'm grateful for the opportunity to watch you at your work. I'm only here to learn."

Nevertheless, Paul was back the following week, and the week after that, observing, listening; and in the fourth week, he ran up his true colors, saying, "I want you all to know about, and share in, what I consider my 'fiduciary trust.' " We looked from one to the other, perplexed. "I feel a responsibility to our shareholders," he explained. "In a real way they have put their resources in our hands, resources that can mean a decent education for a child, or even survival for an old person."

I whispered to Hugh, "Orphans and widows? Is that what he's getting at?"

Hugh only smiled, but I summoned my vision of our new stockholders, bland and smugly forty, sunning themselves on the sterns of their yachts. I glared at Peeling.

Telling Andy, I said, "He threatened us today. He's demoralizing the whole editorial floor."

"Aren't you imagining a lot of it?" she asked. "Paul's brash and naive, but I can't believe he's really sinister."

"Oh, he *is,* Andy. He's destructive. He doesn't have a notion about our *real* 'fiduciary trust,' the one to our authors — the ghosts as well as the live ones."

"Did you *say* that?"

"No."

"Maybe you should have. Hugh might have liked it."

A suspicion she was right stirred in me, but I shook my head.

"Why don't you talk to Hugh?" she asked.

"He's been had, Andy. Hugh was listening to Peeling say things I never imagined I'd hear in a publisher's office. 'Now we want to publish books that are going to sell,' he told us, 'and conversely, we don't want to publish books that are *not* going to sell.' Hugh was a stone."

Andy laughed. "Maybe Paul's beginning to grasp the problem."

"No, he's methodically trying to rid the place of publishing taste and courage so as to make way for the mediocre ideas and writing-to-formula that his graph tells him reach the most readers."

"I'm not saying Paul's right, but as Joel says, you do have to get on with him."

"How do you get on with a man from business school? How do you get on with a man who believes in computers, for Christ's sake? And graphs. He *loves* graphs. On Friday he stared at me for a long time with that cryptic expression of his and then asked, 'How many people are reporting to you, Lloyd?' Then I knew he'd been brooding about some formula for efficiency they use at United. Christ I don't *know* how many people are reporting to me. Do I count the readers? The editorial secretaries? What the hell difference does it make anyway?"

"I'm sure he *thinks* he has perfectly good standards of his own, and some kind of responsibility to Bill Stickney and to Hugh . . ."

"After the executive committee meeting, he asked me back to his office and there, spread on his desk, was a list of options and advances we've paid out. He'd ticked mine. He showed me

— little red checks. 'All right, Lloyd,' he said, 'now what are the earnings prospects for these books of yours? You've got something like eighty thousand dollars out in advances right now, and I'd like to know what you think these books are going to earn over the next eighteen months.' "

"What did you say?"

"That it *depends* — on whether the books are delivered and, once they are, how they *do*. I was angry enough so I was sputtering and I hit him in the eye with a fleck of saliva. You know what he said? He said, 'but you must have *some* idea.' "

From the start, Peeling's role in the executive committee was plain. His voice was that of the new money and his view of our future was so assertive I could almost believe he'd been there.

When I brought up Joel's plan for the new paperback lines, he took to it at once, saying, "If Joel's right about Philip Lerner, and I suspect he is, we may as well hire Lerner and let him build a whole new outfit for us. I'd back him with whatever he needs to get going."

But there our entente ended, and I found myself bristling every time he opened his mouth. He would be bringing us some new ideas, he announced, and this was his first; he asked if each editor would single out his successful books over recent years and indicate the reasons why these books had sold well. He was convinced, he told us, that in this way he could arrive at a demographic chart of American readers, their whereabouts, their nature, their density, and the sort of books that most appealed to them.

"We've done all that," I told him. "It was figured out years ago. So all we have to do is hang a sign over the front door that says from now on we're just interested in manuscripts about Lincoln's doctor's dog."

Peeling smiled. "While you've been busy editing, Lloyd, there've been some interesting changes in the world. There are marvels of all kinds to tell us things we ought to know about our business."

"Not this business," I replied. "Computers can't find intelligent readers. They're like Indians in the woods."

"You'll be surprised how readily Crowninshield's can be brought out of the nineteenth century, with a little cooperation among us."

"And if you let the computers in here to tell us what to publish, we're going to wind up with a grab bag of pedestrian books and authors. The Crowninshield imprint means something, Paul. Don't you understand?"

"I wouldn't be here if I didn't understand the way a business is run most efficiently. Thinking about that, studying it, extrapolating it, is what I've been doing for ten years, Lloyd. That's *my* department."

The consequences of these meetings was a sea change in me. I felt clumsy and beleaguered. I lingered over dressing and breakfast, often missed my train and was late for work. Once there, I procrastinated over unimportant decisions. I would sit at my desk, willing my arm to reach for the telephone and make a call that needed making, and it was as if my arm were weighted with the knowledge that it didn't matter if I did or not. There was such a weariness in my bones, and my senses were numb to every activity around me. I wanted only to go home.

Occasionally I didn't go into town at all. Canceling my appointments I would spend the day at home. But a reminder of some office matter would provoke a seizure like dull pain. The first wave receded, but the next would be more acute, and with each recurrence the agony mounted, sapping my strength until I had no core at all. I could not face the simplest chores. Reading the paper was too much effort.

I found there was nothing that a house or a field or woods or friends or a son or even a wife can do for a man in the undertow of acedia. It pulls him out beyond his depth until he is in water that has no bottom. Days pass, each like the other. Weeks seem months. Time itself no longer has meaning.

"You know, you could have a heart to heart with Will," Andy proposed one Sunday. "It would do you both some good. Now he's really going off to camp, he's worried about it."

"A first time. It's always that way."

"Tell him that."

"Yes, I will. Not now, but later." While I intended to have that talk when he came down from his room, Will stayed there most of the morning, reading and playing his records. When Andy drove him out, I watched him linger on the steps for a few minutes, brooding, finally pedaling off aimlessly on his bicycle — and I let him go.

Then the phone rang, and to my surprise, the voice was Hugh Severance's saying, "Oh, Lloyd, I'm glad to catch you. I was wondering if I could drop in on you and Andy. Would it be an inconvenience? Are you busy with pruning or something equally important? I know how it is with Saturdays."

"No, Hugh. We're not doing anything."

"Good. I'll be in your neighborhood about eleven."

Waiting for Hugh, wondering why he would come calling, I decided it was to fire me. "It has to be," I told Andy. "I'm trying to think of alternatives, but there are no plausible ones."

"But why would he do it here? Why involve me in it?"

"I don't know. Maybe because it does involve you, and he's trying to be humane about it."

"It's hardly that."

Hugh came onto our porch in his slouchy, country hat and old hacking coat, wiping his boots carefully on the mat, shaking hands, looking as though he might bestow a kiss on the anxious Andy's cheek and, once inside, glancing around admiringly at the Cushing portraits and saying "You're good to let me barge in like this."

He *was* nervous, as I had not seen him before, walking around our living room, peering at Andy's ceramics, saying, "Oh, these are awfully good, Andy," and then, spying the liquor tray, asking, "Could I make myself a splash of something? I seem to need it."

When Will turned up to complain he would be missing a

party at his friend Mark's tomorrow unless his departure were put off, Hugh inquired and soon had Will admitting he was anxious about camp, now that departure was only a few hours away.

"Oh, camp's great fun," Hugh assured him. "How long will you be going for, Will?"

"Two weeks," Will replied.

"That seems long, doesn't it, Will, from this end, but once you get there . . . Oh, you'll have a fine time."

There was assurance in the spectacle of Will describing Hemlock and the canoeing he was anticipating, and in Hugh's demonstration of the proper paddle stroke, recalled from his Nile voyage. However, when Will went to pack his duffel bag, Hugh settled by the big window and looked across the pond into our back woods, grave and tense again.

Andy sat with folded hands, watching him. As silence thickened around us, a fog of suspense, I longed to clear it, to tell Hugh that I knew what he had come to say, but he spoke first.

"How do you think Joel's getting on?"

"All right, I guess. I haven't seen him in a week."

"Is he as disappointed as you with the new arrangements?"

"No, but he hadn't been encouraged as I was."

"True."

"And I gather the new management likes his paperback ideas."

"Well, Joel's indefatigable, isn't he?" Hugh said, in what I took as a rebuke. He swallowed some whiskey and seemed to relax, to drift toward pleasanter thoughts. These, it turned out, concerned the manuscript of *Fulgencio's Game,* which had grown by three chapters, so that I now had nearly half the book in hand. The consul, his young wife, the Cuban despot, were growing into complex, fascinating characters, fulfilling that promise I had seen. "Well, you've struck a lode, it seems, with your Bryce book. Edmond Pigott tells me he's pleased with it. You've certainly been quiet about it."

"I haven't seen it all. I don't want to crow too early."

"It sounds awfully interesting, Lloyd. Could I have a look?"

I was confused now. Was he still unable to get to the point, or was he really interested now in the Bryce? Could it be that keen nose which had brought him, sniffing out a prize of a new author?

"Of course you can see the Bryce," I said. "I can't give it to you now. The manuscript's at the office, but I doubt it's going to be a big seller. It may not even show up on Paul Peeling's graph."

Hugh grinned. "All right, Lloyd. This is what I came for. Say what you like about Peeling — just between us."

I hesitated, weighing discretion, wondering if telling Hugh what I really felt would not be the submitting of my resignation, but after the months of anxiety and depression I felt an urgency to be done with them and to speak my mind. "I don't think I can work with him," I said. "He doesn't understand what an editor does. He doesn't understand that editing cannot be reduced to cost accounting. He doesn't understand how much depends on luck and human nature." I looked at Hugh squarely. "Now, that raises a question, and I think I know the answer to it."

"But Peeling's intelligent, Lloyd, and he's anxious to learn. You'll have to take that on faith, I'm afraid, but I'm sure of it."

"He's only been in the office a month, but so far he hasn't been much of a student."

Hugh smiled. "Perhaps we can change that. I've been busy with the transition and letting editorial problems slide, I'm afraid."

"I'm confused. I thought you'd come over to fire me."

Hugh laughed. "You've every reason to feel ignored, Lloyd, but I hope you'll believe this. In our work, nothing is final, nothing is quite as it seems. Real progress from one point to another is seldom in a straight line. Progress zigs and zags and is only understandable when you have in mind that our destination is always moving away from us, shifting this way and that. I'm not so foolish as to believe I can set a course for it, but I can keep up a controversy over which direction to steer."

"Is the course different now than it was before the merger?"

Hugh smiled, made his tipsy gesture. "I'm concerned about new things. For example, Bill Stickney said at lunch yesterday that we ought to move. He pointed out that our parcel of land on Forty-eighth Street is too expensive for publishing, and the old building too inefficient, that we'd be better off to put the service functions in New Jersey and take space in an office building for our editorial and promotion work."

"That's Peeling and his graph."

"Still, it may be very sound economically. New York real estate is valuable. We do have to take it into account."

"But these people have no concept of the firm's tradition. Does he know who Louis Sullivan was?"

"Of course he does. Bill Stickney is a knowledgeable man. He's also a practical one. That's not necessarily a fault."

"But it can be, in a place where taste matters."

Hugh hunched his shoulders in discomfort. "If you wonder, Lloyd, whether I've lost my senses going into partnership with Stickney, I haven't — though of course one never really knows about such things. Our business is changing, and lovely as it is, our building was made for another era."

"That's exactly why it's important. Because it's substantial, as we are. It has the integrity and character to survive."

"Our survival — and I do know about this, Lloyd — has come from anticipating the future, in a very practical way. It's the balance sheet and not the masonry that makes for publishing longevity. In the end it's capital, enough to get from one good harvest to the next. Each year that takes more money. We do need outside resources. But I'm not going to sit by and watch Crowninshield's become a second-rate house."

"Are you telling me to start speaking my mind in the executive committee?"

"You tend to say things I agree with. I'll back you up when you do, Lloyd."

"Then you didn't come to fire me?"

"No. It's the other way around. I've come to ask you to stay. I want you to go along with our new consortium, if that's what we're to call it. However much you feel betrayed by the reorganization and by me, I want you to stay with us. I want you to do that for me, if you will. However much you see it as a thwarting of your own plans, I hope you'll give ours a chance. Don't quit us. You have a great deal that we need."

We were silent. I heard a dog bark at some distance from the house and, from upstairs, Will's voice calling for his mother's help, and then I said, "Of course I won't quit."

"Good." Hugh stood, brusque and invulnerable again. "I haven't sold Crowninshield's out, and I don't want you to believe that I have." He made for the door, retrieving his hat from the bench and pausing on the step to say, "I have an idea Paul can be more receptive. I'll look into that on Monday, and if the building thing comes up at the next meeting I hope you'll hear the argument and then, if you continue to feel as you do about the move, and if I do too, we may just make a common cause of it." He waved and was off toward his car.

Watching him drive away, Andy asked, "So? What was that really all about?"

"Well, it's puzzling isn't it, but there's the move for one thing. He doesn't like it and wants me to say so for him. Then he's anxious about Joel for some reason and he thinks I know what he's up to. And then the Bryce. He only found out yesterday that Pigott was taking it in England. He believes in Pigott and so he thinks I may have a hit with it. That's all it takes, just a little dusting of success on you and it changes everything."

"Oh, Lloyd, Hugh's too wise for that."

"Whatever, it's better than I expected. Maybe he has changed his mind about United and wants me to bully them back a little. I wouldn't mind that."

We drove together, Will and I, down to Noroton and wandered onto the pier. To the west a yellow haze skirted the bridges and the towers of the city.

At thirteen, Will was a round kid with a tummy and a puffiness about him, as though he had just awakened. But his mother's high cheekbones were emerging. So was another

Cushing characteristic, the slightly raked eyelid hinges, like French accents, that gave his face a newly challenging expression.

He had been tensing as we walked along the planks. Now he sat at the pier's brink, legs dangling, looking away across the Sound, waiting.

"Still a little anxious about Hemlock, Will?"

He sucked his lips and shrugged.

"You know you'll be O.K., don't you?"

"Sure." It was noncommital. A falling inflection seemed to turn me away.

"Maybe it's stupid of me to bring it up. Your mother tells me I shouldn't. But if you're even a little worried about being lonely up there, I want to talk about it and let you know it isn't strange. Practically everybody has trouble with going away the first time. I remember going away to camp and it can be a real pain — all the know-it-all counselors and the strange kids, having to eat and sleep and go to the bathroom side by side. You feel like an animal in a stable. Don't be surprised by that, Will. Everybody has it the first time. It's agonizing — right up there with seasickness and first love — but you just wait and it'll pass."

"Don't worry," Will said. "I'll be all right."

"I know. Of course you will. But this is a big moment, your going off on your own for the first time. I want to be in on that, Will. I've been there too. I know how it is."

He had found a bottle cap and was pressing it into the pocket of his hand, intrigued with the white, crown imprint it made there. Now he scaled it across the water and we watched it plop, flip once, glinting before it sank. "Sure," Will said. "I know."

"I get busy with my work. I've got into this habit of shutting myself up with a manuscript or whatever's on my mind, but I hope you know none of it is as important as our talking about what's on your mind. You know that, don't you?"

"Sure."

"What are the things that worry you, Will?"

"Nothing."

"Oh, come on. Everybody worries. Schoolwork? You could be doing much better, you know. You've got a good mind."

He shrugged.

"I don't know how to help you there," I said. "Not unless we *do* talk about it and get some kind of understanding. What do you think I could do that would help you, Will?"

He shook his head indifferently.

"What have I done that was wrong? Was I wrong to punish you for not doing as well as I know you can?"

"I guess not."

"Was it wrong not to?"

"When you didn't that time . . ." he said. "I was expecting a spanking, and when you didn't . . . I guess that was worse."

"But it didn't have any *more* effect on you?"

Will was silent. A bleakness settled in his eyes and he seemed to shrink from me. He looked cornered and helpless, as though I had taken my belt to him. Now he looked yearningly toward the parking lot. There was no word left to say. I rose and Will followed me to the car.

When Andy asked, I reported, "No, not too well. I couldn't get much out of him. I guess he'll be all right, though. He doesn't seem worried about going away. Still, I am frustrated about not being able to talk to him. I tried, God knows. It was as if there were a wall there. I don't know, maybe it's just too early to expect . . ."

"Or too late," she said.

That spring, Charles Cushing, a characteristically healthy man, had suffered from indigestion and lost some weight. Hospital tests had found a stomach tumor, and although this had turned out to be benign, he remained depressed and asked if Andy could come down to Georgetown for a visit.

We had delayed going to the Vineyard until Will's return from camp. Our plan was to go up at the beginning of August, but at her father's appeal, Andy said to me, "I've got to go down and be with him for a few days. I do hate abandoning you and Will, just when we're ready to get off to the Vineyard."

"You have to, Andy," I said. "Maybe Will and I can go up as planned. I'll try to take Friday off, and we'll get the house open anyway. It'll be a camp out, a good thing for us."

Andy seemed doubtful. "I wish you luck."

"We'll be fine. I'll call Doug Spang and make sure the water's on and there's wood for the stove, maybe ask if he'll get us in some canned stuff. We won't starve."

When I put it to Will, he was acquiescent, asking if he'd be able to drive the car along some of the back roads.

"I thought we'd leave the car in Woods Hole," I said, "so we won't have to worry about getting on the ferry. We can rent bikes in Vineyard Haven. You know, if the weather's good we can put the dinghy in the water and have a sail."

On Thursday, setting out for Georgetown, Andy told Will to look after me, while I explained to him that I planned to be home in time for us to have supper together and pack. We would have to be up early on Friday, leaving plenty of time to catch the two o'clock ferry from Woods Hole. It would be fourteen miles to Chilmark and we'd want to do them in daylight.

At the office, I called Doug Spang and learned that both water and electricity had been turned on. The weather had been rainy but the weekend forecast was hopeful. The key was on the hook behind the back door.

Then, late in the day, I found I had to stop by a party for an English agent, so I called Will at home. "I'm going to be late," I told him, "but I'll be on the eight-twenty-five for sure. Can you handle supper for yourself?"

"Uh-huh."

"Who's that?" I asked. "I hear somebody's voice."

"Mark."

"Oh, good. Maybe Mark can stay and have supper with you. Can you do hot dogs?"

"Maybe," Will said. I heard Mark's voice again and then Will asked, "Hey, Daddy, do we *have* to go to Chilmark tomorrow?"

"We don't *have* to do anything. I thought you wanted to go."

"Well, it's this way . . ." Will hesitated, laughed in discomfort. "There's something I'd rather do."

"What?"

"The Surfriders are going to be in Orange tomorrow night. This big concert. Kids are coming from all over. I mean not just from around here, but as far away as Ohio."

"If you want to — but you know the house is ready for us, and there are things we ought to do."

"Won't they wait?"

"To tell the truth, Will, I was counting on it. I'd hoped we could have some time together over the weekend. With Mummy away, it's an opportunity that doesn't come along too often. Won't there be another concert?"

"Not like this one."

"Well, something similar? Nearly as good?"

"You know who the Surfriders *are*?"

"No. But look, Will, I've got to go now. I have somebody waiting. Will you do this? Hold up on deciding. We can talk about it when I get home."

"O.K. — but I'd really like to hear the Surfriders."

"At least keep it open about Chilmark, will you?"

"O.K."

At nine, when I reached Oenoke Road, I found the house dark and, entering, my footsteps rang with a particular hollowness. Turning on lights in the hall and living room I sensed a desolation there. In the kitchen, skewered on a carving fork, was a note — "Gone to Mark's for supper. Maybe I'll spend the night."

Mark's sister answered and presently Will's voice came on, preoccupied, irritable at this summons from the television screen, saying, "No. Don't come over for me. Mrs. Ogleby wants me to stay. I've got my bike. I'll be home in the morning."

The trash bin, which Will had been charged with emptying, overflowed. The boys had left dirty knives and glasses on the counter. Putting them in the dishwasher, I found the glasses smelled of whiskey and, looking into the liquor cabinet, I suspected a bottle of bourbon was missing.

I wandered from room to room, feeling abandoned and undeservedly so. While I knew it was not reasonable, my resentment groped toward Andy, for leaving me alone in my own, cold house.

The following morning was a lovely one, sunny and warm, but Will did not show up. When I called, Helen Ogleby told me, "No, Lloyd. The boys have gone. They were going to a concert in Orange. Didn't Will tell you?"

I spent the day waiting, trying to sublimate my rage in chores. I woke at two o'clock on Saturday morning to the sound of water running in the house. Will was in the bathroom, and his face, bright with sunburn, cringed at the sight of me.

"Where in hell have you been?"

"Orange. Like I told you."

"Why did you go off without giving me a chance? You said you'd let me talk to you about going to the Vineyard."

"We didn't know. It just happened. We wanted to see if we'd have any luck hitching. We were just going to try it and *see* if anybody'd stop for us. Nobody did for half an hour and then this truck did, and we got in. I thought there'd be a place to call, but there wasn't. It was a huge great jam, thousands of cars, and people walking . . . like a war."

"You said we could talk about it. That was our agreement."

Will stared at the soap in his hand, the wristlets of gray lather. "I didn't know." His jaw set and the muscle at its corner tensed.

"You did know. Helen Ogleby knew you were going. You knew I was counting on going to the Vineyard with you."

As his eyes crept toward me I could see them filling with hostility. "I told you why."

"You didn't tell me anything. You just went."

"I told you I wanted to see the Surfriders. I wanted to go with Mark."

"I'm your father. You don't seem to understand that."

He looked away, peered at his reflection in the mirror.

"Do you, Will? Do you understand, God damn it?"

Will nodded.

"What? What do you understand?"

"That you're my father."

"And what does that mean to you?"

"I don't know."

"It means you do what I tell you, not what Mark Ogleby tells you. He's not your father. Do you understand that?"

Will did not reply. He was looking into the mirror at his reflection, withdrawing behind passiveness and letting my wrath wash over him. I could feel waves of insolence flowing from him, and my response, something like hatred, was first an impulse to strike him into submission, then only to weep for his stubbornness. He was not going to concede me anything. Then I realized that he had won, that I was no match for Will and he knew that, had known it from the start.

"Why?" I tried to quell the shivering in my voice and in my heart. "Why are you punishing me? What did I do?"

He was mute. He had me. There was nothing more to say.

Later, turning in my bed, I thought of things I might have said, threatening things, placating things, to reach him, and all of them were futile. We could not communicate, Will and I, not without Andy as mediator.

Perhaps he would outgrow whatever lay between us, I thought. Maybe going away to school would do it, reorient him in a world of which he was not the center.

As first light and the voices of birds crept through the blinds, I thought of Andy, wished her back soon, tonight if possible. "Come back," I pleaded, "and spread your salve between us please. Soothe this fury that lies between my son and me."

☙ 13 ❧

Charles Cushing was operated on for stomach cancer the following summer, and he died on the first of September. Although Andy took this loss with mature resignation, it also struck her to the roots. That she was no longer the daughter of a living man wrought a subtle change in our relationship, as though she had been a bit of a daughter to me as well, and she was now reeling in whatever cord that had been between us.

At the same time, Will had gone off to Housatonic School, leaving the house notably empty, so that in a sense she was no longer a mother either. It seemed as if the simultaneous relinquishing of these roles had driven away the prevailing fair weather of Andy's disposition and had made way for an unsettled climate.

Clouds and storms came up without warning, provoked by an innocent remark. Our quarrel over the firing of Molly Givens, the errant schoolmarm, was a typical one.

"Maybe New Canaan's too small for Molly," I had suggested. "Maybe it's time for her to move on."

"She's done a lot for this town. She's done a lot for Will, incidentally."

"I'm being practical. People don't forget a night in the slammer."

"Oh, you're so funny about it. Molly Givens is really small potatoes to you, isn't she?"

"And Clip Ogleby sees her in a clearer light?"

"He understands what's going on. This could be Salem with a witch. It's worse somehow, because everybody knows Molly's a good woman and that policeman's a vindictive, stupid man. Yet they let him put her in jail."

"If you mean the townspeople, they could hardly prevent that. It was two in the morning and most of us were asleep."

"You know what I mean. He knew he could get away with it."

"Molly was drunk and, as I remember, she called him a dumb prick."

"He could have driven her home. He knew just how humiliating it would be for her to spend a night in jail. My God, Lloyd, they never use that jail. It's to scare little boys. It's a joke, that jail."

"People we know, rarely spend the night there, but I'm sure they do use it."

"Tell me why no one is standing up for Molly now. Not a person on the school board would, and yet she's a fine teacher, the best in the elementary school. She gets kids excited about what they're doing and they love her for that. They respect her and they're going to miss her. Isn't that the important thing about a schoolteacher, that she's good at teaching school?"

"Oh, Andy, you know the answer."

"You're Molly's friend. You always said you were Molly's friend."

"She drinks too much."

"So do a lot of people in New Canaan — but I can't think of one who's lost his job because of it."

"Well, it can't be helped. Certain events are just unfortunate and it's a waste of energy trying to fix them. We don't have enough time to right all the wrongs."

"None of this matters to you. You don't really live in this town as I do. You live in New York and you have a whole different set of glossy values."

"Not true."

"You're not really interested in what happens to Molly Givens. While you talk about it you're thinking of who you're having lunch with tomorrow."

She was furious. I felt that if I reached out to touch her, Andy's flesh would flinch from mine. She sprang from her chair to clear away her dishes and silver and carry them to the kitchen. Presently, the door beyond banged as she went into her studio.

I sat for a while wondering if my indifference to town affairs was the fulcrum of our dispute, and guessed that it lay deeper — in Andy's awareness that a part of her life was over, that she had lost two important roles and was bewildered about how to fill that emptiness.

When I had loaded and started the dishwasher I went into the studio and found Andy at her work table. The elephant, begun three months ago, stood at the far end. It was unaltered since the last time I had seen it, head and trunk roughed in the clay, but the hindquarters, which had displeased her, lay demolished, her finger marks wrung into flank and leg, the armature bare from trunk to tail.

Andy had wound a sheet of paper into the roller of my old typewriter and she was staring at it, hands in her lap. Moving behind her I saw that she had been typing a petition, a statement followed by tiers of dotted lines for signatures.

"Andy, I'm not indifferent. You must know that. But you *are* more involved. Why is that? Is it because she's a woman, and you're able to identify with her in a way that I can't? Any truth in that?"

Andy considered. "Yes. I suppose there is. I suppose I am identifying with Molly. I suppose I see my own frustration in it, my own feeling of ineffectiveness. That's what infuriates me."

I sat down in the sling chair and looked at the ceramics hung on the studio walls and standing on wooden crates or on the shelves she had nailed up.

"How are you coming on the show?"

"I'm not. I called it off."

"Why?"

"I don't have enough. I'd need at least thirty pieces. I don't have half that many."

"January's three months off."

"Some of my things are only munchkins."

"I don't believe that."

Going off to school, Will had dismantled his room, taking banners and flintlock, but he had left behind the bas-relief of *Gypsy*, his grandfather's Seawanhaka, with her sail full-bellied. Andy had done this while a schoolgirl and it hung beside the polychrome tiger, churning itself to butter, which she had made for Will's sixth birthday.

Prowling the shelf were later arrivals, a lynx, an otter, a fox, which she had coaxed from a wildlife handbook to distract the manic Cub Scouts when they had denned here.

As goals and touchdowns pre-empted Will's fancies, Andy had been left to explore her own, and these were displayed upon the wall and trestle table, glassy, richly colored ceramics in her whimsically innocent style — Godiva, Lorelei with sailor, fig-leafed Eve with Adam; then the pregnant ones, eggs within eggs, mothers within mothers *en abîme,* Jonah within the whale, and most recently the sleeping Molly Bloom dreaming of Blazes Boylan.

Looking at Jonah now, at the composure she had put in that pale face peering out from between whalebones, I said, "You're wrong, you know. That's good. It's craft at least. Maybe art, for all I know."

She smiled. "Well, that's good of you to say . . . but, really, you think it's all occupational therapy for me. You're annoyed when I get any recognition."

"That's not true. But it is hard to make any reliable judgment on what one's wife is up to. Other feelings mess one up."

"I know which feelings those are."

"Not all possessive ones. Nothing would please me more than to see you busy with work that's important to you. I want to come home and hear about the money somebody's paid to have one of your pieces, or that you're off to Paris to collect your blue ribbon from the Beaux Arts. Do you really think *I'd* get sick the night before your plane left? I mean my idea of a happy marriage is one where a husband and wife go off to their professional worlds in the morning and come together at night to tell each other how it's been."

"I wonder. I wonder how you'd react if I really did that."

"Try me. Put your show on."

Resting her chin in a hand she pointed to "Mothers within Mothers." "Yesterday, a friend said that was cute. She thought she was complimenting me, you know, but it made me want to smash it. I'm terribly afraid her thoughtless remark was absolutely right."

"What do you care what she thinks?"

"I don't, but I think she's telling me a truth, the kind we can't see for ourselves, and you're too prudent to tell me."

"Truth? About it's worth? But there *is* no truth about that. You set your own standards and you don't listen to what anybody says about the results unless it's what you want to hear."

"Oh, but there's a difference, Lloyd. I don't want to be an amateur, a lady playing at art. That's ridiculous. I have the same contempt for that as you do."

"Well, come on, Andy. You have to be a little realistic. You're starting late. You've never been to art school. It's what you can reasonably accomplish with what you have."

"Don't patronize me, Lloyd. That's not the way you think at all. You admire people who're good at what they do."

"Of course, but you're not doing ceramics for *me*. Look at Kay and her four years of torture with that novel. She's rewritten it as many times. That really lovely girl turned mean over it, and it still isn't very good, but she did wake up to the truth about it, that it isn't supposed to make people admire her, but is only to be the best book she can write. So then, for the first time, she felt good about the book and about herself as a writer."

"Baloney. What's changed Kay is getting a contract."

"O.K., that helps. Still, like everything else that's been beyond reach, when you get it you're not satisfied."

"What I'm saying is that the kind of woman you admire is the professional. You don't have any use for women who can't do anything, or women who do things ineptly. You dote on the Kay Rossbachs and you compare me to them. Yes you do, and I don't like that, being compared to Kay, having her held up to me as a model."

"Christ — I can't say anything right," I said, and went to do my reading.

When she came to bed, Andy said, "I think I know now. I think I know what I want to do. I want to look for a job."

"You mean a real job — nine to five?"

"And twelve months a year. What's keeping me now? The laundry'll get done. Don't worry about that. There'll be something to eat on the table."

"Wouldn't you miss the Vineyard?"

"Of course. We all would. But that isn't the only consideration. I can't see anybody taking me seriously about a job if I don't turn up during July and August. We can stay here. People do."

"If we don't take the Spang cottage next summer, someone else will. I've always thought we'd buy that some day."

"I love the Vineyard and all the rituals of opening and closing the cottage. I love the cycle of the week, even the rainy and lonely days, waiting for Friday. I love all that as you do, but it's getting in my way."

"It needn't. You can find something part-time."

"I don't want a part-time job. I want a whole one, all my own."

"The important part about a job isn't where you do it."

"But it *is*, Lloyd. What I envy you most is your other life, all the complicated relationships you have with people in the office and agents and authors and competitors. Every day there's some new intrigue or project under way, and you have a part in it. Knowing you have all that to yourself, and I'm barely looking in on it, is so unfair."

"All that stuff at the office is mostly a pain in the ass."

"The lunches — at the San Marino and the Argenteuil?"

"Particularly the lunches. One day I'll drown in hollandaise sauce."

"I'm starved, for just a teaspoon of hollandaise sauce."

"What kind of job?"

"Maybe something in publishing."

"Publishing? Why my field?"

"Why not? It's what you trained me in. It's the profession you *gave* me, remember? Or wasn't that true? Did you merely want me for a back scratcher?"

"Not at all, but I have a feeling it's bad for marriage, going to bed with another editor."

"Why? Because you're afraid I'll be a better one?"

"Or worse — I dunno. Maybe it's tradition. Maybe it's some inadequacy I can't face, but still it makes me queasy."

"Oh, don't worry, I won't come within a mile of Crownin-shield's. You won't even hear about me, you can be sure of that. But I think I'll try around, perhaps at the magazines, or the big book places like Doubleday's. Do you think anybody'd give me a job as a reader?"

"Reader's jobs are hard to get, you know. They don't hire strangers off the street, and it's dull work if you can get it. I don't quite see why you'd want it. I thought you had itches and cravings of your own. Be selfish. It has to interest you."

"Publishing interests me. I know I'm a pretty good reader, and I've come to think that publishing *is* the vocation. Writing's important. Words can change a mind. Sometimes they change a million minds. There's a lovely leverage."

"Well, anyway, I'd go at it cautiously if I were you. No sense bringing down all our world we've taken such care to build."

"I'll let you know," Andy said, turning out the light, "before I do that."

Lying there beside Andy, listening to her breathing slowly into the rhythm of sleep, I found myself questioning if I was as evenhanded as I believed about Andy and her work or if, unconsciously, I rationalized while I busied myself with sandbagging the ramparts of my custom and privilege. It was a wakeful thought and I had to put it out of mind before I too could drift toward sleep.

That October of 1964, Andy did look around for a job in publishing. Several days a week she went in on the train with me to visit personnel offices. In the evening she reported on indifferent receptionists, the hours spent knee to knee with other applicants, filling out forms and awaiting a perfunctory interview. As the weeks went by she had a message from the publishing community, that she was a little too imposing for the clerical jobs and not experienced enough for the editorial and promotional ones.

She abandoned the trips to town and wrote letters of inquiry with a waning optimism. It was at this point that I bumped into Ethan Poole on the concourse at Grand Central.

He paused, one eye on the clock, to ask, "How are the Erskines faring?"

"We're fine, Ethan. Andy's turning pro. Has she been in to see you on her job hunt?"

"No, she hasn't," he replied. "But I've always thought her the better of the pair. If she'd like to take a short trip with me, tell her to drop by sometime."

"Seriously, Ethan?"

"Sure. Mia's going off for an operation, and then she's hoping to renew herself with a couple of months in Italy. It's just temporary, but it's a start. We've started a lot of prominent publishers."

"I'll tell her," I called after him as he waved and scurried toward his train.

The following week, Andy went to work for Ethan Poole, and within a few days she was a changed, a radiant, woman.

*

"Oh, Lloyd." It was Hugh Severance in my doorway, shambling in to perch negligently on my radiator. "I'm chasing off to London tomorrow after the Hume papers. They're to be released on Friday and there's a chance we can get the rights. I've talked with members of the family, and a lawyer. Edmond Pigott may be helpful too. Incidentally, any messages for him about your Bryce book?"

In fact I was concerned about Bryce. There had been nothing from him for some time. When I wrote to inquire, the response came from Istanbul, saying he was with a girl there, enjoying himself, promising to be back at work in a month. But I said to Hugh, "I'm more optimistic than ever. Aren't you?"

"Oh, yes." He frowned in the effort of recall, and then said, "Yes, I think it's awfully good — fine." Nodding, he sighed. "But I think you're right about it not being a big one. Too abstruse. Don't you agree?"

"I'm counting on good reviews."

"Oh, no doubt." He was moving on.

"You can tell Edmond Pigott I'm hoping for a finished manuscript next year, but whenever it comes in, it'll be worth the wait."

"I'll do so."

"Hugh?" I asked, checking him in my doorway, "will you miss the executive committee meeting tomorrow?"

"I'm afraid so." Uneasiness appeared in his eyes. "Oh, I'm going to let Peeling run the meeting. It seemed wisest to give up that inch. He wanted it, and I don't believe he'll get into too much trouble."

"Where will you be?"

"The Connaught."

"Shall I let you know if he decides to sell the building and ship us to Canarsie?"

Hugh smiled. "Yes, let me know if he does anything like that."

"In my opinion, your softening up of Peeling didn't take. He needs a booster."

Hugh was expressionless. "You may have to wait until I get back for that."

My phone rang. It was Corinne Perry asking, "Is Mr. Severance there, Lloyd? I have Edmond Pigott calling."

"Ah-h," Hugh said, and left me, coattails aflap, the last I was to see of him for five weeks.

Coming into the executive committee meeting on Thursday, Paul Peeling hesitated at Hugh's place, then took his customary one opposite. As he spread his graphs and print-outs on the big table, he shot me a friendly glance before saying, "Hugh has asked me not to get into the real estate matter seriously, but it's in the air and it may be useful to exchange views in an informal way. What *are* yours, Lloyd?"

"I don't believe we'd be the same house moved into an egg-crate office. This building has its effect on us and our authors, one you can't draw on a graph."

Surprisingly, Peeling agreed. "Yes, certainly, the message of the stones is a consideration. We certainly will have that in mind."

I was further disarmed by the conciliatory way in which he dealt with the rest of the agenda, and I was unprepared for the final item. At twelve, as we were recalling lunch plans, he said, "Oh, one thing more. Before Hugh left, we talked about enlarging this committee."

"Surely not in his absence?" I said.

He smiled. "Not without his consent, of course."

"I'd like to see Joel Rossbach here, and at the proper time I'll nominate him, but first I want to know that Hugh is in favor of a larger group."

"I think you'll find he is," Peeling said and, with a glance at his watch, adjourned the meeting.

I had assumed Hugh would return the following week but when Tuesday came with no sign of him I called Corinne Perry.

"I don't know exactly," she replied. "He called this morning to say there was no decision as yet on the Hume papers but he's enjoying himself and if there were no emergencies here he'd wait and see."

"Corinne, next time he calls will you say there might be an emergency and I'd like a word or two?"

"Shall I say what it is?"

"The additional executive committee member."

Flavia Moore, that barometer of Crowninshield weather, was remote. She complained of a cold, muttered about not coming in tomorrow, and then turned on me like a shrewish wife. "Why don't you stand up to Peeling? Why don't you tell him he's demolishing Crowninshield's? Make him understand. Make Hugh understand."

"Hugh's in England."

Flavia pointed at the phone. "Call him. That's what that thing there is for."

"I'm waiting for a call. I've told Corinne I want to talk to Hugh."

She smiled and contempt oozed from the corners of her mouth. "You might want to tell him how I feel about working here now. I don't need this job. There are a million jobs in this city. I work here because I like *you*, or I used to like you because I used to like what you were doing and the way you did it. But I don't like being shat on, which, in case you didn't notice, is what's happening. Unless you tell me there's to be a change in that, I won't be in tomorrow. I'll be doing something else. I don't know what. They say Jamaica's great this time of year, or I might look around for a job. Let me know, will you? I'll be home tonight . . ." And Flavia left me with a toss of her glossy, dark hair.

Carried along in the ebb tide toward the station, I was a castaway. Staring out the train window, unable to read, I gradually turned my feelings of dependency and trust in Flavia, to ones of betrayal.

Andy had further balm at home, saying, "Oh, well, I know how you feel about Flavia, but she's not irreplaceable, Lloyd. She's really too ambitious and too pretty a girl to be satisfied as a secretary . . . even *your* secretary. Perfectly frankly, I think she fancied herself your manipulator. I'm not exactly miserable over Flavia's leaving."

"You're right. I don't need her."

Next day I had a note from Flavia, written in her round hand on initialed stationery. "Dear Lloyd, I know you must be thinking evil thoughts about me today, as I am about myself. That was a bad performance I put on for my farewell last night, but please be a little indulgent. My real problems are personal ones, and it was from these I was reacting so nastily. Forgive me, and know I'll be rooting for you. Ever, F."

On Thursday, Paul Peeling again presided over the executive committee meeting, this time reporting with pride on progress in our new paperback division. He put particular emphasis on Lerner's role and none on Joel's.

Again, at the meeting's close, he spoke of enlarging the committee. "It seems to me that the various departments are well represented here and the person we need is someone with a perspective on our problems, someone from the financial community with a particular knowledge of publishing."

"I don't like that at all," I said, "and I know Hugh feels as I do. This is a book publishing company and it should be run by book men, by editors who understand what a good book is and that good books are the foundation of Crowninshield's. I don't believe a Wall Streeter can grasp that idea. What's more, I don't think we should continue this discussion without Hugh Severance. I don't believe you understand how he feels about it."

"But I do," Paul said. "I talked with Hugh this morning. He happens to be very much in favor of having a financial expert on this committee."

Waiting for the elevator with me, Joel asked about the meeting.

"Evil portents of every sort," I said. "And what *about* the paper lines? We got an earful on Lerner."

"Then you may know more than I. He and Peeling had lunch together yesterday."

"Without you?"

Joel nodded.

"If Hugh isn't back soon, he'll find just a hole here."

"Has it occurred to you, Lloyd, that he's away on purpose?"

"No. Whatever Hugh is, he's not chicken."

Andy felt as I did. "*Hiding* in London? No, I think Hugh wants you to do what you're doing, oppose Peeling, be the loyal opposition. Hugh's sympathetic to you, and if you're only patient . . ."

"But why doesn't he *tell* me that? Why would he call in, talk to Peeling, and ignore my message?"

"You can't be sure why, Lloyd. It could be Corinne. You say she's never been a particular friend."

"Corinne would be a friend if Hugh were encouraging me. Corinne's a weather vane, a damned accurate one, and the wind is blowing wrong for me. Ethan must be having a good chuckle over me these days."

"He doesn't know about any of this."

"Then he's the only one who doesn't. It shows on me. Flavia saw it and ran. The other secretaries see it. In the elevator they look away, out of embarrassment for me. Total strangers in the street see it and hurry by. Dogs put their tails between their legs and run . . ."

Andy laughed. "At least you can be funny about it."

"I'm not being funny about it."

Matthew Weld was the name of Peeling's candidate for the executive committee. I saw it first on a memorandum which awaited me that Friday morning. It had been set squarely in the center of my desk.

To: Lloyd Erskine
FROM: Paul Peeling

Matthew Weld is a junior partner in the brokerage firm of Truslow, Hanks & Co. He is an expert in publishing stocks and has a reputation for knowledge of our business and an ability to forecast the most successful operations. Also, he is a director of Winmill & Co., the Philadelphia textbook house.

I feel sure you will agree that Mr. Weld's special qualities will be an asset to our thinking on the executive committee, and if it is at all possible we should avail ourselves of them. I have spoken with Mr. Weld about this and I believe we can persuade him to join us. I shall appreciate your prompt approval so that we can have him with us at our meeting next week. P.P.

"Tell me, Corinne," I said. "Did Hugh ever get my message? Did you tell him that when he called I wanted to talk to him?"

She squirmed and twirled her telephone dial. "Yes, Lloyd, I did tell him. But he's busy with the Hume papers. He must have decided it could wait until his return."

"But not Paul Peeling."

She opened her hands as though to say there was no accounting for Hugh's priorities.

"Does Hugh know about putting this man Weld on the executive committee?"

"I couldn't say."

I found Paul Peeling speaking into his Dictaphone, but he looked up affably as I came into his office and he put the microphone aside.

"I'm a little baffled by this message about your friend from Wall Street," I said, closing the door on the curious gaze of his secretary.

"Sit down, Lloyd."

"First, I don't understand why you'd want to bring in someone from outside. Don't you think we know enough to run our company?"

"You know the answer, Lloyd. Matt Weld understands our business, and he has a different perspective on it."

"I know that perspective and I'm not interested in it. I'm interested in authors, in their rights and privileges and in their knowing that the people here are concerned about them. The more money men we get on the executive committee, the worse the list."

Paul smiled. "Your reaction doesn't surprise me, Lloyd. I

know you feel that way about it, but you're in the minority. And I think you'll come around."

I waved the memorandum. "First I'll want assurances from you and Weld that this isn't the start of a merger with this text house in Philadelphia. I'll certainly want to ask him some questions before voting on him, but I'll keep an open mind."

Peeling was shaking his head. "That won't be necessary. The other members of the committee have already met Mr. Weld, and they're in substantial agreement."

"What do you mean? Everyone but me?"

"Yes."

"I don't understand." I folded the memorandum in half. "Why was I excluded?"

"An oversight. I'm sorry."

"Hugh has met Mr. Weld?"

Paul nodded.

"And approves?"

He smiled. "Of course."

I had folded the memorandum into a glider, which I now launched at Paul Peeling's heart. It fell short, on his desk, and he laughed.

As I walked out I said, "I don't."

I passed through corridors, through shoals of desks and busy people, hearing the voices as though in a dream. Drifting toward my office I was grateful it would be empty, that Flavia was not there to see me in this hour. I no longer cared about the rest, except to avoid their pity.

Alone at my desk, I told the operator I wanted to speak with Mr. Severance in London and I listened while she passed through the relay of overseas operators and, within a few minutes, reached the Connaught.

"Who's calling?" Hugh's voice surprised me. I recognized perforations of fatigue, but it was strong, as though anticipating good news, clear as a photograph.

"It's Mr. Erskine," the Crowninshield operator said, "Mr. Erskine in New York."

"Just a moment . . ." Hugh's voice had turned uncertain, drifted off, but I could still hear it in a distant conversation. Then a new voice, male and English, came on. "Could I take a message for Mr. Severance?"

"When do you expect him?" our operator was asking, but I burst through her. "I must speak to him," I said. "Isn't he there with you? He answered. I heard his voice."

There was a silence in which I imagined Hugh shaking his head at the speaker.

"He's not available just now. Sorry. Could I take a message for Mr. Severance?"

"No message. Thank you, operator."

Flavia's typewriter was hooded, but I sat before it in her chair, a Danish one she had seen in a West Village shop window. I remembered the lunch hour in which we had brought it here in a taxi. Unveiling the machine, I put carbon between three Crowninshield letterheads. I wanted a copy for my bureau drawer. I wrote:

To: Hugh Severance
From: Lloyd Erskine

Our conversation at my house three months ago suggested an understanding between us, but in your absence Paul Peeling has asked me to approve the appointment of a Mr. Weld to the executive committee.

Apparently Mr. Weld is known to you and the other members, but he is not known to me and I cannot pass judgment on him.

I have tried repeatedly to reach you about this and my failure is notice enough that it is time for my resignation, which I submit herewith.

I signed it and put the original and a copy for Peeling into the mail basket. At my desk, staring into the outer office, I was aware of how still it had become. They were leaving me alone. Just beyond my door lay a quiet zone. My sickroom had been posted. Beware the plague of failure.

I was wondering who I must take leave of and thought of Joel, but he was not in his office. On his pad I wrote, "I just quit, L." Then I took my umbrella and raincoat from my closet and left the building without a word to anyone.

I had barely got home when Joel called to say, "You can't do that, Lloyd. You can't resign. There's a battle going on here and you're important to it — don't you know that?"

"It's lost," I said. "If there ever was a battle, it's over and we never had a chance."

Then I went into a semi-trance, listening to Andy's solace and the familiar sounds of the house — its phone, the closing of its drawers and doors — through a pillow of indifference.

For a week I expected a call from Hugh, telling me it had all been a misunderstanding, that he'd had no idea of my indignation, that he hadn't the least intention of accepting my resignation. Then, as the days wore away with no word, I relinquished those last hopes and turned to rationalizing.

"Hugh doesn't want a winner," I told Andy. "He thinks he does. He says he does. But in the center of that black heart is a king who refuses to die, who cannot choose a successor."

"And there's the force of United," she said. "Maybe he's not strong enough to stand up to that."

"Hugh's strong enough. He thinks he can manipulate Stickney, take his money, a million and a half dollars mind you, and also keep his publishing house intact — and I'm the sacrifice for that. I think he set me up for that, goaded me into being an irritant to Peeling so Peeling would complain about me to Stickney and then — in a demonstration of his own tractableness and team play, and to persuade them he *has* been bought — Hugh dumps me."

That night I dreamed I was taking charge in the aftermath of a subway accident, speaking to the passengers from a box in the middle of a car, calming them. From a clipboard in my hand which lists the procedures necessary for our rescue, I am assigning each person a task. It goes well. They are attentive to their orders and move off to execute them. Near me, watching, are several young women. One particularly pretty one distracts me, for her sweater is open, exposing full, long breasts which she looks down upon from time to time, as though inviting me to touch one — and I do, feeling its softness, and surprising length, the nipple taut and thin-skinned as a balloon.

I hear noise and laughter in an adjoining car and silence it with a sharp word. Then I re-examine my clipboard to find I have reached the bottom of the list. In fact we are already successful, for our car door has opened onto a platform and I dismiss everyone, accepting their thanks as they go. I am going to follow the girl with the long breasts until I realize that Hugh Severance is standing on the platform. He has been watching me, and he is smiling his approval. I am proud about that, and exhilarated, until I understand that it is not yet dawn and I am in New Canaan, lying beside my sleeping wife, and the fact is — Hugh has fired me.

But then I did hear from Hugh — a note saying, "Dear Lloyd, I have just returned to the office and am dismayed to find your letter of resignation. I cannot tell you how this has upset me, nor what a loss it means to all of us here. I wonder if you will have lunch with me next week so that I can make some explanation. Wednesday at one? Jack and Charlie's on West Fifty-second?"

The choice of that expensive restaurant heartened me. It was a place for courtship and celebration and I wondered if he had some proposal to make me. But on Wednesday morning, Corinne called to ask if the Brussels would do as well.

It was there, at a table backed by a large mirror, I awaited Hugh, saluting editors and agents as they settled at their rendezvous, tasting their first drinks of the day and fanning up the coals of a relationship.

He was twenty minutes late, apologizing as he sat down across from me. "I'm sorry, Lloyd." He took a watch from an envelope and fastened it on his wrist. "I thought I had plenty of time to pick this up at Cartier's and then of course there was a line, and trouble finding it."

It was the icebreaking inconsequence, the prelude to business, and served to cover Hugh's discomfort.

When I admired his suit, Hugh said, "They're getting awfully expensive, the London tailors. I've been going to Smallbones for years. I'll admit I like all the ceremony of it, the acting out of some renaissance play about masters and servants. Like anything that's well done, there's a mystique to it. Still, you get what you pay for in a suit. I had this made" — he peered into a breast pocket for the date — "in 1951. It's thirteen years old. I get a pleasure out of dress, as you do. Where'd you get that tie, by the way? I was admiring that tie."

"Hermès. I blew myself to it when I went to work for you."

"Ah-h." Hugh fidgeted. "I suppose it's simple vanity, caring about how you look, but it's always disappointed me that Hugh Jr. is so indifferent to it."

The waiter set oysters before us, and as though this were the signal for substantive talk, Hugh asked, "What do you really think of this plan of Joel's and Hugh Jr.'s? Be candid. Do they have the stuff? You know just how hard, how nearly impossible, it is to start a house nowadays?"

"Are they?"

"Really?" Hugh was astonished. "You don't know? That hadn't occurred to me. I haven't been *officially* told, but raising money in this town leads you to a very small clan. I was told by a banker friend ... Joel and Hugh Jr. are seeking investors who might be willing to come up with three quarters of a million dollars to back a new house. You really didn't know?"

"No. Has Joel quit?"

"Joel's let me know how unhappy he is in being kept off the executive committee, and now in Peeling's making off with Lerner. I suspect I'll have his resignation the moment he gets that money together. Aren't you in touch with Joel?"

"I guess not. Won't you be short-handed?"

"Yes, but of course we'll manage." Hugh looked at me

closely. "I have an idea you *wouldn't* come back to us, Lloyd."

"Why did you want me out of Crowninshield's, Hugh?"

"Ah-h." He looked away. "Well, I didn't."

"Peeling did."

He cocked his head. "It was Paul, surely, who pointed out the unpleasant fact that on balance your sales record shows a loss for last year, slight but a loss — the two novels."

"And the theater book," I added. "That was a sales bust too. But my God, Hugh, can't Peeling get it through his calculating head that good publishing is failure, that we must crash a dozen hopes to get one that flies? He doesn't seem to realize that each of these books introduces an author we think is going to have an effect on American letters. He hasn't even discovered that over the years, my books have made money for Crowninshield's."

Hugh nodded. "I tend to agree with what you're saying, but there *are* two sides to it, and I wonder, Lloyd, if we can't, if we mustn't, be a little more efficient about it. Bill Stickney thinks we can, and we must give Peeling a chance to prove it."

"No, Hugh, absolutely not. I cannot work with a man, *under* a man, actually, who is so indifferent to what I mean by publishing. He might as well be making sausage."

"Yes, that's how you feel, I know. You've made that clear enough, and I have too much respect for you to ask that you endure Crowninshield's agonies just now. After we're through this transition period, perhaps there'll be a time when it'll be right for you to come back." His eye caught the waiter's and he signaled for a check.

Home again, I accepted the custodial duties, the shopping, tidying, chauffeuring that Andy had performed over the years — each night awaiting her at the station platform. She was among the first to get off the train, swinging my attaché case and full of the day's doings.

"I think I found a live one today," she told me one evening as we drove home. "It's poetry, a Welshman I've never heard of, but I think he's awfully good. I've got the proofs here.

Heinemann's doing it in England, and, oh, wouldn't I love to get Ethan to say yes."

"Good luck."

"He might, you know, if I keep at him. Will you tell me what you think?"

"I don't think I can read anything, Andy. The thought makes me weary."

I had slept most of the day, and still felt drowsy. This morning, driving back from the station, I had promised myself to cope with the porch cornerposts, to scrape away at the bases to see if they needed carpentry or if some putty and paint would do, but I never got to the cornerposts.

Making the bed, I was drawn to it. The crumpled sheets opened like a mother's arms. In jeans and workshirt I had lain down and drifted into half-sleep, aware of sounds, wind threshing in branches, the passing of the refuse truck for which I had failed to put out our cans, the postman's deposit in the mailbox, even the phone, which rang eight times at my ear.

I thought of Hugh, busy in his office, and I wondered who sat at my desk, devastated by how easily the world moved without me, how soon the hole where one had been closed over.

I remembered an evening when, darting along Forty-fourth Street toward my train, I had almost stepped on a suicide, a body fallen from a window of the Yale Club, just covered with a sheet and filling a crack in the pavement with scarlet. Passing again next morning, I had marveled at how all had vanished. There was not a stain. The parade of shiny shoes danced on across that target of a man's life.

At dinner Andy was saying, "You know I've been thinking that even if Mia does come back on schedule, Ethan might keep me on. I don't cost much and I think he's getting to like having me around. I don't gripe about the menial chores. I do standby on the switchboard for Helen's lunch hour. And Ethan thinks I'm smart. He listens to me, anyway. He had me working on a mailing piece for his river book and he liked what I did . . ."

The more I nodded glumly, the more Andy tried to herd me

into her own enthusiasm, and while I did not want to puncture it, I felt it dragging me further into my own despair.

I cleared the table, carrying our dishes into the kitchen, opening the door of the dishwasher with Andy's voice trailing me, saying, "You will have a look at my Welshman, won't you?"

"No," I said. "I can't do that. I'm not up to making judgments, and I can't do these dishes either. It was all I could do to get to the station for you." I looked at the sponge in my hand and flung it toward the sink. "I can't do this, can't keep house for us."

Drying my hands I went into the library and stretched out on the sofa, laying a forearm across my eyes to shut out the light from the foyer. Hearing Andy finishing up the dishes, I gave myself to the undertow of self-pity.

Afterward she came into the library and sat down at the desk to say, "I'm sorry. I shouldn't have loaded all that onto you. I thought you wanted to keep busy."

"It isn't working. Every surface and corner of this house, every rail and doorknob, reminds me . . . I'm getting more depressed."

"Why not come into town tomorrow?"

"For what?"

"Call someone. Call Joel. Go have lunch with him."

"He'll think I'm begging for a job . . . and I would be, in spite of myself."

"Elena then. Go see Elena. She'll have some ideas."

"Can't. Don't want anyone's pity, or charity."

"You'll have another job — probably a better one."

"I don't think so."

"Of course you will. You're an intelligent man and a good editor. You can have another job whenever you want it, whenever you're ready to ask."

It was like telling a man who had just lost his girl that there were plenty more in the world.

"It'll take time," she went on. "Maybe you should get away for a couple of days. Would you like that? Would you like to go somewhere over the weekend?"

"No. I can't think where."

Because I had slept most of the day, I could not sleep that night, and toward morning I woke Andy and we talked quietly about what could be done to change this new pattern of our lives, to make my custodial role acceptable. She volunteered to do her own driving and to take an earlier train home so as to do the shopping.

"If you really don't feel up to job hunting right now," she suggested, "why don't you take a trip. It's your chance to see the places in Scotland you've always talked about, the ones you and your father were going to visit."

Strangely, her suggestion of a European trip brought me a first sliver of optimism. Over breakfast I said, "You've got me thinking about Crete . . . I might come in with you today and see how much it would cost."

"Crete? That would be expensive."

"We could find the money."

"We? You want *me* to come?"

"This is important to me, don't you understand?"

"Yes," Andy said, glancing at the kitchen clock. "So is my job. I'll have to leave now if I'm going to catch the eight-eleven. Will you want the car?"

"Take it. I'm just going back to bed."

There were more days then, in which I scarcely ate and did not sleep at all, but lay like a corpse on the study couch, let my beard grow to an ugly stubble, and turned mute. I lacked the energy to form words with lips and tongue, to greet Andy when she came home and stood in the door.

She conceded. "All right, Lloyd. I can't stand any more of this. If you want, I'll go off with you for a couple of weeks. At least I'll put it up to Ethan."

"You won't say it's for me."

"No, I won't tell him that. I'll tell him I've always wanted to see Crete. Will that make you happy?"

"Yes," I said. And sure enough it did.

⁓ 14 ⁓

AT HAGHIA TRIADA, the rubble of palace walls rolled away toward an olive grove and a mist-bound arm of the sea. Andy had been admiring the stone block on which she sat, observing that the hand that had dressed it had been dust for three thousand years.

On our departure, Will's most recent report card had come from Housatonic School, telling of a likable boy who majored in indifference and was content with C's. Now she was writing him a postcard. I was recalling that she had not uttered a resentful word about having quit her job for this excursion, nor about the two thousand dollars we had splurged on it, nor indeed had she hinted at any painful parallel between it and the Formosa trip her mother had failed to make. Moreover, she had been showing me up as a tourist, studying her Michelin, trotting after the guides, and drinking-in the Minoan tax structure with all the ardor of original discovery.

"What are you telling him?"

"About Michael Ventris and Linear B."

"If you can do it in thirty words, there's a job waiting for you at the Digest."

"Well, not the whole thing, of course, but a taste — and maybe it will tie in with his history. It always helps to relate the real world with what you're studying."

A man in coveralls, who had been circling us and raking indifferently, now approached. There was something wrong with an eye and he exuded villainy in every gesture. Opening a claw, he offered a fragment of earthenware.

"I find." He nodded at a patch of grass behind him and added an apprehensive glance toward the administration building. "Hundred drachma."

"Let's see it again," Andy said.

He permitted a second glance, long enough for us to make out a rim and part of a handle.

"Well, no, actually," I said, shaking my head in case he didn't understand the words, "we're just looking."

Instead of smiling at our wariness, he left us brusquely and, half an hour later, as we drove out of the car park, he was there, glaring at us from under a dusty cap.

When we stopped for supper at Phaistos, we spoke of the groundskeeper again, wondering how I could possibly have offended him, and if a tip would have made things right between us.

The road was dark as we resumed our way to Heraklion and, noticing that a pair of headlights had appeared in the mirror, I watched them.

Andy laughed. "That's old evil eye, isn't it, with his cargo of revenge."

"Ridiculous, all right, but I can't get it out of my head that he *is* following us, for obscure reasons of his own. I know he'll be there forever, and there's absolutely nothing to be done about it."

"Honestly, now, we've imagined the whole thing. He's home in bed and that angry look is for his wife."

In the mirror, the headlights were a little closer. "I haven't thought of this for years," I said, "but my father once told me a story about the curse of King Tut's tomb. It was very much in the news because the Carnarvon expedition had found it and broken the seal, and in fact some of the people in the party did die soon afterward. My father's story had the two of us as members of the expedition. Leaving the desert on camelback, we see twin blue flames behind us, burning eyes in the night. We hurry away but then in Cairo we see them again, from the window of our hotel room. They're at the edge of the city, still coming. We close our shutters and lock our door until it's time to go to the boat.

"The boat is English, a Cunarder, with a band playing and courteous stewards. Once we're at sea, headed for New York, we feel safe, all danger left behind in Egypt, but then at night, when I'm getting into my bunk, I pause and go to the porthole to look out at the dark sea, and there they are, that pair of fiery blue eyes, following."

"He told you that . . . as a *bedtime* story?"

"Well, he didn't expect me to take it seriously, but it did scare the wits out of me, for years afterward — and it still does. I don't know why."

"It's a scary story."

"I'm not afraid of curses now."

"But you are of fate."

"Of what?"

"Of your father's fate."

The car in our mirror, a Volkswagen with two girls in front, overtook us and hurried on.

"Yes," I said.

"And you shouldn't be, you know. There's no reason. Why do you dread becoming your father so? He was a wonderful man."

"Because he never once asserted himself. Because people grazed on him. They ate him away, and it was the world's loss. I don't know what's to become of me but I'll make sure it isn't that."

"I have my own idea of him, Lloyd. I think if he'd wanted to prevail in the world, he would have. You love him to this day. That in itself tells me he wasn't a failure, and you could do lots worse."

"I might. But I wonder about doing worse — if it's even the point. Maybe the point is we mustn't repeat our fathers' mistakes."

In Heraklion, the man from the car rental office took us to a taverna where, at midnight, the waiters began the dancing. They were broad-shouldered, thin-waisted fellows, handsome in a unique, two-dimensional way, as though cut by scroll saw from flat, flexible stock. All in a line, dancing that spirited *hasapiko*, arms wide, feet prancing on the stone floor, they seemed like sea birds in flight.

By noon next day we were at Knossos. I was resting on a step of King Minos' palace. The guide's account of Evans's reconstruction had combined with my hangover to produce a weariness, and yet I was intrigued by what I had just seen. The cup bearers, who for thirty centuries had paraded on King Minos' bathroom walls, were unforgettable. What had struck me was their resemblance to the wasp-waisted waiters we had seen dancing a few hours before.

Then, looking down at the gypsum step on which I sat, still white and sparkling in the Cretan sunshine despite the interval between Minos' tread and mine, I recognized the crystalline pattern, tiny, irregular trapezoids. It was identical to that of the recently laid floor at our hotel in Heraklion.

These commonplace observations had the force of revelation. Up to this moment I had been living as though history began in 1920, as though King Minos and his cup bearers and step builders had never been.

I had shared in that particular American innocence which persuades us that we are original and that all that has occurred prior to our birth was a sequence of blunders committed by such incompetents as our parents, that only with us has the millennium begun.

This sense of the past broke upon me like sudden dawn and in its light I could see my own experience, until now seemingly lonely and tragic, as common and oddly heartening — its very futility, if not divine, at least comic.

In that spring of 1965, our Cretan experience was just the tonic for me. With each day I grew more forward-looking, and as I watched Piraeus and the Adriatic melt away beneath us, I said to Andy, "I've been denying old friends and competitors the opportunity to employ me. On Monday they're going to get a break. I'm hustling a job."

"Me too," she said.

"Where will you try — Poole's again?"

"No. Ethan was hiring my replacement as I left."

"Ethan has a soft spot for you. Go see him."

"I won't go back there. *I* have too much pride, but I'm going other places."

"Fine. We'll be a search team. We can help each other."

"I don't want any help, thanks."

"You're foolish. You wouldn't have got the job with Ethan if I hadn't bumped into him in Grand Central."

"That's exactly why. I don't want to be in any debt to you for the job I take now."

On top of the accumulated mail was a note from Susie Ogleby who had been plant-sitting for us. "Mr. Rossbach wants you to call him when you get in, even if it's late."

Joel was effervescent. "Was it great? I want to hear all about it. You're lucky to have had the time for a vacation because you won't have another for years. I'll explain. What are you doing tomorrow?"

"I'm going to hunt for a job."

"No, you're not. You're coming in with us. Can you meet me about eleven — at the Century?"

I had been avoiding the Century. It was such a symbol of my green years in the publishing community. Billy Maxwell had put me up then, saying, "Oh, you've got to be in, Lloyd — for me, of course. I want my friends in. But it's important for you. The Century's the only club in town where you're likely to have an intelligent conversation with men you scarcely know. Besides, it's a bench mark for an editor. It means that your competitors not only admire you, they like you."

So, out of affection and gratitude, Billy had campaigned to get me in, found a seconder in Eric Tappan, an editor at Random House, then took me to lunch with each of the seven members of the admissions committee, so that I was elected in record time, within three months of my proposal.

Saul Diamond had asked me to second Joel. It was just after the Polly Dupee incident and to do so seemed an hypocrisy, but Andy had said, "You must. I know how you feel about Joel now, but he means a lot to you. He always will." He was a member within the year.

My present misgivings about the Century grew from awareness of the rights I had forfeited with my job. I suspected the Century was one of them, that friends encountered here would see me wearing the placard *unemployed* and recognize, not the Lloyd Erskine they had known, but an Erskine in need.

I passed under the club colors, the white lamp on its blue field, pushed warily on the heavy oak door, but as Daniel came to take my coat, I could find no reservation in his earnest welcome.

"Yes," I explained, "I've been away," and felt a powerful sense of self restored.

Then Joel came dancing toward me across the marble to pump my hand and draw me off to a corner of the periodicals room where, hands clasped, he erupted with his news.

"I think..." He gave my knee a palping. "Yes, I think we're going to do it, Lloyd. I haven't spoken to you until now because I didn't want to start false hares, but this week we have our grubstake."

"Whose?"

"Hughie's of course. To his father's distress, he's selling his Crowninshield shock. Not the least of our pleasures is going to be showing Hugh Severance a thing or two..." Joel grinned, eyebrows raised for confirmation. "Then Kay's brother, Dick Sondheim, is putting in a hundred thousand dollars, and Kay's persuaded her father to do the same. It's her inheritance, so she'll have a share in the company too, but no, we will not publish her. Kay stipulated that. She's a smart girl."

"If you're asking me to invest..."

Joel shook his head. "I know you're not rich. There are plenty of rich men, but very few good editors, even fewer of

them with the kind of respect you have in the community,
Lloyd. I want you as a partner. I want you to join Hughie
and me in founding a publishing house. You know our virtues
and our faults and you've lived with them, you may even know
how to get the best out of them. I think we three do agree on
the kind of house we want to work for and there's only one
way to assure that now — run it ourselves. A small list, maybe
thirty titles a year to start, but of such quality that our name
on the spine of a book will mean excellence. I don't know
what we'll be able to pay ourselves, maybe only a bare living
for a while, but I have such faith in you, in all three of us for
that matter, I suspect that in ten years you'll be a rich man.
Oh, look, I know money doesn't mean much to you. None of
us would be in this business if it did. But, Lloyd, founding a
house, getting it to go against the odds, that's a chance we get
no more than once."

I nodded.

"You want time to think it over?"

"Is there a prospectus? Some kind of plan?"

From his pocket, Joel produced an envelope with my name
on it. "Hughie and I drew it up this morning. The three of
us as partners, with fifty-one percent of the stock at a dollar a
share — the balance to the investors at a hundred. We're capi-
talizing at a million, which should see us through three years."

"How much more do you need?"

"We're not halfway. There are people with venture capital
who'll welcome the chance to invest in you as a publisher.
Think about it for a minute. It's a smart gamble. Old friends?
New friends?"

"I'll think."

"Then call them. Make a date for lunch as soon as they'll
see you. It's important to *them*, Lloyd. This house of ours is
going to make some people a lot of money."

"I'm beginning to believe you," I said.

"That means you're coming — because you're too smart not
to. It's what I've always wanted and it's what you've always
wanted."

"Whose name is going to be on it?"

"None of ours. That's a vanity to be avoided, I think. Maybe something with a literary flavor."

Joel sat back, eyes searching the fusty volumes on the shelves, the cord of magazines freighting the great trestle table, the Hudson River landscapes and the portraits of bald, whiskered past-presidents. My own gaze fell on the nearest frame. It held a yellowing political cartoon, that of a supine giant, waking to behold the stakes and guys that restrain him, and the Lilliputians at their work.

"Gulliver," I said, pointing him out. "Gulliver House."

"That's great," Joel said. "See how we need you?"

Starting Gulliver House, those rosy months of 1965, was the most exhilarating experience of my life. Every act, whether it was pursuing a rich friend as an investor, or shopping for a brownstone that could be made into an interesting headquarters, or seeking a book for our first list, was filled with original joy, as though we were remaking the world.

Although Andy was pleased by the upturn in my own fortunes, sharing in my new problems and offering advice about them, she lagged in keeping the promise to herself of searching out a satisfying job. When I asked, she'd say, "Oh, next week," and in the fast stream of my own affairs, I did not worry about it.

As a result of my venture into Wall Street, Loomis Pitcher, with two friends, put up two hundred and fifty thousand dollars, making me as responsible for Gulliver's capitalization as my two partners.

During the week, each of us did his own prospecting, calling on the agents, assembling manuscripts at the Rossbachs' apartment on Cornelia Street, where Kay logged them in and filed our reports.

We saved each Friday for a self-congratulatory luncheon at Charles's, sharing experiences, discussing the books and authors that tempted us, projecting their earnings and endurance, growing more inebriated from our prospects than from the wine.

There was a feeling between us that every painful moment of our Crowninshield experience would be vindicated in our triumvirate and that our unique combination of idealism, vitality, and shrewdness would change the color of the publishing world.

We could not help rejoicing in our mutiny, the knowledge that every achievement would be a tweak for Hugh and for every person who had ever ignored, patronized, or doubted us. We were so sure of ourselves that failure was inconceivable.

Kay often joined our table at Charles's, sharing in the excitement of our discoveries, in laughter at the absurdities of our newly acknowledged power, and delighting us with her "Gullys," trinket awards for the coup, or the gaffe, of the week.

Perhaps it was because he lacked Joel's charm, and my immoderate curiosity about people, that Hughie shied from intimacy with agents. Making the rounds, retelling the marketplace gossip, which sometimes leads to a chance at a desirable author, was a chore for him.

As our search for books progressed, Hughie admitted this, and added, "We know that sales is going to be the crucial job, and I'll volunteer for it. I'll make myself the housekeeper, the office tyrant, while you guys hustle the manuscripts, but I'll want to be in on major editorial decisions."

"I'll volunter for whatever you like," I said. "Advertising? Subsidiary rights?"

"You're the *mensh*, Lloyd," Joel said. "That's the important thing. You're our good, gray head, our idealist. Now if you want to mess with advertising, that's fine — you'll be good at it. But don't forget your role, because it's opposed to mine. I'm the *macher*. I'm brash and aggressive, and that makes us a fine editorial team, playing to, and against, each other." Turning to Hughie he said, "And that's where you come in. You're the *chachem*, you adjudicate and reconcile, when we can't do that ourselves."

"A paradise," I said, "where never is heard a discouraging word."

Our acquisition plan did evolve from that facetious luncheon exchange, Joel and I dividing up the agencies and agreeing to find fifteen books each for our debut in the spring of 1966.

I felt sure that with our small, independent house, free of corporate pressure, we could bring along a strong, significant, and, in the end, profitable list — if we cleaved to quality. We would win some and lose some but I was certain that if we could publish a dozen promising tyros annually, as well as the usual standby books for our backlist, six or seven years would leave us with a score of established, productive authors, and a reputation that would attract more of them.

From the stream of manuscripts now flowing to us, I chose several youngsters with book enough and talent enough for a debut with us, laying down options or advances of three and four thousand dollars — and went to work with the authors.

Joel had an entirely different idea, that we must present some writers of known reputation, investing in them as necessary. At one lunch, he told of his interest in Luke Pentecost, a science fiction writer whose underground reputation he felt was ready to flourish at street level.

"I've tried to read Pentecost," I said. "Isn't it kid's stuff?"

Joel shook his head. "The scholars are writing about him, saying the future of fiction is in fiction of the future. Believe me, he's going to be big. We'll have to bid for him."

"Is the new book good?"

"We'll have to take that on faith, because it isn't written yet. But there'll be one. He's got a couple of chapters. Gus Fodor mentions it here . . ." Joel produced a clipping from the *New Republic*. "*Dimming of the Sun* is the title."

"How much is he asking?"

"I want to offer him fifteen thousand."

"That's a lot. What's he earn on a book?"

"On the last book, only a couple of thousand, but you know, Lloyd, he's beginning to pay off in paperback. I expect a boom in Pentecost." Confronting mine, Joel's eyes turned a churlish shade. "Are you going to take *that* line? You know, Lloyd, you can't always work a book out in terms of past performance."

"Oh, I *like* a gamble. We *have* to gamble. But you don't

like this guy any better than I do, Joel. I don't hear any enthusiasm about his work. He's singled out by a dubious critic. You're going on what other people say. If that's nose . . ."

"Hunch," Joel said. "It's hunch and I've got to play it."

I looked to Hughie. "O.K., Mr. Chachem. What do you say?"

Hughie considered, peering at the polka dots in Joel's tie. "I guess we've each got a right to a flyer. If Joel's so sure, I want to bet on Luke Pentecost."

"O.K.," I said. "Then so do I."

"How did it go?" I asked a week later. "Are we publishing Pentecost?"

"I offered him the fifteen," Joel replied.

"And he's turned you down? Well, maybe you're in luck."

"Luke wanted to accept it, but he's thinking it over."

"Afraid of a new house?"

"Luke's broke and behind on his alimony payments. A friend, a neighbor of his out in Easthampton, is advising him. He may even be running-off an auction. He told Luke he could get fifty thousand."

"Christ," I said. "Not of our money, he can't. It's insane — for a book that isn't even written."

"I've seen a couple of chapters. It's going to be O.K. I know what I'm doing. We'll go the fifty if we have to."

"Now wait, Joel. Hughie and I are in on this too."

"We want to announce ourselves, don't we? We can't piddle around forever. We need a star to open shop with, to cause talk, to attract other writers."

"A star? Luke Pentecost? *What* other writers?"

"You'll have to trust me on that."

I fumed about the Pentecost that night, but Andy said, "Give Joel the chance to learn. You don't know. Nobody knows if Pentecost is worth a lot of money. If he's being stupid, he's going to learn from the experience."

"We can't afford such costly lessons, Andy. I've bought five authors with the same amount of money."

"Joel has a right to be seriously wrong once. Of course if he goes *on* doing foolish things you'll have to assert your authority. If there's a boss, I guess you're it."

Next day, Joel signed a contract with Luke Pentecost, obligating us to pay fifty thousand dollars for a collection of published stories which would appear on our first list, to be followed the next year by the novel, *Dimming of the Sun.*

Joel was jubilant, asking us by for drinks to meet Pentecost and his girl and at the same time proposing we get a story about our signing him up into *Publishers Weekly.*

"A story now?" I asked. "You want to announce our grand opening?"

"Why not?" he said. "Let's blow the horn, tell the world we're ready to go."

"I think it's too early. I think we should have more books and a place of business before we stick our heads up."

"Nobody believes we're really going to start. I'm for a press conference."

"Suppose nobody comes to it."

"They'll come," Joel said.

We settled on a Wednesday afternoon at Hughie's high-ceilinged apartment on Seventy-ninth Street and sent out invitations for three o'clock. The three of us turned up to admire the buffet Nancy Severance had set out, and to wait, nervously, for arrivals.

At three thirty, a girl from *P.W.* came, and shortly afterwards, a man from the *Times.* Both accepted the announcement we had prepared and asked us what we thought of our prospects. I was replying with a modest statement about proving our editorial judgment when Joel interrupted to tell them about Luke Pentecost. As he went on describing what he felt was our good fortune in acquiring him, I had difficulty keeping a rein on my irritation.

Then, as our two guests left, there was a call from NBC, asking if the mobile unit could film an interview with us for *Today.*

Going down in the elevator, Joel said, "This is terrific, you know. A couple of minutes on *Today* is worth a hundred thousand dollars in publicity."

"Whatever it's worth," I suggested, "let's not blow it all on Pentecost. You're obsessed with him. There are going to be other books on the list . . . I hope."

"Yours?" Joel said. "If you want to talk about yours, go ahead."

"Let's talk about the house, about *our* plans, you know? Not just yours."

As we walked through the lobby, Joel glared at me as though I were a backward child. They were waiting in the street and a crowd had gathered to watch the camera crew set up equipment at the curbside.

"We just want two minutes," the director said, holding out a microphone. "Tell us what you're up to. Which of you is the spokesman?"

Joel pointed to me. "He's the boss. He gets to do the talking."

My resentment surged forth. "No," I said. "You tell 'em about it. This is your idea. Tell 'em all about Luke Pentecost. We can talk about Gulliver House some other time."

Joel grinned. He turned immediately and spoke into the microphone. "Being new is not necessarily a virtue in the publishing business," he said, "but we think, in our case, it is. Each of us has worked at a distinguished house, one that attracts fine authors. That's a good reputation to have, and yet we've found it restrictive. It has prevented us from taking some innovative actions that we think will be good and healthy for all of us. I don't mean just for Hugh Severance, Jr., and Lloyd Erskine and myself here, the partners in this new venture of Gulliver House, but for all of the authors and readers we are going to acquire."

Joel was, as always, articulate, facile, and persuasively urgent. When the director signaled him to stop he did, and, still smiling, he turned to me and said, "Some *mench*."

*

We were looking at a vacant brownstone and we had paused on its steps while the agent sorted through his keys. I glanced up Sixty-first Street and, in the corner of my eye, appeared a silhouette, that of a young woman, a taut leash, and an eager dog. There was a carelessness in the way she moved that stirred memory, and a sense of coincidence. I realized it was Flavia Moore, and waved.

When we caught up with the others, they were still on the ground floor in what had been a formal dining room. "Oh, yes, it still works," the agent was explaining to Joel. "If you were to use it you'd want to have the flue checked. That's a handsome mantel, by the way. I don't know if you'd care to keep it."

"It takes up wall space," Hughie observed.

George, Flavia's poodle, sniffed the hearth, the bits of fallen plaster that littered the scarred parquet. It was a visit to George's veterinarian on Sixty-second which brought her from Gramercy Park, Flavia explained as she toured the room, peering at the stair rail with its missing balusters and at the murky hallway beyond. "What would this be?" she asked.

"Reception room," I said at once. I had been imagining it, complete, as though the shape and feel of it had existed in my head for a long time. Clean, white plaster, like the frosting of a cake, hung with the season's jacket drawings. Light fell from glass pools recessed in the ceiling, upon the comings and goings of people bearing manuscripts and folios of artwork, on printers and salesmen and out-of-town reviewers and publishers from abroad.

The light itself was magical, opaque, warm as June, and it favored a teak chest with a square, Chinese lamp. I marveled at my detailed vision of this reception room, as though I had waited here myself for admission. Oddly too, I was thinking of my father, of bringing him into the imagined warmth. It was such a peculiar fancy to occur to me here in this unheated, gutted old house, and yet it elated me.

On the parlor floor I found them laying out a ground plan — editorial here at the head of the stairs, the heart of the place.

210

There could be an office for each of us here. Two in front, looking down into Sixty-first Street, and one in the rear, with a view of the garden.

"What shall we do," I asked, "draw straws?"

"No," Joel said. "We take our pick. Which do you want?"

"It's pleasant to look into the street, see what's going on, but if you divide the front room, they'll be narrow offices, and the back one, though smaller, has quiet. I think I'd prefer it, but . . ."

"Fine with me," Hughie said.

"It's yours," Joel said, squinting into the fretwork of ailanthus branches. "Think of the money you're going to make us staring at that tree."

At The Bank, a neighborhood bar on Second Avenue, Flavia asked, "What kind of list?"

"Small, classy. Twenty titles a season. We're going to prove there's still a demand for quality. We'll publish books we want to do, whatever the market for them, and we'll publish bread-and-butter books as well, but only if we believe in them. It'll be the kind of house, on a small scale, that Crowninshield's was fifty years ago."

"Who's the boss?"

"I'm the first, in a kind of rotating chairmanship. We've divided the functions — Hughie, the sales; Joel, the manufacturing. I'll do subsidiary rights and, God help me, advertising."

"Who takes the books?"

"Joel and I, with Hughie as tie breaker. I'm free, really, to do fifteen books a year. Hughie'll make an annual California trip, while Joel and I will alternate to London. We have our difficulties, but we're all exuberant, and I can hardly believe that just three months ago, life seemed so glum."

On the bench beside Flavia, George watched me while she fondled his ears. "You trust Joel's taste?"

"He makes mistakes, like the rest of us, but he's good — a sixth sense."

"And Hughie?"

"Hughie's not so sensitive, not as clever as Joel is, but he's intelligent. He's hard nosed and he'll be good at making the house run."

"And he's putting up most of the money?"

"All of us have brought in money."

Whiskey had warmed me, lent some picturesqueness to The Bank's gloom, its black varnish and the fluorescent blue of the television screen. The bleakness of the day no longer seemed forbidding.

"How are *you?*" I asked.

"All right, I guess." She seemed to be weighing a confidence and then said, "My husband is a composer. He's talented, but easily discouraged."

"I understand that."

"I don't think you do, really. You have a good idea of your own worth and intelligence."

"Do I? Does anyone?"

"Yes. You believe in yourself. You have vitality. Ernest is twenty-seven, but alongside you, he's an old man."

Flavia smiled, finished her drink, looked as though she wished I'd buy her another, but she patted George off the seat onto the floor and stood up.

"I think you're going to do it," she said.

"What?"

"Make some kind of wonderful publishing history."

"The odds are all against us. You know that."

"No." She shook her head with certainty. "Not against the three of you. Collectively you're a powerhouse. Your timing's right — experience behind you, a full head of energy, and you *can't* fail. I mean you're mutineers. If you go back, it's to the brig."

"Would you like to come along, Flavia?"

"You mean it?"

"Of course."

"Oh, wow, Lloyd. Would I *ever.*"

⊸§ 15 ⃛

GOOD NEWS, like bad, tends to come in bunches and create in the innocent mind an unwarranted optimism. The early Gulliver years of the mid-sixties were good-news years. Each day brought some new cause for rejoicing.

Miraculously, the Literary Guild took Luke Pentecost's short story collection. On the strength of this, Joel flew off on our first London mission, reporting back within a few days that he had acquired American rights to the winner of the Prix Goncourt.

The golden brush had touched us all and the news spread. Polly Dupee, feeling Crowninshield's had bungled her critical success with the *Berenson,* offered us her new book on the Met. Although Morgan Bryce had not been heard from for a full year, when he returned he atoned with two fine new chapters. *Fulgencio's Game* would be Crowninshield's book but Elena Wallace held out some hope that Bryce too might ultimately come to us.

Even my first novels did well. Leonard Oakes, an author I had been following since early Crowninshield years, had given me *The Frog Pond* and we'd published it in early 1966 to a few favorable reviews and a very small sale, but then, to our delight, it appeared as one of the dozen nominees for the National Book Award.

I am told that it was a fluke, that only because of a deadlock between the judges over the two principal candidates did our very dark frog get into the jumping at all. There was an epidemic of acrimony at other houses over the outcome, and over the rumor that one of the judges had agreed on *The Frog Pond* in order to catch his train.

Nevertheless, *The Frog Pond* did win the fiction award and that announcement set off a week of jubilation on Sixty-first Street. After the NBA ceremony there was an all-night party at Gulliver House. At its height, the bashful Lenny Oakes, the only one in a reflective temper, told me that he was writing a second novel, much grander in design than *The Frog Pond,* and in his opinion vastly better. It was to be called *Lucy Paradise.*

But while the sense of assurance grew at Gulliver's, at home, Andy's waned, as though she were its counterweight. The pride that had kept her from asking Ethan Poole for a leave to make our Cretan holiday, kept her from asking him to rehire her. But even as she admitted to the hundreds of alternatives, she did nothing about them. Months of procrastination became over a year of it, and I felt she had starved her incentive.

Hardly a week passed in which I didn't encourage her, saying, "Go and make the rounds. Try Crowninshield's. You want me to call them for you?"

"No. I can do it. I will."

But I knew it was unlikely I would find Andy brushed and panoplied, list of prospects in hand, ready to board the 8:10 with me. She wanted to do things, to be engaged with people and be admired by them, while at the same time she honored the habitual, instinctive circle of her privacy. It seemed as though her very determination to break it, or perhaps my urging her to do so, made it flame the higher, like Wotan's ring.

I wondered if that difference between us, her reticence toward adventure, was simply a lower level of curiosity about people and places which came from a characteristic contentment. But she was no longer content.

When I speculated that this was essentially an inhibition, one that went back to her father's notions of what a lady did, and did not do, she accepted it saying, "Yes, it probably does have to do with my father and his ideas of what makes a woman unattractive, like a loud voice and being ridiculous or open to criticism in some way, but it's you too, you know. You always discourage me. You don't really want me committed to a job that might interfere with your plans."

"Not true. I want to see you working at something you like and I'll help you if you let me know how."

Going into town next morning, I was still thinking of Andy's dilemma, guessing she would kick herself for every passed up chance. But even if I were partly responsible, in some way the source of her inhibition, I could do no more than suggest. Surely I had no more influence than that, nor responsibility, did I?

The agents, sensing the excitement on Sixty-first Street, were coming around with fresh and tempting proposals. I had always known Duncan Woolley as the keeper of a fine, literary stable of clients, and I was particularly anxious to have access to it. I liked Duncan. He was a few years older than I, with exquisite, snobbish tastes, and for years we had lunched every few weeks. We talked about personal things. I told him about Will, the pleasures and pain he brought me, and listened to his concerns over a daughter of Will's age. We spoke too of food and music and women and people in our business and, of course, the literary scene. Without ever saying so, we had reached an understanding that, when the time was right, when one of his desirable clients was ready for a move, my courting of him would be rewarded.

Duncan's reward arrived in the shape of a mammoth novel, *The Crown of Priapus,* by one of his most sought-after clients, Oliver Swimming. I had often asked Duncan if Swimming was happy at Harper's, where he sold pitifully despite consistent praise by the critics. Here was Duncan Woolley's answer.

Flavia was elated at the prospect of publishing Oliver Swimming. I had to pry the manuscript from her hands, and on the train I opened it with the expectation due a long-awaited gift. Nevertheless the early pages seemed obscure and patronizing and I remembered that although I had admired his first, I had been unable to finish Swimming's most recent book.

At home I sat up reading it until late, offering swatches to Andy, becoming more bewildered and exasperated as I made my way through the self-conscious exposition and the improbable adventures of a Roman god.

"Well, I don't really like it," Andy said in returning a section. "Do you suppose he's serious about it?"

"Yes, and for all I know he's James Joyce and this is the new *Ulysses,* but I'm uneasy with it." I skimmed the last hundred pages and closed the box undecided. Surely I would get an opinion from Flavia and Hughie before making a decision, but I wished Joel were here as well.

As it turned out, neither Flavia nor Hughie was much help. "I don't think you'd go *wrong* with Swimming," Flavia reported when she had finished it. "But the trouble is, Duncan's going to want a display of enthusiasm, some real money, and I don't think this is nearly up to his earlier books. He's a good writer, but this is so smart-ass . . . as though he were defying readers to like him. I bet you Harper's turned it down."

While Hughie was reading it, I called Pitney Gates at Harper's and asked about Swimming.

"Oh-ho," Gates laughed. "So you've got *The Crown of Priapus,* have you? We wondered. No, we didn't turn it down. We made Duncan what we thought was a decent offer, based somewhat on past performance, naturally, and I'm not in a position to tell you the figure, you understand."

"Of course," I said. "And Duncan's shopping around for a better deal. Can I ask if your offer stands?"

Gates hesitated. "Oh, I *think* so. We've put a lot into him you know."

"Thanks, Pitney," I said. "You're a friend."

The following morning Hughie said, "I don't know what Oliver Swimming is smoking these days but I'd like to know, because I could get a nice price for it in the Village. But the book has a phony smell to it. I don't think I could sell it."

I called Duncan while the courage was in me. "Duncan, this is a painful thing to say, but we're bewildered by the Swimming. I know I've told you a dozen times that we'd dip deep in our jeans for a chance at him, and I had every expectation . . ."

"Oh, please, don't fret about it, Lloyd. You don't like it. You're under no obligation. Just send it back."

"I think it would be a mistake all around to take him, feeling as we do that this is a tour de force but not his best . . ."

"I disagree there, but no point in arguing over it, Lloyd."

"What most distresses me is that you're disappointed in me and won't send us any more of your good people."

Duncan laughed. "Not a chance, Lloyd. In fact I'm sending you a choice one this afternoon. I'm determined to do some business with Gulliver House."

"Who?"

"Bushrod Ketcham. You know him?"

"By reputation, of course. And I shook hands with him once, at the National Book Awards."

"This is not a novel. It's his autobiography. He happens to be free, and this is a first offer. But, mind you, I'm going to want a good price on this one, Lloyd."

The Bushrod Ketcham manuscript turned out to be a thousand disheveled pages, a confessional by a literary has-been, a man who had been celebrated and spoiled for his early novels in the thirties and had had the misfortune to outlive his reputation. It was a vain and flatulent book, but it had plums of perceptive reminiscence and self-revelation.

Flavia and Hughie were favorably impressed, but Kay Rossbach, who had come in to look through Joel's mail, was most enthusiastic.

"Lloyd, you've got to get the money for it," she said. "How much do you suppose Duncan wants?"

"Ketcham's in debt and probably won't write another book, so I'll guess twenty-five thousand and that, I'm afraid, is just too much for us."

"There must be another way. Could you get a paperback house to go along with us?"

I nodded. "I thought of Phil Lerner, how he's an investor. He's promised a report by the end of the week."

It had the feel of a bad morning with its implacable sky and a rain that had settled in forever. From my window I contemplated a gray world standing in a filthy puddle. The telephone rang with the special tolling of bad news.

To be sure, it was Phil Lerner calling to say, "I liked the Ketcham myself. If it were up to me, Lloyd, I'd string along, but some of the others felt it wasn't of special interest. A whole new generation doesn't even *know* Bushrod, and the older ones think he's dead. Now, we agree you'll do well with it. You'll find the audience. But, perfectly frankly, I think we're put off by the shape it's in. It's a mess and needs to be cut by half. Bushrod must be going soft. What is he — seventy? All of that, I guess, and he's lived each one hard. Now, I want to see this again, — when you're in galleys."

"But we can't afford it."

There was a silence. "Well, I'd really like to help you out, but I'm afraid this bet is yours. Let me know, will you, Lloyd?"

"Oh sure, Phil."

Still brooding about my luck, I heard a voice from the door say, "Hi." It was Kay Rossbach in slicker and boots, dripping into my new rug and looking like a young fisherman in off the sea. "You look down."

"Bad news from Lerner. He didn't bite on Bushrod Ketcham. They want to see it cut first."

"Well, what did you expect? The reprinters are such unimaginative oafs, really. Of course, it does need a lot of work. Why don't you cut it?"

"It's a job. I don't have that kind of time, to say nothing of that kind of money."

"Even so, maybe you should try it on your own. Go to the bank for a loan. Put up Andy's fur coat. Show the bastards."

I laughed, delighted with her spirit. "What do you hear from Joel?"

"He called last night to say he'd be a day later. He's coming on Wednesday."

"If you're free, I'll take you to lunch."

While we waited for a table in the swarming bar of Le Cheval Blanc, Kay was saying, "Oh, Joel's having a glorious time. He's been to dinner with every publisher in London, and he went to some marvelous after-theater party of Joe Farquharson's and met the whole cast of the Old Vic's *Macbeth*. He's gone to Frankfurt for a day. That's the delay. It's disgusting he's off having such a glorious time while we're here getting rained on."

"I wish he'd been here last week. I'm still uncomfortable about the Swimming."

"Oh, dear. I did tell him." Kay seemed to bite her tongue.

"And what? He thinks we should have taken it?"

She took a quick sip of her Dubonnet and nodded.

"Oh, for Christ's sake."

Kay made a birdlike gesture. "Well, you know Joel. He's in a particularly oracular state of mind. I think staying in expensive hotels has this effect on him, but he thinks Oliver Swimming is ripe for his harvest."

"Now, that really pisses me off, Kay. Second-guessing us without even reading it. Did you tell him what you thought?"

"Yup."

"Ripe. That's exactly the word for that pretentious, overwritten book. Andy couldn't even read it."

Madame beckoned us along the corridor to a corner table in the back room. Across from us, Mia Penrose waved. As I watched Kay pondering the menu I thought how pretty she was, cameolike, with her milky complexion and exquisite features. There was such an intensity about Kay, the darting of her black eyes, as though she must make up in energy for her small displacement.

I didn't believe I was attracted to Kay, yet forces worked between us and there might be something to Andy's jealousy. As she finished her discussion with the waiter I allowed myself a momentary fantasy of making love with her.

Surrendering her menu, a real Kay Rossbach rested her chin on folded hands and smiled at me.

"You seem different, Kay — happier. Are you?"

"I am. I'd forgotten what it was like."

"Getting on with the writing?"

She shook her head. "Haven't been near the typewriter in a month, and I don't know what to make of that. I should be suffering tons of guilt, but I'm not. Maybe I've *had* my book."

"It was a good one."

"Your note was sweet, Lloyd. One of the few nice things that happened."

"I meant it. The *Times* review was unnecessary and wrong-headed."

"Well, it is out of my system, and that could be why Joel and I are getting on now. It was ugly, you know. We fought over everything, talked with the lawyers, very nearly split." She impaled a slice of salmon on her fork and ate it thoughtfully. "But now, working on the juvenile list has had this really marvelous effect, not just on me you know, but on both of us. It's so good to feel important."

I nodded. "Andy's going through the career crisis too. She wants to be in publishing, but she's not finding anything. She's feeling blue about it and has about given up. She's jealous of you incidentally."

"Is she? Why?"

"Because I admire you. Because you accomplish things."

Kay smiled. "*Do* you want her to succeed?"

"Of course. I want her to be happy, if only for selfish reasons."

"But *un*consciously, aren't you making it as hard as you can for her — willing her to stay on the bench so she'll go on pampering you? Of course you don't know you're doing it, but look at the record. You train her up to be your reader, infect her with all your publishing enthusiasm, tell her she's learning how to go out and do it on her own — and then you discourage her, tell her that if she does it she'll threaten you, that she must stick to nursing or clay-modeling — isn't that right? And when she *did* get a job you got her to quit it, right? She was your Crete companion? A matter of priority, wasn't it? I think you ought to face up to that, Lloyd. It isn't Andy's womanliness that's holding her down, it's your purdah. Who are you really looking out for?"

After a minute I said, "That's hard to swallow, but I guess it's possible."

"Get Andy a job. You can do that. There's a test for *you*. See how you feel about giving her a real break." Kay squinted at me.

"At Gulliver's?"

"Why not?"

"Because she doesn't want my help. She wants to do it all on her own."

"Oh, pooh. It'll be professional as hell. We'll see to that."

"I wonder," I said. "Do you suppose Andy could edit the Bushrod Ketcham?"

"I'm sure he's a difficult man, but Andy has that cool, chaste authority he'd respect."

As I sat sipping my wine, thinking about it, my reservations weakened. The idea of our being the masters of Gulliver House with the power to do such things, the power to help each other, led me to think this was a feasible plan, as good for Gulliver's as it would be for Andy.

By the time we left the restaurant I was ready to see if we could get the Ketcham book at a reasonable price and to persuade Andy to edit it. Strolling up Lexington with Kay, we found that the rain had stopped and the air was misty with the promise of a reappearing sun.

*

That evening I said to Andy, "Gulliver's has a proposition to make you. It wasn't my idea, by the way. Originally, anyway, it was Kay's. How would you like to work on the Ketcham book? Lots of ifs — if we can get it cheap, if Ketcham agrees to a lot of work. It needs a third cut out, more if you can get it, and some rewriting. He's said to be a difficult man. What do you say?"

She took some time to think. "Gulliver's? Is that a good idea? Does Kay really think so?"

"So she says, and after all, *she's* doing it. It'll be all business. We'll pay you the going fee."

Laying a spoon on the stovetop, she said, "Who'll be the boss?"

"He will. It's a matter of how much you can get him to do."

"But who decides what we want him to do?"

"You. And if you want my advice, I'll be ready to give it. I can tell you now where some mushy spots are. If Duncan is reasonable, I'll bring home the manuscript and you can see for yourself."

Andy nodded slowly, then more certainly. "Well, first, I think Kay's great to think I can do it, and second, I don't want to get my hopes up and have it fizzle, but of course I'll do it if you all want me. It sounds like heaven."

After supper I described Ketcham's growing up on the South Side of Chicago and then, with the success of his first book, coming to Greenwich Village in the thirties and knowing everyone — O'Neill and Edna Millay, Dos Passos and Maxwell Anderson, Oliver La Farge and Edna Ferber — having a dozen love affairs, before the creeping failure and the alcoholism, then finding the comeback trail. Much of it was seamy and all of it self-serving, but still it was a unique view of a literary generation.

"Oh, I think I can do something with *that*," she said.

"Andy's going to edit the Bushy Ketcham?" Flavia arched an eyebrow.

"It wasn't my idea. It was Kay's. But it's going to be fine.

We've been through all the doubts, and I did have a number. In the end, you know, the essential thing is whether Andy's qualified, and she is. She certainly will be conscientious about it. Why?"

"Oh, I don't know. I was wondering, what if she doesn't get on with Bushy. Isn't he a trial? What if Andy doesn't work out?"

"She'll work out."

"Ah-h," Flavia stretched, smiling. "I see."

Joel returned to us in a black hat that gave him more the air of a Hungarian diplomat than an editor, but he was jauntier than ever. At our first luncheon he described the five titles he had bought. They were a promising bag and I envied him the successful trip, eager for my own turn.

I was expecting some grumbling about the Swimming, but he offered none. Instead he congratulated me on the Ketcham and my persuading Andy to work on it.

Duncan Woolley did agree to our offer and I called Andy to say she could start when she was ready.

"Oh, I'm so pleased," she said. "I was afraid it would fall through."

"When you're ready to talk to Ketcham, just call him. Buy him a lunch. He's here in town and waiting to see you."

That evening, when I brought home the manuscript, Andy skipped through it while we were having drinks and she was putting the final touches on supper, pausing to read passages and once turning up her nose to say, "I don't think *that's* very good. He seems fuzzy. Is it the drink or old age?"

"He'll rewrite. You'll just have to pay out a little tact and, of course, psych yourself into liking it."

"Well, that," she said, "may take some doing."

After dinner she skimmed the *Times*, glanced through a magazine, and then went to the phone to make some calls. From my reading chair I could hear her talking about the raise for teachers which would be coming up at some meeting.

When she returned, she took up the Ketcham manuscript

and as soon as she started to read, I saw anxiousness webbing around her eyes. Her lips turned in with it, as though she were about to shout the letter *m*.

"Want some advice?"

She looked up.

"Just read it as though you'd found it lying on the seat beside you, and enjoy it. Don't worry about what to do with it now."

"I'll manage," she said. "Don't worry."

Later, falling asleep, I was aware that, beside me, Andy was far from it, and that there was little I could, or should, do to help. I knew fear of failure as an old enemy of my own. I wondered if hers was the same, a dread of the damage it would do to her sense of capability, which had not yet been put to the test. Or if, possibly, it was the other, from the distaff side, fear of succeeding.

In the morning, as I left for work, she was already at the manuscript again, and that evening she disappeared into the studio with it and I saw that she was filling a legal pad with notes.

She volunteered no information about it, but when I asked, she spoke of the colorful incidents, Bushrod's boxing with Hemingway in Paris, his affair with an actress in California which ended his first marriage, and a drinking bout in Chicago. I sensed a faint distaste and she did say that Bushrod came through as self-indulgent, and she wanted to prune some of that away.

Andy came into town with me one morning, looking smart in her new green coat and alligator pumps, the Ketcham swinging from her shoulder in a leather bag she had bought for the purpose. I didn't press her about plans.

As she made herself some notes, Andy said, "I don't know what train I'll be taking out — something midafternoon if I can. It depends on how I get on with Bushy. We're going to have lunch. I'll see if we can do some work on the manuscript first, but I gather he has terrible hangovers, so maybe the afternoon will be better."

"We could clear you a place at the office."

"Maybe." We were gliding into the station and she stood in the aisle so as to be among the first off. "I'll call if I need it. I'd just as soon not be around any more than I have to. My office" — she patted the leather bag — "is here."

"Good luck," I said, and as she walked off toward the booths on the main concourse, she gave me an airy wave.

I had no word from Andy throughout the day, and at six, walking along the platform, looking to see which car to enter, I was surprised to find her peering from a window.

"How was lunch?" I asked, putting my briefcase in the rack and sitting beside her.

"It was all *right*."

"Where'd you go?"

"I was all set to take him to the Russian Tea Room, but he insisted on Christ Cella's. He was already there when I arrived, and into his second martini. It was so expensive I didn't have the money, so *he* paid."

"He probably enjoyed that."

"I didn't. He wasn't making much sense — then, or afterward when we went to his apartment so I could show him my suggestions. And he smells. He has halitosis."

"An occupational hazard. Be glad you're not his dentist. Did it work out? Will he do what you want?"

"He's thinking it over. I guess he'll do some of the things." The train had started to move and she watched the columns slip by her window. "Oh, I know, whether I like him or not isn't really the issue, but in this case the book *is* Bushy, and the bad parts are so obviously the bad parts of the man — all the sucking up to big names and taking swipes at people who have snubbed him."

"Are there *no* good parts? Ethan always used to say there's no book so bad you can't find *something* to admire."

"Sure. He's often funny. He can tell a story beautifully, and there are good things. I mean I can understand our wanting to publish it, but I do think we have to comb it out. That's what I want to do."

"Don't you find anything admirable in Bushy?"

"He's sixty-eight and I'm sure he think's he's still irresistible."

"He gave you a little chase?"

"Nothing I couldn't handle." Her indignation thawed under a wan smile. "Oh, it's a job. I do know that, and I want to do it well." From her shoulder bag she brought forth some books, Moss Hart's, the Van Doren and Mencken autobiographies. "I'm going to read these while Bushy's reflecting, and by gum I'm going to know what a good memoir looks like the next time I see him."

Over the next few days, Andy was full of discoveries about Jessica Mitford and Edith Sitwell, and I waited to hear what the next step would be, but beyond reporting afternoon appointments with Ketcham, she was mum.

As I returned from lunch one day, Flavia looked up from the manuscript in her lap to say, "I think Bushy's unhappy." She settled in the chair beside my desk and watched the pendulum swing of her foot. "Duncan Woolley called — he was hesitant, all ers and ahs. Is he like that?"

"As a rule, he's headlong."

"I asked if I could help, and that seemed to make him more nervous. I told him I was privy to all the crannies of your intent, but he said no, it was a matter he must discuss with you — but it did have to do with the Ketcham, and would you call him when you came in." Flavia raised her eyebrows and smiled her I-told-you-so smile.

"I don't like the sound of it."

"What's wrong with your wife?" Flavia asked. "Doesn't she know that authors have a special license to be obnoxious?"

"No, she doesn't know that. Also, she's super-anxious, which may have just the wrong effect on a difficult man."

Flavia watched me, smiling, as though there were something she wanted to, but dared not, say.

"What?" I asked.

"Do you think she has the right effect on you? Or shouldn't I ask that?"

"Maybe you shouldn't, but in fact she does. Andy's a rock. She expects good behavior in herself and the people around her, and as a rule she gets it."

Flavia smiled. "Not everyone's taste runs to rocky ladies. That's lucky for me."

"Thank you for calling back, Lloyd," Duncan said. "Could we talk for a few minutes this afternoon?"

"Right now."

"I could do this over the phone, but it's something of a delicate nature, I'm afraid. Look, if you come up here, I'll give you a cup of tea."

An hour later I was taking the cup from him, saying, "I can guess what this is all about. Ketcham is not too happy with Andy?"

Duncan settled in his armchair, sipped, brooded, and then replied, "Well, I think he *likes* Andy. I shouldn't be surprised if he's a bit *gone* on her. No one could dislike Andy. That's a given and I hope you'll tell her so for me. She has class and Bushrod is susceptible to class. It's my hunch that Andy reminds him of some woman out of his past who attracted him and then tried to reform him, but I don't pry with him, or with any of my clients. I'm a doctor and a clergyman, of course, if they want one. My God, what a profession this is, and it's simply too late to change." He sighed tragically and poured himself more tea. "But Bushrod *says* he's intimidated by Andy. He feels she's trying to clean him up and make him more presentable. 'I've had these all-wool ladies in my life,' he puts it, 'and God damn it I don't need any more of 'em. I thought I was through all that when I passed sixty.' Well, I don't know what to say, Lloyd. Puts us in an awkward situation. Perhaps you'll want to get out of the contract?"

"No. Certainly not. If it's just Andy, I'm sure she'll understand. Gulliver's has agreed to publish Mr. Ketcham and if Andy's not the right editor, we must find another."

"I suppose it would be awkward for *you* now."

"Yes."

"What about young Hugh Severance? Could he do it?"

"If that's a solution, he will."

Explaining it to Andy was not so easy, and by the time I had reached New Canaan, seeing her waving from the platform, I still hadn't an idea of how I was going to put it to her.

As she drove out of the lot, telling radiantly about a victory of the committee that had been defending the right of a grade teacher to refuse to teach a disruptive student, she had never seemed so vulnerable. But as we arrived in the garage and Andy turned to get her purse and a package in the back seat, I decided to do it now.

"Andy," I said, "I'm going to ask you to be wholly professional now, while I tell you something."

She looked at me queerly, cocking her head, already sensing, I think, what was coming. "What?"

"It's business, just business, and not to be taken personally, because it isn't personal. I went up to Duncan's office today and found that Ketcham isn't happy with the way the book's going. Duncan says he'd feel better if I got in on it and did some of the work with him ... But what's important for you to understand, is that it's not that he doesn't like you, in fact it's the reverse. Duncan suspects you remind him of some dark lady of his past who rejected him somehow. But none of that, and none of us, matters. It's only the book and how best to do it. So ..." I eased a long sigh from having set down my burden. "So don't fret about it, Andy. We'll pay you, and maybe we can find you something else, a book without Bushy traps."

She was staring ahead through the windshield at the rakes and shovels, the coil of garden hose, all hung on their gibbets and bathed in the glare of our headlamps.

"You're firing me," Andy said at last. "I've never been fired before in my life. Give me a minute to get all the way around it."

We sat there, listening to a ticking in the cooling engine and a stirring of leaves through the open garage door. "Somehow," she said, "you could have done that better."

Then, gathering her things, she got out quickly, radiating a new, dangerous tension, and hurried up the stairs. I followed, wondering if I should, could, take her in my arms. But there was no chance. She was putting something in the refrigerator and she slammed the door hard, and when she turned, there was such a look of hatred in her face.

"I'm going into the studio for a while," she said, "and I don't feel like making supper tonight. Do you think you can manage?"

"I'm sure of it."

As Andy walked off, slamming the studio door, latching it, I made myself a drink, and then hamburger and a salad. When I had cleaned up the night's reading, I went to bed. I saw her studio light still burning and about midnight I heard her climb the stairs to make up the bed in Will's room.

⊰ 16 ⊱

IN JUNE, readying books for the fall, I began working late, long after the others had gone for the day, doing up the last of the correspondence, talking with Flavia about the manuscripts we were considering, about editors and the courageous and cowardly decisions they had made and how these had affected their careers.

Sometimes we would stop off for a drink at The Bank, and Flavia would linger past eight, even though she had a husband awaiting her on Gramercy Park.

One evening, while we sat in the office, I realized that Flavia had been talking for some time but I had lost track of what she was saying. Guessing this, she asked, "What's the matter?"

"I'm not sure." I spread the fingers of a hand on my knee. "I'm very tense, and I want to kiss you."

I stood up, walked around the desk to where she was sitting with a copy of the *New York Review of Books* open in her lap and, leaning down, I kissed her briefly, chastely, on the mouth.

Flavia accepted the kiss without surprise. She smiled as I returned, sheepishly, and sat down again behind my desk.

"Sorry," I said, "but obviously that was the trouble. I'm better already."

Watching me, Flavia's eyes grew rounder. I could not tell from her expression, which was emergent, tolerant, if she was angry or amused, but then she folded the *New York Review,* dropped it in the basket, and stood.

"How about a real kiss?" she asked.

In full view of the Sixtieth Street apartment windows, we embraced. There was an instant of awkwardness, as though lip, arm, and breast were taken unawares, but then, with only the slightest adjustment, we closed perfectly, two crenulated pieces of puzzle snugging. In the bonding, Flavia sighed, and I felt that until this moment I had been incomplete, and that I had just been made whole.

It would always be so with her. She seemed to withhold nothing, not a strand of her glossy hair, nor a thought, nor a beat of her heart. She gave the whole; every facet of mind and body was focused and responsive. Even in talking to Flavia she was like a cupped radar antenna, concentrating every vector on me, seeing through to the essence of me, seeking and provoking the center in me. When she stood beside me, it was as though she conformed to the outline of my body, touching all along it, and when we embraced she seemed to fit even closer, filling the very core of my navel, melting into, being absorbed by, my body.

From the time of that unexpected kiss, Flavia's obligations in Gramercy Park seemed to weigh less upon her than ever. Each night we talked on into the early evening, about books and about ourselves. Once, answering the phone, I heard a voice say, "This is Ernest Moore. Is Flavia still there? She's not home yet and I'm worried."

It was nine and I hesitated before saying, "Yes, she's here. I'm sorry. We had some work."

When Flavia spoke to him, she was abrupt. "Yes," she said, "some things came up at the last minute. No, you go ahead. Don't wait for me."

She replaced the receiver thoughtfully, momentarily gone from me, and I shrank from this wind of the real world. Our hours together had been enchanted and insubstantial. Here was the collision I had dreaded, a jealous, resentful husband, waiting.

But Flavia returned to me saying, "I'm going to have to deal with this soon. It's been a bad marriage for a couple of years, but you're not to worry. It's my problem."

"It's mine as well," I said. "I must have something to do with it."

"No. You don't. You're a help to me, that's all."

"That's a comfort."

We sat, hands within hands, never so sober, nor so aware that our relationship was taking on substance and did bear on the rest of our lives.

"My marriage has been pretty disappointing too — over the past year or so," I said. "There's been a growing apart, as though we'd fulfilled our function and there was little left but the habit, the juice gone."

"You mean sex?"

"No, not that at all." I felt a qualm at this confidence, this admission of Flavia into Andy's and my bedroom. Also, I was suspicious of my testimony. I would be liable to some dishonesty in courting Flavia's sympathy. Still, I let the injured man speak and was nearly persuaded by what he said. "It's the rest," I went on. "It's the talking and sharing things, laughing at them, as you and I do. Andy and I don't laugh together. She's become very grave and resentful, as though I've done damage to her. When I admire, or dislike, something, she takes the opposite view as though she were afraid of agreeing with me. So we can't have an intelligent conversation anymore. We just spar, and that's boring and pointless, so we rarely talk now."

"But you've been married for twenty years. Surely it wasn't always this way."

"No. It's recent, and I know we're not alone. It's the national epidemic. I'm sure that women always go through an episode of futility when the children go off. They're used to having lives dependent on them — winding everybody up for the day, sending them off. It's like early retirement, with all the depression *that* brings along — only now we have a revolution telling them it needn't be that way, and someone's to blame."

My pleasure with Flavia Moore was not entirely perverse. Now I could hardly wait to get to the office, to find Flavia there, fresh as spring flowers. Sharing the morning mail with her was joy enough. We would laugh over the surprises, the successes, even the failures it brought, because we felt that together we were proof against any serious damage.

We slept together for the first time on September 11th. We had stopped by Flavia's apartment to pick up a manuscript I was to read that night, and when I paused in the living room to admire the summery, green and white painting of the Tillsbury dunes, she made me a drink. This time, when we kissed, all the playfulness was gone. There was a terrible urgency to it. Fleetingly I wondered where Ernest Moore was, if we might hear his key in the door lock, but anxiety dissolved in fervor. We made love on the sofa like a pair of animals, ravenous, gasping, and quick.

Ferocity left Flavia serene, and me, helplessly in love. I was lightheaded, eternal as a child. Custom-dulled acts became fresh, newly minted. Walking a familiar street brought discoveries and delights. The act of walking itself had become pneumatic. From the waist down I seemed to be turning into a kangaroo. Pouncing through crowds on my way to work I felt like snatching every person I passed, hugging them and telling them what it was like to be *alive*.

Time had gone erratic, creeping through the late hours of the morning until noon, when we left the office separately. Twenty minutes later, as we met at Gramercy Park, it stopped altogether. I would move about these rooms, touching the books, the clothing, the photographs of another man, finding our collusion against Ernest Moore profoundly exhilarating.

Yet the sensation of the noon hour's infinity was more glorious, as though even time moved at my will. At the hour's start I knew there was enough of it for us to touch until we tired of touching, to tell each other the trifles we had observed, the bits of gossip we had heard, all the inconsequences of our pasts.

The illusion did not fade until our hour was three quarters gone, until I saw that the clock on Flavia's dresser had actually started, its hand accelerating, whirring away our store of moments in conspiracy against us. It seemed to leap from its pinion and strike me straight through the heart.

Throughout all these days of the autumn, I was incandescent, every sense alert for her. The name *Flavia* lay on my tongue, waiting to be spoken. My ears were alert for its mention. It was a talisman, bringing me a sense of safety, and of peril, both irresistible.

Without the least hesitation, and only a fleeting guilt, I undertook the conspiracy against my wife. I justified it through feelings of another loyalty to the woman who fed my spirit, and in the belief that Flavia offered a promise of a whole new life, a life within a life, and a miraculous defiance of time's millstones.

Any other course seemed cowardly. Besides, I reasoned, I had been provoked. In Andy's resentment over her victimization, she had deserted me, left me alone, in need of admiration and affection. Surely these were man's rights. Most important, I was in love, more powerfully than I had believed possible. Even if I had willed it otherwise, I could not help myself.

I lied to Andy, inventing meetings with authors and agents, so that I could be with Flavia for a whole evening. We would go from the office to a movie that had interesting notices, and then hurry to her apartment with all the suppressed excitement of a shared deception.

As we went along darkened streets I held her hand, kissed her in the taxi, in the elevator, sometimes on the subway platform or street corners while we waited for the light's change. Assured there was no possibility of interruption by Ernest, that Flavia was eager as I to make love, I lost every inhibition.

I laid open her dress, peeled it to her waist, fondled and kissed her breasts until she felt for my rising penis, unzipping my fly to release it into her ardent hand, and then, mindless with urgency, we stripped and made love. Sitting on the edge of her bed, she spread her childishly rubbery, gorgeous legs to me as she kissed me, gasped with pleasure as I sucked at her nipples and plunged into her again and again, and finally threw back her long hair to cry out in a wail of rapture, as she came all around me.

She would dispel my moment of melancholy with a whispered assurance that sex had never been so fine for her. Then she would be up, quickly gathering her dress and underwear as she left me, to reappear a moment later in slacks and sweater, to make us drinks and put on a record, and resume being my comrade.

Bare feet curled beneath her, glass in hand, she told me that she could no longer endure her marriage. She shrank from her husband's touch and had provoked nightly quarrels so as not to have to share a bed with him. She asked how I managed with Andy and took my confusion to mean that I felt no revulsion toward her and could love — make love with — two women simultaneously.

It was certainly true that I could make love to Andy, often with more vigor and pleasure than in the past, even though, in the act, I might confuse her with Flavia. In fact, in the darkness, touching Andy's flesh, feeling my penis thicken to her touch, rising to meet her need, she seemed to be all the women of my imagining, all desire and charity, in one.

Flavia felt this lingering attraction to Andy unnatural and set me an example, explaining that Ernest had become increasingly dependent on her and diffident about his work, and in fact he was on the point of being fired from the City Center. While she had lost respect for him, she still liked him, felt for him, and despised herself for hurting him, as she had just done by insisting he move out.

She needed time to be alone, she had told him, time to think out her own problems, and she could not do so in his presence. Typically, he had been so inept at finding himself an apartment, that last weekend she had marched off, *Times* classified section in hand, and found him a place in the Village.

I was strangely joyless at the news Flavia was planning to divorce Ernest. Now I was free to come to her any time I could get away from my wife, she said, and I felt more anxiety than release toward this new era of the single deception.

It would be *too* easy, and I would be alone with my guilt and twin obligation. I knew that what I had been enjoying was precarious, and yet I was reluctant to accept change of any kind. I had a sense that the party was coming to an end, and a number of bills were soon to be presented.

One Saturday, hoping to spend an hour with Flavia, I called her from a drugstore phone and was surprised by a male voice. "Hay-lo," it said, in the hollow tone of a betrayed man speaking from the midst of ruin.

I struggled for some acceptable ground between us, and finding none, I hung up. Immediately I felt my heart plunge as though it were sinking through the filthy floor of the smothering booth. I recognized the feeling for what it was — knowledge of my own cowardice.

Nor was I relieved of it when, next day, I did reach Flavia and learned that Ernest had come by to pick up some shirts and had been left in charge of the apartment while she went on some errands. She had warned him I might call and had told him to say she would return in a few minutes. "Yes," Ernest had reported. "He called, but he hung up."

It was my first acquaintance with this sort of shame. I had suffered plenty of regret at mental and physical shortcomings — the humiliations of fumbling a ball, having studied the wrong book, forgotten a friend's name — but all these could be shelved as mechanical failures. Here I felt a spot of rottenness at my core, a sneakiness that might spread through me like a virus. I had taken it for granted that my prime strength was less an intellectual than a moral one, a good heart and spirit, a candor, the willingness to open my doors to everyone, without fear of what they might find. This belief was the essence of my confidence and I guessed that once it was shaken, in the smallest way, I would be a different, and possibly doomed, man.

I promised myself no further cowardice, that beyond protecting Andy from unnecessary pain, which I continued to view as my motive in being secretive at all, I would be open and direct in every act.

But now a new Flavia began to emerge from the one who had

seemed so miraculous an extension of myself — a Flavia self-propelled. It was as though I had been dancing with a girl who had been following me so expertly she seemed to anticipate every step, so facile she was scarcely credible, more wish than flesh — only to discover she had subtly, yet unmistakably, changed her response, drawing me now with some force in the direction of *her* choice, trying to lead *me*.

"Why must you go home?" she asked one night as I disengaged myself to grope at bedside for my undershorts. "I really hate your getting up and leaving now as if I were some whore. Andy knows where you are. Why don't you just relax and enjoy yourself?"

I hesitated, looking over my shoulder to see that Flavia had half risen, one arm gathering the flowered sheet beneath her breasts, the other supporting her, still warm, tousled, sleepy with love, exuding a delicious fragrance of perfume, sweat, and semen. She was watching, smiling, daring, and yet she was so exquisitely soft, so urgently needing to be touched that it was an act of will for me to stand and draw on my clothes.

"She doesn't know," I said.

"If that's true, she's dumber than I think — dumber than you think she is too."

"Of course she's not dumb," I said. "But Andy thinks the best of people. There isn't a suspicious thought in her head. I wish there were. I'd feel better about it."

Flavia laughed. She bowed, so that her long, black hair made a curtain across her face, then tossed it back, securing it behind an ear with her fingers and reaching to the table for a cigarette. "You needn't feel guilty, Lloyd."

"Why?"

"If Andy doesn't know, it's because she doesn't want to know. While she doesn't know, it's trivial. I don't matter." Flavia lit the cigarette, blew a thoughtful stream of smoke through a tiny hole between her lips. "Is she right, Lloyd? Don't I matter?"

"Oh, my God, darling." Dropping back onto the bed, I drew her close, kissed her mouth, an eyelid, the softness beneath her jaw. When I drew back to look at her, she was smiling at me, tenderly now, and she said in a whisper, "Then I think you ought to tell her."

But I did not tell Andy. I did not tell her because it would change every assumption between us and demand an answer to the question, "What next?" I had no idea what that answer was, but I had just enough objectivity to realize that I did not know as much about Flavia as I did about Andy and that to leave all we had put together over twenty years for this alluring girl, would be an adventurous, perhaps foolhardy, even ludicrous, act.

And yet to ignore such promptings of my heart was to reject life. I was caught between wanting to follow my emotions, and distrusting them. Time, I felt, was my only ally. Perhaps the clock held a revelation for me.

Sometimes I clung to the belief that my affair with Flavia held the possibility of rejuvenating our marriage, that somehow my renewed vitality would touch Andy. I conjured a fantasy in which I "kept two women happy," while they competed for my favor and made the decision I dreaded to make for myself.

It was otherwise. In New Canaan, Andy and I made the neighborhood rounds as another pair of domestic animals and, in familiar living rooms, among old acquaintances, we behaved as we always had, with affection understood between us. But when we were alone, we turned sullen. When I came back from the city at midnight, she did not remark on it. She seemed insulated, wrapped in her preoccupation and indifferent to my odd hours. When I asked her to read a manuscript, she took it without interest and, next day, returned it, saying she hadn't the time.

"What *is* eating you?" I asked.

"I quit my job at Poole's for you, remember? For my pains I was fired. I'm still sore about that, and I can't give you cheerful service in return. Not anymore, I can't. I think you'd better count on my being a pain until I find some new purpose."

"What might that new purpose be?"

"Some cause that will take my brains and put them to work. Oh, I'm looking, Lloyd. I'm looking all the time."

She had taken to retiring early, often without a word to me. When I came into the bedroom, I would find her not asleep, surely, but curled on her side like a crustacean, giving off waves of resentment.

Lying beside her, I might be angry, or I might grope toward an understanding of her feelings of betrayal, how she felt relinquished by the men in her life and overwhelmed by the world's indifference, how she had fastened the rage onto me.

That she did not know the enormity of my treachery left me appalled. Recognizing myself in the villain's role, I could not believe it was I.

But then I would tell myself that if Andy was in fact drowning, rescue lay only in her swimming. To answer her cry for help was to offer myself as victim, which I felt was, in some obscure way, her objective.

✌ 17 ☙

W<small>HEN</small> W<small>ILL</small> <small>HAD GONE OFF</small> to Housatonic School, I had believed that exposure to other boys his age and to the comparatively wholesome men and women who taught there, would dispel his indifference and reveal the responsive young man beneath.

Thus the phone call from Housatonic's headmaster shook my foundation stones. "I'm sorry to be intruding on your business day with this kind of unpleasantness," said Amory Winship, "but Will has broken one of our organic rules. He was found smoking marijuana and there is a possibility he'll be expelled. I wonder if you and Mrs. Erskine could come up to school and let me explain?"

The following morning, Andy and I set out for the Berkshires, following the route — Danbury, Kent, Canaan — that had meant seeing Will in Saturday circumstances. Habitually, going to Housatonic stirred boyish feelings of my own. The sound of cheering at the game, the sight of ruptured sofas and bureau photographs in dormitory rooms, evoked old anticipations of holidays and the "real life" that lay in store.

But this morning I was feeling all my years and an overwhelming disappointment in Will. I could not imagine any happy outcome of this day.

"I don't see how he could have brought that stuff back to

school with him," Andy was saying. "I simply don't believe it."

"You don't believe the kids have it at their parties? Where have you been?"

"It's not that. I don't believe Will is so foolish."

"Will's confessed. You won't persuade Winship he didn't smoke it."

"Then why are we asked to come?"

"To pack him up, I guess."

"But he didn't *say* that. He wants to talk. I think that's hopeful."

"Well, he said expelled, and I'm prepared for that. If Will's foolish enough to trade Housatonic and a shot at college for a puff of grass, that's what he wants. If he wants high school and its opportunity for pinball and rock concerts, that's his choice. It's a free country for a seventeen-year-old, just as it is for me. Nobody *has* to make anything of his life."

"You're so angry, you're not making any sense."

"Maybe it'll be good for him. He takes everything for granted. I don't think he can conceive of going hungry, or that he might have to work at some filthy, boring job just to survive."

"If you think going to high school is going to give Will your point of view, you're mistaken. Only you can do that."

"He's not been working. He's getting such lousy grades no college will want him."

"I worry about that too, that it's my fault somehow, but really, Lloyd, that's what a father's for."

"What can I do? I can't *tell* Will anything. All I can do is provide the example."

"You could do for him what your father did for you. You've forgotten what you learned from him."

"I scarcely saw my father."

"But when you did you knew how much he cared about you. You always keep Will away."

"I don't keep him away, but he has to come to me. He has to show a *little* curiosity."

"Will admires you. Do you doubt that for a minute?"

"Yes. Will rebels against me. He always has."

"But that's *you*, Lloyd. You have to show him the way. You could start today. Don't wait for him to meet you on your ground. He won't, you know. He has his own pride. You never understand his enormous need for you to love him."

"This is a game of whose fault it is, and it isn't anyone's. We do the best we can. Kids make out with the worst of parents."

We drove along in uneasy armistice, thinking our private thoughts. Mine, perhaps Andy's too, were taking shape as suspicions that Will's difficulty lay in our own discord and that that was the place to start.

I could hear Flavia asking, "How much are you willing to risk, Lloyd? How much comfort and custom can you give up to realize your potential? Do you know how much you're hobbled by anxiety over what they'll think in New Canaan and Chilmark and the Century bar, and by what *Andy* thinks? You don't have any idea of what it would be like to be free of all that harness. Oh, Lloyd, if you can be *you*, what an editor you'll be. Don't you see you *have* to? That's your *liberation* movement and you ought to be as committed to it as Andy is to hers. Too old? Oh, Lloyd, come *on*. You're a child. You'll *never* grow old."

And then I imagined Joel's voice counseling, "Oh, no, Lloyd. You don't have to worry about Andy. She's an attractive woman. Andy'll do very well. You can be sure of that. She's probably just as eager to be free. Don't feel guilt about it, for Christ's sake. That's where the tragedy lies, in people hanging together out of guilt. Guilt is pumped into you Wasps from birth so you'll be miserable in this life and saved in the next, but I promise you it doesn't count for a damn thing in either one."

It was as though I had been rehearsing the words for weeks, getting them down for a performance whose time had not been set. Now it was at hand.

"Andy," I said. "It's time we faced up to the real trouble. You're bitter about me. You feel I'm responsible for your unhappiness, for your not having a job you like. I react in the

only way I can, by fighting back. If we keep on we'll be scream-
ing and blacking each other's eyes."

She was looking ahead, showing nothing, accepting this as
rhetoric, a fresh skirmish in the endless battle. "I'll face up to
anything you like."

"Maybe we'd be happier if we separated, Andy. We aren't
manacled."

I could feel her eyes on me, digesting this bluntness. "You
mean that, Lloyd?" Her voice had gone soft and vulnerable.
"Do you really mean that?"

"I mean that I'm miserable, and I'm making you the same.
I see us turning more bitter every day. I don't know what else
to propose."

She considered this and then said, "I know I'm cross. Sometimes I wonder how you do put up with it. I really do. I think
it'll pass. I think I'm growing through something, and all I need
is a little help." She reached out and put a hand on my arm in
such a tender gesture that I could not go on.

"This work for Clip Ogleby's campaign is doing some good,"
she said. "I haven't thought about the Ketcham business in a
week."

"That was surely a mistake."

"Oh, it was. I'll never work at Gulliver's again. No more
riding on your handlebars." She spoke with new buoyancy.
"But the committee job is going to lead somewhere after the
election."

"Only if Clip wins, and you know the odds on that," I said
sourly.

"Lloyd, give me some encouragement. I'm having to climb
out from under a lifetime of obedience training. I'm finding
that was the wrong kind, and how late it is for me to know that
and act on it. Changing turns out to be like moving a mountain by the spoonful. It's endless and I'm not even sure you'll
like me when I've done it. But I've got to, of course, whether
you like me or not. It's the only way for us, do you see?"

"Not really."

"Well, it's an answer to what you said about being unhappy. Give me some time, Lloyd."

We were driving through the gates, up the serpentine road, past the lake and the hockey rink. Will, first among the boys we saw, was coming out of Main. He made his way toward us slowly, carrying his head a little to one side.

He smiled, though, with a touching mixture of contrition and gladness to see us. There was a moment's pretense that our appearance made this some kind of holiday, but as all three of us walked along the terrace, past the chapel, making reluctant progress toward the headmaster's house, Will sobered.

"It's true," he said. "I smoked part of a joint as it was passed around. But I didn't bring the stuff and I'm not going to say who did. On Sunday we were up in the woods. We had cigarettes and this one joint. I know it was dumb — but at the time it was just something to break the monotony. It gets so dull here after a while. Eunice, Mrs. Colfax" — he named his betrayer with corrosive scorn — "was out birding and saw us. Then later, when they had the inquisition, I was the only one who owned up to the dope. That's what makes me mad, because each of us had at least a toke. If I'd wanted to lie with the others . . ."

Will in trouble, Will without his armor of apathy, was a vulnerable, appealing son. Walking by his side, I could recall my own schoolboy mischief and the sweet agony of punishment which followed.

A cadet officer, returning from a visit to the dentist, had seen us hitchhiking, miles from school. That evening, standing at attention, I had felt the soak-slip folded into my hand. Stealing a look, I had read my name and the bold letters, AWOL. Beneath my feet the pavement had trembled.

Awaiting justice, Wally Badger and I had enjoyed the awe of other cadets, hated and swore vengeance on the informer, and quailed at the thought of our audience with Colonel Emmett.

I still recall the long wait outside his office, how Wally had emerged, shaken, his voice weak, seeming half his normal size, to report, "I'm canned. I'm going home."

In my turn, standing before the yellow desk while Colonel Emmett's fingers had played with a saber letter-opener and massaged the tension in the blue jawline, I had heard him say, "Erskine, you know the rules. A cadet who goes absent without leave is fired. Badger doesn't surprise me, but you have a good record and I'm disappointed. Your father's disappointed too."

The link to Dan. My coming home in dishonor. What a sweet-sick plunge of remorse it still held. What a betrayal for the barren adventure of a fifteen mile trip to nowhere.

Yet now, thinking back, I could see my need for that trip, how an irresistible wind had blown me up the road beyond the soccer field to thumb an oncoming car, knowing the ride I wanted was all the way to New York and the one-room apartment Dan had taken on West End Avenue.

I was puzzled by Will's stubbornness though, by that absoluteness of principle which had led him to own up while the others pleaded innocent. In Will's shoes, I suspected, I would have gone with the others. I had to admire that inflexible sense of honor, as I admired it in Andy, and realized how much Will was his mother's son.

Winship, young for a headmaster, sturdy and coachlike, gave Andy and me a sober welcome to his study and sent Will to his dormitory.

"Drugs at a boys' school are serious business," he began, "particularly at a small, Spartan one such as ours. We can't have that going on, no matter what the consequence . . . We're into an area where a state law is broken. If we were to call in the police, you know, poor Will would be on his way to jail. I don't know if we have the right not to do so."

"The school means a lot to Will," Andy said. "He's very loyal."

"Yes, I know. And let me say this, Mrs. Erskine. Will's not a gifted student, nor a natural athlete, but he has a quality I admire equally. He hangs on. He's sure of his worth, and so am I. I'm not at all eager to lose Will."

"Mr. Winship," I said. "I understand that you have little choice, that it comes down to condoning what you fail to punish. But I've had a chance to talk to Will, and I have no doubt that what he tells me is the truth. He says he smoked some marijuana, but he didn't bring it to school, and he was not alone in smoking it. I hope that isn't revealing a confidence. His whole point is not to accuse the others, but he feels his honesty has made him the one to bear the punishment for all."

Winship nodded. "I'm afraid there is confusion about that. I do have to go by the book you know, but I'm reluctant to do an unfairness. That's why I wanted you to come up, to see if we can devise some discipline that will discourage a recurrence and yet be fair."

"I wonder . . . Would it be possible to look at it from the boys' point of view for a minute — the fact that they don't see pot in the same light we do, that it is very much a symbol of changing standards? The law itself, the state law you mention, is in moral question, at least in . . ."

Winship raised a hand to stop me. "I don't think you and I should get lost in that swamp. Let's say I'm aware of a variety of opinions on the seriousness of the crime. Also, your coming up today is a big help to me. With your concern, I may be able to work out something short of expulsion — perhaps a probationary period, a confinement to school grounds, exclusion from team athletics . . ."

So Andy was proved right. The headmaster decided on a public announcement before the school. There would be further questioning of the other boys, a meeting of the faculty, and penance a-plenty, but Will was to stay at Housatonic.

I had a further revelation. When I walked with Will around the path in the woods, explaining the terms of his sentence, I went on to press him about getting down to work. "You can do that now," I said. "You can redeem yourself all the way by getting your grades up so you'll have some appeal to these college admission guys."

"Daddy, I do all I can," Will said. "You know I get up to study while it's still dark. I read an assignment two or three times. But I don't remember it as well as some of the others who read it once. I don't get it down on the test paper. No matter what, I can't get better than a C."

I knew this for the moment of understanding it was, that he had opened to me, and I tried to respond to it, saying, "It must be the *way* you're reading, Will. You've got a good head. It has to do with concentration, not letting your mind wander while you study. You have to get aggressive toward information. You know what I mean?"

But by the time we had returned to the car, Will had closed again, like a shutter. Still, I had seen beyond the alien son to the one who was hobbled by self-doubt, and by some demand that I, or Andy, had put on him, one he felt he had already failed.

⤙ 18 ⤚

PUBLISHING PARTIES are an occupational hazard. They're a burden to those who must go to them and a source of envy to those who are left out. Brendan Gill says that everything happens at parties, by which, I take it, he means that, for the curious and gregarious, parties are not a waste of good time, offering, as they do, rewards of information and opportunity.

When Andy and I were asked to Hugh's party for *Fulgencio's Game,* Flavia dropped the invitation on my blotter with manifest pique.

"After all, I found Morgan. If it weren't for me there wouldn't *be* a Crowninshield party for him. It's so unfair. Can't I go, somehow?"

"I could ask Corinne. She'll have the list."

"Corinne? Oh, for God's sake — she'll think of five good reasons why I shouldn't be invited."

"Or I'll ask Hugh, if you like. He doesn't have it in for you. You certainly ought to go if you want."

"Oh, forget it. I despise pushy women."

"Whatever you say."

I was relieved. Morgan Bryce was coming from England for his publication and I wanted to be at the party, but I was not comfortable enough in my adulterer's role to enjoy a scene that included both Andy and Flavia.

Entering my office on the afternoon of the party, I found Flavia sitting on a corner of my desk and, to my surprise, Morgan Bryce, tilting back in my chair, chatting with her.

I had not seen Morgan in over a year and he was paler, heavier, as though he took poor care of himself, and there was a negligence, a weary arrogance, as though the good reviews had had their effect. It was an air of renown, a certainty the world would come to him. I was more pleased than offended by his appropriating my desk, my chair, and Flavia.

"Morgan, I had no idea you were coming by."

Slowly, he brought his attention around to me and stood, beaming, to take my hand. "Lloyd, I did want to see your quarters, and they let me out of the interview early — I was that rude to the girl. We'll be seeing each other tonight? You're bringing Andy?"

"She's coming in especially."

"Well, I'm impressed with all this." He moved to the window seat to stretch his surprisingly long legs and scanned the shelf of our recently published titles. "You're clearly doing very well."

"We *are* getting some good books now. It won't surprise you, Morgan, that I hope someday we'll publish you."

"Conceivable, isn't it?" He smiled. "Flavia's been most persuasive."

"Have I?" She was back at her own desk, holding a copy of the *Book Review* with its prominent review of *Fulgencio's Game.* "I thought I was just telling you how good the book is."

"Ah-h. Well, same thing. I'll be watching Crowninshield's very carefully, I can tell you, to see if Hugh can come up with equal praise."

When Morgan and I decided to go out for a drink, Flavia tagged along and, within a few minutes of our taking a table at The Bank, she had her invitation to the party. Over her protests, Morgan insisted that she come and assured her that Hugh and Enid would know he had asked her.

"Not for me," I said when Morgan ordered a second round.

"I've got to meet Andy. Would you want to come along to Grand Central with me?"

Flavia frowned at the notion, and Morgan said, "No, thanks, I must change my shirt."

It was a red gingham shirt and he was still wearing it at the party which took place at the Severance house on Beekman Place. The party was opulent, made up of Crowninshield people with a seasoning of reviewers and booksellers. I found Sid Broyles and Alice Margolies eager to hear about developments at Gulliver House. That was a pleasure, feeling the concern and sympathy my former associates had felt for me become admiration.

I watched Flavia make her courtesies with Enid and Hugh, then swim through the throng like a slippery fish, greeting friends, flirting, laughing, even having a word with Andy, and I had a sense that she was showing me her independence. Once, while she talked with Dexter Barnes, I caught her eye and she winked, as though to say, "You didn't want me here, but you see — I always get my way."

For all her darting and plunging, Flavia was never far from Morgan Bryce and I felt she was working that sadistic device as well, courting my jealousy. She was successful too.

When Andy told me that since she had to drive to Hartford in the morning she would take the eight o'clock train to New Canaan, I suggested that I wanted to see more of Morgan and would follow on a later one, or even stay in town for the night.

On the way to get my coat I said to Flavia, "I'm taking Andy to the train, and we can have dinner if you like. If Hugh's made no plans for Morgan, you might get him to join us."

"Oh?" she said. "Well, maybe. We'll see how it works out."

When I returned to Beekman Place, most of the guests had gone. On the doorstep, Alice Margolies said, "Oh, Morgan went off with your secretary. They had a purposeful look about them. I think I heard him offer to drop her off, or was it the other way?"

At ten, backed against the Gramercy Park fence, I could see the small lamp in Flavia's living room was burning and though

I waited for half an hour, it cast no human shadows. There was no answer to her doorbell nor her telephone. I waited for another half hour in the lobby of the Algonquin, where Morgan was stopping. Behind the early edition of the *Times* I kept one eye on the door, another on the elevator, but they did not appear.

I slept in the Gulliver House guest room but at eight in the morning I was at Flavia's door, ringing until she came, cross and sleepy, to let me in.

In her bedroom, she drew the covers over her head, murmuring, "No. No, I guess we *forgot* you were coming back. You were gone for hours."

"Half an hour, maybe three quarters. Andy missed a train."

"We didn't know. I thought you'd gone to New Canaan."

"Where did you go?"

"To some bar. No, I don't know. Please, Lloyd, stop it. We just talked. We were having a good time. All right, yes, he did come up. For one drink. He'd brought me home, for God's sake. No, I don't know what time. Lloyd, what are you thinking, that he laid me? Don't dear, please don't."

And I believed her even though, when I kissed her, there was a scent of what I thought was semen on her breath.

In December of 1968 we decided on a Christmas party. Hughie had looked after the Bushrod Ketcham memoir and now we were delighted to find it on the season's gift lists. Joel, who had multiplying hopes for a book he had picked up in England, was in a celebrating mood, while I was carrying a weathered banner for Oakes's *Lucy Paradise,* a book we had published that fall to the bafflement of most reviewers. The single encomium, in *Time,* came too late to stem a flurry of returns.

I was sure the public indifference to *Lucy Paradise* was mistaken, that if the book was marred by Oakes's overambition, it was still a fine one, a sequel to an NBA winner, and the second book of an important American novelist. I wrote letters to the trade saying so. Within the house I insisted on ads in Chicago and California, and a second printing to go with a *Publishers Weekly* announcement of our faith in the book.

So far, *Lucy* had failed to budge. Phil Lerner's was the only bid for reprint rights and it was so low I had spurned it, but I found reason for continued hope. A British sale had been followed by an inquiry about television rights and another about academic discount for a course in contemporary fiction.

The Christmas party seemed a good way to say that *Lucy* was alive and would yet thrive.

Hugh Severance had never visited Gulliver House and we invited him, suspecting he would be enticed by curiosity. Nevertheless, with the party at high tide, I was surprised to glance up and see Hugh, in full radiance, coming through our door.

"Well, this has the look of prosperity about it," he said. "Everything going smoothly, Lloyd?"

"Oh, never better, Hugh."

"Really? Getting along with one another? No scraps?"

"I guess we're too well acquainted for that."

As Joel came to join us, Hugh said, "Lloyd tells me you're doing beautifully, and I'm pleased of course, as I take some of the credit for that."

"And the best is yet to be, Hugh," Joel said enthusiastically. "I've just bought a fascinating Russian book, by a refugee. *Women of Red Square* it's called, about the ladies who influence the Kremlin. And it seems they do, just as in Washington."

"What's this? What's this?" Hughie asked as he arrived. "The old man looking for a job?"

Hugh was delighted. "No, not this week. Just checking up is all. Joel says you have a big Kremlin book coming, and Lloyd tells me I've missed my chance to pick up some Gulliver stock at a good price. I hope there's a thorn or two on your rosebush. It would be a suspect rosebush without." Hugh was smiling at me. "By the way, I saw your letter about the Oakes book. What a good way to get some mileage out of the *Time* review. How's it going?"

"Fine," I said. "Good signs. Gollancz has just taken it in England."

"Ah-h." Hugh was enjoying my discomfort even as he reassured me. "I don't imagine those disappointing reviews have really hurt you. You probably have some good reprint offers."

"I'm hopeful."

"And your sales are holding up, I dare say." He turned to his son. "What *are* you selling of the *Lucy Paradise?*"

"We're doing fine." Hughie turned wary. "Yes, fine."

"How many?" Hugh insisted. "How many this week?"

Hughie hesitated. "That's for me, and the salesmen, to know."

"Oh-ho." Aware he had touched a quick, Hugh smiled. "Did you overdo it? Getting a few back? Did you really have ten thousand copies out when you went back to press? Well — you can't be sure. If Lloyd keeps up the attack you may prove the reviewers wrong. God knows they are often enough."

"In this case they weren't." Hughie was pink with aggravation and he turned a particularly hostile glance on me. "Anyway, I don't want to talk about it here. This is a party."

To me, Hugh said, "Was I rubbing it in? I didn't intend that. I do think that letter will work to your advantage."

"Well, I hope so."

As Hugh and Joel moved off toward the bar, Hughie glared at me, pipe stem clamped so furiousy between his teeth I expected to hear a crack. "God damn it," he snapped, "we *are* overprinted on that Oakes book of yours and he knows it. What's more we should have taken Lerner's five thousand. He knows that too."

"Not necessarily. We'll come out all right."

"Didn't you see? The old man was laughing at us. From now on you can leave the print orders to me." Hughie spotted his father now centered in a new circle of admirers and he stomped off, making erratic progress toward him.

Later, I felt a hand on my sleeve, and I turned to find it was Hugh's. "I've got to be going along, Lloyd, but I do want to say my hat's off to you, all three of you. Gulliver's looks a very healthy child."

"Coming from you, that's really heartening."

"Incidentally, Lloyd. If you have a spare moment later in the week, come in and see me, will you? There are a couple of ideas I'd like to put up to you." He looked at his watch and said, "Oh my, I'm due uptown in five minutes. I'll be in serious trouble with Enid." With a smile and a wave, he was gone, taking some of the party's expectancy with him.

Next day, turning into Crowninshield's, I wondered if I was about to enjoy some revelations of Hugh's own state of mind, whether he was happy with his new associates, and whether he missed the old ones.

Corinne's smile was of the first magnitude. "Go right in, Lloyd. Hugh's waiting." Indeed he was, coming to greet me, brown eyes glowing welcome, beckoning me toward the nest of armchairs reserved for important visitors.

"It's like coming home," I said. "Nothing *seems* changed. I expected you'd be up in United's tower."

"No, not yet. I find I'm a little frightened of heights myself, but you'll be glad to know we're still battling it out at the meetings. I found myself quoting you this morning."

"You're winning, I hope. I don't want to hear that Paul Peeling's making any ground."

Hugh laughed. "No doubt we'll be arguing real estate forever, one of Parkinson's laws, to avoid more urgent business."

"That urgent business used to be inviting."

"Oh, it still is. Actually, I doubt you'll find significant change there. Perhaps your old adversaries have lost a tooth or two. Peeling's learning a few things about the business. Stickney's gone on to other enthusiasms, as I was sure he would, and Weld is proving useful."

Reaching for the new Crowninshield list, he offered it to me, and I flipped through, noting two titles of my own. "Everything," Hugh said, "goes along much as before."

"Then what's our business today, Hugh?"

"Oh, nothing much. I'm interested in how you're all getting on. I don't manage to pry much out of young Hugh. Fathers seem to have difficulty communicating with their sons. Do you find that so?"

"It *is* a surprise. I was certain when Will got to school age we'd be fairly pal-sy, but we draw further apart — except when trouble brings us close."

"Trouble?"

"Yes, he got into a little, at Housatonic. For an hour or so, Will and I were very much the brothers I'd had in mind."

Hugh nodded. "That's a good little school. We thought seriously about it for young Hugh." He seemed to be recalling some crisis in his son's education, but then went on, reflectively. "Perhaps in the end, our sons mature enough to talk to us openly, but only when they realize the conflict is a fairer one than they had imagined — and getting fairer for them daily."

We were silent, aware of office machines, bells, and voices at a distance, yet comfortable together.

"You wanted to ask about Gulliver's?"

Leaning forward, Hugh got out pouch and pipe. "Joel seems to be having a run of luck — first with his Luke Pentecost and now this Russian book. That'll go well, I expect." He searched my face. "You've certainly had your share too, with your new fiction. It's a list I'd be proud to have at Crowninshield's, and that biography of Faulkner was a crackerjack. How'd you get hold of that?"

"Through the author's wife. I had an option on her novel. When that didn't work out, she told me what her husband was up to."

Hugh laughed. "That's too much luck for one year. Tell me, what's your overall view? Do you think you're going to make it, Lloyd?"

"Yes."

"I was guessing you might be through the honeymoon stage and facing up to your lack of a backlist to float you. It's not easy having to produce a dozen moneymakers every season to survive."

"True. We're always falling a little short, having to go back to friends, and finding them less friendly, less eager to see us. It keeps me awake some nights — but I've never been much of a sleeper."

"Getting on all right with Joel?"

"Yes."

"He can be difficult when his luck's running." Hugh leaned back, enjoying some puffs from his pipe. "But then you're tolerant of your fellow man, Lloyd. That's one of the reasons you're missed around here."

"Am I?"

"Don't ever doubt it." The spectacles had slipped down his nose and, peering over the tops, Hugh's expression was benign. "Incidentally, when the fun of it does wear thin — and I can promise you it will — I trust you'll come back and see me. I'd have something to suggest." He raised his thick eyebrows.

"That's good to know."

"But it's a bit too soon for that, is it?"

"Yes." While Hugh peered into the bowl of his pipe and decided it needed rekindling, I felt bold enough to ask, "Do you have any regrets about letting in the United people? Hasn't that changed the nature of Crowninshield's?"

He pondered before replying, "*Times* have changed. The business has changed. But I don't believe I have, nor has my relation to this place. I've learned to adapt, but I still do the essentials. I've been doing them for thirty years and I know how." He put his long, delicately made, brown-specked hand flat on the table between us. "I tell you, Lloyd, I like sticking my head in the lion's mouth. It keeps me young. But I never plan on having it bitten off. Did you think I was in danger?"

"I did."

"I *will* leave it in too long one day, surely. But that's the joy of it." He searched me again. "Are you getting your share of the joy at Gulliver's?"

"Much of the time, just as here, is spent in anguish over decisions. I'm not sure I like making decisions unless, of course, they're the right ones."

"No one does, Lloyd."

There was a sound, like a whisper, as Corinne opened the sliding panel to say, "Your lunch is at twelve-thirty, Mr. Severance."

"Oh, thanks, Corinne." Hugh's stretch was the dismissal signal.

"Was there anything else?"

"Oh, yes," Hugh said in rising. "I guess it goes without saying. I've just heard from Edmond Pigott there's to be a new Bryce book, nonfiction, about his father and mother. Should be interesting, and I think we'll do well with it here at Crowninshield's. That's all."

I smiled. "No poaching, you mean?"

"Yes. I felt we should have an understanding on that."

"You have an option, of course. But you may not want to do the book."

"That's always possible." Hugh had taken his overcoat from the closet and, in putting it on, reached under the tails to give his jacket a downward snap. His eyes had regained their metallic luster. "But don't assume so, Lloyd. Give you a lift uptown?"

"No thanks, Hugh."

⋙ 19 ⋘

APRIL 11, 1969, was our fourth anniversary and in my calendar I had marked the noon hour as that of our birthday luncheon. I chose the restaurant, the San Marino, and presumed that Kay Rossbach would again provide her sumptuous, fourteen-layer Cointreau cake crowned by Gully and the Lilliputians.

But as I called for a reservation, Joel appeared at my desk to say that Kay had a cold and must be excused. There would be just the three of us. That was the first disappointment. While I knew the year-end figures were going to fall short of expectations, I had no idea of what was coming.

Joel, the last to arrive, came to the table preoccupied, muttering that one was always mistaken in imagining the traffic could not grow any worse. Hughie was grave as the Buddha. Looking at him, I was struck by an increasing resemblance to his father, a gray dappling at the temples, the nose emerging from flesh, cartilaginous, ornithic. The mouth, always cautious, was today stitched with gloom.

The first round of drinks and my toast to another year's survival failed to bring the good spirits and laughter of the former birthdays to our table.

"Buck up, you guys," I told them. "It's only money. We knew we couldn't increase earnings every year. There are bound to be some bad ones."

Joel and Hughie exchanged a glance, as though they had agreed on something and were uncertain about sharing it with me.

"What is it?" I asked. "What's it all about?"

From his breast pocket, Hughie brought forth a Gulliver letterhead and delivered it to me. "These are the estimated profit and loss figures that will go out to the stockholders on Monday. Read 'em and weep, Lloyd. We're going to be about sixty thousand bucks in the hole."

It was a letter to be signed by the three of us and it showed a projected operating loss for the fiscal year of a little over a hundred thousand dollars, only fractionally offset by the new juvenile department's success and two favorable reprint sales.

"Unless you know a good magician, that sixty thousand will come out of operating capital for next year," Joel said. "So we have some unpleasant decisions to make here today. That's why we're grumpy. We'll have to cut back on next year's list."

"By about half," Hughie said. "Which means twenty books at most. We have that many signed up, so we can quit reading manuscripts and go for a nice rest."

"We can take a fat salary cut," Joel suggested. "That won't do it all, but it'll help. Think you can live on about ten thousand next year, Lloyd?"

"No, but I suppose we can make some economies all across the board. We've hired new people recently and they may be a luxury. They're doing jobs we did at the start."

"If you mean Joe Driver," Hughie said, "forget it. Joe's auction of the Pentecost is what keeps this year from total disaster."

"And if you're thinking of Charlie Schranz," Joel said, "I am like-minded. He's doing beautiful books. However disappointing the content, they're uniformly handsome. That's our Charlie."

"Well, I certainly don't think we ought to make our economies in the *list*. That's cutting off our arms. There are books I want to do. I'm signing up a novel tomorrow."

"Oh, Christ, don't," Hughie said. "We're drowning in your two-thousand copy novels."

"Now that makes me mad, Hughie. What are you telling me?"

"We're telling you this is going to hurt," Joel said. "We're trying to impress that on you."

"You've done that. And what hurts is that you seem to have reached a decision without even consulting me. I gather you've known about these figures and talked about them and drawn up this letter without me. What *is* this? Why haven't you showed this to me until now? Why have you left me out?"

"You weren't in the office," Hughie said.

"You were off with Elena I think," Joel said.

"Well, I'll tell you something. It's a mistake to have a partners' meeting when one of the partners is away on business."

"When I drew up the figures," Hughie said, "they worried me. I wanted to talk about them, and Joel happened to be there. You weren't. It wasn't a meeting. *This* is a meeting."

"I thought it was a birthday party. Some party."

"Wine!" Joel beckoned to Mario. "Some birthday wine for us, please. You must have some of that good Orvieto. Could you bring us a nice cold bottle?"

"No wonder Kay didn't come," I said. "She knew it was no lunch for a cake. Everybody knew, didn't they? Everybody but me."

"A cake too!" Joel called. "Would you have anything like a birthday cake for Mr. Erskine?"

"No cake," I said. "Something more austere for me, please. Would you have a wormy apple, Mario?"

"If you had let me know, Mr. Erskine . . ." Mario said. "But there is no birthday cake. We have *zuppa inglese,* and profiteroles . . ."

"Ah-h, profiteroles." Joel clapped his hands. "They're good here. The very dark chocolate, like the White Tower's."

"White Tower's?"

"In London. It's the best Greek restaurant in the world."

"Oh, forgive my ignorance. I haven't enjoyed your broadening travel experiences, but if you say they're as good here, I'll have the profiteroles."

There was an instant's silence before Hughie laughed. Then Joel grinned, and our camaraderie was abruptly restored. With the wine, the good lunch, and four years' habit, we reverted to banter and entertainment, Joel telling a long, amusing story about Blanche Knopf's tyrannical Haitian cook and the luncheon party for Simone de Beauvoir.

But as we were finishing our entrées, Hughie brought us back to business. "A week from Friday we have the stockholders' meeting," he reminded us. "What do we tell 'em? That we'll need another hundred thousand dollars to get through next year?"

"That has a nice lilt to it," Joel said. "How does that sound to you, Lloyd? Can you learn the harmony to that by a week from Friday?"

"We'll have some explaining to do," Hughie said, "before they cough up another dime willingly. We'll need to say what went wrong this year and how we're going to correct it next. We're going to have to show we know our weak spots and what we can do to fix them."

"Oh, let's be honest about it," Joel said with a sharp look at me. "Overhead isn't our problem. We have a really skinny operation. The trouble is we're doing too many books that lose money. We know beforehand they aren't going to make a profit. Come on, Lloyd, look at the record. This year your three first novels were all clinkers."

"They were good books."

"That may be." Joel returned my gaze evenly. "But they didn't even meet their plate costs. You can't run a business that way."

"We have to take on authors and books we believe in. Some are going to prove out. One of those authors will write us a big book."

"You passed up the big book a couple of years ago."

"The Swimming?" I cried, stung. "You mean Oliver Swimming? *Crown of Priapus* is a pretentious, bad book. We all agreed to that."

"It had big reviews, favorable reviews, all over," Joel insisted.

"And bad ones too," I replied. "The perceptive ones were bad. Come on, Hughie. You were in on it, say something."

"We were wrong," Hughie said. "We should have taken that book."

"Why? Because it made money? Look, I know we have to turn a profit on the list, but we didn't start Gulliver House to publish books that simply make money. We could do that anywhere. We agreed to publish the best books we could find, and that's what our name would stand for. There's bound to be some difference of taste between us. I don't happen to agree with Joel about Luke Pentecost. Pentecost is more interested in his quirky propaganda than in character . . ."

"Luke Pentecost has made us a lot of money," Joel said. "I'm sorry about that. I apologize. I'll try not to do it again. I'll try not to bring in any more profitable books. If you like I can do public penance at the stockholders' meeting. I'll show my hair shirt. Each of the stockholders can have a go at my bare back with the cat-o'-nine-tails, one stroke for each thousand of overcall."

To Hughie I said, "Of course we have to make money, but we don't have to abandon our editorial policy. We don't have to publish junk . . . or do you also think we do?"

"Of course not. Neither does Joel."

"I wouldn't know how else to operate," I said. "I can only choose the books I believe in, books I think are good books."

"The thing is," Hughie said. "You aren't always right about that."

"Neither are you," I said. "All three of us do stupid things. I'll admit to my share. But I was working on the assumption that you don't make a remark like that to your partner." I stood. My hand was trembling as I took a twenty from my wallet and dropped it beside Joel's plate. "That should cover my lunch, but I'm not enjoying it and I'm not staying for any more of this shit."

"Hey," Joel called after me. "Don't go away mad. What about your profiteroles?"

From the checkroom I saw they were both watching me, Hughie with an apprehensive smile, Joel's hand raised in propitiation.

At the paperback stand in Grand Central, I browsed, thinking that I ought to go back to the office and come to an understanding with Joel and Hughie, but I was not sure what that understanding should be. On impulse, I went down to the lower level and boarded the 2:40 for New Canaan.

A shake, a cedar shingle, has a life expectancy of fourteen years. New from the bundle, it has one of the most enticing perfumes I know. Sweet as a cut into fresh bread, or the woods after a rain, and yet with a hint of bitterness — it is like longing.

The smell is only one of the appeals of my wood-shingled roof. It is a violation of the town fire code. I can renew the entire roof only with thin, industrial leaves of asphalt. But I can patch it. I can pry up the adjoining, overlapping shingles, trying to avoid splitting them as I squeeze beneath to extract their nails and to replace the soggy, fourteen-year veterans.

Despite the splinters and bruised knees, there is a satisfaction in driving home the final nails, sealing in the comfort and shelter below, standing off to view the patch, like a fresh bandage on a piece of good surgery which, given time, will heal and be one with the rest.

The roof, the mossy section at the southwest corner, drew me aloft. There, ripping away, making a four-foot clearing, chips and rusty nails showering down onto the azaleas, I found some focus for my anxieties.

From here I saw the Ogleby wagon approaching. Helen Ogleby was driving, Andy beside her, and they both got out to observe me.

"How come you're home so early?" Andy called.

"The world was too much with me."

"What are you doing?"

"Therapy."

"Don't take too many pains, Lloyd," Helen called. "Andy has plans for that roof."

As Helen drove away, I expected Andy's curiosity to bring her up the ladder, but instead our back door slammed.

I found Andy in the kitchen, looking at a booklet of photographs and diagrams of a solar heater.

"It's the Solveg," she said. "It's Swedish and I think we ought to get one. We could pay for it in a year the way fuel costs are going."

"I've had a scrap with Joel and Hughie," I said. "I'm trying to decide what to do."

Andy looked up, puzzled, then back at the book, turned a page. "Do? What do you mean?"

"We're in trouble, the kind everyone's predicted from the start. We can't meet our running expenses. According to my partners, it's my books that are the dead weight, and I made a mistake in passing up the Swimming — *that* piece of junk. Well, it's my books that give Gulliver's its class — four titles on the *Times* list of the hundred best books of the year, those stunning reviews of Mary Whetstone's novel. Jesus, they forget the NBA for Oakes's *Frog Pond*. That's what brings good books to us. That's what *attracts* the commercial books. They know that as well as I do, and they refuse to acknowledge it."

"So? Do you want to look for another job?"

"Of course not, but I can't play scapegoat for them. That's not in the agreement."

"Well . . ." Andy turned another page. "If you're asking my opinion . . ."

"I am, and I wish you'd stop looking at that catalog. This is important."

She looked up but kept a finger between the pages. "I don't think you're in any position to quit. If they're being unkind, I suppose it's because you're in financial trouble. That's realistic, isn't it? You're always telling me to be realistic about my work. I guess you have to live with realism too. You can't have people stroking you *all* the time. There's probably more truth in what they're telling you than you like to admit. Your books *have* lost money. There's no denying it. Why not just accept that and figure out a way to do better."

"Thanks. Now you can go back to Ogleby's solar heaters."

"Well, you asked me."

"I'm in a fight with them, don't you understand? We're down to some compromise of principle, and I'm not giving in to them. As for cutting back the list, I'll refuse. I'm going to propose we raise more money. Our reputation is excellent. If our backers aren't willing to provide for us, we can get it elsewhere. I'll have to ask Loomy about that."

Andy's eyes dropped to the catalog and she turned another page.

I answered the pantry phone. It was Joel's voice, saying, "Lloyd, I'm really very sorry about lunch today. I was rude and insensitive. You must know how I feel about you, and all that roughhouse was to be taken in context. Hughie and I had decided you needed an alarm, that's all. You know how he is. I mean you do realize that any possibility of failure is a hundred times worse for him than for you or me. He has a nightmare about Gulliver's fizzling and his having to crawl back to his old man for help. I'd had a full dose of his panic, and it got to me."

"I *am* sore," I said. "I suspect I'll continue to be. Since I left you I've been thinking what I ought to do about it. We certainly can't work together as partners unless we're equal and trust each other in every way."

"That's why I called you."

"I feel you've been keeping me out of financial sessions."

"You haven't been interested."

"That isn't true."

"From now on we won't mention the word money unless you're there. How's that?"

"I'm serious. I don't think it's time for cutting back, nor for timidity of any kind. If we do need more money to operate next year, we'll raise it. If the backers aren't willing to provide it, we must find more backers. I was just going to call Pitcher about that, the possibility of going public."

"I think he'll tell you it's too early for that. Phil Lerner and Dick Sondheim were talking about it last week and they felt . . ."

"Oh? Another financial meeting? When *are* they?"

"No, no. Just in the most casual way. Jesus, Lloyd."

"Joel, I'm not going to be pushed around. That letter is not to go out to the stockholders until I've had a chance to talk to Pitcher and think about ways of raising more capital. And another thing. While I'm airing grievances, this is a good time to bring up the London trips. You'll recall it was supposed to alternate between us. This is the third year running for you, isn't it?"

"I've continued to do the London trip because I've built up the associations. The British publishers and agents know me now, and there's an advantage for all of us in that."

"It's important for me too, you know, to keep up with the London people. As it happens, there's a particular reason for me to go this year. The new Bryce is finished, and if I were in London there's just a chance we might get it. That would gladden our treasurer's heart. As for keeping up the house contacts, I can do that too."

There was a hesitation. "We'll talk about it — O.K.?"

"We certainly will."

A few minutes later, Hughie called, saying, "Lloyd, I had no idea you'd be offended. I thought we understood each other better. I was just trying to make it clear we're shook up. If I was too blunt . . ."

"Not a matter of bluntness," I said. "I'm all for that. I want to be in on these decisions, that's all. I've just been telling Joel that I want to reopen the financing business tomorrow. Will you be available around eleven?"

"I can be."

"Good," I said. "Good night, Hughie."

Upstairs I found Andy getting ready for bed. At the moment I entered the room she was taking off her brassiere. She dropped it across the stool at her dressing table. As she bent forward, peeling panties over buttocks, the mirror reflected a softness, the bluish white of her breasts and thighs, and she returned my glance there, surprised by my sudden desire. She went briskly toward the bathroom, closing the door behind her.

I undressed, put on pajama bottoms, and opened the door. Andy was deep in her bath. Green water lapped at her chin and the islands of her knees. Hair ends floated about her shoulders. She looked up from her steamy pool, challenging me, as though I had violated some reverie.

"Tell me about the solar heat," I said.

"You're not interested."

"Yes. Now I am. I got the stuff that was bothering me off my chest in a couple of phone calls. Now I can focus on solar heat. What's it all about?"

She watched me suspiciously. "Oh, you know what it is — a reflector on the roof that picks up energy from the sun and stores it."

"When the sun shines."

"Yes, of course when the sun shines. This Swedish one is efficient enough so Clip thinks it can save half our fuel bills."

"Is that what he does in New York? I thought he was raising money for the Democratic party."

"You see? You didn't want to know. You just wanted to ridicule it. It doesn't have anything to do with the committee."

"Well, why not? Why is he diddling with Swedish plumbing when he's supposed to be doing Connecticut politics? Why isn't he talking about taxes and jobs now? I thought that was why he opened an office in town, to get to those guys while they're at work."

"I knew you were going to do that — knock him. Clip is a sensitive man." She rose suddenly, dripping, bending to open the drain and snatching a towel from the rack to wrap herself. Standing before the misty mirror, she frisked the wet tendrils of her hair. "He listens to people when they talk. He isn't so focused on his job that he can't respond to the people around him — has enough interest in his son not to be offensive about his girl."

"I didn't like Will's girl." I closed the toilet lid and settled on it. "You don't seem to have the least notion of what's happening to me — that everybody is turning on me and for the first time in my life I haven't any idea who I am. I don't know if I'm some huge fake of an editor, if I ever knew anything about the job, or if I just had a streak of luck and deceived everyone, myself included, until I got found out, first by Hugh Severance, now by Joel and Hughie. And you're indifferent. No — you seem to rejoice in it."

She tucked the towel more firmly around her and selected a toothbrush from a cup on the basin's rim. "You forget that I was fired from that place. You fired me. Do you really expect me to ignore that and keep up with all the squabbles and infatuations you have among yourselves?"

"I'm in trouble. Don't you understand — or don't you care?"

"What do you want me to do about it? Tell you you're right and everyone else is wrong? What about me for a change?"

"What *about* you? I think you've given up."

"Oh-h, you're so wrong, Lloyd. I'm just beginning to look out for myself."

"In Stamford? That's pastime. That's a crush on a man who flatters you."

"You can't conceive of a different way from yours, can you? You can't imagine a person sincerely interested in a better society and working for it. You can't imagine a woman might find that worthwhile."

As Andy started for the door, I reached for her arm and she recoiled, snatching it away. "Leave me alone," she said. "I'm going to sleep in the guest room."

Rage boiled into her face, twisting it in a contempt and ugliness that called forth my own anger. My hand rose in a threat but it was stayed by strong cords of inhibition.

"Go on," she said. "Do it. I'll hit you back harder."

I lunged for her, gathering her around the waist, taking her weight on my hip, lifting her off the floor, half carrying her, half falling through the bathroom door and onto the bedroom carpet beyond. I was trying to struggle on top, to get a lock on arm or neck, but to my surprise her weight and strength matched mine and she was struggling free of me. Her loose hand came crashing full into my face, stunning nose, cutting tooth into lip. Her other hand ripped at my pajama cord as her own towel fell away.

Naked, we rolled across the floor, clutching at each other and struggling to get free. As shock and numbness waned and I tasted blood, felt the torn flesh, I was appalled that she had struck me in the face with such vengeance and I willed reprisal — a handful of her hair, a vicious retaliating crunch of my own bone into her vulnerable parts, a torturing of soft breast, swaying, open to my hand — but I could not, as though some schoolboy referee stood by, cheeks puffed and whistle at the ready.

I was trying to pull her left arm behind her back, to twist it against her shoulder joint, and as she gave slowly to my hammerlock, comprehending it, her teeth closed on my ear, sharply enough so that I hesitated, let up the pressure on her arm enough for her to snatch it free, and we rolled apart, righting ourselves to face off again, crouched, gasping, and I sprang, taking her at the waist and carrying her off balance, struggling to pin her shoulders to floor while her legs, flailing powerfully, bucked me from one side to the other. As I grasped her wrists, forced them out and down, her grimacing, spitting face whipped from side to side, and then her knee came up like a piston head, thudding hard into my genitals. I gasped at the lightning of pain which split me to my chest. I rolled off, doubled, groaning.

Andy was up and closing on me, her face fierce.

"Enough," I cried out, arm raised defensively. "This is ridiculous." I struggled to my feet, panting, catching breath, dabbing at trickles of blood, feeling eyes and mouth for damage that would need explanation tomorrow. The victor bent to pick up her towel.

✧ 20 ✧

I SHY FROM BIG DECISIONS. I neglect them, put them off, trusting in Providence to push the door of choice. I believe in fate, a predetermined order to our lives, and fear too great an interference there. Like a character, only occasionally a principal one, in a sprawling, episodic novel of my times, I hesitate to encroach upon the author, who has a far greater understanding of my destiny than I.

So, from the summer of 1967 into the autumn of 1970, I was unable to alter the double course of my life. My heart went home with Flavia Moore, and often I did too, but twenty years of habit, a distaste for nastiness, for unkindness and expense, as well as a deep admiration for and commitment to Andy, kept me commuting home to my house on Oenoke Ridge Road, going out to meetings and parties, acting my old role while I rehearsed for a new one.

Sometimes Flavia was understanding, saying, "Oh, I *know*, Lloyd. I wouldn't love you as I do if you could close Andy out of your life so quickly. Of course you have a tremendous feeling for her and you can't bring a twenty-year marriage down in one thumping crash. I know it'll take time, but I'll wait for you, however long it takes, years if I must — because we're so

absolutely right. Meantime I'm happy being with you whenever I can."

"All the same," I said to her, "I can't see so pretty a girl
sitting alone in her apartment night after night while I get up
the nerve to break off with my wife. Won't there be other
guys? Flavia, how steadfast *is* your heart?"

She smiled, one eye narrowing coquettishly. "Don't ask. Oh,
Lloyd, don't ask that."

But she insisted that Andy knew. She would say that at least
once in the course of our ritual, twilight drink at The Bank.
It was often at the exact moment when the hand of the wall
clock reached the half-hour mark, when to let it slip for another
moment would give me a reprieve, another thirty minutes with
her knee against mine, my hand in hers, a mingling of pleasure
and guilt.

Then she would say, "Oh, don't agonize so. She knows.
Andy knows where you are. She knows we're together."

I did not really believe that Andy knew — at least not ex-
plicitly. Oh, she knew I was close to Flavia, that Flavia knew
all I did about my work and responded to Gulliver events like
some other part of my own brain. She also knew that I found
her physically attractive and enjoyed being with her for that
reason.

Still, I don't think it had occurred to Andy that Flavia and I
were lovers. She was so sure that I was bound to her by inde-
structible emotions, and by my own word. She trusted me,
trusted Flavia too for that matter, and simply could not accept
what was so close and so obvious. I wore my faithlessness like
a scarlet carnation.

But what I could not do in a stroke, I could do by inches, by
the steady pressure of desire, and the hope of starting anew.
I wanted the truth out now. I wanted to be caught. I took
ever greater risks, making my real relationship to Flavia ever
more apparent. Over the painfully long weekends I called her
from the house. During the week I took her places where we
were likely to be seen by New Canaan friends, and I took her

along to the American Booksellers Association meeting in Washington that spring.

When, in passing, I mentioned this to Andy, she caught me up. "Flavia was with you?" she asked. "You took her along? Isn't that rather silly? Doesn't it make for dangerous talk at the office, particularly at a time when you're feeling vulnerable there?"

"I don't see the risk. Everyone knows how I depend on her."

"It's more than depending if you take her along on trips. You're being a fool over that girl. She makes you do just what she wants."

"I guess that's true, Andy. I'm drawn to her because she makes me feel good. I need that more than ever now."

"Just so you know — she uses you. She twists you right around her little finger, and I'm sure the people at the office find it just as distasteful as I do."

"You don't understand how much I'm attracted to Flavia."

It was a critical wounding. I saw the effect in her eyes, but she said, "Well, go ahead then. Why don't you have an affair with her and get it out of your system?"

"I am." In the silence between us I heard a tock, a faint but unmistakable cracking of heartwood.

"You've slept with her?"

"For some time."

"And then you've come to me?"

"Yes."

"I don't understand. But it disgusts me — more than I can possibly tell you."

"It seems to work well enough."

"Where do you go with her — some hotel room?"

"Her apartment."

"While Ernest is out?"

"At first, yes. But Ernest is gone. They've separated."

"What do you want to do — marry her?"

"It's in her mind. She's mentioned it."

"Is it in yours? Is that what you want?"

And here my woodsman's courage failed. The crest was moving across the sky and the terrible noise was all around, a wrenching and cracking of the trunk. "No," I said. "I haven't got so far yet. I'm only enjoying myself."

"Go on, then. I'll be doing the same."

"All right."

"You've been so sneaky about this. I suppose everybody at the office knows. Everyone knows but me. I'm the last."

"I don't know that they know. If they know, I doubt they care."

"Joel knows. Kay knows. Hughie knows. They've all been laughing, haven't they? Having a good laugh about me?"

"No one laughs about this."

"You're going *on* with it?"

"Yes. I guess so. If I go to London I'll need someone to help with the reading. She's never been abroad, and she wants to come along."

"*She* wants? I don't care what that *cunt* wants." Andy was staring toward the light on the piano and I saw tears leaking silently and copiously across her face. After a few minutes she rose and walked to the Chinese bowl and, seizing it, she hurled it against the mantelpiece, where it shattered and rained down upon the hearth.

Turning to me she said, "Take off your clothes."

We went into the bedroom together, solemnly, as though to judgment, and there we made love in terrible anger and passion.

Joel was on hands and knees before his office fireplace, tinkering with his capricious damper. Beside him lay a neat bundle of kindling.

"Elena's seen a rough draft of Morgan Bryce's new book," I said. "It's nonfiction. The family. She thinks it's going to be a sensation."

"So?" Joel sat up, brushing soot from his hands.

"She's sending it to Hugh, of course, but there's a chance, if I were to go and see Morgan, we might get it."

Rising and going to his desk, he said, "You really think Hugh would let Bryce go?"

"He might. If it were *too* sensational."

"Scandalous, you mean? Law suits? Then we won't want it either."

"You've never been enthusiastic about Morgan."

"You mean I've never been *right* about Bryce. Ah-h well . . ." Joel smiled. "I never claimed to be infallible. And listen, if you can get it by going to London, I'm all for you. I'm not against your going to London, Lloyd. I'm against my not going — but I'm keeping an open mind." He tried the soil in his potted dracaena and thoughtfully irrigated it from a toby jug. "When would you want to go — next month? March, I find, is best. You avoid the Frankfurt crush and the British aren't all off on holiday yet. Of course, everyone else from New York will be there too, but that's what you want, isn't it, to have everyone know? Let me think a few minutes. Let me sort through the little deviousnesses I had in mind and see which you might perform. Incidentally" — he was tilting back in his chair now, rocking, studying the oval of molding overhead — "did you hear the cheerful news on financing? Phil Lerner came by last night and told Hughie he'd had a good year and might spot us some operating expenses."

"Lerner? That's remarkable. What's he want in return?"

"I presume he's just concerned about his investment in us, but we'd surely hear from him about running a taut publishing business. Maybe we should take a lesson from Phil. He's no shnook."

"Maybe. Maybe he *has* something to tell us."

"I'm glad you feel that way," Joel said, nodding, and began some notes on his desk pad. "Well, here we go on London. There's Deutsch. I put the needle in André regularly for a chance at Heinrich Böll. Can you give him a prod?"

"Sure. Give me all your errands."

Joel smiled. "You're taking Flavia?"

"She's never been — never abroad at all. And she'll be useful."

"I'm sure."

"She's paying her own way."

"Have a good trip."

As I left the office, Philip Lerner was coming through the front door and I paused to ask, "Is this true, Phil, that you're optimistic about us?"

Eyes brightening, he said, "Oh, I like what you fellows have done with Gulliver — and you know, Lloyd, you could turn a profit next year if you tightened up here and there. Comb that backlist and you'd turn up some reprint sales."

"You going to bail us out?"

He considered, nodded. "Sure. I'd want to secure it of course — against stock. Think about it."

Later, telling Loomis Pitcher about it, he said, "Yes, I guess it's encouraging. Lerner knows more about survival than any of us, but . . ."

"What?"

"Looking at it in the coldest, most actuarial light, Gulliver's is not an attractive investment. That may change for better or worse, but we've learned what a lot of push it takes to get a new house rolling. What do *you* think of Gulliver's future?"

"Earnings?"

"I know about them. I was thinking about how you guys are getting on. What does financial trouble do to the relationship? Do you lie awake nights blaming each other?"

"Yes."

"Well, Christ, Lloyd. Is it worth it — to have your own imprint? Any one of you can have a perfectly good job at a going outfit — just for the asking."

"Yes. We are quarreling, calling the kettle black, but I'm sure none of us wants to quit, however tough it gets."

"O.K. then, I'd take Lerner's money, but I'd be careful of his getting more control. If there's any new stock issued, all the investors should be in on it."

~§ 21 §~

FLAVIA LOOKED STUNNING, easily the prettiest, most desirable girl in the bar of the White Tower. It was a new dress, some kind of gray wool, but flowered, cinched with a wide, russet belt and a huge, harness brass. She looked a Londoner born.

"You've been shopping," I said, planting a kiss on her cheek. "It's lovely. Where'd you get it?"

"Harrod's. I didn't intend to. I just put my nose in to see what it was like and" — she looked into her lap — "it spoke to me. 'Yank,' it said, 'take me home,' so I did."

"It was a good idea. What's that you're drinking?"

"Pym's. Number one."

"You've gone mad dog." I asked the bar man for a martini. "What else did you do today?"

"The works. The changing-of-the-guard and then an hour at the Tate. A sandwich at Fortnum's, which was crowded as you said, and to the Abbey this afternoon, topped off with a stroll in Hyde Park. The Serpentine was wholly lovely — the light, oh my! I even squeezed in some work. Two books came — a thing about Charles the First, from Heinemann's I think, much too special, and a novel from Edmond Pigott, which is a clinker. Don't waste your time. Anything on Morgan?"

"Rumors. One goes that he has a runaway girl down there.

While her family tries to ransom her, she and Morgan perform unspeakable acts for an audience."

She laughed. "I bet he made that one up."

"It does have his mark, doesn't it?"

"Did you call Zoe?"

"She thinks Edmond might let me look at his manuscript — as a friend, you know. We'll see. I'm having lunch with him tomorrow."

"Who else did you see?"

"A gaggle of publishers. All affable. I've got a pocketful of notes and five books. My case feels as if it had bricks in it, which is probably about right. Maybe I'll just leave it in the check room. The glamor does wear off as you trudge around. Whoosh. I'm *tired*." I took a grateful sip of my martini. "It's good to see *you're* enjoying it."

Her face darkened. "Well, yes. I love it, just as you said, maybe more, but is it going to be like this, me doing the sights all day and then back to the hotel at night for a wade through the slush pile?"

"Wait till I get a night's rest. I haven't forgotten about the theater. Maybe tomorrow."

"Don't we get out with some of these biggies you see? I thought they had you out to Hampstead Heath or somewhere for a taste of the real Yorkshire pudding and a look at their hollyhocks."

"Joel said Alan MacLean will ask us. I'm seeing Alan on Thursday, but I can't very well put it up to him."

"If Andy were along you'd be having all sorts of social life, wouldn't you? Inviting people for dinner and going off to stay with them for the weekend?"

"If Andy were here I'd be eating in a less good restaurant."

"I like the restaurant."

"We'll do all sorts of marvelous things. I can take some time off later in the week. We could go up to Oxford."

"Do you think I could come along to lunch tomorrow?"

"With Edmond? It's at a club, a men's club."

"Oh."

We were seated for dinner in the largest of the restaurant's several rooms and we could watch the diners being led through to the others, a parade of good-looking, affluent men and women, and Flavia's spirits revived as we ordered and then weighed the matter of a white wine to go with her sole and my veal.

I had begun a game of identifying the occupations of the men as they passed into the back room, or up the stairs to the right of us.

"Doctor," Flavia said of a man with a beard, "a really expensive, Harley Street gynecologist. I know by the misogynous curl of the nether lip. No question. And that one's a baker, a big English muffin tycoon. What *do* they call English muffins here? American muffins? Is it like French leave?"

"That's Joe," I said, waving. "Your English muffin man is Joe McGrath. You know, the *Symbolist Review*."

"No," she said. "I don't know."

Joe's glance swept by, lingering just long enough to gather in Flavia beside me, but he did not falter in his progress through the room.

"Well," she said. "So much for Joe. He's an old buddy?"

"He used to live in New York."

"He knows Andy?"

"Yes."

"That's why, in case you're wondering."

"I don't think he was sure who I was. Does it matter? You want me to get him? Bring him back?"

"No." She had turned overcast again. "Never mind."

"Look, you're not going to spoil this. We've come to London for a good time together. This is one of the best restaurants in the world. What's the matter now?"

"The matter is that I don't like my role. I don't like being tucked under the rug at the Connaught. I don't like being your dirty little secret. Can't you see that?"

"Darling." It was an awkward word on my lips, but it

started tears to my eyes. "I love you. You know that. What more do you want to know?"

"What you're going to do about it."

"I'm going to ask you to marry me when I can. That's what I'm going to do. We've been over this. I'm planting the idea of divorce, getting Andy used to it — but I have to do this gradually. I can't simply poleax her. Don't you understand?"

"Oh, do I ever. I suffer every day over what I've done to Ernest Moore. My God, when I think about his loneliness and misery and realize I've brought it all on him, that I'm responsible for that . . . If you only knew how I loathe myself for making people unhappy. But Lloyd, I can't help it. None of us can help it. You can't go on living with someone you don't love. That's even crueler. Don't you see?"

"How do you know that? If you change your partner every time you change your heart, don't you wind up as miserable as if you stick it out? Given that the courts are behind in their work, how can they keep up with all the changing hearts? How is yours, by the way — changing?"

"I'm getting rid of it," she said. "It just gets me in trouble. Why? Are you worried about it?"

"I worry about everything."

"In that case," she said carefully, "I think I'd better go home."

"You must stop this now, Flavia. It's not like you to whine and make a fuss. We're here together with the whole of London to ourselves. You're not really going to spoil it are you?"

She whirled the wine in her glass, studying it, sipped it, turned to look at me. "No," she said with a distracted smile, "I won't spoil it for you."

But back at the Connaught, where I had hoped to get in some reading before I grew too sleepy to concentrate, I felt Flavia was eluding me, changing from the woman who was effortlessly understanding and responsive into a woman who resisted me and made of every opportunity a difficulty.

Perching on the windowsill I said, "What *is* this? Suddenly you're doing some kind of number. I don't understand. Are you ill?"

"No."

"Why are you being so abrasive?" I rose and went to her. In spite of her quizzical expression, I was sure of myself and took her hands, pulling her to her feet. She came to me like a helpless ship being snubbed into her berth, and as I put my arms around her I said, "I love you, Flavia. More than ever. More than anyone. You know that."

When I kissed her she was warm but passive, and after a moment she took her lips from mine to lay her head against my shoulder, as though she were thinking. Then, pressing her hands gently against my chest, she released herself. With the slightest shake of her head she moved off to get her wrapper and disappeared into the bath.

As I looked through the proofs on the desk I was thinking that it would be all right once we got into bed, where all difficulties could be resolved. But when Flavia emerged from the bath, she moved around the room with an unaccustomed primness. Finding a blanket in the top of the mirrored wardrobe, she said, "You're not going to like this, but I'm sleeping on that thing."

"Flavia, don't be ridiculous. If you don't want to make love, that's all right. There's no need to camp out."

She went on with her work at the sofa, tucking the blanket around the cushions and taking a pillow from the bed. When it was finished, she crawled in, pulling covers to her chin and turning away from me.

In pajamas, I knelt beside her, trying to kiss her once more.

"Please, no, Lloyd," she said. "Allow me this tonight. We'll figure it out in the morning."

I tried to read for a while, turning occasionally to look at her, curled there like a child. I said aloud, "God damn it!" but she did not reply. I lay awake for an hour or more, listening to her breathing, and to the sound of traffic in Carlos Place.

The passing of cars became infrequent and tires whispered on pavement wet with early morning rain.

The moment I caught sight of Edmond Pigott awaiting me in a semicircle of the Garrick's dark, leather chairs, wire-rimmed spectacles descendent, an amiable, pedagogic bird with his beak in the *Observer,* I felt confident of his friendship, the justice of my case, the persuasiveness of my tongue, and the likelihood of some favorable outcome.

Edmond's joy at seeing me was equally reassuring. "How marvelous," he bubbled, "to have you here at last. Must get you a drink." A jingle at the table bell brought an elderly steward wearing military decorations at his breast. When I had ordered, Edmond went on, "And you didn't bring Andy? What a pity. You're a fine chap, Lloyd, but somehow more ornamental with your lovely wife along. I was hoping to construct some kind of party around you two."

"I'm sorry. You should have warned me, Edmond. But of course, if it's simple loveliness you want, I can offer my assistant. She's here to do the reading."

"Ah-h." Edmond's eyebrows arched, just perceptibly. "The dark-haired girl."

"You remember Flavia, Flavia Moore?" I was anticipating the joy a little party at Edmond's would bring her.

"Oh, very well. Yes, we must see about that. Must see what nights we're free. How *is* Andy? Doing her ceramics is she?"

"Actually, she seems to be turning to politics. She has a part-time job in the county Democratic office in Stamford."

He nodded approval. "And how's it going at Gulliver's?"

"Very well, really, given the difficulties. Everyone says you can't do quality books and last long enough to build a backlist, but I think we're doing just that, Edmond. We've been lucky. One book always gallops up to the rescue. It isn't luck so much as good will. Friends, like yourself, tend to steer us a choice one."

"I'll try not to disappoint you there. Have you had a look at that novel I sent round? It's interesting I think."

"No more than a glance, I'm afraid. Flavia read it. I gather it's intelligent. Probably good reviews, but I doubt we'd sell it. It's a risk, Edmond. When we take a risk now, it must be on a big book."

"Still, you can't have all big ones."

"I'm looking for *one* big one."

Edmond smiled as if he'd read the name Bryce in my mind, but he welcomed the matronly waitress who hovered with menus. "Ah, good, here's our chance to order. The vichyssoise is *quite* good."

When this was done I said, "Edmond, I know you well enough to go right to it. I want to know whatever you can tell me about Morgan Bryce's book. I feel I have a right to ask."

"Yes, I rather thought that was what you had up your sleeve, and I'd like to help, but I'm not altogether sure . . ."

"You mean that it's Crowninshield's option."

"That, yes."

"And I'm his editor. It was my enthusiasm for Morgan that brought him to Crowninshield's when *nobody* was interested. I brought Morgan to you. I think he'll want to come to Gulliver's for this book, particularly if he's made to see that these ethics of editor and author are more important than the legal ones. My God, *nobody* pays any attention to options anymore."

"I'm not so sure of that," he said.

"Edmond, you know the realities."

"Yes, there are many. One of them is what's best for an author who, thanks to you, has his choice of American publishers. How would *you* advise him in his own best interests?"

"That he couldn't possibly do any better than to be with a young house, one wholly committed to pushing his new book because the house's very survival depends upon it."

"But, however remote, there's a chance Gulliver's will fail. You've had good luck but you're just now getting into the endurance test. Can you survive some lean years?" Edmond blinked. "It's a risk, surely. You're taking it willingly, but I don't see why Morgan Bryce should take it as well."

"He'll benefit from the risk exactly as we will, suffer from caution exactly as we might."

Edmond considered. "Well, I can see no harm in telling you this. He's calling it *Fitchy Gules*."

"What are fitchy gules?"

"Heraldry. The fitchy is a cross sharpened at the point, like a dagger. Gules is its color — red. From the family arms. The book is about his mother, his being a bastard, of course, and about his father's attitude toward both of them. It's moving — almost too much so, you know. There will surely be problems."

"Not in the writing, certainly. He cannot write a bad sentence, let alone a bad book."

"No, but we have a rather different sense of taste here. I think Hugh is sensitive to that. It's conceivable Hugh won't want to do it."

"Hugh is sometimes numb on fiction, but never on autobiography. He won't pass it up."

Edmond smiled. "So, in spite of the palace revolt, you keep an admiration for Hugh?"

"Never more so," I said. "He's sixty-three and he seems like a youth, doesn't he? I'll confess that the moment I'm through with lunch here, I'm going up to his tailor, hoping he'll make me look something like Hugh."

"I'm glad to hear that. Important to keep up with our friends. They're trusts, really."

"Specifically, what are the problems with the Bryce?"

"The book may offend. There's a question of libel. People, still alive, may be hurt. I don't see that's necessary. If Morgan wants to do this explicit homosexual stuff, why not in fiction? Or leave it out. I've suggested both."

"And what does Morgan say?"

"He doesn't. No answer at all, to *three* letters. I've asked him to come and have a talk about it. No response. I'm sure he's still down in Sussex. All sorts of stories."

"I've heard some. I cabled him from New York and hoped there'd be something waiting at the hotel, but nothing so far." We were finishing lunch with mangoes and Stilton cheese. "Edmond, will you let me see it — not as a publisher, but as a friend, his and yours?"

"I can hardly do that until I have some authority, until I know Hugh's plans."

"Where does Hugh stand on revisions?"

"I hope he'll go along with us. Much stronger case if we stand together on it."

"Supposing Morgan refuses?"

"I hope he won't."

"But if he does?"

"We shall have to see our counselors."

"If they advise caution?"

"We could hardly go against their advice."

"I was thinking of going down there. Perhaps I'll rent a car and see if I can smoke him out."

Still smiling, Edmond said, "Clearly we aren't going to resolve the Morgan Bryce problem at this luncheon, are we?" He stole a look at his watch. "I'm afraid we must be getting along then — you to your tailor and I to some chores in Great Russell Street."

At the Garrick's door we stood looking into the sluggish traffic for an empty cab and I was wondering if he had forgotten about the invitation, if the idea of having Flavia and me around had escaped him, or if he had withdrawn it.

"Tell me, Edmond," I said. "Did I speak out of turn?"

"Not at all. I understand perfectly."

"Good. I had the feeling I'd offended you somehow, disappointed you in some way, and couldn't make out if it had to do with Hugh, or Andy, or whatever."

"Not a bit of it. Oh, there's one now. You'd better hop for it. There's a chap across the way looking."

"It's yours, Edmond. I'm going to walk."

"Right-o." He touched me on the elbow and dashed, coattails flying, toward the empty cab. It crossed my mind that he knew something, had heard, or picked it up in the telepathy that passes through the publishing community, crossing the ocean as easily as it crosses Madison Avenue, that all was not well at Gulliver's. It was a nettling thought.

Walking through Piccadilly Circus, which was giddy as a midway with pretty, long-legged girls and spurious continentals in floppy hats and sherpa coats, I felt the onset of depression. Edmond had eluded me, made off in that cab with some small but essential hope. I felt the ache of rejection and it led backward, like a fly line disappearing into the mists of memory but hooked into something forgotten yet still alive, sliding through the dark, submarine caves and tunnels of my subconsciousness.

I could not shake the thought that he had censured me, countering my request that he entertain Flavia with a dose of disapproval. But of course that was ridiculous. If ethics were on Edmond's mind, they were of a different sort. He had disagreed tartly about honoring options and at that moment had taken the moral high ground. I had never quite regained it.

Then it occurred to me that what Edmond had in mind was, not ethics at all, but Hugh Severance. Of course Edmond was wary of offending Hugh. Whatever the future of Gulliver's, Hugh was a far more menacing enemy than I. In that instant of perception I was even more determined to have Morgan Bryce's book.

In the Albemarle Arcade, a ticket broker, a gnome of a man in a stiff collar, assured me, "Oh, yes, sir, I think you'll enjoy the *Richard*. Haven't seen it m'self, but customers tell me Sir Ralph is very good indeed. I can give you two in the stalls, and nice they are, full center. Seven o'clock curtain, mind. That'll be four pounds ten, sir."

With his slip in my pocket I felt newly armored for the night before me. Sir Ralph held the key to Flavia's contrary heart, and if it went well — probably just fatigue last night — we could go on to the Café Royale for supper, get caught up in all the civilized pleasure of this town. Something interesting was going to happen. I could feel it.

Turning in at Smallbones on Savile Row, I found the sales-room empty, but I was happy enough to be left alone here un-der the tolerant gaze of the stag heads. On the great, carved table in the center of the room, lay bolts of cheviot and shet-land. The smell of the cloth was as warm and live as a bakery's. The patterns — glenurquharts, saxonys and barleycorns, her-ringbones, homespuns and donegals — and colors — rich, au-tumn browns, haughty grays, pale, feminine biscuits, and faded roses — started an obscure hunger. My fingers explored the harsh gorse of a pinkish Harris, and the cloying, pussy willow evanescence of a beige cashmere, the silkiness of a plump, Cam-bridge flannel.

Glass cases showed buttery pigskin gloves, foulard scarves, crimson stockings, and pale, robin's egg shirting. There was a huge fireplace in the wall opposite, and blazoned across its man-telpiece, reaching into the adjoining panels of smoky, black walnut, were the arms of a dozen kings and queens. Victoria? I wondered if Mr. Smallbones had personally drawn his meas-ure across the royal buttocks, and if so, what toasts had rung out in consequence at the guildhall.

"It's Mr. *Erskine* . . ." The marbled welcome of Brian Small-bones was approaching. "How very nice to see you on British soil for a change. Are you staying with us long?"

"Just a few days I'm afraid. Long enough to see if there's any-thing that looks right for our readers."

"Do I have it correctly, that you've gone off with young Mr. Severance to start your own firm? That's exciting, surely."

"All of that."

"Do you still see anything of Mr. Severance Senior?"

"Not as much, of course."

"I hope he's well. Always such a pleasure for us to see Mr. Severance. A joy, you know, to make clothes for him. He does wear them well." Brian Smallbones pocketed his hands. "Well, sir, is there anything we can do for *you* this trip?"

My eye swept the fabrics covetously. "I'm not at all sure I need anything . . . and yet, I just passed a fellow in a very dark, gray suit. I think there was a small stripe. It looked very well."

Smallbones smiled. "Oh, yes, it *is* difficult to match an Oxford flannel for all-round wear in town, sir." He moved smartly to the wall racks and brought down two bolts which he flung open across the table. "Now this is actually a mill-finish worsted, but it's so tightly loomed — just feel this, sir — that it has the hand of a fine flannel. And do you see the stripe? It's a hairline, but double, sir. It does lend a certain formality, I think, and it would go awfully well on you, sir, if I may say so."

Left alone in the fitting room, I contemplated Smallbones's truncated, walnut horse, and tried its saddle. Seeing myself in the mirror, a middle-aged child at play in this shop, I laughed. It was a fun-house, an escape from the reality that lay just beyond the door.

My eye lit upon a pair of whipcord riding breeches which lay folded across a hanger bar, awaiting adjustment to some horseman's hindquarters. They were of an especially creamy color — thick, Devonshire cream at that — and although I had no interest in horses, the breeches attracted me and I dismounted. The material was soft as a puppy. With a finger I traced the wide fairing of the outseam, wondering why I felt such peculiar emotional stirrings.

There was a way one walked in breeches like these. Rapid, authoritative, alarming. Boots, tall, of polished calf, with a rippling at the ankle, encased them. The heels, resonant as castanets, made a beat — crump, crump — on dark, hardwood floors, evoking awe and longing. Above my strutting illusion, I recognized the face. It was that of Colonel Cornelius Emmett, headmaster of Montague School.

Military tailors. I had read it on the window. All these Savile Row masters must have apprenticed on uniforms, learning to give the human jelly a martial cast, transform it into a shape for admiration, one to go with the music and colors. Given the human beast, with its knobs and sagging flesh, theirs was an act of magic.

But for the customer, it was a child's game, this love of the illusion in the mirror, the costuming, the love of dressing-up.

How it fanned the actor's flame in all of us, the ham within that plays at manliness.

Still waiting for Brian Smallbones and his fitter, I had another recollection. At first it seemed gratuitous, unrelated to the hobbyhorse and thoughts of Colonel Emmett. I was remembering the Boltons, the childless couple who lived next door. On summer mornings I would mount their back steps and find Mrs. Bolton, Aunt Anita I took to calling her, busy with shears or paintbrush, recovering a lampshade or brightening a chair.

Her eyes were dark circled, as though she slept little, but they fastened on me earnestly when I spoke, and in return I listened while she puffed on a sequence of Turkish cigarettes, pursed her lips to sip inky coffee, and exposed the shifting currents of her own thoughts.

"You are what you eat," she told me, and read me excerpts from the *Journal of Natural Foods*. "You are what celestial forces command," she said, and read my horoscope from the *Bridgeport Post*.

Harvey, Dr. Bolton, was a gentle man with indistinct features, sparse, sandy hair, and a speckling of freckles. When Mother and I were asked to join the Boltons for a Sunday drive, I sat in the front seat of the gray Lincoln with him and listened to the chatter of the two women behind. I wished he would point out things that interested him, or decide our route, but he was too engrossed at the wheel. He was as unassuming as his wife was assertive.

But in midsummer, during the first two weeks of August, a change took place in Harvey Bolton, as dramatic as that of a chrysalis. On a Friday afternoon he would appear on the porch, arrayed for the summer encampment of the Connecticut National Guard. A Sam Browne belt — a great girth of dark leather, brass prongs, and rings — now corseted him up into a fasces of purpose. On the brim of his campaign hat bobbed the two gold acorns of a captain. Setting a cock in that hat, he was off up the path, and the Lincoln itself was possessed of new urgency as it headed for Niantic and Camp Cross.

When he invited Mother and me to the Sunday evening parade, I sat cross-legged on the grass and watched the columns of guardsmen stepping out to the Sousa march, marveling at the arms and legs in cadence, the plumbline company front, all the random, male energy unified, and I sensed the beauty of its might.

Afterward, Mother, Aunt Anita, and I walked along the sour-smelling company streets to find him. In the square tent, its fly and sides rolled to catch a breeze, we sipped the iced tea he had summoned from the officers' mess, and watched the captain as he peeled off puttees and moist tunic, revealing a khaki shirt, darkened at armpits and chest by swampy continents. And as he cooled, he became gentle, prudent Harvey Bolton again.

Brian Smallbones was back, bringing Mr. Tanner, the fitter, a narrow, exquisite man, who set-to with his tape measure, re-calibrating me, calling off the figures with an air of important discovery.

Enjoying all this attention in the three-way mirror, I was aware of a shadow, that of a man passing the dressing room door. Glancing up, I caught a fragment of shoulder, no more, but it startled me — a string plucked and set vibrating. While I had not seen the man whole, I was sure he was well set up, that he walked with a thrust, his head forward, and now I strained to hear a voice.

Presently there were several, at the cashier's perhaps, an inquiry and a polite response. I heard a familiar chord, confirming those shoulders.

"When you have a minute, Mr. Smallbones," I said, "would you put your head out and see who it is that's just come into the shop?"

Mr. Tanner paused and Brian Smallbones looked into the corridor. "Why, it's Mr. Severance. Would you excuse me . . ."

As I was putting on my jacket, Hugh appeared in the doorway. I thought his smile affectionate. "Well, Lloyd, they looking after you all right?"

"Hello, Hugh. This is a surprise. I had no idea . . ."

"I have you there. I knew you were here . . ." He chuckled. "Well, not at Smallbones, but in London."

"From Hughie?"

"No." Hugh squinted, recalling. "It was Philip Lerner, I think. Anyway, it was all over town. You have good publicity."

"Yours is preferable. Slipping into town unexpectedly. That's the way to work."

"Finding anything?"

"Not yet. It's hard to know."

"Well, perhaps we can pool our information. Can we get together sometime? Andy with you?"

"No. As a matter of fact, Flavia Moore is here, doing some reading for me."

"Ah-h. Well, maybe I can get you both to come around for dinner. Not tonight. I'm engaged tonight, but tomorrow perhaps. I'm at Claridge's."

"I think that'll be all right. I'm at the Connaught."

"Around seven?"

"We'll be there."

Zoe Farquharson, Morgan Bryce's agent, was Joel's friend and I was bringing her a gift from him, a can of maple syrup, hoping to learn something more about Morgan's book and to get her advice on going down to Sussex in search of him.

On the telephone, she said she could make a few moments at four but doubted there was much to tell me. She had heard nothing from Morgan in several weeks. She never knew what blackness he was up to. He had become very strange in the past year. He was at his father's old place, West Dean, digging around in the family skeletons and doing his best to keep clear of one estranged wife who was after him about money. One didn't know what to believe, there was such gossip.

Zoe Farquharson's office was next to Chatto's in William IV Street, and although I arrived at four exactly, I never saw her.

As I settled in the waiting room, a secretary brought me a message to call Flavia at the Connaught.

Flavia's voice was giddy. "Guess who's just turned up, looking for you?"

"Andy?"

She laughed. "Not yet. Andy's not due in till tomorrow. It's Morgan. He got your cable. He's here with me now, and he's going off to have dinner with Hugh. Hadn't you better dash right over?"

With hope rising like a bird in my chest, I jogged along St. Martin's Place and into Leicester Square where I eyed the underground station, the charging, elephantine buses with their fascinating destinations. Only Will Shakespeare, leaning negligently against a lectern atop his column, saw me, and my relief at finding an empty cab.

Alighting at the Connaught, I noticed the Stingray. It was purple and crass alongside the black Rollses and Bentleys, an affront to the cockaded doorman. From the entrance of the chapel-like bar, I heard Morgan's derisive, determinedly American, drawl.

He bulged his rumpled suit, as though he had put on another ten pounds. He wore a black shirt and a dreadful, figured white tie. His hand moved with that particular Bryce indolence to comb a thatch of untidy red hair from over his right eye, and Flavia was intent. Neither was aware of me until I sat down at the table.

"Hi," Flavia said. "You're out of breath."

"I ran some of the way."

"Lloyd." Shaking off his air of suffrance, Morgan Bryce grinned and offered his big, soft hand. "What are you doing here with this beautiful girl?"

"We've come to solve the mystery," I said. "Nobody would tell us about the new book. We've come to find out about that —and to lay the rumors. I hear you're operating a home for runaway girls."

He laughed. "Well, there was a girl. I seem to need them. But that's mostly my smoke screen. I've been working."

"What's really been happening with you, Morgan?"

He nodded. "We should keep in better touch, Lloyd. I trust you, you know. How you doing?"

"I'm doing beautifully. It's my first London trip — and having a grand time of it."

"You'd never get here working for Hugh, would you?"

"Not likely."

"Is he still doing a good job?"

"It's hard to knock Hugh."

"I know that, but this week I may give it a try. You know I'm seeing him tonight?"

"The old fox. He said he was busy, but not why."

"You *saw* Hugh?" Flavia asked.

"At the tailor's. He asked us to dinner tomorrow."

"Lloyd," Morgan asked, "is Hugh a good editor? Between us."

"Of course he's good. He's shrewd about what he knows, and he knows biography. Of course he doesn't do much editing now. He passes that on. He's an acquisitionist. Why?"

"You know how I admire the man. Hugh's really why I went with you for *Fulgencio*. I wanted to be published by him. But to tell you the truth, he's behaving very strangely. I have a letter from him saying he 'likes' *Fitchy Gules* but wants revisions . . ." From a pocket, Morgan produced a Crowninshield letterhead, unfolded it and contemplated it. "They're radical. I don't agree with them, and what's more, some of these phrases are the same, word for word, as Pigott's. I have Edmond Pigott's report, and Hugh's cribbed from it. I wonder if he's *read* my book. It's long . . . and he's busy. What do you think?"

"He doesn't read any more than he has to."

"I'm just a little pissed off at Hugh. Wouldn't it piss you off, Lloyd, to be told to change your book by a man who hasn't read it? If he's going to tell me something that will improve my book, I'll listen to that, but I won't be ganged up on by these people, and I won't change a fucking word to make life easier for them, or to avoid hurting feelings. I'm writing this one for me."

"I can't respond to that very well without having seen the book. I asked Elena for a look before I left New York, and I asked Edmond today, and I was going to ask Zoe . . ."

"You didn't ask me."

"You have a copy?"

Morgan swung a rucksack onto the table and brought forth a pair of dirty red socks, a tennis shoe, then a red box containing a manuscript tied with a green cord. They were thin, legal sheets, and I guessed at about six hundred of them. "Here," he said. "It's my ribbon copy. Help yourself."

I saw that the pages were dense with type. "How long can I have?"

"Actually, it would be very useful to know what you think from a skimming. Could you just give it a sniff and tell me whatever comes to mind? Could you do that *before* I see Hugh?" He looked at his watch. "I'm supposed to meet him at Claridge's around seven."

"That'll work out," I said to Flavia. "We have theater tickets."

"Oh?" she said. "Do we?"

Morgan asked, "What can you do for me in two hours?"

"I'll go upstairs and give it a try. What do you want to know?"

"How good is it? Where do I stand? How tough can I be on Hugh?"

"Where'll you be?"

"We'll go for a little ride," Flavia said. "Morgan has a car. I'll get him to drive me around the park. We'll call you at quarter to seven."

"Another drink first," Morgan said, beckoning the waiter.

Leaving, with *Fitchy Gules* under an arm, I cast a backward glance and saw Flavia laugh at something Morgan had said.

Upstairs, I promptly lost myself in *Fitchy Gules*. By the end of the first chapter, I was so held that even though I knew I must grasp the whole in an hour and a half, I could not skip a word. It was written around his mother who, as the handsome, free-spirited daughter of a teacher-poet from Amherst,

Massachusetts, had become an able journalist. She had gone from the *Boston Post* to the *New York Tribune,* first as a local, then a foreign, news reporter. A Cuban assignment gave her the material for her single book, *The Seven Days at Camaguey,* and her Russian assignment introduced her to Crispin Bryce, whose father was publisher of the *London Daily Mail.*

The body of the book dealt with her ten-year love affair with him, her growing doubts he would leave his wife for her. This was Rosemary Knollwood, a beauty, a woman of influence, and a lesbian. I began to see the portrait of a joyous, guileless woman, crushed by a charming, cynical predator, not so much a wicked man as the instrument of his family's wealth and prestige. At first I felt it was false, that under the surface of Morgan's elegant prose his own bias was apparent, but then as he went into the character with ever more understanding, I accepted the premise as one might a fictional point of view. In the end I felt that what made the book so effective was its very immoderateness.

I began to see places where, as editor, I would have suggestions, and as I began to list these I saw it was ten minutes to seven. We would be late to the theater. Flavia had not called as promised, so, gathering the manuscript, I hurried down the wide staircase and into the bar. There was no sign of them.

On Carlos Place, I found the purple Stingray gone. "Yes, sir," the doorman reported, "the lady went along with the gentleman."

I walked up to watch the carousel of taxis circling Grosvenor Square, then back to scour the lobby and the bar again, and up Mount Street to South Audley, peering into the pub at the corner. Returning to the Connaught's entrance, I patrolled Carlos Place, telling myself that of the next ten cars turning in, one would surely be a purple Stingray. But at half-past seven there was still no sign of it. I left a message at the door that I would return in half an hour and set out, the manuscript of *Fitchy Gules* still under my arm, for Claridge's.

"A Stingray?" the Claridge's doorman repeated. "Purple, sir? No, sir."

"Could such a car get into your garage, perhaps, without your seeing it?"

"Not likely, sir."

I stood at the entrance to Claridge's restaurant, searching the tables, creeping farther across the threshold until the maître d'hôtel offered help.

"Could you tell me please, did a Mr. Severance, Mr. Hugh Severance, have a reservation?"

He was distracted by two smart-looking couples bustling up in a flurry of French ebullience. "Could you wait here just a moment, sir, and I'll see?" he said, smiling at the French party and leading it forth toward a table.

Left alone I moved to his desk and ran my eye down the dinner list. I was having trouble with the handwriting when I was interrupted by a second member of the staff.

"Mr. Severance?" the man said. "Yes, I think he did, sir." Looking over my shoulder he lay a finger on the name. "There it is. A party of two. You're the gentleman?"

"No, just curious," I said, backing off toward the lobby, "not me."

But as I retreated I saw that I was being intercepted by the triumphant maître d'hôtel. He was leading Hugh Severance and announcing, "*Here* we are, sir."

I saw Hugh's expression turn from vexation to astonishment. "Good Lord, it's you, Lloyd. I was expecting someone else. Isn't it tomorrow?"

"Tomorrow? Oh, is it?"

"Are you alone?"

"So it seems."

"Well," Hugh frowned at his watch. "Unless I'm hopelessly confused, I was meant to dine with your friend Bryce. He's over an hour late. I think perhaps I'm stood up. Look, have you had dinner? Come on then. He's got a table waiting."

Hungarian violins, flattering mirrors, cream of asparagus walls, rosebud bouquets, made an incongruous setting for this stag meal and sent my thoughts to wander among the taxis and the buses, the Rovers and the Triumphs, whirling through

Hyde Park and Green, Regent's and St. James's in the soft night, carrying everyone in London to a lover.

Somewhere out there, my girl was leaving me. I was feeling the vertigo and the mourning of it, and just as I told myself this was true and must be faced, like any loss, some other voice within me denied it, saying she would be back. There would be some sensible explanation, and the cycle of hope and despair would start again.

I had a vision of them, together in the dark, driving through countryside now, sharing the excitement of escape — touching, laughing, planning what they were going to do, her hand in his.

Just beyond us, in an alcove, a dark-haired girl in a black dress asked for "Zigeuner," and the violins played it twice for her. The narrow straps made valleys in her white shoulders and the man with her touched her wrist, fingers straddling an emerald bracelet. Everything about her reminded me of Flavia, and the loneliness she had left me.

I felt some part of Flavia everywhere, in the flirting melody of the strings, the whiffs of perfume and sauces, the sight of wine poured in a glass, even in the sound of Hugh's voice, as he spoke of Crowninshield's.

"Not too bad, you know, the new building," he was saying. "It's damned convenient, and I have a gorgeous view, straight up Park Avenue. I don't really miss the old air shaft. I like old things of course, but I don't like the idea of *living* in the past, as though we were artifacts in a museum. We have to keep up to the minute, live as close to the future as we can. It's good psychology. Don't you agree, Lloyd, and good business?"

Nodding, I was aware of the weight of *Fitchy Gules* on my knees, and the irony of that.

"Bill Stickney," Hugh was saying, "having moved us into the tower, seems to have lost interest in publishing. He does come to meetings." Hugh had ordered cigars and he was offering me one. "But his focus has moved on, to rare earth oxides, I think it is, along with computer memory and such. I suppose Paul Peeling will be leaving us before long." He puffed up his cigar in luxuriant clouds. "It occurs to me you might want to think about the new Crowninshield's, Lloyd."

My agony, surely apparent to Hugh, only made him the more sanguine. For me, speech was an effort, but I gathered myself to say, "If that's an offer of a job, Hugh, you know I'm quite happy at Gulliver's."

"Well, I wonder about that, Lloyd." Hugh directed the waiter to pour me a snifter of the cognac he had ordered. "I wonder if you're as happy at Gulliver's as you think you are."

"Explain, Hugh."

"Are you in touch with your office, Lloyd? Any idea what's been going on since you left town?" He took some puffs, studied the white ash and tipped it into the tray. "Philip Lerner tells me he's taken an interest. He's been showing your partners how to cut costs, and it's my impression you're on the list of economies."

"They've cut my salary?"

"More in the nature of tying a hand, the kind of penance you're sure to find unpleasant, maybe insupportable."

"You mean I'm fired?"

"Oh, I don't think they would, or even could, do that. Could they?"

"Tonight," I said, "I can believe in every kind of perfidy."

*

Dear Lloyd,

I have this thing about the southern coast. The Royal Pavilion in Brighton is some kind of shrine for me, and Morgan has agreed to drive around Devon and Sussex until I tire of them. So, that's where I'll be.

This will seem callous and silly to you, but actually I've thought it through carefully. I shouldn't have come with you, and now that I've done this, I can hardly go back with you.

I haven't entirely thought it through about the job, but I suspect I'd better quit. We could probably keep that part going because I'll always have the most tremendous liking and respect for you, but I'm pretty sure you belong with Andy. I'm certain of this — that though you'd like to give her up for me, right now you lack the courage, and I'm not the sort of girl to dangle on slender hopes. Anyway, patching it up with Andy will surely be easier for you if I'm not around.

This is impossible,

but of course,

love,

F.

Her note looked up from the center of the desk and her clothes and valise were gone. Overlooked, a black, cashmere sweater lay on a shelf and I sat down with it, smelling her scent, crushing its softness in my hands and finally burying my face and weeping into it.

In the morning I called to cancel my appointments, returned the dozen submissions, and checked out of the Connaught. In the afternoon I rented a small, gray Hillman, packed it with my belongings, and drove out of London toward the south.

Morgan Bryce's address — The Hermitage, West Dean, nr. Midhurst, Sussex — took me along the A24 through the gray towns of Leatherhead and Dorking, then through the mists and soaked, green wealds hemmed by bare, black oaks, toward the Sussex Downs, rising like faint hopes.

Early evening brought me through stone gates where a freshly painted sign pointed to The Stables. As the driveway climbed, I had a glimpse of battlements, a manor house with square towers and a belfry.

A girl in a white dress stood in the middle of the road, waving me into a field where there were a number of cars.

"I'm looking for The Hermitage," I said.

"It's already started you know. You're late."

"For what?"

"The concert."

"I'm looking for The Hermitage — Mr. Bryce's."

"Oh." Her expression turned suspicious. "Is that the son, the writer?"

"That's right."

"I think he does have a place. It's the turn at the gate, the way you've come."

Half an hour later I found a stone house set between two ponds. It was half in ruins as well as dark and locked, but shining my headlights through a window, I made out a desk with a jar of pencils and a volume of the O.E.D.

At The Stables, a soprano, a tenor, and a baritone were singing a modern opera about a cat, and I prowled through the intermission crowd — students of the music school, now the tenant of West Dean, and its patrons from Chichester. No one I asked knew of Morgan Bryce.

At The Angel in Midhurst, the proprietor did know him. "Yes, Mr. Bryce comes in here once or twice a week, when he does his wash. Goes across to the launderette, and then comes in for a pint, often with a young lady. He has an eye for the young ladies."

During the three days I waited at The Angel, driving out each day to West Dean, sometimes as far as Bognor Regis and Brighton, looking for a purple Stingray, I thought despair in every shape. I thought of suicide, of swimming from the pier at Hove straight toward France until my strength gave way to the tides and current.

Most agonizing was the fantasy that when I did find Flavia, she would have come to her senses and would plead to be forgiven. While I knew this for the wish it was, I was masochist enough to have to prove it beyond all possible doubt.

On Friday morning, I found the Stingray. It was in The Angel's courtyard, and I caught up with Morgan Bryce in the launderette as he was removing clothes, some Flavia's, from the single dryer.

"Where is she?"

"My God, Lloyd." He was full of concern. As he put a hand on my shoulder I disposed of one fantasy, that I might drive a fist into his pale, dissolute face. "She's home, at my place. I feel awful about this. You've got to know it wasn't my idea. I wanted to come back and explain — *that* at least, you know. She wouldn't do it. I had to be lookout for you while she packed her clothes. For one thing, I wanted to find out what you thought."

"What I *thought?* I was catatonic, Morgan — crazy with jealousy."

"I don't mean that. I mean *Fitchy Gules.*"

"Oh, for Christ's sake. This has driven everything else from my mind."

Stuffing the laundry into his rucksack, he said, "God knows, she's an attractive woman. I can see how you'd get attached to Flavia, but I'm rationalizing my own role by believing I'm doing you one hell of a favor."

"A what?" I was following him across the street toward the pub entrance to The Angel.

"She's a bright girl and a damned pretty one, but she's really fucking you up, isn't she? I mean your marriage."

"That's over. Finished. I was going to marry Flavia until you came along."

"I doubt that. You've got too much sense."

"No, I don't."

"Why would you marry her? She's not that kind of girl."

"What kind do you think she is? What are *your* plans for her?"

"Plans? What do I want with plans?"

"All right. Just do this for me, Morgan. Will you tell Flavia I have to see her before I leave. Only ten minutes."

"Yes, I'll do that." He asked for two pints of bitter. "Now, what about my book? What do you think of it? You must remember something."

"I have it upstairs. I'll give it to you."

"But what did you think?"

"That it's very good. There are wonderful things in it. Much more of a book, much more of you in it than in *Fulgencio.* You've done a marvelous portrait of your mother. I wouldn't change a word of that. You have a problem in the ending. I was thinking maybe you could put that first. But it's powerful. What I was going to say to you is, don't let anyone bowdlerize it."

Morgan sipped, nodded. "I tell you what, Lloyd. I want you to do this book. I'm going to tell Zoe that."

"I'm not sure what'll happen when I get back to New York."

"Well, you're sure of one thing, that if you want to publish *Fitchy Gules*, it's yours."

Flavia came alone. She was anxious, swinging across the flags of the courtyard in the flowered wool dress, but as she saw me waiting, holding her sweater, she smiled, from the long habit of it.

"How was the trip?" I asked.

"It was really lovely. Palm trees in Torquay — can you imagine?" As we sat down together, she looked at me sympathetically. "How are you?"

"Don't ask."

"You'll be all right once you're home."

I shook my head. "It's all coming apart at the office. I'm going back tomorrow. Do you want to come along, Flavia? I really think I can forgive you anything."

"No."

"What do you see in him?"

She shrugged.

"I mean physically, he's such a slob. But then I never have understood what it is about a man that attracts a woman."

"He does something strange to me. When he talks, he moves me somehow. We're very alike, he and I."

"You're just one of the transients to him. I don't think he cares about you at all. You're just another lay."

"I know."

"And you're letting me go for *that?*"

"I'm letting you go because it isn't working out."

"It could, Flavia. It would."

"We're bad for each other now. You're scared of me, and rightly. You don't want to leave Andy. I know that, even if you don't."

"I've wrecked all that."

"You can put it all together again."

I shook my head. "I don't want to." I realized I was clutching her sweater, still in my lap. "Hugh had some news for me. He says I'm the victim of a conspiracy. It seems Joel and Hughie let me come to London so they could fix me. I'm the sacrifice to economy. When I get back, I'm in for a fight."

"You're up to it. You're a match for both of them."

"With you, yes."

Flavia shook her head. "You'll manage, Lloyd. Maybe Gulliver's *is* going down the drain. Think of it — good riddance to me and Gulliver's, all in one round-trip to London. What a deal." She leaned across the table to kiss me. "I'm going to miss you."

"Don't forget your sweater," I said.

She opened her hands to catch it, and with it under her arm she went swiftly out of the pub.

The proprietor came over to ask, "Will that be all, sir?"

"Yes," I said. "I guess that's all."

Driving back to London, I felt oddly remote from the man whose several lives had collapsed, as though the impact were too great to accept. Knowing this for a temporary remission, I rejoiced in my limbo, observing the quilted fields through which I passed, the truncated roof lines of the barns, a man in a leather apron, carrying pails.

Also I sensed I was not alone, that my father was close. I could feel his presence beside me, hear his voice admiring the Hillman's fittings, then the countryside. I could feel his eyes upon me.

"Dad, what kind of man am I?"

"You're my son."

"But have I failed you?"

"No. On the contrary, I'm proud, Lloyd. You must know that."

"Now? When all my selfishness and blundering have met me here, had their reckoning, left me disgraced in every way that I can imagine? What can you possibly find to admire?"

"Oh, it's not so bad as that. Think of me. You always do

when you need to. You look at my life and see the waste of it. That's why you're determined to go another way. It's for me, I know, and for us."

"Dad, I've lost. I've lost everything."

"The reality's always got some disappointment in it, but you don't dread reality. What I merely dreamed, you've done."

"If I were back at the ways' crossing, I'd take another."

"You've come some distance on this one. I'm proud of that. Think, we're here in England. Look there, Lloyd, the church. It must be Norman. Let's stop a minute."

The steep, sway-backed roof and brooding steeple followed some ethereal line that touched the spirit. Its slates and thick stones were lichened, green as the churchyard itself. While we watched, a man and two women emerged from the church door. They were old, dressed in unaccustomed clothing for some rite. For an instant they stood blinking in the sudden brightness, before separating, scurrying off to resume their day's work.

"Just there," he said, as we drove on, "in that glimpse. That was worth the journey."

"What did I lose, Dad? Something precious? Did the ambition consume what I most loved about you? Is that what's cost me a wife, a son, a friend? Could that be? Why so silent? Do you know? Do you know what Andy knows?"

But he had gone.

⧉ 22 ⧉

I DID NOT HOPE to find welcome on Oenoke Ridge Road. In fact I was surprised that the house itself stood as I had left it, late afternoon sun reddening the chimney stones and calling attention to the flaking paint of the kitchen window frame.

I needed my key, and in the chilly hall I stood for a minute, listening. "Hello?" I called. "Anyone home?"

I nudged the arrow of the thermostat to sixty-five and the furnace whispered in answer. Seizing my bag, I climbed the stairs and paused at the bedroom threshold, looking in. The bed was trimly made and the hand of the clock on Andy's table swept round and round, counting off minutes.

In search of the luggage rack, I tugged at the closet door and it rolled open to reveal the clothes rod with its dangling skeletons of empty hangers. I groaned.

Her note was propped against the telephone.

Lloyd,

I have a new job and expect to be busy with it for the next several months. I will be staying with the Oglebys until I find a place of my own. I ask only that you not telephone, nor try to see me. Whatever we must settle, and there will be many things, let that be by letter.

                                                        Andy

A weariness fell upon me like an avalanche. It was all I could do to get my shoes and jacket off before crawling onto the bed, where I slept deeply for a few hours and then woke, hoping for morning, to find it was not yet midnight.

Next day I reached Gulliver House at quarter to nine and, waving off greetings, went to my office. My mail was pushed aside to make way for someone's papers, a list of titles, notes, figures, two letters addressed to Philip Lerner.

I found Joel at his desk and he looked up affably to say, "Well, how did it go, Lloyd? Was it all you'd hoped?"

"And more," I said. "I see Lerner's been using my office. Does he work here now? What the hell's going on?"

There was a moment's anxiousness in his eyes, a glance toward the door for Hughie's support, but Joel recovered promptly. His hands opened to the ceiling and he smiled assurance. "I'll tell you whatever you want to know, Lloyd. Phil's been helpful. He's made good suggestions and we're planning changes. Sit down for God's sake. Oh... here's Hughie."

"Well..." Hughie approached, gingerly offering a hand. "Glad you're back. Have a good time?"

"So, so. Joel's just telling me about changes. I don't know about them. You must be eager to have my approval."

Slumping in a chair by the window, Hughie confronted me coolly. "Yes, we've been making plans for next year and we hope you'll want to go along with them."

"Go along? What's that mean?"

"It means we're redefining our duties very specifically around here. Did you see the memo?"

Joel shuffled among his papers, plucking out a Gulliver letterhead. There was a portentous knell in his throat as he said, "Here."

April 26, 1971

To: The stockholders of Gulliver House, Inc.

FROM: Hugh Severance, Jr.

In the light of present needs for our company's renewal, I have felt obliged to draw up a plan for more efficient performance of essential publishing functions at Gulliver House, and I submit that plan herewith.

Beginning with the first of next month, each of the company's executives will have more clearly prescribed areas of responsibility and authority.

Joel Rossbach is designated Executive Editor. He will also undertake the title and responsibilities of Director of Subsidiary Rights. Hugh Severance, Jr., while maintaining his present title as Sales Manager, will be named Publisher. Lloyd Erskine will continue with his duties as editor.

Henceforth, all editorial decisions must be approved by the Executive Editor and the Publisher.

H.S. Jr.

I folded it, put it back on Joel's desk. "Well, that's clear enough."

Joel gave an immense sigh. "It wasn't pleasant, having to do that, believe me."

Hughie said, "It's just that from now on we'll be in on decisions about the advances you pay out."

"That's bullshit," I said. "That isn't what you say here. This strips me, makes me the messenger boy. You've forgotten we're equal partners."

Joel shrugged and looked into his lap.

To Hughie I said, "Last week your father told me why I'd got to London. It was so you could make my funeral arrangements. Here it is, on this paper, and I cannot believe that friends behave so treacherously."

"Friendship doesn't have anything to do with this, Lloyd," Hughie replied. "Don't get the two mixed up. When a business like ours is sinking, nothing stands in the way of plugging the holes."

"That's frank, Hughie. I'm grateful for frankness. Now I'll

tell *you* something. You'll need my approval for this, and you won't have it."

"You're outvoted, Lloyd," Hughie said. "Two of us, only one of you."

"I hope we can settle this among ourselves, like gents," I said, "but if we can't, if you really want a scrap, we'll be going to the stockholders for support. We're fairly evenly divided there, so I don't know how it will come out, but Loomis Pitcher says I can win. Meantime, let's get rid of this nasty little document." Crumpling the memorandum I dropped it into Joel's wastebasket.

Back in my own office, I was looking at accumulated mail when Philip Lerner appeared in the doorway. "I'm sorry about that stuff of mine, Lloyd," he said. "I didn't expect you in until tomorrow."

"Are you working here, now?"

"No. I just look in from time to time, when I can be of help. How's everything in London?"

"Yes, I gather you've been very helpful, making suggestions on how to save money and so on. I'm looking forward to hearing about them. I hope I'll like them better than those editorial proposals I've just rejected. My partners can't ignore me — nor can you. Make sure you understand that."

I brushed by him, then past Joel, who was waiting on the landing to say, "You *are* my friend, and your friendship means more to me than any business, Lloyd — but we do have to survive here. That's all. We haven't mounted a conspiracy."

"Then what have you been doing?" I asked. "How would you describe it?"

"Trying to get the message into your head. We can no longer afford the carelessness we've been practicing for three years. We've been unrealistic. You, in particular, have been unrealistic. We thought you had the Perkins touch, that books you liked would naturally become successful. Well, they don't, necessarily. That's all we're trying to tell you. Now don't overreact."

I went down the stairs and out the front door, turning east on

Sixty-first Street. As I neared Third Avenue I heard footsteps overtaking me and turned to find they were Philip Lerner's.

"Can I buy you a drink?" he asked. He pointed across the avenue at The Bank. "How about there?"

"No, I'm in sort of a hurry. I have to see my friend Pitcher."

"Ah-h," Phil said, studying the uptown crawl of traffic. "Maybe I can save you some time there. It might be useful for you to know that your partners do have the clout — if it should come to that."

"Come to what? What are you talking about?"

"The memorandum, the editorial changes. They can make that stick. I thought you'd want to know."

"I don't believe it."

"Lately, I've acquired more shares."

"Whose?"

He was reading the inscriptions on a moving van, the cities it served, the annual sum it paid in road taxes, as though he might find my answer there. "Well, let's say it's one of your guys'."

"No, it isn't."

"Why should I lie to you, Lloyd?"

"Pitcher would have told me."

"Pitcher." He shrugged. "Pitcher doesn't know everything."

"If that's true," I said, "I'll quit — and if you're going back to Gulliver House, you can tell my partners."

"Lloyd, you don't mean that. You've put too much of yourself into the firm."

Over his shoulder I saw the phone booth standing empty and I said, "Excuse me. I have to make a call."

Phil Lerner was still with me as I felt for change and examined the phone for signs that it functioned. "Listen, Lloyd," he persisted, "you'll think better of this in the morning. I know you will. But if you really do want out . . . You know I can understand that — how you might want to wash your hands of Gulliver. I wouldn't blame you, actually. Now if you do feel that way, will you give me a call? I'll have a proposition to make you."

"What kind?"

"I'll make you a decent price for your stock. Remember, it's not going to be easy to unload. The word's not good on Gulliver."

"Phil, I'd sooner give it away. I don't know what you have in mind for Gulliver House, but I'm certainly not going to help. People who trusted me still have a stake in it."

"Forget it." He turned away. "I was just trying to do you a favor."

I reached Loomis Pitcher as he was leaving his office, and told him, "I thought I was doing O.K. until a couple of minutes ago when Phil Lerner caught up with me on the street corner. He says they *do* have the leverage, that he's bought some of our people's shares."

"Whose shares? Did he say?"

"No."

"I think he's bluffing, but I'll see what I can find out. Do you want to have a drink around six-thirty?"

"Yes."

"Where are you staying?"

"It's going to be lonely in New Canaan. Andy's left me."

"I've got plenty of room."

Loomis Pitcher let me into his apartment on Seventy-second Street with a grave nod. "Lerner told you the truth. Last Monday he took my ex-friend Frank Spencer to lunch, told him what an illness there is at Gulliver House, and offered him two hundred dollars apiece for his shares. Oh, Frank knew he'd done a bad thing all right. He was *afraid* to tell me. Well, there it is."

"A real conspiracy."

"It looks that way."

"I can't go back there."

He took my valise into the room that was to be mine, then led the way into his library. Uncapping the bourbon, he said,

"Still, it's Lerner's conspiracy. He did the dirty work. His enthusiasm never did make sense to me — but I think Rossbach and Severance are all right."

"They went along with him, Loomy."

"You might give them a chance. Listen to what they have to say. We're all in trouble, Lloyd. Why run out in the middle of the row?"

"Loomy, I'd cut off a hand rather than let you down, but I cannot go back to Gulliver House. Tomorrow I'm looking for another job."

"I always salute attitudes," Loomy said. "I'm all for displays of indignation, honor, and such. Of course they *are* a luxury. That shouldn't bother you though — unless there's some place you want to go."

Next day, my first call was on Roscoe Boone, the affable Managing Editor of Stavenger and Company. He paused in the midst of a busy morning to welcome me, and then to entertain me with the house gossip, recent spinnings in the affairs of love and influence which webbed the corners at Stavenger's. One episode had led to the departure of an editor, and I opened myself to invitation.

"Roscoe," I said, "maybe you've heard about the differences between us at Gulliver House. I'm going to leave."

"Oh? I'm sorry to hear." Roscoe frowned and I detected a scurrying of the guard, a rattle of drawbridge chain. "That's tough luck."

"So I *am* interested in whatever proposal you have to make."

"Proposal?"

"You did tell me that if I ever wanted to come with you, I had only to ask. Did you say that — or did I just dream it?"

"Oh, I meant that, Lloyd. I'd really like to have you with us, and so would Potter. He's told me so. But right now . . ."

"You just said there was an opening."

"Yes. Well, we'll probably close ranks for the time being. You know how it is, with the government revoking the library subsidies. We're already heavy on the editorial side. I mean we're letting people *go*. But listen, you're very employable, Lloyd. I'll ask around."

The grimy, utilitarian lobby with its work-horse elevator cab, had been done over in mirrors and beige plastic. Luther, the grouchy operator, had been replaced by a panel of buttons, but up on seven, I found Ethan Poole confidently resisting change.

"Ghastly," he told me. "I close my eyes as I walk through. I'm planning to come in some weekend and restore the lovely, dirty cracked tile and bring Luther back from happy retirement."

"I'm retiring too," I said.

Ethan looked uncomfortable, but he offered me an apple, took one himself and tossed it twice before biting into it. "How's Andy?"

"She has a job with a foundation, and I think she's doing fine, though I don't know firsthand."

"I'm sorry you don't. That's a fine girl, and they're getting scarce."

"I know."

"It's a wise man who knows his own luck."

"I've run out of it at Gulliver House too, Ethan. My partners and I aren't getting along."

"Surprise you?"

"Yes."

He laughed. "You're learning, Bub. Keep it up and you'll be earning your keep in this business."

"You have the strangest effect on me, Ethan, like going back to school, as though time flowed backward. I'm nearly fifty."

"That's a sprout. I have fifteen years on you, and I'm still learning something new — maybe every *other* day now."

"Ethan, I'm out of a job. Do you have any vocational advice?"

He examined his apple core, found a last nibble on it, and dropped it in his basket. "I'll have to give that some thought."

"Will you?"

He waited before allowing me a considered nod. "You interested in coming back to this garret, Lloyd?"

"What about that bridge I burned? Is it negotiable?"

He raised an eyebrow. "That depends. What makes it appealing to you? I'd like to know that, in any case. There was a time when you'd outgrown us. Did you find out anything I ought to know up there at Crowninshield's?"

"I missed the human touch, whatever that is. They seem to starve it. I wouldn't have believed that without seeing it."

"Would it be fair to say though, that after a couple of rounds with the Severance boys, you still think of us as amateurs?"

"Better than that."

"Be honest now. You do admire all that efficiency."

"Excellence, yes. That's what survival depends on."

"I can't argue against excellence, but I smell our difference, right in there. You like the way we bet our hunches here, our comfortable follies, but in the end you'll be making us over — to go with the lobby downstairs."

I smiled. "That's unkind."

"I know."

"You'd want me to come back with something, wouldn't you — some benefit of my experience?"

"I wonder," Ethan said. "I wonder if any of us can come back."

When I rose to go, he followed me to the door and we stood for a minute, hand in hand, Ethan regarding me with that delicate, affectionate smile that made me feel like a child.

"You think about it too," he said. "I suspect it's *you* that's burned that bridge."

Waiting for Elena Wallace at the Argenteuil bar, I kept an eye on the door as it swung with lunchers, each pink with anticipation. The mood was catching, laying a rosy veneer on my unease. Here she came, too, smiling confidence and all's well. The captain went scurrying for her table as though she were true royalty, while clusters of patrons and waiters parted miraculously before her.

When we were seated she patted me soothingly as though she knew the details of my plight. "You must tell me all about London, Lloyd. I've had mystifying messages from Morgan, but I gather you saw him."

"Briefly."

"You mustn't be shy with me, Lloyd. I'm an old gypsy fortuneteller, and I know all about such things. You're having your difficulties and there's no need to go into them unless you want to."

"I'm out of Gulliver's, that's all."

"And well out," Elena said, raising her glass in salute. "Here's to you — and don't look so morose, Lloyd. I can tell you exactly what to do, and I'm going to, whether I'm invited to or not. You can begin by helping me with this." Groping in the pouch at her feet, she brought forth the scarlet box of manuscript I had left at The Angel in Midhurst. "The revised manuscript came in the mail today, along with this for you."

It was a note on a page torn from a copybook.

Lloyd,

I won't feel right about publishing *Fitchy* until you've had a chance to reflect on my need for you. That's important to both of us and makes small beans of the rest. I've told Elena I want you to publish *Fitchy Gules* wherever you are. If you're not interested, I'll regret it, but I'll understand. Incidentally, Flavia's left here. I'd guess she'll be back in New York by the time you read this.

Ever, Morgan

"He wants you to have *Fitchy Gules*," Elena said, "and I'll try to see that you do. Do you like this book?"

"In spite of myself, I do." I opened the box to the title page and felt a frisking of excitement. I flipped some pages, read some lines. "Like a thief, browsing in Cartier's."

"Are you aware that Hugh wants you back at Crowninshield's?"

"We talked about it in London."

"Why not go? Oh, I know how you feel about Mr. Peeling.

There are Mr. Peelings everywhere, Lloyd. You know that.
Perhaps that's a good reason in itself for going back, like get-
ing up on a horse that's thrown you. Think of it, Lloyd.
There's much in timing. It may be just right for you."

"I'll pay a call on Hugh," I promised.

Hugh Severance glanced up from the pages of a contract and
waggled a hand in greeting. Pointing to a book on the edge of
his desk, he said, "Have a look at that, Lloyd, while I finish
this fine print."

It was a copy of *The Millionaires,* by a *Wall Street Journal*
reporter. Its pages exuded the freshness of ink and glue as I
flipped them, discovering biographies of six men who had made
their fortunes in a dramatic way.

"Whose is this, Hugh? Is it yours?"

He put down his pen and smiled. "Peeling's."

"You're asking my opinion?"

"I am."

I put the book back on his desk. "Well, it's not my kind of
thing, you know."

"The advance sale is over twenty thousand." He glanced at
the daily sales sheet. "Twenty-two eight, as of this morning."

"If it were twice that, and I were ten times as anxious to get
back to work, I'd still not be interested in how the ambitious
get rich."

"A lot of people are, Lloyd."

"Are you, Hugh?"

"No . . ." he said thoughtfully. "Perhaps that's why I wanted
you to see it. It's merchandise. I hoped you'd tell me so." Mischief sparkled in the brown eyes. "Well, how did you find
things at Gulliver House?"

"You're a good soothsayer. I've quit."

"What are your plans?"

"Does your offer stand, Hugh?"

"Sure." Hugh made a church steeple of his slender fingers
and pressed it against his lower lip. "You could start right off
with Morgan Bryce's book."

"Did Elena tell you I've read it?"

Hugh nodded. "Think it'll go?"

"There'll be libel problems, but there's no question the book will do well. I did see Morgan after you and I had dinner. Now I have a note from him, asking me to be the editor — wherever I go."

"Well, of course Bryce is bound by contract. If he's hazy on that, I'm sure Elena isn't."

"What will the future be like here, Hugh?"

"Salary you mean? Title? What do you want?"

"To do my stuff. I just want to edit books. I don't want to squander my energy in cabals."

"Oh?" Hugh's eyes widened in dissent. "You want to be left alone — really? Editing is publishing, Lloyd. You're always fighting for the privilege of doing the books you want, in the way that you want. You have to be willing to lay down your pencil and take up your brass knucks every few years. It's change, and you have to deal with that, or they come along and stuff you. Meeting change in this business is the most important part of doing it. You know that, even if you won't admit it. Simple survival in the rapids is the whole point. You're managing well enough, but you'd better be sure you know that and don't believe that pond water is going to satisfy you. It's in the ponds we drown."

Corinne Perry's window opened. "Excuse me, Mr. Severance, but Mr. Aldrich is here."

"I'll be right with him." H.S. tilted back in his chair. "Think it over, Lloyd, and let me know by Friday, will you?"

Loomis Pitcher came home at seven. I heard him whistling cheerfully in the hall and then he appeared in my doorway to ask, "Get a job?"

"One offer," I sighed from the depths of my chair. "I can go back to Crowninshield's, along with Morgan Bryce."

"You sound glum about it."

"I'm a little shook, discovering I'm not so good as I'd thought. For years a guy at Stavenger's has been telling me if I ever wanted a job I had only to ask. I did, and he turned me down. Ethan Poole was more gracious, but he didn't want me either. A month ago, I felt lucky, able, sought. That was a mirage, Loomy. We editors get a little power; people flatter us and we come to believe the flattery and to live on it and drift further from the truth about ourselves. I'm beginning to think Hughie and Joel are right, that as an editor I'm a liability."

"You're as good as you ever were."

"Which is not much, and the worst of it is, I've deceived not only myself, but you too."

"I think you're a good editor, Lloyd, and so do Joel Rossbach and Hughie Severance — or so they tell me. I stopped in at Gulliver House this afternoon to talk about Lerner and those shares."

"What did they say?"

"That the sale was news to them. They were even skeptical about it."

"I don't believe it, do you?"

Loomy shrugged. "When I left, they were two sober guys."

I looked out the apartment window into the night sky where the red lights of a plane, moving slowly down the leg of a holding pattern, appeared from a break in the clouds and vanished again. I was wondering if we were all three deceived. I guessed that Philip Lerner was cunning enough. I went on to ponder Hugh's prescience and the relish with which he had shared it over the dinner table at Claridge's.

"You don't suppose this is Hugh's game," I said, "his fine Italian hand moving the pieces?"

"I could," Loomy said. "Does that make you want to play it?"

"Lloyd, is that you?" It was Hughie's unusually anxious voice calling at eight in the morning. "We've been looking all over for you. What is this about your quitting us?"

"I was betrayed, Hughie."

There was a conspicuous silence before Hughie resumed. "I'm not proud of myself. I won't say you're entirely wrong about that — but we didn't, and we don't, want you to leave Gulliver's. You've got to believe that, Lloyd. You might also consider that you're being unnecessarily difficult yourself. Now, I'll try to explain everything to your satisfaction, if you'll give me a chance. We want you to come down here and talk it over sensibly. Will you do that? Can you make it at ten?"

"O.K., Hughie. I'll be there."

Passing my office, I lookèd in. It was empty, neat, recent mail lying open, awaiting attention.

"Here we are," Joel called from the end of the hall, waving me into his office where Hughie, rarely one for such amenities, was pouring coffee.

When we had settled ourselves around the desk, Joel asked, "Have you really been looking for another job?"

"I was all over town yesterday, and the best offer I had was to go back to Crowninshield's."

"Hugh?" Joel asked. "Hugh wanted you back?"

"I don't know if it's me or Morgan Bryce's book he wants, but yes, Hugh offered me a job."

"What about Morgan Bryce's book?"

"Morgan's told Elena he wants me to have *Fitchy Gules* — wherever I am."

"I didn't know that," Hughie said, "but it would be fine having Bryce on our list."

"Will you get it?" Joel asked.

"Only if I go to Crowninshield's. Elena and Hugh are seeing to that. So if *Fitchy Gules* is why you want me now, forget it."

"We want you," Hughie said, "because you're too good a man to lose. The memo was intended to restrain you, that was all. It was not intended to make you angry, surely not to make you quit. Let's try and forget the memo. It won't come up again."

Joel said, "I don't blame you for seeing more plotting in that exchange of shares into Lerner's hands, but that really wasn't our doing." He tilted back in his chair and smiled. "You know the leverage of those shares will be nil so long as we hang together, and we'll hang together once we understand why he wants them."

"Why does he?"

"Well, of course if things get any worse around here he'll be able to buy in all he wants at his price, and own us. Now, we wouldn't want that, would we — not even if he's acting for himself."

"No," I said, "nor even if he's acting for Hugh Severance."

"Particularly, if he's acting for Hugh Severance," Hughie said.

"In either case you've persuaded me," I said. "I'll just go and have a look at my mail."

≼ 23 ≽

MY NAME AND ADDRESS in Andy's unmistakable, round, firm hand startled me.

> Lloyd,
>   I've just come from seeing Will. He and Sharon are planning to marry sometime next month. Since you took such a dislike to her, he doesn't know whether to tell you or not. I think he's tormented by that, as he is by our split, and by your continuing indifference to him.
>   You could still make up for your failures with Will, if you'd go to him — for his sake and yours. In any case, don't tell me what, if anything, you do about it. I really don't want to hear from you.
>
>   Andy

I wrote Will, saying I would be in Boston the coming Friday and would try to look him up for lunch. There was no response, but I went up anyway, taking the MTA to Kendall Square and emerging, just at noon, into the gray alley district of Cambridge. Half way down Hayward Street I found The Big Noise, its storefront newly painted a daisy yellow.

Within, I was buffeted by a gale of sound, electronic instruments laced by a terrorized wailing. At the counter, a young black man was waiting on a single customer, but he looked up, asking, "You Mr. Erskine?"

"Yes. Is Will around?"

"Will's out back." He pointed to the cork-faced door behind him.

Passing through it, I found myself in a large, brick-walled garage ringed with workbenches, each with its canopied, fluorescent light shining on spools of colored wire and strewn tools. The sound of baroque string music poured from two speakers overhead.

For a moment I thought I was alone here, and then I saw him. Will, his back to me, was seated at a table and partially obscured by a pallet stacked with cartons. Approaching, I saw that he looked well, that his beard was trimmed, his hair shorter.

As I came up, determined to embrace him, he turned, rose and with the dawn of a smile said, "I didn't know if you'd come."

"I said I would." Since he seemed to back away, not even offering a hand, I hesitated. Then I reached to put my arms around him but he was unprepared and we teetered, awkward, off balance, until we stepped apart. Nodding at the ledger, I said, "Don't you want to finish what you're doing?"

"It'll keep."

I looked around the room. "You're busy here. What are you doing?"

"Making speakers." He led me to the nearest bench and pointed out a nest of cones. "Charlie, one of my partners, designs these. They're pressed in Woburn. We do the assembly here." He moved around the benches, touching bits of metal and plastic, telling me the names and sources.

"How are you doing?" I asked.

"We're getting orders. We'll make some money this year. We'll have a little return on our investment."

"But that's great, Will. I didn't know you'd put money in the business. Where'd you get it?"

"Well, you know, Dave, Sharon's father. He was interested and loaned it to me."

I nodded. "If Dave *hadn't*, would you have asked me?"

"Oh look, Daddy, I might lose it. We could still lose it all."

"Sure, I know."

I left my briefcase on his desk and we walked soberly up into the square. At a tavern, Johnny John's, we took a booth in the back where a matronly waitress greeted Will, brought us beer, and recommended the haddock.

"Where's Sharon?" I asked Will. "Any chance I'll see her?"

"She works."

"I could stay over. Maybe we could all have dinner."

"I don't think so."

"That's why I came up, Will. To tell you I'm for you, you know. You and Sharon."

"You didn't used to be."

"It's true. We didn't get off on the right foot. That happens. I sensed a little hostility, didn't I?"

"She thought *you* were hostile."

"I didn't intend that."

"Well, she's not the kind of girl you'd like. She isn't social. She knows that. And she doesn't play up to you."

"She's bold. She wants things. And I did have reservations, Will. I don't deny that, but they were on your account. You had no job, and I worried about your taking on that much woman. I was trying to sound the cautionary note, do my fatherly thing."

He watched me, his eyes glinting with old resentment. "You were afraid," he said. "You were afraid you'd have to support us. You won't, you know. I'd starve first — and so would Sharon."

Stung, I leaned back and sighed. "No, Will. I don't mean that."

"You do mean that. You're always afraid I'm going to be a cargo and a shame to you. I'm always thwarting your wish for a facsimile son, a kid who'll parrot you, add to your fame, impress everybody with you."

"I must have hoped many things for you. Whatever they were, I've forgotten them. Today it's only that you have the good sense and the guts to get the better of life, and some pleasure from it — just for you. Don't do anything for me. My father said that to me once, and I couldn't believe he meant it. I mean it, Will, and today I see that's exactly what you're doing. I'm only sorry I'm not in on The Big Noise, nor a member of the wedding."

He thought, sipped at his beer and said, "It's not going to be much of a wedding, but you can come if you want. Are you and Mummy up for a family ceremony?"

"Yes, I think so. It's your welfare that's our only line now-adays."

"I'll keep it open." He grinned. "Don't worry."

"She tells me I've failed you, Will. I can believe that, but I don't know how, nor when. If I knew, it might help me. Do you have any idea?"

Will shook his head.

"There must be some time, some incident when you saw me suddenly as a disappointment, a turning when you decided that my ideas were all wrong. Do you remember?"

He looked uncomfortable, embarrassed, and again he shook his head.

I pressed him. "What *did* you think of me as a kid? How did you see me? Was I ogreish, the man who came home oc-casionally and took your mother away from you? Were you jealous?"

"No."

"Or some kind of fake — a pompous man, strutting around, demanding that everyone shape up, then revealing myself as foolish and incompetent? When did you discover my feet were clay?"

Will shrugged. "I still think of you with the chain saw, felling trees in the swamp, bringing those huge things crashing down out of the sky. Even now I'm surprised to find my eyes on a level with yours. I know I can never measure up to you. Remember giving me the toy saw, with it's string of BBs for a chain — and how I tried to cut a tree with it? Somewhere in there I knew I was a disappointment to you, that you'd always have the real chain saw and I'd always have the toy that wouldn't even scratch the furniture, and all the time you were doing this number on me, expecting me to bring down trees like you — and despising me when I couldn't."

"Surely *now* you know that's not true."

He sighed. "What you think as a child cuts deep in the heart."

"If I ever doubted you, Will, I've come around, all the way. I admire you. I have an idea you'll succeed where I've failed."

"You're talking about failure again," Will said. "You dread it as though it were the plague. Did you ever think maybe it isn't all that bad? That maybe you ought to try it once and see? Maybe you *don't* die of it."

"Maybe not, but it's painful, failing you, as my father never failed me."

"You haven't," Will said.

"I've sent you looking for me in other men. And now, you see, you're becoming the man for me to admire and marvel at."

We sat for a while longer in Johnny John's, wondering if, at last, we understood each other. Then we walked back to The Big Noise where men were now at their benches and the music from the speakers was loud and aggressive.

As I took my briefcase from Will's hand, I asked, "What was that playing when I came in, do you know?"

"Vivaldi. *The Four Seasons.*"

"It was lovely. Do you like it?"

"Yes," he said. "I chose it."

"I thought you were an incorrigible rock fan."

"I like that too," he said, smiling, "but I had an idea you were coming."

When Will let me out, we embraced there on the threshold of The Big Noise, this time without awkwardness.

❧ 24 ❧

"H I." There was a silence, so that I had to ask, "You there?"

"Yes."

"How are you?"

She hesitated, then said, "I'm fine. I'm very well indeed."

"Good. I want to check my guesswork. You're through with the house?"

"I'll never set foot in it again."

"That's what I . . ."

"If I could put a curse on it . . . If I could make it catch fire and burn to ashes . . ."

"With me in it, I'm sure."

"I hate that house for all the deception that took place there. I hate it for the poisoning that took place there. But it hasn't destroyed me, Lloyd."

"I'm sure it hasn't. Is it O.K. with you if I sell it?"

"I'll want a full accounting."

"There's an offer. Ninety thousand. We could probably get . . ."

"Take it."

"There's the furniture."

"Sell it. I don't want to see it again."

"You sure? Won't you be taking your own apartment?"

She sighed. "Well . . . I may. I *am* thinking of that. I might

want a few things, a bed and a chair or two. Do I need to
come?"

"I can't do it all."

The door's latch resisted as though it knew my waning right
to it, and then gave onto a chill hall with the reek of dampness
and dust. The day, a November Saturday, was bright, the air
filled with yellow leaves and the cries of the new neighbors'
children. I opened the windows on the south side and began
to work in the study, taking books from the shelves, filling
the cartons, one set for the New Canaan library, another for
storage.

Packing memory away had me thinking of my fate, how it lay
before me, patiently awaiting my arrival, some mixture of earli-
est perceivings, forgotten anxieties and yearnings, a nucleus of
my blood, and I guessed that it embraced a stable union with
one woman, a relationship that *kept,* the lasting an end in itself.

I filled the last of the twenty cartons and lugged the two I
was taking to town out to the car. It was one o'clock, warm and
pleasant now. I sat on the porch steps to open the picnic kit I
had brought. I ate a sandwich, drank some coffee, looking up
Oenoke Ridge Road for a sign of Andy's arrival.

I was thinking that *all* relationships between men and women
deteriorate, from the moment they are assumed. Each partner
must balance arctic loneliness, the need to share misfortune
and joy, against the exploitation that rides with affection.
Every relationship, unless in perfect balance, is exploitative.
Nothing without its price.

Back at work, I began tagging the large pieces in the living
room, piano and breakfront, marking them for Mr. Farber's
appraisal. I was unable to decide about the smaller pieces,
chairs and tables that might do for an apartment in town,
things I would store until I could decide on the shape my life
would take.

Frustration crept over me, a need to weep. In our bedroom,
I looked out into the tops of the maples — bare but for a few

tawny leaves at the branch tips — and up the road again. Then I stretched out on the bed, touching the oak headboard we had bought in Brattleboro, tracing its carving with my fingertips and remembering the nights, some six thousand of them, each bounded by the touch of Andy's body. That warmth, the exchange of heat between us, was what I missed, that reservoir of animal need, the mortising comfort of bodies.

I had lost the keen edge of jealousy and wished her the restorative of another man's love, yet the tidal pull of her body was strong as ever, unaffected by alienations.

Sometimes, lying beside Andy on this bed, I had perceived her in anatomical diagram, and persuaded myself that her thoracic zone, seat of her sensibilities, her fastidiousness, all the fondnesses and loathings we had shaped together, was still sympathetic to me. Only her head had turned hostile. It grimaced at me, angry and taunting. I could hear the anger, scolding me to change, when I could not change. Once, at some impasse between us, I lay beside her here and thought of severing the head, sending it rolling, bowling down an alley toward a collision with the pins.

Even now, I could not isolate the failure, the central misunderstanding between us. Had it happened with Flavia, that howling violation of her trust? But I was certain that Flavia was a result and not a cause. Perhaps the misunderstanding had been there from the beginning. Perhaps from the start we had carried separate notions of the contract between us.

My own was the traditional one which, in 1950, Andy certainly shared. We were a partnership. While her responsibility was the household, and mine the career, we divvied and joined in all of it. I made clam sauce and scrubbed pots and bought baby clothes, just as Andy read manuscripts, quarreled with reviews, and drank up the gossip of publishing parties.

But, for all the reciprocity, I had believed there was a specialization to the sexes, that the roles were not interchangeable, that mine was aggressive, that of the runner, while Andy's was protective, that of the coach.

In midlife, Andy had astonished me by turning up at the

starting line. It baffled, and then disheartened me, not that I feared she might outrun me or, by trailing the field, embarrass me, though both were possible, but I could not see how she could run herself without neglecting by half her charities to me. I wondered if *I* could run on such austerity, if her hope for and belief in me were not the essence of my own spirit.

Whether the cause was her running or, as Andy believed, my egoism and indifference to her, the result was worse than I had imagined. Her once powerful interest in the books, the authors, the people who consumed my thoughts at Gulliver House, had become perfunctory. The loss of that fascination in what I was doing was like an act of major surgery, leaving a great hole where a vital organ had functioned.

I saw betrayal in Andy's failure to honor the obligations, the happy combining of which had once made our marriage a professional one, a partnership which recognized the emotional and vocational needs of a mature man and woman. It seemed to me that this failure entitled me, in a simple act of survival, to another woman.

At times, even Andy admitted that it did. In the rare moments when she could take my view, she marveled at my tolerance, just as I did when I could imagine myself Andy, and feel her resentment, her disappointment, her sense of being gypped out of first-class citizenship in our publishing world.

But of course, neither of us could hold the other's view for long. Our sense of grievance was too painful. I know Andy felt it like a nail in the good shoes of our marriage, which she must discard for want of a cobbler.

Her anger, directed as much toward herself as toward me, was untouched by reason. It boiled to a hatred so caustic it could destroy everything — order, civilization, even the love that stood in its way.

Like every aggrieved revolutionary, she stood in the midst of the rubble, crying out for the compassion of her oppressors. She cried out to me in self-pity, for I was the spokesman, if not the enemy itself. While I understood her appeal, I found I could not respond to it beyond saying just that, that I understood.

Hers was not only a rebellion against me, but against the way she had been brought up. School, friends, and father, particularly father, had urged upon Andy the coach's role. But there had always been a thread of insurgency woven into Andy's fabric. It was that which had drawn me to her and, indeed, her to me. Her father's firmness about that Harlem adventure had catalyzed it once, had made me into the shape of her rebellion, encouraged her to think of *me* (there's an irony) and marriage (there's another) as freedom.

"So this is how you get the job done?" A real Andy, smiling, thumb under the strap of an unfamiliar shoulder bag, stood in the bedroom doorway. "I thought you'd have it all loaded onto Mr. Farber's truck."

"Well, as a matter of fact . . ." I felt caught at some mischief and struggled up to sit on the bed's edge, smoothing hair and straightening tie. "I didn't hear you. How did you get here?"

"Taxi, from the station. He let me off out front."

"I'd have come."

She shook her head. "I get where I'm going on my own."

"Ah-h. I see."

Standing, looking at her for the first time in two months, I felt a need to touch — a kiss for habit's sake, some pressure of hands at least, but nothing seemed appropriate, and she did not come toward me.

"Well," I said, "I've packed the books, but I couldn't get on with the rest of the stuff, not knowing what you wanted."

"We may as well start here." Andy sat by the dressing table and, producing a red marker, wrote her initials, ACE, on one of the tags and fastened it to the knob of a drawer. "I decided I want this. I've never really used it, but this apartment I'm thinking of has a good-sized bedroom, and there's a place for it." Peering into the closet, she said, "Oh, thank heavens, there's the box of tennis dresses. I was afraid I'd lost them somewhere."

She seemed to have a zest for the work, and I followed her from bedroom to bedroom, then down through the dining and living rooms, consigning pieces to storage or to Mr. Farber, with a dispatch and a sang-froid I could not match. She knew exactly what she wanted, the small bureau, standing lamp, sewing machine, the portrait of her father, and she went to the task of wrapping and boxing the silver and china, dividing it between us, as though she had thought out each step beforehand.

In the kitchen she said, "I wasn't sure whether we could get most of this done today, but I think we can, particularly if you'll decide about everything here. I really don't want any of it. I'd like to start all over on these utility things." She had a finger on a copper tea kettle we had bought in Provincetown with the seven dollars budgeted for a lobster dinner on the pier.

"You in a rush?"

Andy looked at the range clock. "There's a six-something train. I mustn't be later."

"Six-eighteen. That gives you better than an hour, and I'll run you down, unless that's an infringement of your emancipation."

"No." She smiled. "I guess that'll be all right."

"How about some tea?"

"O.K. Tea would be fine."

Waiting for the water to boil, I said, "How's the job? Will says it's going well."

"I love it."

"What do you do? Tell me about FIS."

"It's a foundation. It's private, but the State Department gives its blessing. We encourage people to study abroad, offer scholarships to qualified students. I'm part of that, deciding which are the qualified ones. It's mostly writing to teachers in Wisconsin."

"That sounds very — worthy."

She laughed. "But dull?"

"No, I meant important. Why must you . . ."

"Dull is what you mean. I know that film on your eyes."

"Oh, Christ. What do you want of me? I can't suddenly turn ardent over something I don't know about."

"*Whatever* I do, if it isn't *for* you, you're going to find it boring."

I poured boiling water over the leaves. "Here, have some tea. I really don't want to scrap, Andy. Not today. We've done all that."

She took her cup to the table and sat down, looking out into the garden, gone scruffy and tangled with dry weeds. "No," she said. "I guess I was just telling myself how hopeless it is. You'll never change. You'll never be able to share."

I brought my cup to the table and sat across from her. Quietly, I said, "Not if by share you mean submit, and that *is* what you mean, isn't it?"

"I mean that I wanted you to accept me as an equal. No — you *don't*. Neither does anyone else in your publishing world, and I'm outraged by that, to the center of my bones. It isn't fair, and that's why I'm angry, being made out to be second best when I'm really not."

"Nobody's made you out to be second best."

"Listen, I *know*. Time and again I've had my self-esteem shrunk to a raisin, but I won't be used again. And I don't want any favors — only to be recognized on my own merits."

"I wonder. Do you really mean you don't want any quarter? In the end I always hear you asking to be loved for yourself, and not for what you do. Isn't that what you really mean by sharing?"

"No," she said, cracking her cup down in the saucer. "You really don't understand at all. And you don't want to."

"I do though. I'm listening."

"You know, Lloyd, your notions about publishing *are* contagious. I'm trying to cure myself, and it's hard."

"What notions?"

"That it's the only kind of accomplishment that matters."

"I don't think that."

"Oh, yes, you do, and I know that. Anyway, the point I'm

trying to make is that I've always wanted your approval. It's been a need, like food and drink. I've always wanted you to think I'm wonderful."

"I do."

"You used to, but I don't believe you do anymore — and I can't really live without that. I'd rather be somewhere else now that I've found there are other streams, other fish, and that I swim quite well among them."

"Yes, well I guess that need goes two ways."

"Does it? Tell me."

"I guess my need is for — affection and approval, of course — but really more than that, a continuity, a pattern of shared experience that keeps with time, that makes sense of the rest — some interdependence of emotion where I belong. It always seemed to me that a family was the least a man could ask of life. Jesus, there's an illusion."

"Not necessarily, not if you . . ."

"Not if what?"

"It's hopeless." She shook her head. "If you could see a wife as the center of her own pattern, but you can't, Lloyd. You think women are different from you, and they aren't you know, except in the most superficial ways." She rose, taking her cup to the sink and said, "It's nearly six. I have to get that box of summer things from upstairs."

"I'll bring it to you," I said. "No sense in carrying it on the train. I'll bring it in to you with the chair and dressing table."

She put on her coat and said, "All right. If you don't mind, Lloyd."

◄§ 25 §►

SENSING HE HAD LOST the battle for Gulliver House, Philip Lerner retreated to his warehouse in New Jersey and, simultaneously, the cloud that had borne such a resemblance to Hugh Severance was dispelled. The knowledge that we three had mustered in time to meet a crisis in our history and had blundered through to a critical victory, cleared the office air of old tensions and oppressiveness. Now we shared the day's difficulties and laughter came easily to us. Just pushing open Gulliver's door in the morning was a good feeling, better for the seasoning than it had been at our beginning.

Shortly after my return, the manuscript of *Fitchy Gules* arrived on my desk, along with a note from Elena Wallace.

Dear Lloyd,
   I am truly unhappy to be offering you the opportunity to publish *Fitchy Gules* under these circumstances. However, Morgan Bryce has insisted I do so. It is a violation of his option to Crowninshield's, and of my word as well as his. I have explained all this to Hugh Severance, proposing that I drop Bryce as a client, but Hugh, ever the gentleman, has deferred to you. So be it. One thing more; as an advance against royalties for this book, I am asking fifty thousand dollars.
                                                        Yours, Elena

In order that Joel and Hughie might read the manuscript simultaneously, I had a copy made at once. They agreed to do so over the weekend so that we could meet on Monday morning at nine-thirty and come to an agreement about publication.

Awaiting this meeting, I felt that *Fitchy Gules'* arrival was a sign. Miraculously, luck was turning my way, changing prior agonies into an investment about to pay its dividends.

On Monday morning, we gathered around Hughie's desk. Joel had folded his *Times* to the crossword puzzle and was filling its blanks with conspicuous facility. It was deliberate insouciance and flushed up old annoyances with him.

Hughie was grave, and the first to speak. "Lloyd, I know that you want us to take on this book of Morgan Bryce's with a lot of gusto, and I promise you I spent a good part of the weekend trying to raise it, but I must admit it scares me. If I have it right, Crispin Bryce, the father, is still alive and so are Peggy Cramm and some of the others he describes. I sense they're all litigious people and won't like what Morgan says about them. He's laid plenty of ground here for legal action. What's Pigott doing?"

"When I saw him, Pigott was hoping to join with the American publisher in persuading Morgan to modify the stronger stuff. We can deal with that."

Hughie kneaded his lower lip. "In any case I'd want a strong warranty clause."

"I wonder," Joel said putting aside the puzzle. "What good is a warranty from Morgan Bryce? *He* doesn't have any money. If suit were brought in this country, the publisher alone would be liable. Besides . . ." Joel fidgeted. He hesitated to offend me but clearly he had something even more unpleasant to say. "I can't believe Elena's serious in asking fifty grand for it. We'd do a trade sale of ten thousand at most. I don't expect you'll agree with me, Lloyd, but I think she's asking twice what it's worth."

"She won't haggle."

"To be honest, Lloyd, I find Bryce's tone kind of nasty. I'm uncomfortable with the book and I'd as soon see Hugh have it."

My response to this unexpected disappointment was, first, suspicion they had got together to thwart me, and then a rush of anger. My thoughts turned to contingencies. Indeed I reached for the copy of *Fitchy Gules* in its scarlet box, held it in my lap, weighing it, thinking I might gather up the manuscript and my hat and get on to Crowninshield's with both.

But then, with my partners eyeing me apprehensively, I reflected that whether Joel and Hughie were right or not, they had come to their conclusions with as much experience and deliberation as I. Their judgment weighed no less than my own — and I must trust it.

"Painful it is," I sighed. "But I'll tell Elena we're turning down *Fitchy Gules*. The world is full of books."

Joel was dumb with dismay, but Hughie sighed his relief and said, "Good for you."

I carried the manuscript back to my office where I wrote Morgan Bryce a note explaining our decision and another, similar one, to Elena. When I had finished these desolate acts and sent the box of manuscript on its way, I felt a lifting of my bereavement. Later in the day I had a sense of exhilaration, as though I had shed some weights. The decision began to seem right and inevitable, whatever became of *Fitchy Gules,* and I did feel certain that my share of good books would be coming around. There was plenty of time for that.

⤚ 26 ⤛

At five-fifteen I left Gulliver House, joining the parade of the homeward bound, surprised at my own sense of anticipation. I headed downtown, toward a garage in Rockefeller Center, pausing at Madison for the light.

In a shop window, one filled with television sets and cameras, I caught a reflection of myself and was startled to find it colorless. In a field of many hues, my face was pale, framed by tufts of gray. A wattling over the collar persisted even as I turned this way and that, hoping to find it a shadow in the glass itself.

I was struck by the resemblance to my father. Involuntarily, my mouth opened and became his as I remembered it, as I often dreamed it, that dark hole crying fears for my safety at sea.

Then it seemed to call out to me, in his hollow, mock Delphic voice, "Lloyd, Lloyd, you could not foil fate. You must have known that from the first, from the last time, when I lay wasted on the hospital pillow. *I* am your destiny — and you're nearly there, don't you see? It was all arranged, long before you were born. There was never a way to change it."

The traffic signal went green and the crowd surged on but I stood rooted, disputing my reflection, "Death, you mean. I know that. I never imagined I could struggle free of the old equalizer. But life, yes. I can affect life. Look, I've edited a hundred books, built a house, had a marriage and reproduced myself, made some history, loved some people, cut a place uniquely mine here in the center of this city."

Rising over the stream of green and yellow vehicles, the avenue's buildings stood like books on the shelf of my life, this year's structures replacing those all but faded from my recollection. But there were many comrades left — Brooks Brothers, the old CBS building where I had worked one summer when I was in college, and Four-Fifteen, where Ralph, amiable as ever, cut my hair.

There were those that housed the agents, old MCA, Harold Ober's, and Curtis Brown. There was Esquire and Newsweek, Viking and Random House, where friends worked, where I knew the texture of the chairs in the reception room and the location of the lavatory. There were the St. Regis and the Waldorf, whose lobbies provided me with sheltered short cuts in the rain. The taste and smell of the air was headier here than anywhere in the city.

You walked to a beat here, a syncopation. Some youngsters could pick up the step in a week, dance to it like old-timers who knew the likelihood of hailing an empty cab on this corner, at this hour, under these weather conditions.

I knew these things, knew them for trivia and yet sure signs of buoyancy. I was proud that I could dance on the pavement in perfect time to that music. The pavement was mine.

"Nor is life over," I said. "There's more to come." Now I found that a change in the shadows had taken away my reflection. I moved until I caught it again, this time in the mirrored shop sign, and I found myself younger, the wattling lessened to a suspicion.

A moment of dramatic beauty had touched the city. The red sun had come to rest on the Palisades and flooded the gorge of Fifty-first Street with a roseate, Olympian light. Passing faces emerged in vivid relief. Branches of the young plane trees glinted lavender and gold. There was a sense that some magical event was occurring, and everyone shared in the hush and wonder of it.

The heavenly light waned and I crossed the street. Midway in the block, it struck me that although I knew I would end as time's victim, I rode a wave of fresh strength, not the profligate kind of youth, but another of endurance and certainty. I knew there would be time enough — not enough for compromise or retreat — but time to use the strength, time for binding myself to people and to ideas I believed in, standing for them, scrapping for them, and so to wring some victory out of this life.

There would be time for more disappointment and pain too, and even for love, though maybe of a different, a more generous, kind.

"Who should I say?" There was frost on the receptionist's vowels, a repellent for petitioners.

"*Mr.* Erskine."

"Oh?" Her eyes flickered disbelief and I watched her with a hostility of my own as she dialed.

Looking through the glass panel beyond, I sighted Andy. She stood at a desk, fingers spread on its edge. The man seated there spoke without looking up from what he was writing.

He was a lanky man with prominent, articulated features. Receding hair gave him a sensitive, scholarly appearance. As I watched, he looked up slowly and smiled, whereupon Andy laughed. Then, hearing her phone, she moved to answer it and his eyes followed the swirl of her skirt. She walked as though she knew that.

"Andy, Mr. Erskine is here."

Now Andy looked through the glass and saw me. Like a child called for by a parent, there was a lag before recognition. She glanced at the clock, which stood at six. She took a few minutes to straighten her desk, to scribble a note, and for a word with the seated man. Then she came through the door saying, "Sorry, I didn't realize it was so late. Any trouble parking?"

"I'm right in front. Illegal, but I thought your things would be safe."

As we wedged into line on FDR Drive, I asked, "Who's the tall fellow?"

"Tall?"

"You know. The one you said good night to. That your boss?"

"Howard? Howard Stern is his name. He's a field representative for us. That's the cushiest job really, if you like to travel, which he does. He's always whipping around the Southern universities or going off to Europe. He's hoping to get to China next year."

There was an intonation, and new expressions like "whipping around," that was not Andy's. I suspected they were Howard's, and I asked, "You see him at all?"

"Why? What an odd thing to ask."

"The way you *were* with him. The way he looked at you. I couldn't help wondering."

There was a shiver of pleasure in the laugh that was her reply. We rode along in silence, accelerating with the traffic, pacing a tug as it pushed its dirty bow wake upriver.

"Well, I congratulate you Andy. You've made it. I could see that through the window."

"Made what? What do you think you saw through the window?"

"That you've climbed the plateau. Good going."

I could feel her studying me, assuring herself I was sincere. As we turned off at Ninety-sixth Street, she seemed to relax, saying, "Well, it *is* true. I love my job at FIS. I do routine things. I type and file and all that, but I'm part of the whole, and I'm treated like a human. It's small enough so there's a feeling of all of us being engaged. Yes, I do like my boss and I do like the others, most of them and, yes, I *do* like Howard Stern."

"Fine," I said, stopping for the light at York and Eighty-sixth Street. "That's fine. What was that address again?"

"Eighty-fourth, five twenty-six. And you're right, I'm attracted. It's so absolutely lovely to feel that, and to feel attractive. You know that."

"Keep an eye out for a space, now," I said. "We might be lucky."

It was a brownstone. Carrying a carton up its stoop I could see across the river to red veins spelling PEARL WICK HAMPERS in the stygian, Flushing sky.

The apartment, a floor-through, was bare except for the pieces — bed, dressing table, and chairs — that Mr. Farber had dropped off earlier in the day. They stood, with a paint-spattered telephone, against the living room wall.

"It was a tree," Andy said, peering from the bedroom window into the garden below, "the ailanthus tree, that got me. There's something reassuring about green leaves that thrive on soot and dog turds."

"What do you pay?"

"Three eighty."

"Not bad. A place I looked at on the West Side was four hundred." I thought of proposing she see it.

"Would you help me put my bed together?" she asked.

I hung my coat in the closet and carried the frame parts from the living room. Attaching the sideboards, fitting the ears into the bedpost slots, I thought of the many times I had done this and how it was always a forward-looking act, a move to new hopes, with a new summer, or a new house, before us.

When we had tugged the mattress onto the box spring, I leaned against the foot and asked, "Is it going to be all right, both of us at the wedding? Can we manage that?"

"I guess so. There's no way around it."

"Did Will tell you we had lunch?"

"Yes. A good one."

"I was impressed — everything coming together for him."

"And I suspect he and Sharon'll be very happy."

"Maybe there was never real doubt about Will. Maybe all our anguish over him was a waste of energy. It would have been good to know that."

"Anyway, Will's going to be just fine," Andy said, and started toward the bathroom.

"Going out?"

"No, I don't plan to. Howard may be by later, with some notes for a grant proposal." She frowned at the dirty floor. "I'd sweep up here if I had a broom."

"There'll be something open. I could go get you one — and a bottle, if you think a drink's a good idea."

"All right," she called above the splashing water. "There's a couple of jelly glasses."

I looked down into Eighty-fourth Street, where a woman watched her cocker appraise a tire, and a cabbie was holding up four bleating cars while he made careful change. I was imagining Andy going to work down these steps, and coming back, leaping from a taxi in the rain, with Howard Stern, perhaps, following her up.

"I guess you're going to be all right here," I said.

"Yes," she called from the kitchen. "Why wouldn't I be?"

"I don't know. I think of you as a dependent. Matter of habit, I guess, putting that down on the income tax for twenty years. Do you *like* living alone, Andy?"

"After years of having to account to somebody, it's lovely not to. If I'm somewhere having a good time, I start to look at my watch and then I think I don't have to go and put the beans on, and that's terrific."

"I'm not sure if I should ask this — or even if I want to know, but I keep wondering. Are you having a love affair?"

She smiled with just a trace of malice. "Well, I have, of course. Did you think that would be hard for me?"

"No but . . . I'm sorry I asked."

"Why?"

"Because it's your business — and because the idea of your making love with someone is still painful to me. I suppose that's a reflex, but there it is."

"Yes, there it is." She was still smiling. "*Now* you know. Anything else?"

"No."

Leaning against the mantel, she surveyed her empty living

room, visualizing a rug laid, curtains and pictures hung. "It's tiny, isn't it, but I can have a few people in for supper, even a little party. I'll need a good sofa for that wall. I'll have to splurge on that."

"Who'll you see? What kind of social life are you planning?"

"Oh, I'm thinking of the office. It's important for us to do some entertaining."

"Parties? Who do you want to please?"

"Our patrons, the foundation people. They're from places like Kansas City and St. Paul, and they're grateful to be taken to someone's house when they come to town. There's a State Department office we work with, and people from European universities who take our students, and sometimes the students themselves. It's wonderful bringing a group together that's just setting out for a year in France, kids from all over the country, feeling the significance of what they're about to do, and brimming with anticipation for it."

"Who's the boss?"

"Mine? You mean Howard?"

"The chief."

"His name is Sloan. He's an ex–college president and good at his job, which is fund raising of course, but he knows all of us, knows when it's time to stop by my desk and ask my opinion of a student from Vanderbilt or of the program at Cologne. He's the kind of guy you want to work for."

"You're dug in, aren't you? That's why I was congratulating you. It shows."

"Good. I'm glad."

On York Avenue, Gristede's was open and we pushed a cart through its aisles, acquiring the broom and some staples for her cupboard. Then we turned down toward Eighty-fourth, pausing at a liquor shop for a bottle of bourbon, feeling oddly clumsy and self-conscious, as though we had first met an hour ago.

Walking along, I was thinking how Andy did seem newly desirable, and that it was because she was feeling good about herself, and because she was absorbed in what she was doing.

Being unconsciously yet wholly wrapped in a task made a woman doubly desirable.

It was a superficial notion and yet it was primordial, the essence of attraction, of quarry and pursuit, and as we turned into Eighty-fourth Street some such reoccurrence seemed possible.

Back in Andy's apartment, I opened the whiskey and made us each a drink. Then, as I sat at her kitchen table, watching her stow her groceries, it occurred to me to propose I stay for supper. The idea had a double appeal — familiar comforts of shared food and drink, and assertion of prime rights. Let Howard Stern beware.

"Here's luck," I said, raising my glass.

"Same to you," Andy said. She was smiling, perhaps reading every last one of these thoughts, yet not allowing me a hint of encouragement. For a second, that seemed an irresistible challenge, but in the next a wave of fatigue washed against me. It was as though I had seen the outcome, glanced into the future and found familiar patterns of the past.

I swallowed the last of my drink, set the glass down, and said, "Will you let me know the number when they hook you up?"

"Yes, if you want."

"I do," I said, and put a quick kiss on her cheek.

It was fully dark as I reached the pavement. I turned west, heading for the car, which I had parked at the York Avenue corner, walking irresolutely, thinking I might turn back, and finally stopping altogether.

The basement windows of a house opposite me were lighted, the shades partly drawn, so I could see within. A man, curly haired, wearing a candy-striped shirt, sat at a table with a woman whose back was to me, and a girl in a gray school jumper.

Dishes and silver had been swept aside, and as I watched, the girl rolled dice from a leather cup, moved a piece some spaces along a colored board, and looked up with a smile of triumph.

The man spoke, and the woman shook her head, laughing. The enormous intimacy of the three touched me, brought a familiar pressure to my heart, and yet I recoiled, stepped back from the scene.

"No," I thought. "I'm such an easy mark for envy. Tonight I want to be alone." I went on again, toward the corner.